THE PENNY

Compiled by the same editor:

THE WILD NIGHT COMPANY
Irish stories of fantasy and horror

THE CLANS OF DARKNESS
Scottish stories of fantasy and horror

THE MAGIC VALLEY TRAVELLERS
Welsh stories of fantasy and horror

GREAT BRITISH TALES OF TERROR

GREAT TALES OF TERROR FROM EUROPE AND AMERICA

THE NIGHTMARE READER

NIGHTFRIGHTS

THE MONSTER MAKERS

THE PENNY DREADFUL

Or,
Strange, Horrid &
Sensational Tales!

Edited by

PETER HAINING

with original illustrations

LONDON
VICTOR GOLLANCZ LTD
1976

85-11730

© SELECTION AND ORIGINAL MATERIAL, PETER HAINING 1975

ISBN 0 575 01779 1

First published January 1975
Second impression January 1976

MADE AND PRINTED IN GREAT BRITAIN BY
THE GARDEN CITY PRESS LIMITED
LETCHWORTH, HERTFORDSHIRE
SG6 1JS

For
David Philips

—who gave generously of his time and his "bloods" so that this collection might be assembled

"It is not enough just to shock and startle by accounts of horror and crime. Such modern writers as confine themselves to this one aim must at least relieve the monotony of their accounts of violence by directing the reader's attention to sexual aberration or to the love life of criminal or detective. The older way to hold the reader's attention, and one that is morally less objectionable, is to arouse his sympathy for the good character, especially the heroine. That this was an essential part of the 'Penny Dreadful' is not often realized."

Margaret Dalziel
Popular Fiction
100 Years Ago

ACKNOWLEDGEMENTS

The compiling of this anthology has involved numerous people and organizations, and while it is not possible to thank all of them, I should particularly like to extend my gratitude to the following: the staffs of the British Museum, The London Library and the University of London Library; G. Ken Chapman for his unfailing kindness and advice, Miss L. A. Slater for the loan of illustrations, and David Philips, without whose enthusiasm and guidance this book would not have been possible. Also Miss Livia Gollancz for so readily supporting the project from its earliest days and finally, of course, my wife, Philippa, for a multitude of services as secretary, typist and enthusiastic collaborator.

PETER HAINING

CONTENTS

		Page
Introduction		13
1	The Terrific Register: "The Monster Of Scotland"	23
2	The Calendar Of Horrors—Edward Lloyd, Publisher: "The Dead Alive"	30
3	The Life Of Dick Turpin—W. M. Clarke, Publisher: "The Robbery Of The Astrologer"	36
4	Robin Hood by Pierce Egan Jnr: "The Ambush Of Death"	50
5	Dombey And Daughter by Renton Nicholson: "The Actor's Tale"	68
6	The Mysteries Of London by G. W. M. Reynolds: "The Body-Snatchers"	83
7	Sweeney Todd by Thomas Peckett Prest: "The Last Batch Of Pies"	95
8	Varney The Vampire by James Malcolm Rymer: "The Resuscitation Of A Vampire"	121
9	Jessie, The Mormon's Daughter by Percy B. St John: "Buried Alive!"	134
10	The Shipwrecked Stranger by Hannah Maria Jones: "The Life Of A Murderer"	146
11	Paul The Poacher by Thomas Frost: "The Abduction"	162
12	The Merry Wives Of London by James Lindridge: "The Episode Of The Knights Of The Round Table"	176
13	Sister Anne by Paul de Kock	195

14	The Raft Of Death by Eugène Sue	212
15	The Mad Wolf by Ned Buntline	229
16	The League Of "The Thirty" by J. H. Ingraham	244
17	The People's Periodical—Edward Lloyd, Publisher: "Confessions Of A Deformed Lunatic"	264
18	Reynolds' Miscellany—G. W. M. Reynolds, Publisher: "The Rosicrucian"	276
19	The London Journal—George Stiff, Publisher: "Stanfield Hall"	293
20	Boys Of England—Edwin Brett, Publisher: "Jack Rushton: Or, Alone In The Pirates' Lair"	302
21	Caractacus, Champion Of The Arena—George Emmett and Harcourt Burrage: "The Arena Of Blood"	317
22	Guy Fawkes by G. A. Sala: "The Vault Of Death"	330
23	Jack Harkaway by Bracebridge Hemyng: "The Road to Adventure"	341

APPENDICES

1	"Penny Packets Of Poison" by James Greenwood	357
2	"Horrible Murder And Human Pie-Makers"	372
3	"To My Readers" by George Reynolds	376
	Bibliography	380

INTRODUCTION

THE "PENNY DREADFUL" is a term most people encounter in childhood and carry subconsciously through the remainder of their lives without ever being quite sure what it means. Heard, invariably, from the lips of a parent, it can be indiscriminately applied to a comic, illustrated magazine or short novel—its implication always dependent on the attitudes of the speaker. In one family it may apply to crudely drawn adventure stories, in another to stories of war and violence, in a third to virtual pornography. Yet, like so many popular phrases, the Penny Dreadful has an established origin and a fascinating history which, though much neglected, does throw light on a particular facet of modern literature.

It was Charles Knight, the renowned 19th-century printer, who boasted that "The penny magazine produced a revolution in popular art throughout the world", and although this term embraces a much larger field of publications than those with which we are concerned here, they are, nonetheless, an important part of it. In fact all these publications were made possible by the advent of three major factors: 1) The introduction in the early years of the 19th century of basic education for everyone; 2) The invention of the rotary steam printing press; 3) The development of paper-making machines. Now, for the first time, even the lowest classes of workers could read—albeit with difficulty—and to meet their needs there were machines available to produce a new kind of literature cheaply enough for even their meagre purses. Existing literature—including the Gothic novel which was then on the wane*—was not what this new readership demanded. They wanted realistic sensation—"anything to please for a few hours, and the less demands it made on the comprehension of the tired worker the better" as Louis James has defined it in his excellent study *Fiction for the Working Man, 1830–1850*. "And so in one fell swoop," Michael Sadleir goes on to tell us in *Nineteenth Century Fiction*, "the Gothic Novel crashed and became the vulgar 'blood'. But the spirit of melodrama and of terror (which is only in rousing guise the spirit of escape) persisted unsubdued, and persists to this day."

The eight-page penny publications which thereafter poured on to the streets of Britain provided exactly the vicarious "escape" which artisan readers sought. The common factor in all was the struggle between good and evil, and while many a reader might have observed a certain flexibility in his own moral code, in the heroes and heroines of the penny publications this was not only inexcusable, but also unthinkable. Their popularity was enormous, eclipsing the sales of even the classics and contemporary works destined for immortality. Writing in a pamphlet in 1935, bookseller C. A. Stonehill commented, "It is highly probable that in its day more people read Thomas Prest's 'First False Step' or 'The Maniac Father' than had ever heard of a book published in the same decade, entitled *Jane Eyre*."

Success for many of the publishers, though, was balanced on a needlepoint. Even paying their authors a pittance (rarely more than fifty pence for an entire issue—if they could not actually get away with no payment at all), employing "sweated labour" to set up the type, and keeping the percentage allowed to the newsagents down to an absolute minimum, any kind of profit margin demanded a sale well in excess of 20,000 copies per issue. Some of the most popular

*The history of the Gothic novel, complete with episodes and stories by many of its greatest authors, is related in Peter Haining's two-volume study, *Great British Tales of Terror* and *Great Tales of Terror from Europe and America*. (U.K. Victor Gollancz Limited 1972; U.S.A. Taplinger 1972.)

sold hundreds of thousands—one or two, like the famous "Black Bess, or The Knight of the Road", sold in the millions —and made their publishers wealthy men; others less fortunate were swiftly bankrupted and even imprisoned if they did not hotfoot it out of the city.

Undoubtedly one of the most important "selling" features of these publications were the lurid engravings—"fierce" plates as they have become known—which decorated the front page of each issue. "The woodcuts and stories perfectly supplement each other," Louis James has written. "The outstretched hands point to the power of destiny, the falling curve of the heroine's body illustrates her helpless innocence, the villain's enormous eyes show devouring lust. Today, when we are deluged with pictorial art, it requires an effort of imagination to see the impact of pictures on early Nineteenth Century readers."

However, while great care was given to this element of the Penny Dreadful, continuity of story got scant attention. As none of the publications had title pages on each issue (such luxuries would have been considered a waste of space by the readers) and the text was tightly packed into two columns per page, episodes could literally finish at the bottom of page eight in mid-sentence to be continued in the next number with the following word. No attempt was made to inform the reader of "what had gone before", and it is not unusual to find a story broken off in the middle and some completely extraneous episode introduced to fill out the number when the author had either lost inspiration or—more likely—disappeared on a drinking spree to relieve the pressures which the prodigious requirements of the work demanded. (E. S. Turner in his *Boys Will Be Boys* recounts the delightful story of a writer who went missing having left his hero bound to a stake, with wild animals encircling him and an avalanche about to fall from above. As the deadline approached for the next episode, several other writers tried to find a means of escape for the hapless man, but without success. "Then", writes Mr Turner, "at the eleventh hour the missing author returned. He took the briefest look at the previous instalment and, without a moment's hesitation, wrote 'With one bound Jack was free'.")

By modern standards, most of these works were atrociously written, appallingly printed and ephemeral to the last degree. Yet their influence and format have been enduring; many a modern publication continues their traditions of lengthy serials, endlessly playing out the stock situation of good and evil balancing and counterbalancing each other. It would be wrong, too, to think that they were solely concerned with crime and criminals—as a number of references would have us believe—for a great many of the more successful issues show a variety of characters, settings and incidents which would do credit to a modern thriller. Nor should we think of them as appealing only to adults; some of the most successful impresarios, such as Edward Lloyd, sought to reach the widest market and tried out potential manuscripts on their young employees. One of Lloyd's contributors, Thomas Frost, recalls in his memoirs, *Forty Years' Recollections* (1880), the dictum employed by Lloyd's editors that "as our publications circulate among a class so different in education and social position to the readers of three volume novels, we sometimes distrust our own judgement and place the manuscript in the hands of an illiterate person—a servant, or machine boy, for instance—and if they pronounce favourably upon it, we think it will do." (This is not to infer that the middle classes and even the nobility were above Penny Dreadfuls—George Reynolds, for one, claimed in several of his works that "the aristocrats were in the habit of borrowing the penny parts from their footmen".)

However, as we shall see in tracing the history of these publications, the market emphasis age-wise does begin to shift noticeably in the 1860s. In *Popular Fiction 100 Years Ago*, Margaret Dalziel notes, "It is true that from the sixties onwards 'Penny Dreadfuls' were directed towards a juvenile public—but, of course, this included many adults, just as the readers of comics do today!"

At this juncture it would perhaps be as well if I emphasized that I am using the term Penny Dreadful to embrace both those types of publication that the experts call "Penny Bloods" and Penny Dreadfuls. The term "Blood" for them is used primarily to refer to the long blood and thunder serials of the 1830s to 1850s, while the "Dreadfuls" emerged later in the 1860s and mostly dealt with the lurid adventures of youthful heroes.* In retelling the story of this facet of literature, I have therefore adopted a chronological order in the selection of items so that the evolution from one style to another can be clearly seen.

As some authorities have pointed out, a number of famous writers of this period contributed to the Penny Dreadfuls but as their work is now mostly available in other editions I could see no point in including them here yet again. Do bear this in mind, though, and if you are so inclined, an interesting hour or two can be spent delving into the stories that Lord Lytton wrote for Edwin Brett's journals and G. P. R. James for George Reynolds' magazines; similarly W. Harrison Ainsworth wrote his *Miser of Shoreditch* for release in penny parts and no less a person than William Makepeace Thackeray is credited with the authorship of the notorious "Blood" "Eliza Brownrigge". Remember, too, that this was a great age for pirating and plagiarism, and there are literally hundreds of copies of the "classics" of the time, ranging from the romances of Mrs Crowe to Charles Dickens' tales of city life.

A lot of the authors represented here will, however, be new names to many readers, and it is a sad fact that, although much that was published in the Penny Dreadfuls was of limited value, there were writers and stories which deserved a better fate. I have tried to unearth as much detail as I can

*John James Wilson, who was the editor of several publications in this category, wrote in 1932: "It was thought at the time these books were published that 'Penny Dreadfuls' were the origin of all youthful crimes and parents not only banned them, but, when discovered, burned them without mercy. Today youthful crimes are put down to the cinema." (One could add television to that!—Editor.)

about my contributors, but facts are few and far between—and often highly contentious. Yet these men and women did serve an enormous public that probably but for them would have been starved of reading matter at a time when literacy—even on the lowest level—was actively being encouraged.

It perhaps hardly needs to be said that not a great many of these publications have survived intact to the present day. Their very production and the careless hands which seized them virtually preclude this. Yet collections exist in several major libraries on both sides of the Atlantic and there are a few collectors with amazingly varied and surprisingly intact ranges of the better products to which I have generously been given access. Because of this it has not been possible to be quite as exhaustive as one would have liked, yet I believe this selection is wide-ranging enough to satisfy the scholar and delight the lay-reader. I have also been able to include specimens from both Europe and America which I think show how widely this style of publication circulated. I should also add that, as primarily an anthologist of macabre literature, I have tended to go more for tales of this inclination in my selections: some of the stories obviously illustrate other aspects of the Penny Dreadful, but by and large my choices are here for their bizarre quality and their ability to entertain a modern audience.

In my research I have drawn on several of the standard authorities for guidance and these are acknowledged in the text. I have also tried through them to reflect the varying public attitude towards these publications and how fluctuating tastes are reflected in much of what was published.* The men behind the Penny Dreadfuls were businessmen out to succeed—make no mistake of that—and their efforts might well be used as a pointer to the changing morality of the latter part of the 19th century.

---

* As an example of one widely quoted viewpoint, I have reprinted an article by James Greenwood who was a noted journalist of the time and "fearless exposer of social evils". See Appendix I.

Finally, I hope that in rescuing some of these publications from oblivion—albeit only in fragments—this book might arouse a more general awareness and study of them among scholars, and add yet another dimension of interest for all lovers of macabre fiction.

PETER HAINING
March 1974

THE PENNY DREADFUL

I

THE TERRIFIC REGISTER

IN THE EARLY years of the 19th century, the famous Gothic novel with its haunted castles, degenerate monasteries, charnel houses, creaking dungeons and supernatural denizens of all shapes and sizes, held the attention of the reading public. This public, however, were a privileged minority; the vast majority of the population of Britain—and Europe and America as well—were illiterate to such an extent that struggling over their own names was about the limit of their capabilities. Equally, those who could read could hardly have afforded the price of these books, should they have wanted them, from their pitiable wages.

Although it is generally accepted that Forster's Education Act of 1870 brought education to the masses in England—both industrial and rural—there was a growing international movement of organizations (most connected with the Church) providing simple schooling in the early years of the century. It was these groups—with their "courses" of spelling, reading and a little calculating—coupled with the invention of the paper-making machine (which went into service in 1820 after some opposition from the trade) and the introduction of the rotary steam printing press, which created a whole new dimension for literature.

There was now a new market of people wanting entertaining reading—and the wherewithal for publishers to provide it at the lowest cost. Presses, which had previously lumbered slowly over hand-made paper to produce high-cost books, could now speed out simple eight-page publications which made a profit for all concerned at just one penny each. As

Louis James has written: "The combination of cheap paper and mechanical printing was the greatest step forward in book production since Caxton." The printers and publishers of the time had only to look around them in the big cities to see the immense market of working-class people who awaited their attention. Obviously great literature was, initially, far above them: they needed excitement and thrills told in the simplest style to relieve the tedium of their day-to-day lives. History was, of course, replete with tales of drama and courage, not to mention the strange and the bizarre, and if these poor people had not actually read the Gothic novels, they were at least aware of their existence. What could be more natural, then, than to take this genre—the genre of sensation and dark deeds—and use it as the starting point for the new publications?

So it was that the first penny papers began to appear—full of gory tales from history, bizarre criminal activities, and frequently grim episodes lifted, piecemeal, from the Gothic novels or publications like the much reprinted *Newgate Calendar*. The potential customer could hardly mistake what he was getting from the titles of just a few of the early arrivals on the scene: *The Tell-Tale* (1823–4), *Legends of Horror* (1825–6) and *The Terrific Register* (1825–7). These publications set many of the standards which were to be commonplace when the Penny Dreadful serial works followed soon after: they pirated and plagiarized anything that was suitable, they carried at least one gruesome engraving, and continuity of reports or explanation of extracts was left at an absolute minimum, if observed at all.

Students who have studied copies of these now exceedingly rare publications which were the first stirring of the Penny Dreadful movement, have noted how they carried a great many simple accounts of men or events which were later to be used as the basis of multi-part serials: take the legends of Robin Hood and Dick Turpin, for instance, which several recounted in simple, yet widely differing reports; or the tales of criminals and brigands which fill *Legends of Horror*. Or more particularly still, the story of the Parisian barber who murdered his clients and made them into meat pies which was published in *The Tell-Tale* and partly inspired the Sweeney Todd story (see Appendix 2).

Another influence on the "Demon Barber" story was undoubtedly the remarkable legend of Sawney Beane, the Man Eater of Scotland, which *The Terrific Register* detailed in issue number 11 of its 104 penny parts (1825). I think it is appropriate that we should begin the collection with this story, as it illustrates not only the bridging of the gap between the Gothic novel and the Penny Dreadful, but also because in Sawney Beane we have perhaps the most infamous character in British history who was in turn to inspire the creation of the most famous figure in penny serial works.

The Monster Of Scotland
Anonymous

Sawney Beane was born in the county of East Lothian, about eight miles east of Edinburgh, in the reign of James VI. His father was a hedger and ditcher, and brought up his son to the same laborious employment. Naturally idle and vicious, he abandoned that place, along with a young woman equally idle and profligate, and they retired to the deserts of Galloway, and took up their habitation by the sea-side. The place which Sawney and his wife selected for their dwelling, was a cave of about a mile in length, and of considerable breadth; so near the sea that the tide often penetrated into the cave above two hundred yards. The entry had many intricate windings and turnings which led to the extremity of the subterraneous dwelling, which was literally "the habitation of horrid cruelty".

Sawney and his wife took shelter in this cave, and commenced their depredations. To prevent the possibility of detection, they murdered every person that they robbed. Destitute also of the means of obtaining any other food, they

The Terrific Register published in 1825 was one of the very first Penny Dreadfuls. The bloodthirsty engraving was the work of a woman, Mary Byfield!

resolved to live upon human flesh. Accordingly, when they had murdered any man, woman, or child, they carried them to their den, quartered them, salted and pickled the members, and dried them for food. In this manner they lived, carrying on their depredations and murder, until they had eight sons and six daughters, eighteen grand-sons and fourteen granddaughters, all the offspring of incest.

But, though they soon became numerous; yet, such was the multitude who fell into their hands, that they had often superabundance of provisions, and would, at a distance from their own habitation, throw legs and arms of dried human bodies into the sea by night. These were often thrown out by the tide, and taken up by the country people, to the great consternation and dismay of all the surrounding inhabitants. Nor could any discover what had befallen the many friends, relations, and neighbours who had unfortunately fallen into the hands of these merciless cannibals.

In proportion as Sawney's family increased, every one that was able, acted his part in their horrid assassinations. They would sometimes attack four or six men on foot, but never more than two upon horseback. To prevent the possibility of escape, they would lay an ambush in every direction, that if they escaped those who first attacked, they might be assailed with renewed fury by another party, and inevitably murdered. By this means, they always secured their prey, and prevented detection.

At last, however, the vast number who were slain, raised the inhabitants of the country, and all the woods and lurking places were carefully searched: and though they often passed by the mouth of the horrible den, it was never once suspected that any human being resided there. In this state of uncertainty and suspense, concerning the authors of such frequent massacres, several innocent travellers and inn-keepers were taken up upon suspicion; because the persons who were missing, had been seen last in their company, or had last resided at their houses. The effect of this well-meant and severe justice, constrained the greater part of the inn-keepers in these parts, to abandon such employments to the great inconvenience of those who travelled through that district.

Meanwhile, the country became depopulated, and the whole nation was surprised, how such numerous and unheard-of villainies and cruelties could be perpetrated, without the least discovery of the abominable actors. At length, Providence interposed in the following manner to terminate the horrid scene; one evening, a man and his wife were riding home upon the same horse from a fair which had been held in the neighbourhood; and being attacked, he made the most vigorous resistance; unfortunately, however, his wife was dragged from behind him, carried to a little distance, and her entrails instantly taken out. Struck with grief and horror, the husband continued to redouble his efforts to escape, and even trod some of them under his horse's feet. Fortunately for him, and for the inhabitants of that part of the country, in the meantime, twenty or thirty in a company came riding home from the same fair. Upon their approach, Sawney and his bloody crew fled into a thick wood, and hastened to their infernal den.

This man, who was the first that had ever escaped out of their hands, related to his neighbours what had happened, and shewed them the mangled body of his wife, which lay at a distance, the blood-thirsty wretches not having time to carry it along with them. They were all struck with astonishment and horror, took him with them to Glasgow, and reported the whole adventure to the chief magistrate of the city. Upon this intelligence, he wrote to the king, informing him of the matter.

In a few days, his majesty in person, accompanied by four hundred men, went in quest of the perpetrators of such cruelties: the man who had his wife murdered before his eyes, went as their guide, with a great number of blood-hounds, that no possible means might be left unattempted to discover the haunts of these execrable villains.

They searched the woods, traversed, and examined the sea-shore; but though they passed by the entrance of their cave, they had no suspicion that any creature resided in that dark and dismal abode. Fortunately, however, some of the blood-hounds entered the cave, raised up an uncommon barking and noise, indicating that they were about to seize their prey. The king and his men returned, but could scarcely conceive how any human being could reside in a place of utter darkness, and where the entrance was difficult and narrow, but as the blood-hounds increased in their vociferation, and refused to return, it occurred to all that the cave ought to be explored to the extremity. Accordingly, a sufficient number of torches were provided. The hounds were permitted to pursue their course; a great number of men penetrated through all the intricacies of the path, and at length arrived at the private residence of these horrible cannibals.

They were followed by all the band, who were shocked to

behold a sight unequalled in Scotland, if not in any part of the universe. Legs, arms, thighs, hands, and feet, of men, women and children, were suspended in rows like dried beef. Some limbs and other members were soaked in pickle; while a great mass of money, both of gold and silver, watches, rings, pistols, cloths, both woollen and linen, with an inconceivable quantity of other articles, were either thrown together in heaps, or suspended on the sides of the cave.

The whole cruel brutal family, to the number formerly mentioned, were seized; the human flesh buried in the sand of the sea-shore; the immense booty carried away, and the king marched to Edinburgh with the prisoners. This new and wretched spectacle attracted the attention of the inhabitants, who flocked from all quarters to see this bloody and unnatural family as they passed along, which had increased, in the space of twenty-five years, to the number of twenty-seven men, and twenty-one women. Arrived in the capital, they were all confined in the Tolbooth under a strong guard; they were next day conducted to the common place of execution in Leith Walk, and executed without any formal trial, it being deemed unnecessary to try those who were avowed enemies to all mankind, and of all social order.

The enormity of their crimes dictated the severity of their death. The men had their privy-members thrown into the fire, their hands and legs were severed from their bodies, and they were permitted to bleed to death. The wretched mother of the whole crew, the daughters and grand-children, after being spectators of the death of the men, were cast into three separate fires, and consumed to ashes. Nor did they, in general, display any signs of repentance or regret, but continued with their last breath, to pour forth the most dreadful curses and imprecations upon all around, and upon all those who were instrumental in bringing them to such well-merited punishment.

2

THE CALENDAR OF HORRORS

Edward Lloyd, Publisher

THE FIRST PUBLISHER to take advantage of the huge potential working-class market was a certain Edward Lloyd who, with the passing of time, has come to be regarded as the "king" of the penny-issue works. Indeed it was his weekly eight-page serials of highwaymen, criminals, pirates and a variety of other dubious characters which first earned the description of Penny Dreadfuls and thereby gave the genre its lasting title.

Lloyd (1815–1890) was the son of a Surrey farmer, who left school at an early age and came to London to set up shop as a bookseller. Even at this tender age he was already an astute businessman, and basing his business initially on books, comic valentines and theatrical portraits, observed how the major publishers of the day, such as William Chambers, were missing the poorest readers. He therefore took up the study of journalism at the Mechanics' Institute in Chancery Lane and began making contacts in the printing works which were then springing up in the Drury Lane area. Gauging the mood of his potential readers exactly, his first penny publications drew on the activities of the criminal fraternity and were embellished with a lurid illustration on the first page. Nothing quite like them had been seen before. His initial venture was the now legendary *Lives of the Most Notorious Highwaymen, Footpads, etc*, the very first Penny Dreadful which began in 1836 and ran for sixty numbers. Its success was instantaneous and Lloyd quickly added to it *The Gem of Romance; or, Tales of Intense Interest* (1836; twenty-eight numbers), *The History of Pirates of all Nations* (1836; seventy-one numbers) and *The Calendar of Horrors* (1836; seventy-six numbers).

To meet the ever-increasing demand for material for these publications, Lloyd recruited a small group of writers of "demonic imagination, prodigious output and an engaging lack of scruple" to quote E. S. Turner. At the head of these was Thomas Peckett Prest, who not only edited several of the above-mentioned periodicals, but also wrote many of his employer's most successful serial works (see Extract 7). Prest delighted in historical accounts of torture, savagery, murder, vice and violence, and utilized these liberally throughout the journals under his control.

Lloyd, however, was not merely content to plough this same furrow. In 1838, he sensed the rising popularity of the young Charles Dickens' stories of the "Pickwick Club" and London life, and instituted the first plagiarisms of his work which were soon to spread like wild-fire throughout the whole publishing industry. He also began a whole range of extremely long and ghoulish penny serials which covered subjects as diverse as witchcraft, "Mary Bateman, the Yorkshire witch", 1840; pirates, "The Black Vulture; or The Rival Brothers", 1840; foreign history, "Julie St Pierre. A Tale of the French Revolution", 1842; sex, "The Maniac Father; or The Victim Of Seduction", 1842; pseudo-morality, "The Bottle; or The First Step to Crime", 1845; gypsies, "Ela the Outcast; or The Gipsey of Rosemary Dell", 1856; vampires, "Varney The Vampire; or The Feast of Blood", 1847; and so on, the list is at least 200 titles long.

To accommodate his huge output, Lloyd moved his offices several times, finally settling in 1843 in Salisbury Square, just off Fleet Street, which location gave yet another title to this style of publishing, "Salisbury Square Fiction". He was also one of the first publishers to introduce Hoe's American printing presses into England—thereby speeding up his production process—and as his fortune grew he established his own paper-making plant in Kent and leased 100,000 acres of land in Algeria for growing esparto grass for the improvement of paper-making. As we progress through this collection, we shall find that the presence of Edward Lloyd is never very far away, and even when he tried to cast off what he considered to be his rather disreputable beginnings by going into newspaper publishing, he was still to be an innovator and prime judge of public taste. Perhaps not entirely fairly, he also had to bear the brunt of most of the attacks on Penny Dreadful fiction, and his later serials are seen to be aimed more specifically at the female market with a noted toning-down of the titles.

To represent Lloyd I have selected a short item from one of his earliest publications, *The Calendar of Horrors* which I am given to understand also appeared in his *Lives of the Most Notorious Highwaymen, Footpads, etc.* If Lloyd had a good story or plot situation he was certainly not reluctant to use it over and over again—nor, it would seem, were his readers averse to reading it more than once.

The Dead Alive;
Or, The Mendicant Robber of Orleans

In 1747, a man was broke alive upon the wheel at Orleans, for a highway robbery, and not having friends to take care of his body, when the executioner concluded he was dead, he gave him to the surgeon, who had him carried to his anatomical theatre, as a subject to lecture on. The thighs, legs, and arms of this unhappy wretch had been broken; yet, on the surgeon's coming to examine him, he found life reviving, and by the application of proper cordials, he was soon brought to his speech.

The surgeon and his pupils, moved by the sufferings and solicitation of the robber, determined on attempting his cure; but he was so mangled that his two thighs and one of his arms were amputated. Notwithstanding this mutilation and

A typical "fierce" engraving for one of Edward Lloyd's early publications, "The Black Vulture, or The Rival Brothers" (1840).

loss of blood, he recovered, and in this situation the surgeon, by his own desire, had him conveyed in a cart fifty leagues from Orleans, where, as he said, he intended to gain his livelihood by begging.

His situation was on the road side, close by a wood, and his deplorable condition excited compassion from all who saw him. In his youth he had served in the army, and he now passed for a soldier, who had lost his limbs by a cannon shot.

A drover returning from market, where he had been selling cattle, was solicited by the robber for charity, and being moved by compassion, threw him a piece of silver. "Alas," said the robber, "I cannot reach it—you see I have neither arms nor legs," (for he had concealed his arm which had been preserved behind his back) "so for the sake of heaven put your charitable donation into my pouch."

The drover approached him, and as he stooped to reach up the money, the sun being shining, he saw a shadow on the ground which caused him to look up, when he perceived the arm of the beggar elevated over his head, and his hand grasping a short iron bar. He arrested the blow in its descent, and seizing the robber, carried him to his cart, into which having thrown him, he drove off to the next town, which was very near, and brought him prisoner before a magistrate.

On searching him a whistle was found in his pocket, which naturally induced a suspicion that he had accomplices in the wood; the magistrate, therefore, instantly ordered a guard to the place where the robber had been seized, and they arrived there within half an hour after the murder of the drover had been attempted.

The guard having concealed themselves behind different trees, the whistle was blown, the sound of which was remarkably shrill and loud: and another whistle was heard from under ground, three men at the same instant rising from the midst of a bushy clump of brambles, and other dwarf shrubs. The soldiers fired on them, and they fell. The bushes were searched, and a descent discovered into a cave. Here were found three young girls and a boy. The girls were kept for the offices of servants, and purposes of lust; the boy scarcely twelve years of age, was son to one of the robbers. The girls in giving evidence deposed, that they had lived nearly three years in the cave, had been carried there by force from the high road, having never seen daylight from the time of their captivity; that dead bodies were frequently carried into the cave, stripped and buried; and that the old soldier was carried out every dry day, and sat by the road side for two or three hours.

On this evidence the murdering mendicant was condemned to suffer a second execution on the wheel. As but one arm remained, it was to be broken by several strokes, in several places, and the *coup de grâce* being denied, he lived in torture nearly five days. When dead, his body was burnt to ashes, and strewed before the winds of heaven.

3

THE LIFE OF DICK TURPIN

W. M. Clarke, Publisher

ONE OF THE first great heroes of the Penny Dreadfuls was the notorious highwayman, Dick Turpin, whose mainly unsavoury exploits were soon buried in a welter of daring adventures. Turpin, whose life had come to an abrupt end on the gallows in 1739, had first been remembered in the chapbooks and songsheets of his period—his dubious ride to York being particularly celebrated in all these publications. Although consistently regarded as a folk hero, it was not until 1834 that he received the great stimulant which was to ensure his popularity for all time: his portrayal in W. Harrison Ainsworth's great novel *Rookwood* which at least bore some resemblance to fact.

The early publishers of the Penny Dreadfuls, as I have indicated, were quick to plagiarize anyone else's success, and a year or so later the market was being flooded with eagerly-received imitations—many depicting Turpin as a basically good character who had been driven to crime by circumstances beyond his control. E. S. Turner has commented on this aspect in his study: "Wage slaves had no intention of spending their scanty leisure hours reading about wage slaves. They wanted to read about fiery individualists, men of spirit who defied harsh laws and oppressive officialdom, even though they finished at the end of a hempen rope." Few of the imitations paid any attention to the facts of Turpin's life —nor, for that matter, did the several stage versions which appeared in London from 1835 onwards—and as the competition hotted up and each writer tried to claim more attention for his work by ridiculing the stories of others, Turpin found himself despatched not only on outrageous missions, but into perilous adventures with Scottish clansmen, Irish bandits and even Red Indians. (In time, too, Turpin found himself beset with female imitators, such as May Turpin, Nan Darrell and the delightfully named Starlight Nell.)

The most successful of all the Turpin penny-parts—allegedly selling two million copies per week—was undoubtedly "Black Bess, or The Knight of the Road", whose "author", Edward Viles, sustained the highwayman's adventures for 254 weeks, writing in the region of two and a half million words.* The work, almost certainly the longest Penny Dreadful by one author, in fact had four main characters, Turpin, Claude Duval, Tom King and "Sixteen String Jack", all of whom plundered and robbed together or rescued each other from the jaws of disaster, with a complete disregard for authenticity.

Edward Lloyd had, of course, been at the head of this vanguard of publishers who profited from the public taste for highwaymen. His *Lives of the Most Notorious Highwaymen* (1836) had played a major part in its development, but it was not until the 1850s that he joined the competition with a vengeance, producing "Gentleman Jack; or Life on the Road" (probably by Thomas Prest, 1852), "Tom King; The Bold Highwayman" (now one of the scarcest of all his publications, 1852) and the long-running "Claude Duval: The Dashing Highwayman" (1854). One of his greatest rivals was W. M. Clarke of Warwick Lane, Paternoster Row, who had

*Montague Summers has maintained that Viles only "fathered" "Black Bess" and that it was in fact the work of J. F. Smith. Although a great many sensational romances appeared under Viles' name, it is alleged that he employed a stable of writers to produce all these works for him. Summers also recounts an interesting story that Robert Louis Stevenson offered Viles the manuscript of *Treasure Island*, but the old man "did not think much of the stuff". He would, however, purchase the tale "to be rewritten by a more competent hand". As all the world has good cause to be aware, Stevenson resisted the temptation and asked for his work back.

realized the attraction of Turpin right from the start and was running his *The Life of Dick Turpin* from 1841.

Clarke, who was also a printer, was one of the few publishers in this area who did not concentrate solely on material for the lower classes and published a wide range of periodicals from educational books to middle-class novels and Penny Dreadfuls. He was also a specialist in what have been described as "paste and scissors magazines"—weekly journals assembled by editors who "lifted" extracts or entire stories from other books and publications. Clarke's "Dick Turpin" is one of the most accomplished and constantly entertaining of the highwaymen stories I have read, and in the episode I have extracted here the anonymous author describes a bizarre robbery by Turpin and an associate from an old astrologer.

(Another hero who perhaps ought to be mentioned in this context is Jack Sheppard, the London apprentice who was sentenced to imprisonment in 1724 for theft and then proceeded to make three extraordinary escapes from prison which made him the focus of widespread public attention. Daniel Defoe was one of the first to write about him, but from 1839 onwards he was fêted in no less than seven Penny Dreadfuls which, Montague Summers tells us in *The Gothic Quest*, "caused a veritable furore and stirred up a storm of adverse criticism against the school of 'criminal romance', severely but very feebly and inconsistently attacked by Thackeray and Forster.")

The Robbery Of The Astrologer

The parlour of the "Jonas and Whale" was in a state of cruel commotion and the passage crowded with curious neighbours, when, amidst the general hubbub—"Landlord! clap to the door!" exclaimed a voice, "Turpin has been traced to this house, with a mail containing stolen plate."

"To this house, quotha!" retorted Landlord Thomas Tankard, angrily; "d'ye think I keep a resort for your

Turpins, Kings, and such nightriders as they? No, no, here be only the club of Bucklersbury, all good men and true; and if this should be Richard Turpin, why I'll testify we had no truck with him here."

"Perhaps not, perhaps not, Master Tankard," replied the voice, which was that of Master Jones, the thieftaker, who was with the pursuing party; "but by your leave, gentlemen, we'll just search old Moses's premises adjacent, and see what turns up there."

The officers set off, but they ransacked the Jew's establishment in vain, no trace of the valuable plate could there be found.

Meanwhile wonders on wonders came on the quiet club, like clap after clap of thunder; for while Master Tankard, with honest zeal to clear himself from the imputation of harbouring or comforting the daring reiver who had thus, as he imagined, brought a slur upon the respectability of "Jonas and Whale", and was busying himself in search of the highwaymen, or at least pretending to do so, the members of the club who had remained behind, whispering about robbers with bated breath, were almost petrified by a shrill scream, followed by cries of "fire! murder! rape! and robbery!" proceeding from the room directly over head. The voice was clearly that of Tankard's better half; and as the ear-piercing lamentations struck on the ears of a group of drinkers below, each looked in his neighbour's face as seeking therein some explanation of what this outcry might forebode. "Now, Master Sagetop," remonstrated one Howlett; "thou'rt a man of war, a valiant trainband captain, go first up the stair and we will follow thee." The prudent herbalist looked as though he had rather

Let I dare not, wait upon I would.

"I'll follow, Master ———" But they were saved further trouble by the descent of Mistress Tankard herself, who opened the door, vociferating—

The dramatic robbery of the astrologer from the very popular *Life of Dick Turpin* published by W. M. Clarke (1841).

"Run, gentlemen, and fetch me Master Liverwort the constable—oh that I should live to see this day—" At length, in reply to twenty clamourous questions, she disburthened her breast of the fact, that while Master Tankard had been running over the neighbourhood seeking the robbers of other people, some one or other of the scoundrels had cleared the shelf in their bedroom of four massive silver tankards, in which vessels it was then the custom to serve spiced ale, mulled wine, &c. to the guests. Poor Tankard shortly after returned—to a sense of his situation as well as his house. So that night the Members of "The United Brethren of Bucklersbury" sat in solemn conclave until an hour beyond twelve, devising means for the capture of the villain who had put this slight upon their citizen sagacity, and cast indignity upon these worthy and brave citizens.

Numerous were the suggestions; in most of which, unfortunately, the propounder was singularly anxious to thurst forward his neighbours into the post of honour and of danger, which they, on the other hand, as resolutely declined. At length, none of their schemes securing a sufficiently unanimous support, it was proposed that a consultation should be had with Ptolemy Horoscope, the Astrologer, anent and concerning the recovery of Tankard's lost plate, and that a subscription should be forthwith made to fee the cunning man for this purpose. This was assented to, as was an acute amendment by Mr Sagetop to the following effect; "that as a reward of £200 was already offered by government for the apprehension of Turpin, that Ptolemy should also be consulted as to the probable success of the enterprise; and should the stars be favourable, the Club should be first reimbursed the amount of their several subscriptions and expenses (out of the said reward of £200), and the remainder be placed to the spending-money of the Club and the replacing of Tankard's silver jugs, should they not (which of course they most probably would) be recovered upon the capture of the robber." This proposition, warmed by the highwayman's punch, which yet "ream'd in their noddles", was received with general applause, and the Club broke up, as well satisfied with the result of their deliberations, as many greater and cleverer assemblages, who have, like them, sold the bear's skin before they caught him.

The subscription of two guineas was duly raised, and it was decided that Master Sagetop, accompanied by Howlett and Tankard, should form a deputation to wait on the mighty seer.

*   *   *

We will now shift the scene to the astrologer's apartments in Little Britain, where, having made their way up a narrow dark staircase, in the spiral turns of which the goodly corpus of Master Thomas Tankard had more than once nearly jammed, the leader of the band, Master Sagetop, arrived at a strong narrow black door, studded with square bosses, imitating immense screw-nuts or nail-heads, but really consisting of small squared pieces of light wood, cunningly glued on and painted over. At the door of this enchanted castle Sagetop thrice rounded with the head of his "staff tipped with horn". The call was answered by a tall, thin figure in a loose gown of foreign damask, with a belt of parchment curiously painted and gilded; who, signifying by a sign of his finger that one only of the party could be admitted at a time, the two others were fain to await, with beating hearts, the result of their neighbour's conference with the interpreter of celestial secrets. The door was cautiously closed, and the astrologer seated himself behind a table whereon lay Haly's *De Judiciis Astrorum, the Trithemius* of Spannheim, Glanville, Regiomontanus, and sundry numbers of *Lilly's Almanack*. He motioned Sagetop to be seated, and fixing his eyes on the folio which lay open before him, became seemingly wrapt in study.

Sagetop looked round the chamber with a creeping, cold, shuddering sensation, as his eye roved from a bleached skull reposing on a Bible, to sundry bottles containing monstrous pickles in the shape of tropical toads, frightful spiders, bats, and centipedes; while, overhead, a hideous shrivelled alligator, a dried serpent or two, and a shark's jaws were suspended, in a group neither picturesque nor pleasing to one ignorant of natural history, and whose only notions were those received through his uneducated senses, to which these all conveyed ideas of satanic ugliness and terror. Poor Sagetop never felt half so uncomfortable when, fifteen years before, on the news of the rising in favour of the Pretender in '15, he was assured by a waggish neighbour that his company of trained hands were ordered for "foreign service", to meet the Popish claimant to the crown. He wriggled and fidgeted, and at length his throat, having filled with phlegm, and his nose with some pungent dust which flew in the apartment, he unwillingly let go a "hem!" followed by a hearty sneeze.

The astrologer looked up. "A'll tell'ee whaat a come about; a'll set'ee up a figure secundos artos, and tell 'ee what to do." The astrologer here began to scrawl sundry ill-favoured signs on the paper before him, while Sagetop looked on in mute wonder to see what might come next.

Not to keep the reader in suspense, it may be here right to explain that Ptolemy Horoscope, who was really a skilful astronomer and learned man, had retired to rest, having "outwatched the bear" over night in his astral studies from his observatory at the top of his dwelling, and had directed his man Parable to call him in case any client should arrive. This precious assistant, however, had long entertained a vehement desire, which his master would never gratify, of seeing and answering enquirers himself, and this he now determined to try his hand at, for having got together a few astrological phrases, Parable considered himself fully qualified to resolve any cases that might be put to him; besides, he doubted not he could pocket a fee, to him the principal end of the science, as well as his master. Having blotted the paper with many marks, he proceeded, "Thy name's Master Sagetop, of Bucklersbury (this wouldn't have surprised anybody, for Parable had many a time and oft dealt at his shop), and thou comest hither concerning the tankards of him who keepeth the 'Jonas and Whale'—good."

Had the City of London been engulfed at his feet, poor Sagetop could not have been more petrified than he was, in his then frame of mind, at these announcements of Parable. He never recollected—how should he?—that the persons of the whole club were known, and that Parable had spied "mine host" on the stairs, whose loss had been bruited about the City for two days, with all sorts of exaggeration. His knees positively shook with awe, and he awaited in gaping wonderment what next might be revealed.

"The cusp of Aldebaran is on the hinder leg of the Great Bear," continued Parable, gravely, "and the fiery triplicitus hath pointed to—but I am wearied from much study," added the knave, raising his head in imitation of his master's style; "what dost thou desire to know?"

"Briefly this," replied Sagetop, "an' it please your wise mastership; but I fear me to speak in thy reverend presence —may I—"

"The aurum potabile, which signifieth gold to drink," interrupted Parable, stretching forward his arm, and pushing a small wooden bowl in the direction of Sagetop, still keeping his eye on his book, "is the needful thing to lengthen life and guard this microcosm against hurts of venomous things, the bits of dragons and toads—Albertus Magus, Nostradamus, Regiomontanus, Albumazar, Hazael, with the —— good, Master Sagetop, good," continued he, drawing back the bowl with his forefinger, and throwing over it a piece of embroidery. "Thou mayest open the door and let in thy friends."

Sagetop felt as a man waking after a suffocating nightmare, and availed himself of the permission with alacrity. The other two entered, each bowing lowly.

"Listen to what the stars say," said Parable, opening an old almanack: "the Asseli denote death by fire, fevers, hanging, disgrace, beheading, and utter ruin—look for thefts, and robberies now about—new moon 16th day, 11h. 18m., at night—something ails the Pope about this time—I wish the Cardinals may sit easy—

> When Pisces doth in heaven appear,
>   And Orion's stars do brightly shine,
> Then draweth to an end the year,
>   And daylight greatly doth decline.

Now guard from attacks, head, face, throat, neck, arms, shoulders, breast, and stomach—Pleiades, Hyades, Castor, Pollux, Praeape, Menkar, Procyon,—you see how it is, my brethren."

"Aye, aye, neighbours, you see how 'tis," said Sagetop, shaking his head very wisely at the rest. "Mr Ptolemy told me all I knew about it before you came in; he tells us, you hear, that Turpin robs in the new moon, at the short days, at eleven at night"; hereat mine host gave a melancholy grunt of assent; "and that he attacks the head and throat, and all the parts he mentioned, with his crew of rogues, with those hard names, though I've heard his gang called quite differently; but to be sure Mr Ptolemy knows best."

"But now, Doctor Horoscope, how may we best know how to secure him?" asked Howlett.

"Why," continued Parable, "that is another question"; and again the bowl was pushed forward, and a crown each chinked in by three of the party, "and 'twill call for much calculation—if Mars be angular with Antares, he shall hardly 'scape death by drowning or assassination—fair and pleasant weather now about June, but expect snow and dark nights about November—Arista giveth honour and riches, and with Rigel good fortune is assured—the bright star Fomahaut, if with the hyleg, doth denote a murderer, who will come to an untimely end—let Poland look to herself; but do you go down, brethren, to the skirts of the forest, and there it shall be revealed to ye—knock him down—a blusterous time will come after this—a sly piece of villainy is brought to light—and the knave discovered—Algol, Hydra, Deneb, Ophiaca, Antares—you see how it is, brethren and friends—he weareth a brown coat."

"Many thanks, many thanks, worshipful Mister Horumscope. A man in a brown coat. Neighbours, we must be well watched and lighted. Good day, Mr Ptolemy. Oh! what a fine thing it be's truly to read the Box Spellarem, as the allmyknack says. Skirts of the forest—sly piece of villany. Neighbours, we're sure of him—I feel as good as if the reward was in my pouch, and if I gain it, I'll give—I'll give—the club a new china punchbowl. Bravo, gallant Master Sagetop", and with these and the like exclamations, the deputation bowed themselves out of the sham astrologer's presence, and threaded their way down his corkscrew stairs into the street.

It was now fast growing dark in the narrow, confined street of Little Britain, and the party did not observe, on the opposite side of the way, beneath the shadow of an overhanging shop-window, two men, who evidently had been awaiting their departure, and who scarcely repressed a laugh as the worthy cits picked their way along the cobble-stone pavement, full of the wisdom they had purchased of Peter Parable.

Scarcely had they turned the corner of one of the projecting houses in the crooked street, when the stouter one observed to his companion—"Ha! ha! well, 'pon my soul, Dick, this is, beyond question, one of the drollest affairs it's ever happened to be my luck to fall in with. But how, in the name of his sooty highness, came you to know that these gulls were coming hither, and to what end are we here?"

"Gently, George, my boy, and you shall know all in good time. The astrologer hath just robbed these muddy-pated knaves, and now we'll pluck the astrologer. They were late yester-morning for such early-to-bed snorers, settling how to take you and I, and the result of their secret-council was known through all Bucklersbury before noon; nay, Foxy Norris brought me word of every syllable of their proceedings, past and intended, which he picked up from the Drawer at the 'Jonas and Whale', before one of the privy-council of cunning men had opened their gummy eyes. Ha! ha! step up softly, George; this is the door, and there's no need of violence in this business. I'm going to consult the astrologer, d'ye see; and by way of reversing his professional practice, shall take a fee of him for my trouble in reading his fortune in the stars."

So saying, the two slowly threaded their way up to the door, by which the worthy deputation of Bucklersbury had just left.

*　　*　　*

"What! more customers?" muttered Parable, as he cast a glance at an ancient horologe, which ticked in the inner chamber, to ascertain whether he might venture on earning another crown or two, without risk of detection by old Ptolemy: the knocking was repeated, and Parable, who had lighted a silver cresset-lamp which hung in the room, unfastened the door to his new visitor. The stranger was a stout man, in a brown horseman's coat, girt about with a leathern belt, and, making a low bow, he seated himself in a chair and looked about him.

"Queer ken this," muttered he; "and no one to tout at the door."

"Well, Master Astrologer, I've heard down in our parts in Essex, that you can tell simple men like me when to begin a weighty affair, and how to conduct it, like; so, do you see, as I've a little venture just now in hand, d'ye see, there's five as good broad gold pieces as was ever coined, if ye can tell me whether it will come off as I wish it, like-eh?"

The astrologer looked up, with his long sallow face, at the querent; he did not like his brusque manner of address; indeed, being yet so young in trading on his "own hook", he was rather "taken aback", as sailors say; he, however, started off, with his eyes fixed on the book—

"Respect and venerate the mighty seer, who, in the cycles and epicycles, the lines, secants, and tangents of the heavens, reads the destinies of weak mortals—Saturn, in the cusp of the fifth house, doth grievously afflict Mercury in quartile—there be leaden thieves abroad, who shall be frustrated in the eastern parts—he comes from Essex—guard well your goods, and look to live-stock—drill beans and sow broadcast—great danger to pigs, poultry, especially calves, about this time—

> For Rigel is a star of fame,
>   And now doth rule with fear;
> While Caput, Algol, and the Whale
>   In conjunct close appear—

ah! I see—the trine configuration is adverse when the regeat or native have a malign promittor—Sagittarius, Taurus, and

Leo, be brute signs, and these, with the vernal Aries and Cancer—the Crab, that doth backward go—do signify"—

During this speech Dick had silently opened the door to his comrade Fielder, who, slipping in on hands and knees, had, in the short space of a few seconds, slipped into a bag he had brought under his cloak, the golden pentacle, the lamen of like precious material, with sundry other apparatus of necromancy, and had taken the magic sword in hand, when a loud report from its handle, sharp as a pistol crack, occasioned him to drop it, and startled the terrified Parable to his feet.

"Sit still, my celestial sage," said Dick, soothingly, putting at the same time a pistol to his ear; "go on with your gibberish—curse me, but you're a funny fellow! Sit still, will ye, or I'll whistle an ounce of lead through your learned numskull!"

Poor Parable needed no interpreter of the stars to tell him he was in danger of death from lead; his jaw dropped on his breast, and his nether end on his master's seat.

At this juncture, while Fielder was looking at the mystic symbol as it lay on the floor, the voice of Ptolemy himself was heard above. "Thou whoreson knave! thou scoundrel meddler! Parable, I say, how darest thou to meddle profanely with—"

"What, impious wretch, fearest thou not that the spirit will rend thee? Aldama! Hezail! Cassiul! Oberion! Vanatha! seize me this impious intruder!" exclaimed the Wizard, as he arrived at the foot of the narrow stairs which led from his dormitory, and espied, by the streaming light from the outer chamber, Fielder standing in the centre of the awful circle itself!

"Pray don't flurry yourself about me," was the answer, in a voice that stopped the torrent of Horoscope's objurgations. "You need call for no other spirits but Geneva, old Triangle; and if you'll make that appear, why, I'll pound it, we'll lay it in the Red Sea down Red Lane, as the little boys call it. Take a seat, most learned magus, here, on the carpet, while I pass this curtain-cord round the bottom of your petticoats, old gentleman; there, that will do; and now just tell me, or I'll solve the secret of your nativity for you in a crack, what the devil's the matter with this queer looking stick, that a gentleman cannot lay hold of it?"

The astrologer was deaf to this question, for he merely entreated the robber to leave him the tools of his art.

"Here, Dick," said Fielder, "is the real necromancer; t'other outside is only a sham!"

To this, Parable, on bended knees, confessed.

Dick and his comrade now bound and blindfolded the two prophets, and laying them side by side on the floor of the inner apartment, they fastened the door, then, having previously relieved Parable of his ill-earned cash, they nailed up the outer-door and departed.

Then, making their way towards Aldgate, they found their horses at the accustomed spot, and while they were riding towards King's Oak, burst out with laughter at their adventure, and the detected knavery of Parable.

4

ROBIN HOOD

by Pierce Egan Jnr

ANOTHER CHARACTER OF legend to enjoy early popularity in the Penny Dreadfuls was Robin Hood, the outlaw of Sherwood Forest. As in the case of Turpin, his success stemmed almost solely from the writing of one man, in this instance Pierce Egan Jnr (1814–1880). Egan was the son of the noted sports reporter for *Bell's Sunday Times*, who wrote several works including the famous *Life in London* (1820), which was an immensely popular weekly publication showing for the first time low life in the capital and from which over sixty later works were to derive including Charles Dickens' *The Pickwick Papers*, and G. W. M. Reynolds' *The Mysteries of London*. The younger Egan almost inevitably followed his father into journalism and though lacking the originality of his parent, was a hard-working and capable author. He first went into print as an illustrator, however, providing the woodcuts for one of his father's books, *The Pilgrims of the Thames* (1838), and then published his own first novel, *Quintin Matsys, The Blacksmith of Antwerp*, based remotely on a European legend, in 1839. He was to leap to the forefront of the Penny Dreadful writers less than a year later when the first of the forty-one parts of his tale "Robin Hood and Little John; or The Merry Men of Sherwood Forest" appeared.

Egan, like his counterparts, used only the bare bones of the legend of the outlaw, but nonetheless public demand quickly mounted to hundreds of thousands of copies per week, and the story was only a few months old when the first of many imitations started to appear. In time a whole Robin Hood industry was in full flood, all drawing to a greater or lesser degree on Egan. Although it was to be re-issued frequently in later years in differing numbers of parts and under new titles, Egan busied himself on other tales of historical fiction taking up such diverse characters as "Wat Tyler" (1840), "Paul Jones the Pirate" (1842), "The Black Prince" (1848) and "Clifton Grey: A Tale of the Crimea" (1854). The success of "Robin Hood" was also repeated when it was later republished abroad in translation and one French version was incorrectly ascribed to Alexandre Dumas.

Hard though he tried, Egan never again achieved quite the success of his early story, although his stature as one of the leading writers in the genre remained undisputed. (The *Dictionary of National Biography* refers to him as "deservedly accounted one of the pioneers of cheap literature".) Despite the accolades, many of his tales are certainly long-winded and insipid—and more than one authority has accused him of showing a complete disregard for historical fact and a predilection for scenes of torture and cruelty. E. S. Turner recounts an amusing story about him in this context concerning the editor of the *London Journal* who tried to drop his gory romances in 1859 and replace him with Sir Walter Scott. Sales, however, plummeted so dramatically thereafter that he had to be hastily summoned and begged to return to the columns of the periodical.

Naturally, I have selected an item from "Robin Hood" for this collection, and it is a nicely self-contained episode in which Robin wreaks bloody vengeance on an adversary.

The Ambush Of Death

It had been ascertained by the Sheriff of Nottingham that Robin Hood with half his men were away in Yorkshire, and he conceived with some shrewdness that it would be possible, with a sufficient number of men, to make an attack upon the merrie men who still remained—clear the wood of them—destroy the haunt—and lie in wait for Robin and the remainder of the men when they returned. He sent to London for a reinforcement of troops, making out a strong case of necessity for them, and they were sent to him; he organized them after his own fashion, and sent them out into the greenwood under the command of him who had brought the men from London. The merrie men, from being connected with so many in Nottingham town, soon were aware of what was in store for them. They concerted measures accordingly, and disposed themselves to receive the troop, who marched on sanguine of success; but when they had arrived at the spot, where the men had prepared to meet them, they were welcomed with a shower of arrows, which committed dreadful slaughter; it was followed by a second and third, each arrow telling with a dreadful precision of aim, without the assailed knowing from whence the shafts came; then the merrie men rushed forth from their coverts with great shouts, and cut down all who offered resistance. A panic seized the troops at this sudden and terrible attack, and they fled without striking a blow in the greatest disorder into Nottingham, with the loss of nearly half their men. Not one of the merrie men received a hurt; and they gathered the bodies of those whom they had slain together, and in the night they bore them into the town, and laid them down at the castle gates, bidding the high sheriff pay them a visit in the greenwood, and they would bring him home in the same fashion, an invitation which, had he received, he would have had no hesitation in at once declining. He was horror-stricken at his ill success, and, while in the midst of his wailing at his misfortune, a Norman, whom he had known at Rouen, called to see him with a stout body of men. To him Fitz Alwine detailed his disaster, and repeated a lying history of the way Robin Hood had served him several times, and excused his own failures by swearing that Robin Hood and his men were invincible.

"Were he the devil himself," said this friend, who was

called Sir Guy of Gisborne, from an estate he possessed there, "an' I took it into my head to pull his horns off, I would do it."

"Not if they were Robin Hood's," said the baron, who hoped to egg on Sir Guy to undertake an enterprise against the bold outlaw.

"If they were the devil's, I tell you," cried Sir Guy, "an' it pleased me to do it."

"Well," returned Fitz Alwine, speaking in a careless tone, "I never knew the man who would not quail before Robin Hood."

"Then you never knew me," cried Sir Guy, with an expression of scorn.

"Oh ho!" laughed Fitz Alwine, "he would make you quail like all the rest."

"Pshaw!" roared Sir Guy; "it is not in the power of mortal or devil to do it: I defy them both alike. Let me meet this Robin Hood, and I will cut off his ears, slit his nose, and hang him up like a swine by the feet."

"By the Mass, then," exclaimed the baron, "I wish thou couldst meet with him; if thou wert able to do that, it would be serving me mightily."

"Tell me where he is to be found, and I will undertake it, my head be the forfeit if I fail," cried Sir Guy.

"I have little doubt but it will," said Fitz Alwine, "for I think it is not in man's power to conquer him."

"You will see," said he, contemptuously. "Where is this mighty man to be found?"

"He is in Barnsdale-wood, some two days' journey hence. I will accompany thee, and join my men with thine. He has only half his crew there, and if we approach cautiously we shall have them all snugly."

"Be it so," returned Sir Guy; "but I will don a yeoman's dress and seek him single-handed, and then you shall find whether he or I am the most invincible."

Delighted that he had such an assistant, Fitz Alwine set to work with alacrity; he got all his men ready, and with Sir

Guy he started off to Barnsdale. It was agreed that he should lead his men to one part of the wood, and that Sir Guy, in the disguise of a yeoman, should take another, endeavour to find Robin Hood, slay him if he could, and in the event of success he was to blow a horn which had a peculiar tone with it, and thereupon the sheriff was to join him, and together they were to do the best they could to slay as many of the merrie men as they could, and take the others prisoners. With this intention, early one morning they quitted Nottingham.

Two days subsequent to this, Robin Hood, lying down beneath his trysting tree, fell into a slumber. Little John seated himself by his side and was conning over the merits of his pleasant wife, Winifred, when a woodwele [a kind of thrush], alighting on a bough above him, began singing with such extraordinary loudness that he could not but take note of it. Robin also from sleeping disturbedly awoke, and sprung suddenly to his feet.

"How now!" cried Little John, startled. "What is the matter with thee, Robin?"

"Why, where am I?—oh, I have been dreaming," he answered, rubbing his eyes and waking himself up. "I have had a dream. I thought I was treated contumeliously by two yeomen; I threw back their scorn with interest, and we came to blows; they conquered me, beat me, and bound me; they were about to slay me, when suddenly a bird alighted on a tree near me, seeming like as it had been made of flame, and it appeared to speak, bidding me be of good cheer. My bands at that moment fell from me and I was free: then I awoke."

"It was odd," said Little John, thoughtfully, "while you were sleeping, a woodwele sat itself on yon bough, and sang so loud it waked you; it fled directly you moved."

"It may mean something," said Robin, scarcely allowing to himself that he was superstitious, and therefore chary of making the remark; "warnings should never be despised, however slight; we will look about us and see what is going on."

Pierce Egan Jnr not only wrote the most popular of the Robin Hood serials (1840), but also provided the gruesome illustrations.

The merrie men now drew nigh in answer to his summons, and bidding them away towards York, which was the only point from which he anticipated danger, he took Little John with him to reconnoitre one part of the wood, while Will Scarlet, with two others, went in the direction of Mansfield. As Robin Hood and Little John proceeded something in the same direction that Will had taken, they saw a yeoman with a capul hide [horse hide] about him as a species of cloak—not infrequently worn by Yorkshire yeoman of that day, especially those who had the charge of horses; he had a sword and dagger by his side, and looked as great a villain as he was in reality.

"Aha!" exclaimed Robin, on seeing him, "here's a stranger; he looks a ruffian—I'll try if he be one; if he is, he hath no business here, and unless he budges pretty quickly, he shall taste the quality of my weapons."

"He looks a dog who will bite," said Little John scanning the stranger from head to foot. "Do you stay, Robin, beneath this tree, and I will go ask him what he doeth here. Marry, I will make him troop quickly."

"No, Little John," uttered Robin, hastily, "I have a fancy for this fellow. I have not had a bout a long while, and, by the Holy Mother, I never should, if thou hadst thy will: thou'rt ever wishing me to send my men before, and I tarry behind. By St Mary, but some day I shall have to set to and beat thee for mere want of practice, only that it may be breaking a good staff, thine head being of such especial thickness. No, Little John, I will trounce this knave myself, for I am sure he is one—he looks one; and do thou go to Will, and bid him back; he is not far from hence. When thou hearest my horn, I shall want thee, but not before."

"Your will is my law," said Little John, turning away somewhat tiffed, because Robin would not suffer him to fight instead of him. Leaving Robin Hood to accost the stranger in his capul hide, we will follow Little John in his path to find Will Scarlet. He wandered on, annoyed that Robin should have taken into his own hands the task of fighting the stranger, for he easily guessed it would come to that, when he wished so much himself to have the pleasure. But a little reflection taught him that he was unjust in being offended where he had no right to take offence, so the fit passed away almost as quickly as it had come; and when he came to consider on what errand he was bound, he found he had wandered considerably out of his path; he, however, bestirred himself, and was soon on the track of Will Scarlet. A long time had not elapsed ere he heard the clashing of weapons, as of men engaged in violent strife; he ran on in the direction from whence the sound emanated, and soon came upon Will Scarlet and his two companions fighting desperately with eight or ten opponents, and the Sheriff of Nottingham advancing swiftly with a large body of men. Little John rushed forward with a loud shout, and getting his bow ready, he took an aim at the sheriff in such an ecstacy of passion that the sudden force used in drawing his bow broke it, and the arrow fell useless to the ground.

"A curse on thee and the tree on which thou grew!" he cried, bitterly, "thou worthless slip of a more worthless tree, to fail me at such a moment as this!"

He darted forward to help his companions. He saw one of them cut down, after opposing three most manfully, without budging a foot. He seized a bow which the unfortunate outlaw had dropped, and took another aim at the sheriff, and exclaimed—

"One shot will I shoot now that shall quiet yonder rascally sheriff, who is coming hither so fast. He shall stop as suddenly as he is advancing."

He drew the bow, and loosed the shaft. The sheriff's quick eye detected the act, and he threw himself flat upon the horse. A retainer, William-a-Trent, who rode close behind him, received it through his body, and fell dead from his horse. That William-a-Trent had been very anxious to be of the expedition against Robin Hood; but it had been better for him:

> "To have been a-bed with sorrowe
> Than to be that day in the greenwood slade
> To meet with Little John's arrowe."

The troop pricked forward more quickly on perceiving one of their companions slain, and Little John threw himself among those who were sore pressing Will Scarlet and his remaining comrade. He hurled one fellow to the ground like lightning, tore a spear from his grasp, and laid about him with tremendous energy and effect. Will Scarlet's companion was cut down, it was impossible to withstand so many opposers, and Will was himself hemmed in. Little John, however, who had seen the second outlaw fall, raged like a lion. He cleared Will in an instant from his assailants, and roared to him to fly.

"Never," cried Will, "while I have breath!"

"Fly, Will, for the Holy Mother's sake!" urged Little John; "seek Robin Hood and get together the merrie men, or there will be more true hearts this day on their backs than the green turf will be glad to receive."

Seeing the truth of Little John's words, Will made a desperate cut at one fellow who blocked his path, and felled him to the earth, and then darted off to find Robin; while Little John gave no ground, and fought like a madman. But it was madness to contend with such numbers, and although his prodigious strength stood him in good stead, there were too many against him to make it of much avail. A long staff was thrust between his legs, in endeavouring to avoid it he was thrown; a body of men threw themselves upon him, and bound him hand and foot. There he lay until the sheriff came up, and one fellow bared his sword to cut off his head on the instant, as he fully expected to receive an immediate command to that effect from Fitz Alwine; but he did not give it. His eye lighted on Little John; with a grim smile he ordered him to be placed on his feet, and said to him with a chuckle—

"I remember you, my forest pole, and you shall remember me before you are sent into the other world."

"I don't forget you," said Little John, gnawing his nether lip, to conceal his rage and shame at being a prisoner. "I hung you like a thieving dog under your own roof—how did you relish your due? Remember you, Robin Hood will be here anon—ask him if he recollects you, and note his reply."

"You mean his head will be here," said the sheriff, grinning. "His carcase will be left to rot in the greenwood, or else to make a meal for the wolves."

"It will never do that," said Little John, "thou'rt only foretelling thine own doom."

"You'll find thy mistake. I will let thee live until his head is brought to thee; then shalt thou speed after him with most uncommon quickness."

"I fear thy threats less than I fear thee, and I fear thee as I fear the miserable worm that trails the ground meeting his death beneath my feet," returned Little John, with cool contempt.

"You shall—you shall—" The Baron was at a loss for a simile, so he would up with "You shall see. I will let thee know thy fate. Thou shalt be wounded, but not to death, and be drawn at my horse's heels up hill and down dale, and then hung on the highest tree in these parts."

"But thou mayst fail of thy villanous purpose, if it pleaseth the Holy Son of God," said Little John, quietly; "so I care not for what thou sayest."

The Baron intended to have made a reply, but so many synonymous sentences rushed to his tongue together, and each strove so hard to get out first, that he found himself bothered; and so, after a little spluttering, he contented himself with saying nothing at all. He waved his hand for Little John to fall back among the troop, and quietly awaited the result of Sir Guy's undertaking.

We must now return to Robin Hood, who, advancing to the stranger with the capul hide, said to him blithely—

"Good morrow, good fellow; methinks, by the stout bow you bear in your hand, you should be a good archer."

"I have lost my way," said the stranger, not heeding Robin's question. "I know nought of this wood."

"I do, every turn," replied Robin. "I will lead thee through it, an' thou tellest me where thou wouldst go."

"I seek an outlaw whom men call Robin Hood," said the stranger. "I had rather meet with him than have the best—"

"What?" asked Robin Hood, observing him hesitate.

"The best forty pounds that ever were coined," he replied, hastily.

"If you come with me, my mighty yeoman, thou shalt soon see him," said Robin Hood, "but if thou'rt in no exceeding haste, we will have some little pastime beneath the greenwood trees here; let us try our skill at woodcraft. We may perhaps light on this Robin Hood at some unlooked-for time, for I can tell thee he is not always to be met with when sought for."

Robin cut down the thin boughs of several shrubs, pared off the leaves, and then stuck them upright in the ground at some distance apart.

"Now, yeoman," he said, "see if thou canst hit with thine arrow, at sixty yards, either of those wands. Lead off, and I will follow thy shot."

"Nay, good fellow," replied the stranger, "if you ask me to do that which seemeth impossible, thou hadst better lead off, and if it is to be done, show how you do it."

Robin shot without appearing to take an aim, and his arrow went within an inch of the slight wand—so close, indeed, that the stranger thought he had hit it; but Robin told him he had not, and made him go on. After several ineffectual essays, he confessed he could not come within a foot of it. Robin then made a small garland of wild flowers and hung it upon one of the wands, bidding the yeoman send his arrow through its centre; he took a long aim at it, and the arrow went through the garland, just ruffling the inner edge.

"Well shot!" said Robin, "but not well enough for a yeoman. You see the thin slip of wand which shows itself through the centre of the garland—I will cleave it with my arrow."

"It cannot be done," said the stranger.

"Behold!" cried Robin, his arrow leaving his bow almost as soon as his words left his lips.

"Wonderfully done!" cried the stranger, decidedly astonished. "Why, good yeoman, an' thy heart be as stout as thine hand, thou art better than this same Robin Hood they talk so much of. What is thy name, that I may remember who hath astonished me with his expertness at the bow."

"Nay, by my faith," said Robin, jovially, "let me know thine, and I will not withhold mine from thee."

"I have a good estate to the west," replied the stranger, "and am called after it Sir Guy of Gisborne. You may marvel to see me in this unknightly apparel, but I have sworn to take Robin Hood, and I bethought me of this disguise as being the more likely to bring me to his presence. Now, what is thy name, yeoman?"

"I have a good estate here," replied Robin; "I have also one in Nottinghamshire; and one in Huntingdonshire, which is kept from me. I am one who cares for or fears no man, especially such a one as thee. I am he whom thou seekest—my name is Robin Hood."

"Then thou shalt die here!" cried Sir Guy, drawing his sword, "and this horn will convey news of thy defeat to those who are near at hand, and will be glad to hear of it. Say thy prayers, Robin Hood; for come what may, I spare thee not. I have sworn to take back thy head, and I will, by Satan!"

"When thou hast conquered me, thou mayst do thy will on my body," said Robin, coolly; "but mark my words, Sir Guy:—thou hast sworn not to spare me—I will not spare thee, if the Blessed Virgin gives me the victory. Thou art a Norman—that seals thy doom. Come on—no quarter—life for the victor, death to the vanquished!"

Not a word more passed between them, but they set to work in good earnest. Sir Guy of Gisborne, in addition to great personal strength, was an accomplished swordsman, and with these qualities he possessed a ruthless stony nature, which would induce him to take every advantage to draw blood, no matter how unknightly or unfair the act, or whether the meanness gained him any advantage; and acting up to this spirit, he attacked Robin fiercely before he had drawn his sword. Robin leaped back to avoid him, and soon had his trusty blade opposed to the knight's; but he lost ground by it, and was forced close to the straggling roots of an oak tree. Sir Guy pressed him hard, for he well knew he had much the advantage of the ground, and he determined to make the most of it; his blows rained hard and fast; they were delivered with a force which made Robin each moment expect to see his own blade shiver at the hilt, but it was a stout blade, and bore all the blows nobly. Robin quickly found that if he remained much longer in his present position, he should stand a very certain chance of being slain; he therefore resolved to use his best efforts to extricate himself, and in his turn attacked Sir Guy; but the knight stood like a rock, and budged not a foot, although Robin kept him well employed in defending himself. After some little time, Robin saw that, without the most tremendous exertion, he could not gain his point, and as this might tell against him if he used it even successfully, he determined to leap lightly on one side, then edge round, and try if possible to place Sir Guy in the same position he had just quitted. No sooner had he come to the conclusion than he determined to act upon it, and just as Sir Guy was delivering a heavy blow, he leaped aside, but his foot caught in a root of the tree just as he jumped, and he fell to the ground. Sir Guy was not the man to let such an opportunity pass without taking advantage of it, and he accordingly with a shout sprung on his prostrate opponent, with the intention of putting an end to the contest at once. Robin perceived the danger of his situation instantly, and cried earnestly—

"Holy Mother of God! Ah! thou dear Lady! it is no man's destiny to die before the time allotted him to live in this world; my hour is not yet come, I feel. Give me strength to win this fight, or die as becomes a man and a true Saxon."

As he uttered these words he felt a sudden vigour pass into his limbs, every sinew seemed strengthened, and dexterously avoiding the fierce blow Sir Guy made at him, he leaped upon his feet and now obtained the advantageous position Sir Guy had previously possessed; he made the most of it, and the clashing of their weapons grew fiercer than ever. At last Robin, making a powerful parry of a blow delivered by Sir Guy with terrific strength, succeeded in whirling his sword far from his grasp, and of burying his own like lightning in his heart. Sir Guy clenched his hands convulsively, and fell dead without a groan. When Robin saw that he had slain his opponent, he offered up a prayer of thankfulness for his success; and when he had done this, he bethought him of what Sir Guy had said relative to bearing his head to those who were near, and who would be glad to hear the tones of the horn which was to convey the news of his defeat.

"By the Mass!" he cried, "it will be as well to see who these folks are that are so near, and with that capul hide I may disguise myself enough for my purpose. Now, Sir Guy, with your permission we will change clothes, and lose no time either about it, for every moment wasted may be of consequence to those connected with me."

So saying, he stripped Sir Guy's body of such habiliments as he deemed necessary, and divesting himself of the corresponding garments on his own person, he clothed himself in the dead man's dress, and threw the capul hide across his shoulders, as he had seen Sir Guy wear it; then, for fear the strangers whom he was about to seek might come and discover the body of their friend while he was looking for them, he dressed Sir Guy in his clothes; he then cut off his head, which he gashed in the face so that it might not be recognized, and bore it with him, in order to make his disguise more complete, as he had heard Sir Guy say he had sworn to carry his (Robin's) head back, as a trophy of his victory. When he had made all his arrangements, and was about to depart, he looked upon the body of Sir Guy, and exclaimed—

"Lie thou there, Sir Guy—lie thou there! thou hast nought to complain of. I have done that for thee which thou didst strive with all thy might to do for me, and therefore be thou not wrathful that I have prevailed; for, beshrew me, if thou had had the hardest knocks, thou hast the better garments— the best Lincoln cloth 'stead of thy Yorkshire woollen. Now will I see what the effect of thy little horn will be, for I will blow a lusty blast; I know not if there be any signal agreed upon, but I will stand the chance of that."

He blew a loud blast, and the horn having a peculiar tone, he concluded there was nothing more needful to distinguish it from any others. It was heard and replied to, and no sooner did the return strike upon his ear than he hastened in the direction whence it proceeded. He was soon close to the baron and his party, and blew a second blast on Sir Guy's horn.

"Hark!" cried Fitz Alwine joyfully, "that betokens good tidings; it is Sir Guy's horn; he hath slain Robin Hood, the vile outlaw."

"A hundred Sir Guys could not do it, an' he fought fairly and like a man!" roared Little John, feeling a horrible misgiving that the baron was speaking the truth, especially as he saw Robin coming down the glade, clad in the capul hide, and imitating Sir Guy's bearing so closely that he had no idea but that it was really the knight who was approaching. "Give me a quarter-staff and let him take his blade, the best steel ever forged, and I will defeat him, if he hath slain Robin: and if he hath, there are as many hands as he hath hairs in his head who will revenge it. He has used some vile means to gain his ends, which no honest man would stoop to do."

"Say thou thy prayers, dog!" cried the sheriff. "Thy master is slain, and so shalt thou be; therefore thou hadst better spend thy remaining moments in prayer than in railing at a noble-hearted knight, who hath slain thy doughty leader as easily as though he were cutting down a reed. Come hither, come hither, thou gallant Sir Guy!" he continued, addressing Robin Hood, whom he saw advancing quickly to him, "thou hast conquered the outlaw—thou hast delivered thy country from the most monstrous villain the world e'er saw—thou hast slain Robin Hood! Ask what thou wilt of me that I can grant, and it shall be thine."

Robin Hood, at a glance, had seen Little John's situation, and smiled as he encountered the fierce glance of defiance and hatred which the latter threw at him, supposing him to be the slayer of his beloved friend and leader. The words of the sheriff alighted on Robin's ear, carrying with them a means of extricating Little John from his situation, and in reply, therefore, he said to the sheriff—

"I have slain him who would have slain me, and since you give me the power of asking a boon of you, I ask but a blow at yonder knave, whom you have there bound. I have slain one; let me see if I cannot prevail over the other."

"If you wish to kill him with your own hand," answered the sheriff, not noticing the change of voice, because he never for an instant supposed, or even thought, that he could be deceived in this manner, "you can, if you list; but this is no boon; ask something else of me."

"I need no other," replied Robin.

"Then shalt thou have thy will; his life is thine."

"I will shrive him first," said Robin; "then will I loose his bonds, and fight with him."

Little John, although he had not detected our hero in his disguise, immediately he heard his voice, knew him, and was in a moment relieved from the most terrible weight of anguish he had ever felt; he gave a long sigh, the effects of the relief he experienced, and waited then patiently and quietly until Robin matured his plan, whatever it might be. He was not long left in uncertainty, for Robin approached him with some haste; but on finding that the sheriff, with several of his followers, were close upon his heels, he stopped suddenly and said abruptly—

"Stand back! stand back, all of you! did I not say I was going to hear his shrift before I fought with him? and ye all know it is not the custom, nor right, that more than one should hear another's shrift. Stand back, I tell you, or I may trounce some of you, even as I have him whose carcase, without this head, lies in yonder glade! There, dogs! take it and glut your eyes with the trunkless head of him who had a stouter heart than any hound among ye!" So saying, he threw the gashed head of Sir Guy into the baron's arms, who as instantly threw it among his men with a roar of terror, as if it had been a ball of red-hot iron; none of them were more eager than their lord to retain possession of it, and it fell to the ground to be kicked from one to the other. Robin had no occasion to say another word: the men, accompanied by the baron, fell back to a more respectful distance, quite as much—possibly more—satisfied with his promise to trounce them, than if he had put his promise into execution. He, as soon as he saw them as far as he considered essential for his purpose, approached Little John, and with a forest knife cut loose his bands, placed in his hand the bow and quiver of arrows which he had taken from Sir Guy (he still retained his own), and then blew the call on his own bugle which summoned his merrie men to his side. He had scarce blown it when a loud shout rung in the air, and Will Scarlet, with a face like his name, came bounding into sight, sword in hand, followed by a body of the merrie men at the top of their speed. The sight of all this came upon the baron's vision like a horrible dream; but it so quickly assumed the appearance of reality, when Robin threw off the capul hide and declared his name, and Little John fitting an arrow to Sir Guy's bow, drew it to the head, only waiting for Robin's order to discharge it, that he "fettled him to be gone", and without stopping to give a command to his men, he spurred his horse hard, and dashed off at full gallop. The men were not long in following his example.

"May the foul fiend have a speedy grip of him!" cried Little John, gnashing his teeth; "but his cowardice shall not save him. I'll bring him down from here." And he prepared to discharge his arrow.

"Hold thy hand!" exclaimed Robin, staying him; "do not

take his life, he has but a little while to live, according to nature; it is of little use to shorten his time here."

"Robin, I cannot let the old rogue escape scathless," cried Little John, excitedly; "I will not kill him, since you wish me not, but I will give him something to remind him of us for some time to come."

As he concluded he discharged his arrow, and judging from the leap which Fitz Alwine gave from the saddle, and the energetic speed with which he drew the arrow from the place where it had hit him, there is little doubt he would find either sitting or riding essentially disagreeable for some time.

With congratulations upon the narrow escape which he had just had for his life, and at which he laughed almost contemptuously, Little John was led by the merrie men to the haunt in Barnsdale Wood, and the remainder of the day was passed in joyous festivity.

5

DOMBEY AND DAUGHTER

by Renton Nicholson

POPULAR THOUGH THE heroes of legend were as subject matter for the early Penny Dreadfuls, all were to be eclipsed by the plagiarisms of Charles Dickens' novels which had suddenly caught the imagination of all stratas of society. How Dickens, the former solicitor's clerk and newspaper reporter, soared to instant popularity with his first book *Sketches by Boz* in 1836, is now part of literary legend, but less well-known is the blatant and shameless way in which most of his works were copied by pirates and published under almost identical titles, while his originals were still in the process of weekly publication. Although the work of authors was supposedly protected for twenty-eight years by the Copyright Act of 1809, publishers of the lower-class periodicals took scant notice of it and, led by proprietors such as Edward Lloyd, plagiarized all and everything that Dickens (and other contemporaries such as Ainsworth, Cockton and Mrs Crowe) wrote. For instance, Dickens' *Sketches by Boz* was followed only months later by Lloyd's "The Sketch Book by Bos" (written by Thomas Prest), his *Oliver Twist* was copied as "The Life and Adventures of Oliver Twiss" and *Nicholas Nickleby* became "Memoirs of Nickelas Nicklebery". *The Pickwick Papers* (1836–7) was almost certainly plagiarized more than any other book of its time and such was the public interest in the stories—real or imitation—that the country was soon full of people wearing Pickwick coats and hats and smoking Pickwick cigars. Dickens tried desperately to protect himself from the pirates and despite one or two minor victories was overwhelmed by the number of publications (and even stage productions) and was left to write bitterly that even in law he was "treated as if I were the robber instead of the robbed".

Such was the voracious public appetite for anything Dickensian that some of the more imaginative pirates even began to lift the most popular characters such as Sam Weller and Mr Pickwick and transport them to different countries—America and the Far East were favourites—for new and still more varied adventures. Supporters of Dickens who attacked these liberties were told, straight-faced, by the pirates that if "Mr Dickens had not thought to venture these characters to far shores, why surely it was the duty of other pens to do so?"

The passing of time has unfortunately confined the vast majority of these plagiarisms to oblivion, but reports and accounts by those who have read large numbers clearly indicate that one of the most successful of all the copies—both in terms of composition and sales—was "Dombey and Daughter" written by Renton Nicholson (1809–1861) and published in twelve parts in 1847 while Dickens' original *Dombey and Son* was still in full flight. *Dombey and Son* is, of course, one of Dickens' most important novels in which he portrays for the first time not just individual villainy but shows evil to be inherent in the very structure of society.

Nicholson, the author of the plagiarism, was an extraordinary character, well-known throughout London and no stranger to the law and to litigation. After a minimum of education, he was apprenticed at the age of twelve to a pawnbroker and thereafter worked in several similar businesses until 1830 when he opened his own jewellery shop. He ran this rapidly into bankruptcy, and was several times committed to prison for insolvency. For a while his style of living was perilous as he tried to earn money by gambling, and was often destitute and had to sleep rough. Then, quite by chance, a London printer, Joseph Last, asked him to be the editor of a publication he was preparing called *The Town* which was to deal with the "flash" or high life of London. For Nicholson, who knew the capital city intimately, this was just the break he needed. The publication quickly caught on, and financed by his success Nicholson opened a public house, The Garrick's Head in Covent Garden over which he presided as the "Lord Chief Baron". Here he created an enormously popular rendezvous for M.P.s, poets, actors, and the more liberal businessmen, and he was addressed as "My Lord" by everyone of whatever station. He also instituted mock trials, elections and debates which were famous for their brilliant displays of repartee and wit. In 1844 the "Judge and Jury Society"—as it was now called—moved to the Cole Hole public house in the Strand, and Nicholson continued to be held in the same high esteem by all his "members"—even those who were forced to take legal action against him for non-payment of bills.

During his life he wrote a number of books—including a biography *Cockney Adventures* (1838) and *Miscellaneous Writings of the Lord Chief Justice* (1849)—but it is for "Dombey and Daughter" that he is still remembered. He mischievously called the tale a "Moral Fiction" and in a dig at Dickens added, "I predict that these pages will be read with pleasure by those whose tastes are not vitiated and who prefer a simple story, representative of real life, to the monstrous productions of a feverish imagination, which of late have been received with unmerited though almost universal applause". The story is, without doubt, a clever evocation of Dickens' style, complete with its plot of a foundling eventually discovered to be an heiress, and its occasional introduction of independent stories told by the major characters.

I have extracted one of these tales hereunder to represent both this particular book and, *in absentia*, the whole school of writers who so callously stole from Dickens—yet by the very extent of their plagiarism only underlined his enormous talent and popularity.

The Actor's Tale

It was about the latter end of the autumn of 1835, when I was professionally pedestrianizing between Exeter and Plymouth. I need hardly say I had not a farthing in my pocket by the time I reached my destination, I had become so tired, and the night was so far advanced, that there was no possibility of procuring even the means of getting a bed. Wearied, hungry, and in a very desponding mood, I stood leaning against a low wall in front of some humble and very suspicious-looking tenements, near one of the outskirts of the town, when a tall, powerfully-built and sturdy fellow suddenly emerged from one of the houses. After eying me earnestly for a few moments, he exclaimed:

"Fine night, sir!"

"Very," replied I, turning round and facing him; "and it's well it is, for I believe I shall have to ramble about the town till morning."

"Indeed!" exclaimed the stranger, coming close up to me, and staring me full in the face; then, after a pause, adding: "Come in to my house, sir; you'll find a good fire there, at all events and perhaps we may even be able to accommodate you with a bed."

Of course, I gladly accepted this invitation, and followed the stranger into his abode, which I then discovered to be the very next to the one in front of which I had been standing. Proceeding along a narrow passage, until we came to its extremity, we entered a spacious apartment, that presented the appearance of a sort of combined kitchen and taproom, though, otherwise, the house bore no affinity to a public-house, being, in fact, a private lodging-house for the accommodation of "travellers" of the lowest class, and of whom the kitchen was completely full. This place was both long and wide, and had a grate with a blazing fire in it at the extreme end, and a lamp fixed to the wall above the mantel-piece. On either side of the apartment, and at the end near the door, were tables and benches, where sat the individuals I have been speaking of—as motley a group as perhaps were ever collected together under one roof. There was an old, hatchet-faced looking fellow, dressed in very ragged seafaring apparel. Next to him sat a female, whom he called his "missis"—a short, thick-set drab of a woman, aged about forty, wretchedly dressed, and exhibiting a countenance that bore the most palpable and painful traces of mental and bodily suffering. Then there was a youngster, a lad of about eighteen, with a remarkably wild, bright eye, and a cocked up nose—his eyes and his limbs, in fact, his whole body, being as restless as a monkey's. He was amusing himself by practising sleight-of-hand with a couple of halfpence. Near him was a tall, good-looking man, of about five-and-twenty, dressed in a shabby-genteel style, but singularly clean and neat, and wearing a white neckcloth beautifully starched, and tied in a bow of the very newest fashion. This fellow assumed the character of a valet out of place, and relied chiefly upon his style of dressing for the pecuniary assistance he obtained. Associated with him, and seated by his side, was a flashily-dressed female, in a very palpable state of inebriation. Opposite to her, with her back to the window, before which fluttered a ragged curtain, sat the landlady of the house, a remarkably tall, Amazonian-made woman, with rather handsome though coarse features, and freckled complexion. I had a faint recollection of having met her somewhere before, in the course of my travels.

"Do you know this gentleman, Polly?" inquired my host.

The woman fixed her gaze upon me for a moment, and then, shaking me by the hand, exclaimed: "Why, to be sure; it's Mr Melville."

Seeing, however, that I was still in great perplexity fully to remember her, she continued:

"Why, don't you recollect the fair at Weldon, and the show that caught fire on the green? You were there with Abram's company, playing in the barn, you know. My husband and I have often talked of you since, I can assure you."

"You recollect us, don't you?" said the husband.

"I do now," said I; the circumstance he had mentioned fully reminding me of the active part I had taken in saving the poor fellow's van and its contents from being utterly destroyed by the flames, and also in my having assisted him in realizing a subscription from the townspeople, on account of the loss he had sustained.

"And so you have given up travelling," said I—

"And turned respectable, you see," replied my host, laughingly; "but, come," continued he, "sit down by the fire, and warm yourself—take this chair; you and I'll have a pipe together, and you shall taste some of my brandy—the right sort, and no mistake."

Saying this, he took up a lighted candle that had been placed on the table for the use of some of the lodgers who were going up to bed, and quitted the room; at which moment, the very musical tones of a female voice were heard in the passage, singing the commencement of the song, "I've journeyed over many lands", with so much spirit, expression, and taste, that my attention was immediately attracted, and I turned my head in the direction from whence the sounds proceeded.

"Here's Kate; a little bit sprung, as usual!" exclaimed the youth with the cocked-up nose.

"What a sweet voice," said I, involuntarily expressing my admiration.

"Poor thing!" whispered my hostess across the table, at the same time significantly putting her finger to her forehead, and adding: "she's a little cranky—Crazy Kate, they call her —you must not mind her."

I nodded assent, and again turning my eyes towards the door, beheld the girl we had been speaking of standing before me. She was a young creature, apparently not more than fifteen, and remarkably interesting in her appearance—a circumstance that arose from the fact of her being very pretty, of a very elegant figure (though rather *petite*), and also from the extraordinary contrast that her style of dress presented, not only to that of other females in the room, but to the common mode of attire among persons in her reckless sphere of life generally. Perhaps I cannot give you a better idea of her, than by saying at once, without entering into minutiæ, that she was dressed precisely in the usual style of a stage ballad-singer, not excepting even the laced bodice, the mittens, the cottage-bonnet, and the streamers of blue ribbon flying at each side of it.

"Would you like to hear a song, sir?" said she, coming up to me, playfully, and prefacing her address with a sort of stage-curtsey; "but," continued she, with the utmost *naiveté*, "I ought hardly to ask you, for you look uncommonly as if you belonged to the player-folks"—a remark which produced considerable laughter, and in which I myself very heartily joined.

I was exceedingly struck with the girl, and felt extremely desirous to hear her sing, but by the time the laughter had subsided, she seemed not only entirely to have forgotten her offer, but the frolicksome vivacity that had given her such a sparkling air on entering the room, had suddenly changed to gloom, and she had seated herself at one end of a bench close to the door, evidently suffering under one of those sudden attacks of melancholy to which persons afflicted as she was (especially when further affected, however slightly, by intoxication) are extremely liable.

"Come, Kate," said my hostess, "what a bad memory you have got; you offered to sing this gentleman a song."

"Did I?" replied the girl, despondingly; "did I say I'd sing? Well, I will; one song, mind—no more"; then throwing back her head against the wall, with one hand resting in her lap, and with the other seemingly tracing with her finger some letters among a quantity of tobacco ashes that had been emptied on the table before her, she began the following song:

An illustration from one of the most accomplished of the Dickens plagiarisms, "Dombey & Daughter" by Renton Nicholson (1847).

The sun was sinking in the west,
  To close the shining day,
The eve when first my eyes were blest
  With sight of Harry May.

We vow'd to love each other long,
  Upon life's chequered way;
And oft my merry mountain song
  Was tuned for Harry May.

The trader with his spreading sails
  Did bear my love away.
And now my broken heart bewails
  The loss of Harry May.

The marriage-bells in happy peal
  A transient joy convey,
For as I list their sounds reveal—
  "Oh, come to Harry May!"

The old moon, when she's shining bright,
  Behind a cloud will stay,
To weep with me in tearful light,
  For my poor Harry May.

And when the great sea-sigh is heard,
  Bowed down by woe I pray;
The whisper of the ocean-bird
  Says—"Mourn for Harry May."

Towards the close of the song, the girl's voice faltered extremely; and as the concluding words of the last stanza died upon her lips, tears gushed down her cheeks, and, burying her face in her hands, she sobbed convulsively.

"Piping again, Kate, eh! What a silly wench you are to be thinking so of a chap that's been food for the sharks long ago," said the youngster with the turned-up nose.

The girl took no notice, but immediately quitted the room in company with the "valet" and his companion, who, at the conclusion of Kate's song, had risen, and taken up the candle that the landlord had brought back to light them up to bed.

"Unhappy creature that," remarked I to mine host, as he took his seat at the end of a form by my side, and proceeded to mix a couple of enormous goblets of brandy-and-water.

"A melancholy sight, indeed; so young and fascinating, too. Evidently been extremely well brought up—the more the pity."

"Do you know anything of her history?" inquired I.

"Only what we have been able to pick up from the girl herself, in her moments of more perfect sanity."

"Well, try the brandy-and-water—genuine, you see"; and then he added, in a sort of half-whisper: "the spirit is so strong, that it is not easy to make it mingle with the water; without some pains, it will float on the surface. Taste it."

"Anybody can tell how you get this," said I, in a whisper, after I had tasted it. "Capital!"

"Is it not? Bless you, we supply all the publicans in the town, and a great many other people besides. Well, about this girl we were speaking of; she has been in Plymouth nearly a year, under precisely the same circumstances in which you see her now. From all we can get out of her, it seems that the cause of her malady is a disappointment in love—some young fellow between whom and herself there arose a passionate attachment; but his friends discovered the acquaintance, and not at all approving of it, they sent him to sea. The vessel was wrecked, and all hands on board perished; an event which, when it came to the knowledge of this poor girl, affected her so deeply, that, on recovering from the appalling paroxysm of the shock, she was found to be insane, just in the same degree as we now see her."

"And you don't even know where she comes from?"

"No."

"But what does she do here?"

"Goes about singing; it's a part of her madness."

"Strange!"

"Yes; at times her mind wanders terribly, and then we have heard her talking to herself about her 'dear Harry'; and from all that can be gleaned, it appears that when her lover was parted from her he managed to send her a letter, informing her he should escape from the service the first opportunity, return to England, and land at this port, Plymouth—though for what actual purpose, or with what intent, it is impossible even to surmise. The girl, it seems, brooded over this letter, until, under the influence of her malady, she actually conceived that her lover had returned, and was waiting to meet her here, the letter produced by his friends relative to his death being a mere fabrication invented by them to deceive her. She eluded the care of her friends, and fled from her home hither, where she is a daily visitor at the docks, to see what vessels come in, and at night she is to be seen at all the taverns and public-houses singing ballads, hoping in the course of her rounds to meet her long absent lover. She takes great pains with that stage style of dress, wishing to make herself as conspicuous as possible, that she may be sure to attract *his* notice."

"A most extraordinary delusion," observed I; "it's a pity she cannot be saved from such a life."

"I don't know that," replied my host; "generally speaking, she appears perfectly happy; and it is only when the fact of her lover's death forces itself upon her, that she seems to suffer much affliction. If she were to be removed from hence, and deprived of the practical indulgence in her delusion, I verily believe she would die from grief—it's meat and drink to her."

"Meat and drink, eh! Very unwholesome nourishment, I am afraid, though, even to say the best of it. Now, this—"

"What, the brandy?" cried he, laying hold of the bottle; "no, there's no delusion about that; it's the real, genuine, unadulterated—"

And here he was interrupted by a violent knocking at the street-door, so loud and aristocratic, that the effect was rather more ludicrous than startling; and turning round to his wife with a facetious air, he exclaimed:

"That must be either the Marquis of Waterford or Prince Albert! The head hotel is full, I suppose; and so, knowing the respectability of my house, they are sending their customers hither."

Then bidding his wife to go and look out a pair of clean sheets that had not got any holes in them, he left the room, to ascertain of what class and quality his clamorous visitors actually were.

There was hardly anybody in the room except myself, the hostess, and a thick-set, Dutch-built, seaman-like looking fellow, stretched out, half asleep, on one of the benches, but who, the instant he heard the knocking, sprang up with a sort of bull-dog growl, as if he scented in the distance some intruders whom he did not at all approve of. Just at that moment was heard the noise, as of a rush, into the house, the moment the door was opened, and the words: "In the queen's name—you know us," uttered in a most determined and authoritative tone; then the sound of heavy and hurried footsteps, and—a couple of Excise-officers, followed closely by the landlord, rushed into the room.

"Quick, quick, the brandy!" exclaimed his wife, just as the officers were entering; and instantly seizing the bottle of brandy and glasses, I dashed them all underneath the grate, and hurriedly raked the broken pieces so as to bury them in the ashes. The officers were just in time to discover what I had done, and after gazing surlily at the remnants, and sniffing up the smell of the brandy, to the great amusement of mine host, turned round fiercely upon me, and began pouring upon me a host of threats and invectives for having been the means of depriving them of their booty.

"Come, come!" exclaimed mine host, "I'll have no bullying here; make your search, if you have got one to make; get what evidence you can, and be off, or else—"

The sentence was finished in dumb-show, by the display of a brace of pistols, which he pulled from his pocket, and proceeded to handle in such a way as to leave no doubt about the nature of the threat intended, and the speedy execution of it. The officers, evidently calmed by this movement, contented themselves with growling out a few oaths, and exhibited their search-warrant, declaring that they meant to search the house.

"Search, and be—!" said my host.

And without giving him time to utter the concluding anathema, the officers abruptly reiterated the avowal of their intent to proceed with the search instantly, and hastened to leave the room for that purpose, followed by the landlord and the sailor whom, it will be remembered, their entrance had awakened from his slumber. In a few minutes afterwards, the officers were heard departing; the landlord sarcastically taking leave of them at the street-door, by regretting they should have had so much useless trouble, and hoping that they would not again inflict upon themselves such laudable anxiety without a better chance of some remunerative profit.

"Got rid of the old scoundrels, at last," exclaimed he, re-entering the room; "and now, we will go out and have a quiet glass together, as we have been prevented from enjoying it at home." After desiring his wife not to sit up for him, and putting the key of the street-door into his pocket, he led me out of the house, down the street, and through a variety of blind turnings, until, at last, we arrived at a corner public-house, into which we made our way by a side entrance; and here I was introduced to the band of smugglers with whom my conductor was associated. We entered a back-parlour, which I found entirely filled by men of the character and description I advert to—rough, athletic, adventurous-looking fellows—some attired in Guernsey shirts, and some in blue jackets, but all dressed in the garb of sailors. My conductor was received very cordially, and on my being introduced to the party as an old acquaintance who had once rendered him most material service under very urgent circumstances, I was instantly greeted with all the cordiality of a friend; and on my companion stating what had occurred with the officers that evening, and also being pleased to say, that I was a very clever actor, every one present evinced such an eagerness to prove his respect for so distinguished a guest, that glasses of brandy-and-water were set before me as fast as I could drink them. I remember little else of the details of that evening, except that, happening, among the variety of songs I was compelled to sing, to give Dibdin's ballad of "Wapping Old Stairs", one of the smugglers asked me whereabouts the stairs were situated, and evinced the most amusing mixture of surprise and credulity on my informing him that they had recently been removed from their original locality, and now formed the ascent to the Duke of York's column—a species of emblematical stepping-stones to glory, which he seemed to think very appropriate, inasmuch as, said he, "If it had not been for the British navy, our armies never would have been able to get a footing anywhere." The night passed on, and my perceptive faculties rapidly became oblivious, until at last I fell asleep, partly under the influence of the liquids I had imbibed, and partly from being wearied by the day's journey.

The next morning, I seemed to have awoke out of a trance. I found myself in one of the beds of a large double-bedded room, very comfortably furnished. The second bed was empty, and did not appear to have been occupied. It was some time before I could recollect the events that had occurred on the preceding night; but at last I succeeded in bringing them to mind, so far as to be able fully to understand that I had been put to bed at a public-house, somewhere in the outskirts of the town, and on getting out of bed, to dress, I found my clothes lying on the floor, just as if somebody had pulled them off for me, and let them drop there. Well, thought I, I had no money to be robbed of, whoever may have performed the office of valet; and then I went on dressing until I had finished, when, taking up my hat, which was lying flat upon the brim, I beheld, to my utter gratification and astonishment, a sovereign lying under it, and placed so conspicuously, that it was utterly impossible I could help seeing it. I concluded instantly that I was indebted for it to the generosity of my *quondam* friend, the smuggler, and hastened down stairs determined to find his abode and go and thank him, but on inquiring of the landlady, all I could learn was that my bed had been paid for by one among a party of strange men who had brought me there in a state of utter insensibility on the previous night. I went out, and endeavoured to retrace my steps in the supposed direction of the smuggler's abode, and I even made inquiries at several lodging-houses of a similar kind, but without success, until at last I became so dreadfully mystified and bewildered respecting the reality of everything which had occurred, that I actually got my sovereign changed for the express purpose of being fully convinced that, at all events as regarded the reality of a piece of coin so valuable, I could not be labouring under any delusion. Strange to say, however, although I remained at Plymouth two or three days, and made considerable search, I was obliged to leave at last without discovering the abode of my friend the smuggler, nor has it since ever fallen to my lot to renew any acquaintance of a similarly romantic and gratifying character.

6

THE MYSTERIES OF LONDON

by G. W. M. Reynolds

ANOTHER WRITER WHO successfully plagiarized Dickens, but possessed sufficient talent and originality of his own to eventually earn recognition as one of the most popular writers of his time, was George William Macarthur Reynolds (1814–1879). Reynolds was one of the most prolific authors in an age renowned for prodigious writing, and while many of his contemporaries are now no more than names in forgotten tomes, a major part of his work is still remembered if not often read. His most famous Dickens' imitation was "Pickwick Abroad", of which one contemporary critic remarked, "It has the same brilliancy of colouring and the same force of feeling which characterizes the works of Dickens." It was as a depictor of the underside of London life that he was to earn his real reputation, however, not forgetting his skilled editorship of several periodicals, including one which bore his own name and to which we shall return later.

Reynolds was the son of a wealthy naval captain who died while he was still a teenager, leaving him a small fortune. Abandoning the army career which he had just commenced at Sandhurst, he took to travelling in Europe and then settled in Paris where, at the age of twenty-one, he revealed his interest for journalism by establishing the *London and Paris Courier*. Sadly, this bold venture failed and with it went most of Reynolds' inheritance. Disillusioned, he returned to London in 1837, to begin earning a living by his pen, and probably supplied several of the cheap publishers with anonymous romances, before winning popular acclaim with "Pickwick Abroad; or The Tour in France", to give it its full title, in 1838.

Reynolds showed that he had learned much from his travels, and the influence of one particular writer, the Frenchman, Eugène Sue, was to be very self-evident when he commenced publication of his most famous penny-part serial, *The Mysteries of London*. (Montague Summers has also suggested that Reynolds was a great admirer of Matthew Lewis's infamous Gothic novel, *The Monk*, and drew on some of its sensational settings and fiery adventures for his later work.) Sue had written a novel, *The Mysteries of Paris*, into which he poured all the degradation, vice and squalor of slum life in the French capital, and Reynolds took the same concept with some of the style of Pierce Egan Snr and moulded it all into a serial story about London. As an avowed Chartist sympathizer, he larded his tale with descriptions of the most appalling conditions under which the poorer classes lived and worked, in stark contrast to the luxury and venal pleasures of the aristocracy. The many and varied adventures of his characters are frequently interrupted by tables illustrating the differences between the two classes, and Reynolds took a particular delight in pouring scorn on factory owners and landlords. To readers of Penny Dreadfuls he became not only a crusader but also a "trump"—one of the highest accolades that could be bestowed on any writer.

Fired by the success of this serial, he embarked on other "Mysteries" and a whole range of subjects as diverse as the theatre, army life, gypsies, ancient history and a profusion of romantic tales. He was avidly read everywhere and not infrequently hailed as "the most popular writer of the time" and Louis James has with some justification called his "The Mysteries of the Court of London"—"the *Forever Amber* of early Victorian fiction".

Because of his popularity it is not surprising to find that Reynolds, just as he had imitated Dickens, became the object of plagiarism himself. He was particularly shamelessly pirated in America and despite lashing out that "these men are infinitely worse than mere pirates; they are downright rogues, imposters, and forgers", he was not only more vigorously plagiarized, but his name was also added to books which he had had nothing whatsoever to do with. (One of Reynolds' statements directed against a plagiarist is reprinted as Appendix 3 at the end of the book.) Despite this, Reynolds continued to produce a vast body of work and on one occasion took on a bet—which he won—to write simultaneously four weekly romances each of eight pages of closely packed type. Unlike many of his contemporaries, Reynolds ended his days in comparative comfort, although his political views had undergone a radical change and he had become a deeply religious person. On his death, *The Bookseller* published an obituary in which they stated he had "written more and sold in far greater numbers than Dickens".

To represent this remarkable man I have naturally chosen an episode from *The Mysteries of London* which, in 1845, was one of the most successful penny-issue works of the time. The extract introduces us to perhaps the most infamous characters of all those who inhabited the streets of the London underworld—the dreaded Resurrection Men.

The Body-Snatchers

There is not probably in all London—not even in Saint Giles's nor the Mint—so great an amount of squalid misery and fearful crime huddled together, as in the joint districts of Spitalfields and Bethnal Green. Between Shoreditch Church and Wentworth Street the most intense pangs of poverty, the most profligate morals, and the most odious crimes, rage with the fury of a pestilence.

Entire streets that are nought but sinks of misery and vice —dark courts, foetid with puddles of black slimy water— alleys, blocked up with heaps of filth, and nauseating with unwholesome odours, constitute, with but little variety, the vast district of which we are speaking.

The Eastern Counties' Railway intersects Spitalfields and Bethnal Green. The traveller upon this line may catch, from the windows of the carriage in which he journeys, a hasty, but alas! too comprehensive glance of the wretchedness and squalor of that portion of London. He may actually obtain a view of the interior and domestic misery peculiar to the neighbourhood—he may penetrate, with his eyes, into the secrets of those abodes of sorrow, vice, and destitution. In summer time the poor always have their windows open, and thus the hideous poverty of their rooms can be readily descried from the summit of the arches on which the railroad is constructed.

And in those rooms may be seen women half naked, some employed in washing the few rags which they possess, others ironing the linen of a more wealthy neighbour, a few preparing the sorry meal, and numbers scolding, swearing, and quarrelling. At many of the windows, men out of work, with matted hair, black beards, and dressed only in filthy shirts and ragged trousers, lounge all the day long, smoking. From not a few of the open casements hang tattered garments to dry in the sun. Around the doors children, unwashed, uncombed, shoeless, dirty, and uncared for—throng in numbers, a rising generation of thieves and vagabonds.

In the districts of Spitalfields and Bethnal Green the police are but little particular with regard to street-stalls. These portable shops are therefore great in number and in nuisance. Fish, fresh and fried, oysters, sweet-stuff, vegetables, fruit, cheap publications, sop-in-the-pan, shrimps and periwinkles, hair-combs, baked potatoes, liver and lights, curds and whey, sheep's heads, haddocks and red-herrings, are the principal comestibles which find vendors and purchasers in the public street. The public-houses and the pawnbrokers also drive an excellent trade in that huge section of London.

In a former chapter we have described the region of Saffron Hill: all the streets and courts of that locality are safe

The Body-Snatchers at work in G. W. M. Reynolds' famous serial, "The Mysteries of London" (1845).

and secure when compared with many in Bethnal Green and Spitalfields. There are lanes and alleys between Shoreditch and Church Street, and in the immediate neighbourhood of the Railway east of Brick Lane, through which a well-dressed person would not wander with a gold chain round his neck, at night, were he prudent.

Leading from the neighbourhood of Church Street up into the Hackney Road, is a sinuous thoroughfare, composed of

Tyssen Street, Turk Street, Virginia Street, and the Bird-cage Walk; and in the vicinity of these narrow and perilous ways are the Wellington Road (bordered by a ditch of black mud), and several vile streets, inhabited by the very lowest of the low, the most filthy of the squalid, and the most profligate of the immoral.

We defy any city upon the face of the earth to produce a district equal in vice, dirt, penury, and fear-inspiring dens, to these which we are now describing.

* * *

The Resurrection Man, the Cracksman, and the Buffer hastened rapidly along the narrow lanes and filthy alleys leading towards Shoreditch Church. They threaded their way in silence, through the jet-black darkness of the night, and without once hesitating as to the particular turnings which they were to follow. Those men were as familiar with that neighbourhood as a person can be with the rooms and passages in his own house.

At length the body-snatchers reached the low wall surmounted with a high railing which encloses Shoreditch churchyard. They were now at the back part of that burial ground, in a narrow and deserted street, whose dark and lonely appearance tended to aid their designs upon an edifice situated in one of the most populous districts in all London.

For some minutes before their arrival an individual, enveloped in a long cloak, was walking up and down beneath the shadow of the wall.

This was the surgeon, whose thirst after science had called into action the energies of the body-snatchers that night.

The Cracksman advanced first, and ascertained that the surgeon had already arrived, and that the coast was otherwise clear.

He then whistled in a low and peculiar manner; and his two confederates came up.

"You have got all your tools?" said the surgeon in a hasty whisper.

"Every one that we require," answered the Resurrection Man.

"For opening a vault inside the church, mind?" added the surgeon, interrogatively.

"You show us the vault, sir, and we'll soon have out the body," said the Resurrection Man.

"All right," whispered the surgeon; "and my own carriage will be in this street at three precisely. We shall have plenty of time—there's no one stirring till five, and it's dark till seven."

The surgeon and the body-snatchers then scaled the railing, and in a few moments stood in the churchyard.

The Resurrection Man addressed himself to his two confederates and the surgeon, and said, "Do you lie snug under the wall here while I go forward and see how we must manage the door." With these words he crept stealthily along, amidst the tomb-stones, towards the church.

The surgeon and the Cracksman seated themselves upon a grave close to the wall; and the Buffer threw himself flat upon his stomach, with his ear towards the ground. He remained in this position for some minutes, and then uttered a species of low growl as if he were answering some signal which caught his ears alone.

"The skeleton-keys won't open the side-door, the Resurrection Man says," whispered the Buffer, raising his head towards the surgeon and the Cracksman.

He then laid his ear close to the ground once more, and resumed his listening posture.

In a few minutes he again replied to a signal; and this time his answer was conveyed by means of a short sharp whistle.

"It appears there is a bolt; and it will take a quarter of an hour to saw through the padlock that holds it," observed the Buffer in a whisper.

Nearly twenty minutes elapsed after this announcement. The surgeon's teeth chattered with the intense cold; and he could not altogether subdue certain feelings of horror at the idea of the business which had brought him thither. The almost mute correspondence which those two men were enabled to carry on together—the methodical precision with which they performed their avocations—and the coolness they exhibited in undertaking a sacrilegious task, made a powerful impression upon his mind. He shuddered from head to foot:—his feelings of aversion were the same as he would have experienced had a loathsome reptile crawled over his naked flesh.

"It's all right now!" suddenly exclaimed the Buffer, rising from the ground. "Come along."

The surgeon and the Cracksman followed the Buffer to the southern side of the church where there was a flight of steps leading up to a side-door in a species of lobby, or lodge. This door was open; and the Resurrection Man was standing inside the lodge.

As soon as they had all entered the sacred edifice, the door was carefully closed once more.

We have before said that the night was cold: but the interior of the church was of a chill so intense, that an icy feeling appeared to penetrate to the very back-bone. The wind murmured down the aisle; and every footstep echoed, like a hollow sound in the distance, throughout the spacious pile.

"Now, sir," said the Resurrection Man to the surgeon, "it is for you to tell us whereabouts we are to begin."

The surgeon groped his way towards the communion-table, and at the northern side of the railings which surrounded it he stopped short.

"I must now be standing," he said, "upon the very stone which you are to remove. You can, however, soon ascertain; for the funeral only took place yesterday morning, and the mortar must be quite soft."

The Resurrection Man stooped down, felt with his hand for the joints of the pavement in that particular spot, and thrust his knife between them.

"Yes," he said, after a few minutes' silence: "this stone

has only been put down a day or two. But do you wish, sir, that all traces of our work should disappear?"

"Certainly! I would not for the world that the family of the deceased should learn that this tomb has been violated. Suspicion would immediately fall upon me; for it would be remembered how earnestly I desired to open the body, and how resolutely my request was refused."

"We must use a candle, then, presently," said the Resurrection Man; "and that is the most dangerous part of the whole proceeding."

"It cannot be helped," returned the surgeon, in a decided tone. "The fact that the side-door has been opened by unfair means must transpire in a day or two; and search will then be made inside the church to ascertain whether those who have been guilty of the sacrilege were thieves or resurrection-men. You see, then, how necessary it is that there should remain no proofs of the violation of a tomb."

"Well and good, sir," said the Resurrection Man. "You command—we obey. Now, then, my mates, to work."

In a moment the Resurrection Man lighted a piece of candle, and placed it in the tin shade before alluded to. The glare which it shed was thereby thrown almost entirely downwards. He then carefully, and with surprising rapidity, examined the joints of the large flag-stone which was to be removed, and on which no inscription had yet been engraved. He observed the manner in which the mortar was laid down, and noticed even the places where it spread a little over the adjoining stones or where it was slightly deficient. This inspection being completed, he extinguished the light, and set to work in company with the Cracksman and the Buffer.

The eyes of the surgeon gradually became accustomed to the obscurity; and he was enabled to observe to some extent the proceedings of the body-snatchers.

These men commenced by pouring vinegar over the mortar round the stone which they were to raise. They then took long clasp-knives, with very thin and flexible blades, from their pockets; and inserted them between the joints of the stones. They moved these knives rapidly backwards and forwards for a few seconds, so as effectually to loosen the mortar, and moistened the interstices several times with the vinegar.

This operation being finished, they introduced the thin and pointed end of a lever between the end of the stone which they were to raise and the one adjoining it. The Resurrection Man, who held the lever, only worked it very gently; but at every fresh effort on his part, the Cracksman and the Buffer introduced each a wedge of wood into the space which thus grew larger and larger. By these means, had the lever suddenly given way, the stone would not have fallen back into its setting. At length it was raised to a sufficient height to admit of its being supported by a thick log about three feet in length.

While these three men were thus proceeding as expeditiously as possible with their task, the surgeon, although a man of a naturally strong mind, could not control the strange feelings which crept upon him. It suddenly appeared to him as if he beheld those men for the first time. That continuation of regular and systematic movements—that silent perseverance, faintly shadowed forth amidst the obscurity of the night, at length assumed so singular a character, that the surgeon felt as if he beheld three demons disinterring a doomed one to carry him off to hell!

He was aroused from this painful reverie by the Resurrection Man, who said to him, "Come and help us remove the stone."

The surgeon applied all his strength to this task; and the huge flag-stone was speedily moved upon two wooden rollers away from the mouth of the grave.

"You are certain that this is the place?" said the Resurrection Man.

"As certain as one can be who stood by the grave for a quarter of an hour in daylight, and who has to recognize it again in total darkness," answered the surgeon. "Besides, the mortar was soft—"

"There might have been another burial close by," interrupted the Resurrection Man; "but we will soon find out whether you are right or not, sir. Was the coffin a wooden one?"

"Yes! an elm coffin, covered with black cloth," replied the surgeon. "I gave the instructions for the funeral myself, being the oldest friend of the family."

The Resurrection Man took one of the long flexible rods which we have before noticed, and thrust it down into the vault. The point penetrated into the lid of a coffin. He drew it back, put the point to his tongue, and tasted it.

"Yes," he said, smacking his lips, "the coffin in this vault is an elm one, and is covered with black cloth."

"I thought I could not be wrong," observed the surgeon.

The body-snatchers then proceeded to raise the coffin, by means of ropes passed underneath it. This was a comparatively easy portion of their task; and in a few moments it was placed upon the flag-stones of the church.

The Resurrection Man took a chisel and opened the lid with considerable care. He then lighted his candle a second time; and the glare fell upon the pale features of the corpse in its narrow shell.

"This is the right one," said the surgeon, casting a hasty glance upon the face of the dead body, which was that of a young girl of about sixteen.

The Resurrection Man extinguished the light; and he and his companions proceeded to lift the corpse out of the coffin.

The polished marble limbs of the deceased were rudely grasped by the sacrilegious hands of the body-snatchers; and, having stripped the corpse stark naked, they tied its neck and heels together by means of a strong cord. They then thrust it into a large sack made for the purpose.

The body-snatchers then applied themselves to the restoration of the vault to its original appearance.

The lid of the coffin was carefully fastened down; and that now tenantless bed was lowered into the tomb. The stone was rolled over the mouth of the vault; and one of the small square boxes previously alluded to, furnished mortar wherewith to fill up the joints. The Resurrection Man lighted his candle a third time, and applied the cement in such a way that even the very workman who laid the stone down after the funeral would not have known that it had been disturbed. Then, as this mortar was a shade fresher and lighter than that originally used, the Resurrection Man scattered over it a thin brown powder, which was furnished by the second box brought away from his house on this occasion. Lastly, a light brush was swept over the scene of these operations, and the necessary precautions were complete.

The clock struck three as the surgeon and the body-snatchers issued from the church, carrying the sack containing the corpse between them.

They reached the wall at the back of the churchyard, and there deposited their burden, while the Cracksman hastened to see if the surgeon's carriage had arrived.

In a few minutes he returned to the railing, and said in a low tone, "All right!"

The body was lifted over the iron barrier and conveyed to the vehicle.

The surgeon counted ten sovereigns into the hands of each of the body-snatchers; and, having taken his seat inside the vehicle, close by his strange freight, was whirled rapidly away towards his own abode.

7

SWEENEY TODD

by Thomas Peckett Prest

IF G. W. M. REYNOLDS was the most popular writer in the penny-issue field, the story of Sweeney Todd, the Demon Barber, was certainly the most popular and enduring of all the original serials. Still today as much a part of criminal mythology as Burke and Hare or Jack the Ripper, Sweeney Todd has been a constant subject for stories, plays, broadcasts, films and even ballet since he first appeared in 1846. There has been much conjecture about the origins of the infamous barber who, one newspaper has stated, achieved such a reputation for vulgarity that the profession he belonged to has ever since been called "hairdressers". Some authorities have credited the legend with German origins, while others have ascribed it to a series of real-life murders in Paris in 1800 when a barber and a baker concealed their murders by processing the corpses of the victims into meat pies. Yet a third school of thought believes that the well-known legend of Sawney Beane, the Man Eater of Scotland, played a major part. Montague Summers has added still further to the conjecture by stating that there may indeed have been a "substratum of truth" in the story as told in the serial, for "there persisted a very old Fleet Street tavern tradition (current long before 1800) that such an individual as Sweeney Todd did exist and his story is only a little exaggerated". He even cites a 1798 account of an old watchman at St Bartholomew's Hospital who used to say that his father "had been murdered for his coin by Sweeney Todd". Perhaps *all* these stories played a part in the final composition, for the author of the Penny Dreadful which began the legend was a devotee of old legends and an habitué of Fleet Street taverns, Thomas Peckett Prest (1810–1879), whom John Medcraft has called "a morbid genius with a wonderful imagination".

In the entire annals of the Penny Dreadful there is perhaps no more bizarre character than Prest, nor any writer more deserving of research to establish his true place in English literature. A man of prodigious output and variety, he was undoubtedly the most important writer in Edward Lloyd's stable of contributors and—despite the difficulty of attribution in the face of so much anonymity of authorship—the creator of some of the most durable of the penny publications. Born into comparative affluence, and related to the Archdeacon of Durham, the Reverend Edward Prest, young Prest displayed an early talent for languages, music and drama. Writing appears to have been an absorbing passion from his youth and we first come across him editing the archdeacon's sermons for the press and adapting French farces for the stage. His musical talent also led him to write lyrics for the theatre and not a few popular music-hall hits of the mid-1850s are credited to him. He was similarly attracted to Fleet Street and early fell in with Edward Lloyd who was to publish much that he wrote either in his journals or as serials. The pressures which work in this field brought to bear on contributors were, however, inexorable, and in middle age Prest succumbed to ill-health, drink and debts. Consumption finally set in and while those who published and sold his work prospered, he died a pauper in 1879 in a cheap lodging house.

As I have indicated, the variety of his work was enormous: he was one of the first major influences on the Penny Dreadful with tales of horror and famous criminals; he penned several of Lloyd's most successful plagiarisms of Dickens, and wrote serials whose titles are now part of the tradition of macabre fiction, "Ela The Outcast" (1841), "Fatherless Fanny" (1841), "The Maniac Father" (1842) and, of course, the Sweeney Todd story which was published by Lloyd under the surprisingly restrained title of "The String of Pearls". (Prest also wrote a number of dramas for the stage, but many of his best tales were stolen by other dramatists and enjoyed huge successes: not the least of these was Sweeney Todd brought to the stage by George Dibdin Pitt.) "The String of Pearls" is certainly one of Prest's most accomplished works, colourful and dramatic with the interest and excitement kept up from issue to issue until the final dénouement. The story of the barber and how he lures unsuspecting victims to their deaths needs no retelling here; suffice it to say that I have selected the closing pages of this mammoth tale, sure in the knowledge that the reader will find them just as enthralling as Prest's original readers did over a century and a quarter ago.

The Last Batch Of Pies

It would have been quite clear to anyone who looked at Sweeney Todd as he took his route from his own shop in Fleet Street to Bell Yard, Temple Bar, that it was not to eat pies he went there.

No; he was intent on very different thoughts indeed, and as he neared the shop of Mrs Lovett, where those delicacies were vended, there was such a diabolical expression upon his face, that, had he not stooped "like grim War to smooth his wrinkled front" before he made his way into the shop, he would, most unquestionably, have excited the violent suspicions of Mrs Lovett, that all was not exactly as it should be, and that the mysterious bond of union that held her and the barber together was not in that blooming state that it had been. When he actually did enter the shop, he was all sweetness and placidity.

Mrs Lovett was behind the counter, for it seldom happened that the shop was free of customers, for when the batches of hot pies were all over, there usually remained such which were devoured cold with avidity enough, by the lawyers'

A contemporary engraving of the infamous Sweeney Todd, now in the British Museum (1846).

clerks, from the offices and chambers in the neighbourhood.

But at nine o'clock, there was a batch of hot pies coming up, for of late Mrs Lovett had fancied that between half-past eight and nine, there was a great turn-out of clerks from Lincoln's Inn, and a pie became a very desirable and comfortable prelude to half-price at the theatre, or any other amusements of the three hours before midnight.

Many people, too, liked them as a relish for supper, and took them home carefully. Indeed, in Lincoln's Inn, it may be said, that the affections of the clerks oscillated between

Lovett's pies and sheep's heads; and it frequently so nicely balanced in their minds, that the two attractions depended upon the toss-up of a halfpenny, whether it was "sang amary" Jameses from Clare-market, or pies from Lovetts. Half-and-half washed both down well.

Mrs Lovett, then, may be supposed to be waiting for the nine o'clock batch of pies when Sweeney Todd, on this most eventful evening, made his appearance. Todd and Mrs Lovett met now with all the familiarity of old acqaintance.

"Ah, Mr Todd," said the lady, "how do you do? Why, we have not seen you for a long time."

"It has been some time; and how are you Mrs Lovett?"

"Quite well, thank you. Of course, you will take a pie?"

Todd made a horrible face, as he replied, "No thank you; it's very foolish, I know when I knew I was going to make a call here, but I have just had a pork chop."

"Had it the bit of kidney in it, sir?" asked one of the lads who were eating cold pies.

"Yes it had."

"Oh, that's what I like! Lor bless you, I'd eat my mother if she was a pork chop, done brown and crisp, and the kidney in it; just fancy it, grilling hot, you know, and just popped on a slice of bread when you are cold and hungry."

"Will you walk in, Mr Todd?" said Mrs Lovett, raising a portion of the counter, by which an opening was made, that enabled Mr Todd to pass into the sacred precincts of the parlour.

The invitation was complied with by Mr Todd, who remarked "that he hadn't above a minute to spare, but that he would sit down while he could stay, since she, Mrs Lovett, was so kind as to ask him".

This extreme suavity of manner, however, left Sweeney Todd when he was in the parlour, and there was nobody to take notice of him but Mrs Lovett, nor did she think it necessary to wreathe her face in smiles, but with something of both anger and agitation in her manner, she said, "And when is all this to have an end, Sweeney Todd? You have been now for these six months promising me such a division of spoils as shall enable me, with an ample independence, once again to appear in the salons of Paris. I ask you now when is that to be?"

"You are very impatient!"

"Impatient, impatient? May I not well be impatient? Do I not run a frightful risk, while you must have the best of the profits? It is useless your pretending to tell me that you do not get much. I know you better, Sweeney Todd; you never strike, unless for profit or revenge."

"Well?"

"Is it well, then, that I should have no account; O God! if you had the dreams I sometimes have?"

"Dreams?"

She did not answer him, but sank into a chair and trembled so violently that he became alarmed, thinking she was very, very unwell. His hand was upon a bell rope, when she motioned him to be still, and then she managed to say in a very faint and nearly inarticulate voice, "You will go to that cupboard. You will see a bottle. I am forced to drink, or I should kill myself or go mad, and denounce you; give it to me, quick—quick, give it to me; it is brandy. That alone stupefies conscience for a time. Give it to me, I say; do not stand gazing at it there, I must and will have it. Yes, yes, I am better now, much better now. It is horrible, very horrible, but I am better, and I say, I must, and I will have an account at once. Oh, Todd, what an enemy you have been to me!"

"You wrong me. The worst enemy you ever had is in your hand."

"No, no, no! I must have that to drown thought!"

"Indeed! Can you be so superstitious? I presume you are afraid of your reception in another world."

"No, no—oh no! You and I do not believe in a hereafter, Sweeney Todd; if we did we should go raving mad, to think what we had sacrificed. Oh no—no, we dare not, we dare not."

"Enough of this," said Todd, somewhat violently, "enough of this; you shall have an account tomorrow evening; and when you find yourself in possession of £20,000, you will not accuse me of having been unmindful of your interest. But see, there is someone in the shop who seems to be inquiring for you."

Mrs Lovett rose and went into the shop. The moment her back was turned, Todd produced the little bottle of poison he had got from the chemist's boy and emptied it into the brandy decanter. He had just succeeded in this manoeuvre, and concealed the bottle again when she returned, and again flung herself into a chair.

"Did I hear you right?" she said, "or is this promise but mere mockery? £20,000—is it possible, that you have so much? Oh, why was not all this dreadful trade left sooner, much less would have done. But when shall I have it—when shall I be enabled to fly from here for ever? Todd, we must live in different countries; I could never bear the chance of seeing you."

"As you please. It don't matter to me at all; you may be off tomorrow night, if you like. I tell you, your share of the eight years work is, and shall be £20,000. You shall have the sum tomorrow, and then you are free to go where you please; it matters not to me one straw where you spend your money. But tell me now, what immediate danger do you apprehend from your new 'cook'?"

"Great and immediate; he has refused to work—a sign that he has got desperate, hopeless and impatient; and then only a few hours ago, I heard him call to me, and he said he had thought better of it, and would bake the nine o'clock batch, which, to my mind, was saying that he had made up his mind to some course which gave him hope, and made it worth his while to temporise with me for a time, to lull suspicion."

"You are a clever woman. Something must and shall be done. I will be here at midnight, and we shall see if a vacancy cannot be made in your establishment."

"It will be necessary, and it is but one more."

"That's all—that's all, and I must say you have a very perfect and philosophic mode of settling the question; avoid the brandy as much as you can, but I suppose you are sure to take some between now and the morning?"

"Quite sure. It is not in this house that I can wean myself of such a habit. I may do so abroad, but not here."

"Oh well, it can't matter; but, as regards the fellow downstairs, I will of course, come and rid you of him. You must keep a good look-out now for the short time you will be here, and good countenance. There, you are wanted again, and I may as well go likewise."

Mrs Lovett and Todd walked from the parlour to the shop together, and when they got there, they found a respectable looking woman and a boy, the latter of whom carried a bundle of printed papers with him; the woman was evidently in great distress of mind.

"A cold pie, ma'am?" said Mrs Lovett.

"Oh dear, no, Mrs Lovett," said the woman; "I know you by sight, mam, though you don't know me. I am Mrs Wrankley, mam, the wife of Mr Wrankley, the tobacconist and I've come to ask a favour of you, Mrs Lovett, to allow one of these bills to be put in your window?"

"Dear me," said Mrs Lovett, "what's it about?"

Mrs Wrankley handed her one of the bills and then seemed so overcome with grief, that she was forced to sink into the chair while it was read, which was done aloud by Mrs Lovett, who, as she did so, now and then stole a glance at Sweeney Todd, who looked as impenetrable and destitute of all emotion, as a block of wood.

"Missing!—Mr John Wrankley, tobacconist of 92, Fleet St. The above gentleman left his home to go over the water, on business, and has not since been heard of. He is supposed to have had some valuable property with him, in the shape of a string of pearls. The said Mr John Wrankley is five feet four inches high, full face, short thick nose, black whiskers, and what is commonly called a bullet-head; thick-set and skittle-made, not very well upon his feet; and whoever will give any information of him at 92, Fleet St. shall be amply rewarded."

"Yes, yes," said Mrs Wrankley, when the reading of the bill was finished. "That's him to a T, my poor, dear, handsome Wrankley! Oh, I shall never be myself again. I have not eaten anything since he went out."

"Then buy a pie, madam," said Mr Todd, as he held one close to her. "Look up, Mrs Wrankley, lift off the top crust madam, and you may take my word for it you will soon see *something* of Mr Wrankley."

The hideous face that Todd made during the utterance of these words quite alarmed the disconsolate widow, but she did partake of the pie for all that. It was very tempting—a veal one, full of coagulated gravy—who could resist it? Not she, certainly, and besides, did not Todd say she should see something of Wrankley? There was hope in his words, at all events, if nothing else.

"Well," she said, "I will hope for the best; he may have been taken ill, and not have had his address in his pocket, poor dear soul, at the time."

"And at all events, madam," said Todd, "you need not be cut up about it, you know; I dare say you will know what has become of him some day, soon."

* * *

Mrs Lovett was a woman of judgment, and when she told Sweeney Todd that the prisoner was getting impatient in the lower regions of that house which was devoted to the manufacture of the delicious pies, she had but guessed rightly his sensations with regard to his present state and future prospects.

We last left that unfortunate young man lying upon the floor of the place where the steaming and tempting manufacture was carried on; and for a time, as a very natural consequence of exhaustion, he slept profoundly.

That sleep, however, if it rested him bodily, likewise rested him mentally; and when he again awoke it was but to feel more acutely the agony of his most singular and cruel situation. There was a clock in the place by which he had been enabled to accurately regulate the time that the various batches of pies should take in cooking, and upon looking up to that he saw that it was upon the hour of six, and consequently it would be three hours more before a batch of pies was wanted.

He looked about him very mournfully for some time, and then he spoke.

"What evil destiny," he said, "has placed me here? Oh, how much better it would have been if I had perished, as I have been nearly perishing several times during the period of my eventful life, than that I should be shut up in this horrible den and starved to death, as in all human probability I shall be, for I loathe the pies. Damn the pies!"

There was a slight noise, and upon his raising his eyes to that part of the place near the roof where there were some iron bars and between which Mrs Lovett was wont to give him some directions, he saw her now detested face.

"Attend," she said; "you will bake an extra batch tonight, at nine precisely."

"What?"

"An extra batch, two hundred at least; do you understand me?"

"Hark ye, Mrs Lovett. You are carrying this sort of thing too far; it won't do, I tell you, Mrs Lovett; I don't know how soon I may be numbered with the dead, but, as I am a living man now, I will make no more of your detestable pies."

"Beware!"

"Beware yourself! I am not one to be frightened at shadows. I say I will leave this place, whether you like it not; I will leave it; and perhaps you will find your power insufficient to keep me here. That there is some frightful mystery at the bottom of all the proceedings here, I am certain, but you shall not make me the victim of it."

"Rash fool!"

"Very well, say what you like, but remember I defy you."

"Then you are tired of your life, and you will find, when too late, what are the consequences of your defiance. But listen to me: when I first engaged you, I told you you might leave when you were tired of the employment."

"You did, and yet you keep me a prisoner here; God knows I'm tired enough of it, besides, I shall starve, for I cannot eat pies eternally; I hate them."

"And they so admired!"

"Yes, when one is not surfeited with them. I am only now subsisting upon baked flour. I cannot eat the pies."

"You are strangely fantastical."

"Perhaps I am. Do you live upon pies, I should like to know, Mrs Lovett?"

"That is altogether beside the question. You shall, if you like, leave this place tomorrow morning, by which time I hope to have got some one else to take your situation, but I cannot be left without anyone to make the pies."

"I don't care for that, I won't make another one."

"We shall see," said Mrs Lovett. "I will come to you in an hour, and see if you persevere in that determination. I advise you as a friend to change, for you will most bitterly repent standing in the way of your own enfranchisement."

"Well, but—she is gone, and what can I do? I am in her power, but shall I tamely submit? No, no, not while I have my arms at liberty, and strength enough left to wield one of these long pokers that stir the coals in the ovens. How foolish of me not to think before that I had such desperate weapons, with which perchance to work my way to freedom."

As he spoke, he poised in his hand one of the long pokers he spoke of, and, after some few minutes spent in consideration, he said to himself, with something of the cheerfulness of hope—

"I am in Bell Yard, and there are houses right and left of this accursed pie-shop, and those houses must have cellars. Now surely with such a weapon as this, a willing heart, and an arm that has not yet quite lost all its powers, I may make my way from this abominable abode."

The very thought of thus achieving his liberty lent him new strength and resolution, so that he felt himself to be quite a different man to what he had been, and he only paused to consider in which direction it would be best to begin his work.

After some reflection upon that line, he considered that it would be better to commence where the meat was kept—that meat of which he always found abundance, and which came from—he knew not where; since, if he went to sleep with little or none of it upon the shelves where it was placed for use, he always found plenty when he awoke.

"Yes," he said, "I will begin there, and work my way to freedom."

Before, however, he commenced operations, he glanced at the clock, and found that it wanted very little now to seven, so that he thought it would be but common prudence to wait until Mrs Lovett had paid him her promised visit, as then, if he said he would make the pies she required, he would, in all probability, be left to himself for two hours, and, he thought, if he did not make good progress in that time towards his liberty, it would be strange indeed.

He sat down, and patiently waited until seven o'clock.

Scarcely had the hour sounded, when he heard the voice of his tormentor and mistress at the grating.

"Well," she said, "have you considered?"

"Oh, yes, I have. Needs must, you know, Mrs Lovett, when a certain person drives. But I have a great favour to ask of you, madam."

"What is it?"

"Why, I feel faint, and if you could let me have a pot of porter, I would undertake to make a batch of pies superior to any you have ever had, and without any grumbling either."

Mrs Lovett was silent for a few moments, and then said:

"If you are supplied with porter, will you continue in your situation?"

"Well, I don't know that; but perhaps I may. At all events, I will make you the nine o'clock batch, you may depend."

"Very well. You shall have it."

She disappeared at these words, and in about ten minutes, a small trapdoor opened in the roof, and there was let down by a cord a foaming pot of porter.

"This is capital," cried the victim of the pies, as he took half of it at a draught. "This is nectar for the gods. Oh, what a relief, to be sure. It puts new life into me."

And so it really seemed, for shouldering the poker, which was more like a javelin than anything else, he at once rushed into the vault where the meat was kept.

"Now," he said, "for a grand effort at freedom, and if I succeed I promise you, Mrs Lovett, that I will come round to the shop, and rather surprise you, madam. Damn the pies!"

He was not slow in discovering that his work would not be the most easy in the world, for every now and then he kept encountering what felt very much like a plate of iron; but he fagged away with right good will, and succeeded after a time in getting down one of the shelves, which was one point gained at all events.

"Now for it," he said. "Now for it; I shall be able to act—to work upon the wall itself, and it must be something unusually strong to prevent me making a breach through it soon."

In order to refresh himself, he finished the porter, and then using his javelin-like poker as a battering-ram, he banged the wall with the end of it for some moments, without producing any effect, until suddenly a portion of it swung open just like a door, and he paused to wonder how that came about.

All was darkness through the aperture, and yet he saw that it was actually a little square door that he had knocked open; and the idea then recurred to him that he had found out how the shelves were supplied with meat, and he had no doubt that there was such a little square door opening at the back of every one of them.

"So," he said, "that mystery is solved, but what part of Mrs Lovett's premises have I come upon now? We shall soon see."

He went boldly into the large cellar, and procured a light—a flaming torch, made of a piece of dry wood, and returning to the opening he had made in the wall, he thrust his head through it, and projected the torch before him.

With a cry of horror he fell backwards, extinguishing the torch in his fall, and he lay for full a quarter of an hour insensible upon the floor. What dreadful sight had he seen that had so chilled his young blood, and frozen up the springs of life?

When he recovered, he looked around him in the dim, borrowed light that came from the other vault, and he shuddered as he said:

"Was it a dream?"

Soon, however, as he rose, he gave up the idea of having been the victim of any delusion of the imagination, for there was the broken shelf, and there the little square opening, through which he had looked and seen what had so transfixed him with horror.

Keeping his face in that direction, as if it would be dreadful to turn his back for a moment upon some frightful object, he made his way into the larger cellar where the ovens were, and then he sat down with a deep groan.

"What shall I do? Oh, what shall I do?" he muttered. "I am doomed—doomed."

"Are the pies doing?" said the voice of Mrs Lovett. "It's eight o'clock."

"Eight, is it?"

"Yes, to be sure, and I want to know if you are bent upon your own destruction or not? I don't hear the furnaces going, and I'm quite sure you have not made the pies."

"Oh, I will keep my word, madam, you may depend. You want two hundred pies at nine o'clock, and you will see that they shall come up quite punctually to the minute."

"Very good. I am glad you are better satisfied than you were."

"I am quite satisfied now, Mrs Lovett. I am quite in a different mood of mind to what I was before. I can assure you, madam, that I have no complaints to make, and I think the place has done me some good; and if at nine o'clock you let down the platform, you shall have the two hundred pies up, as sure as fate, and something else, too," he added to himself, "or I shall be of a very different mind to what I now am."

We have already seen that Mrs Lovett was not deceived by this seeming submission on the part of the "cook", for she used that as an argument with Todd when she was expatiating upon the necessity of getting rid of him that night.

But the cleverest people make mistakes at times and probably when the nine o'clock batch of pies makes its appearance, something may occur at the same time which will surprise a great many more persons than Mrs Lovett and the reader.

But we must not anticipate, merely saying with the eastern sage, what will be will be, and what's impossible does not often come to pass; certain it is that the nine o'clock batch of two hundred pies were made and put in the ovens; and equally certain it is that the "cook" remarked as he did so:

"Yes, I'll do it—it may succeed; nay it must succeed; and if so, woe be to you, Mrs Lovett, and all who are joined with you in this horrible speculation at which I sicken."

*   *   *

Back in Sweeney Todd's barber shop our heroine, Johanna, disguised as an orphan boy, Charley, is sitting alone. Her head is resting upon her hands, and she is thinking of times gone past when she hoped for happiness with Mark Ingestrie who, unbeknownst to her, is the prisoner of Mrs Lovett. When we say alone, we must add that there are two officers very snugly packed in a cupboard prepared for the last chapter in our story.

But Johanna, as her mind wandered back to her last interview with him whom she had loved so well, and clung to so fondly and so constantly, almost for a time forgot where she was and that there was such a person as Sweeney Todd in existence.

"Alas, alas!" she said, "it seems likely enough that by the adoption of this disguise, so unsuited to me, I may achieve vengeance, but nothing more. Where are you, Mark Ingestrie? Oh horror! something seems to tell me that no mortal voice can answer me."

Tears came to her relief; and as she felt them trickling through her fingers, she started as she thought that the hour which Todd had said would expire before he returned must have nearly gone.

"I must control these thoughts," she said, "and this emotion. I must seem that which I am not."

She rose, and ceased weeping; she trimmed the miserable little lamp, and then she was about to go to the door to look for the return of Todd, when that individual, with a slow and sneaking footstep, made his appearance, as if he had been hiding just within the doorway.

Todd hung his hat upon a peg, and then turning his eyes enquiringly upon Johanna, he said:

"Well, has anyone been, Charley?"

"Yes."

"Who? Speak, speak out. Confound you lad, you mumble so I can hardly hear you."

"A gentleman, to be shaved, and he went again. I don't know what puts you in such a passion, Mr Todd; I am sure nothing—"

"What is it to you? Get out of my way will you, and you may begin to think of shutting up I think for we shall have no more customers tonight. I am tired and weary. You are to sleep under the counter, you know."

"Yes, sir, you told me so. I dare say I shall be very comfortable here."

"And you have not been peeping and prying about have you boy?"

"Not at all."

"Not looking even into that cupboard, I suppose, eh? It's not locked, but that's no reason why you should look into it—not that there is any secrets in it, but I object to peeping and prying on principle."

Todd, as he spoke, had advanced towards the cupboard and Johanna thought that in another moment a discovery would undoubtedly take place of the two officers who were there concealed; and probably that would have been the case had not the handle of the shop door been turned at that moment, and a man presented himself, when Todd turned quickly and saw that he was a substantial looking farmer with dirty top boots, as if he had just come off a journey.

"Well, master," said the visitor. "I wants a clean shave."

"Oh," said Todd, not in the best of humours, "it's a bit late, but I suppose you will not like to wait till morning, for I don't know if I have any hot water."

"Oh, cold will do."

"Cold, oh dear no; we never shave in cold water; and if you must you must, so sit down sir, and we will soon settle the business."

"Thank you, thank you. I can't go to bed comfortably without a clean shave, do you see? I have come up from Braintree with beasts on commission, and I'm staying at the Bull's Head, you see."

"Oh, indeed," said Todd, as he adjusted the shaving cloth, "The Bull's Head."

"Yes, master; why I brought up a matter of 220 beasts, I did, do you see, and was on my *pooney*, as good a stepper as you'd wish to see, and I sold 'em all, do you see for 550 *pun*. Ho, ho, good work that, do you see. I've got a missus at home, and a son and a daughter. My girl's called Johanna—ahem!"

Up to this point, Johanna had not suspected that the game had begun and that this was the magistrate who had come to put an end to the mal-practices of Sweeney Todd; but his marked pronunciation of her name at once opened her eyes to that fact, and she knew that something interesting must soon happen.

"And so you sold them all?" said Todd.

"Yes, master, I did, and I've got the money in my pocket now, in bank-notes; I never leave my money about at inns, do you see, master; safe bind, safe find, you see. I carries it about with me."

"A good plan, too," said Todd; "Charley, some hot water, that's a good lad—and—and, Charley."

"Yes, sir?"

"While I am finishing off this gentleman, you may as well just run to the Temple to Mr Serjeant Toldruns and ask for his wig; we shall have to do it in the morning, and may as well have it the first thing in the day to begin upon, and you need not hurry, Charley, as we shall shut up when you come back."

"Very good, sir."

Johanna walked out, but went no further than the shop window, close to which she placed her eyes so that between a pomatum jar and a lot of hair brushes, she could clearly see what was going on.

"A nice looking little lad, that," said Todd's customer.

"Very, sir: an orphan boy; I took him out of charity, poor little fellow; but there, we ought to try to do all the good we can."

"Just so. I'm glad I have come to be shaved here. Mine's rather a strong beard, I think, do you see."

"Why sir, in a manner of speaking," replied Todd, "it is a strong beard. I suppose you didn't come to London alone, sir?"

"Oh yes, quite alone; except the drovers, I had no company with me; why do you ask?"

"Why, sir, I thought if you had any gentlemen with you who might be waiting at the Bull's Head, you would recommend him to me if anything was wanting in any way you know, sir; you might have just left him, saying you were going to Todd, the barber's to have a clean shave, sir."

"No, not at all; the fact is, I did not come out to have a shave, but a walk, and it wasn't until I gave my chin a stroke and found what a beard I had, that I thought of it and then passing your shop, in I popped, do you see."

"Exactly, sir. I comprehend; you are quite alone, in London?"

"Oh quite, but when I come again, I'll come to you to be shaved, you may depend, and I'll recommend you too."

"I'm very much obliged to you," said Todd, as he passed his hand over the chin of his customer. "I'm very much obliged; I find I must give you another lather sir, and I'll get another razor with a keener edge, now that I have taken off all the rough as one may say in a manner of speaking."

"Oh, I shall do."

"No, no, don't move, sir. I shall not detain you a moment, I have my other razors in the next room, and will polish you off now sir, before you will know where you are; you know, sir, you have promised to recommend me, so I must do the best I can with you."

"Well, well, a clean shave is a comfort, but don't be long, for I want to get back, do you see."

"Not a moment, not a moment."

Sweeney Todd walked into his back-parlour, conveying with him the only light that was in the shop, so that the dim glimpse that, up to this time, Johanna from the outside had contrived to see what was going on, was denied to her; and all that met her eyes was impenetrable darkness.

Oh, what a world of anxious agonizing sensations crossed the mind of the young and beautiful girl at that moment. She felt as if some great crisis in her history had arrived, and that she was condemned to look in vain into darkness to see of what it consisted.

We must not, however, allow the reader to remain in the

same state of mystification, which came over the perceptive faculties of Johanna Oakley; but we shall proceed to state clearly and distinctly what did happen in the barber's shop, while he went to get an uncommonly keen razor in his back-parlour.

The moment his back was turned, the seeming farmer who had made such a good thing of his beasts, sprang from the shaving chair, as if he had been electrified; and yet he did not do it with any appearance of fright, nor did he make any noise. It was only astonishingly quick, and then he placed himself close to the window, and waited patiently with his eyes fixed upon the chair, to see what would happen next.

In the space of about a quarter of a minute, there came from the next room, a sound like the rapid drawing back of a heavy bolt, and then in an instant, the shaving chair disappeared beneath the floor; and the circumstances by which Sweeney Todd's customers disappeared was evident.

There was a piece of the flooring turning upon a centre, and the weight of the chair when a bolt was withdrawn, by means of simple leverage from the inner room, weighed down one end of the top, which, by a little apparatus, was to swing completely round, there being another chair on the under surface, which thus became the upper, exactly resembling the one in which the unhappy customer was supposed to be "polished off".

Hence was it that in one moment, as if by magic, Sweeney Todd's visitors disappeared, and there was the empty chair. No doubt, he trusted to a fall of about twenty feet below, on to a stone floor, to be the death of them, or, at all events, to stun them until he could go down to finish the murder, and—*to cut them up for Mrs Lovett's pies!* after robbing them of all money and valuables they might have about them.

In another moment, the sound as of a bolt was again heard, and Sir Richard Brown, who had played the part of the wealthy farmer, feeling that the trap was closed again, seated himself in the new chair that had made its appearance with all the nonchalance in life, as if nothing had happened.

It was a full minute before Todd ventured to look from the parlour into the darkened shop, and then he shook so that he had to hold by the door to steady himself.

"That's done," he said. "That's the last, I hope. It is time I finished; I never felt so nervous since the first time. Then I did quake a little. How quiet he went: I have sometimes had a shriek ringing in my ears for a whole week."

It was a large high-backed piece of furniture, that shaving chair, so that, when Todd crept into the shop with the light in his hand, he had not the remotest idea it was tenanted; but when he got round it, and saw his customer calmly waiting with the lather upon his face, the cry of horror that came gurgling and gushing from his throat was horrible to hear.

"Why, what's the matter," said Sir Richard.

"O God, the dead! the dead! O God!" cried Todd, "this is the beginning of my punishment. Have mercy, Heaven! oh, do not look upon me with those dead eyes."

"Murderer!" shouted Sir Richard, in a voice that rung like the blast of a trumpet through the house.

In an instant he sprang upon Sweeney Todd, and grappled him by the throat. There was a short struggle, and they were down upon the floor together, but Todd's wrists were suddenly laid hold of, and a pair of handcuffs most scientifically put upon him by the officers, who, at the word "murderer", that being a preconcerted signal, came from the cupboard where they had been concealed.

"Secure him well, my men," said the magistrate, "and don't let him lay violent hands upon himself. Ah! Miss Oakley, you are in time. This man is a murderer. I found out all the secret about the chair last night, after twelve, by exploring the vaults under the old church. Thank God, we have stopped his career."

*　　*　　*

It wants five minutes to nine, and Mrs Lovett's shop is filling with persons anxious to devour or to carry away one or more of the nine o'clock batch of savoury, delightful, gushing gravy pies. Many of Mrs Lovett's customers paid her in advance for the pies, in order that they might be quite sure of getting their orders fulfilled when the first batch should make its gracious appearance from the depths below.

"Well, Jiggs," said one of the legal fraternity to another. "How are you today, old fellow. What do you bring it in?"

"Oh! I ain't very blooming. The fact is the count and I, and a few others, made a night of it last evening, and, somehow or another, I don't think whiskey and water, half-and-half, and tripe go well together."

"I should wonder if they did."

"And so I've come for a pie just to settle my stomach; you see, I'm rather delicate."

"Ah! you are just like me, young man, there," said an elderly personage; "I have a delicate stomach, and the slightest thing disagrees with me. A mere idea will make me quite ill."

"Will it, really?"

"Yes; and my wife, she—"

"Oh! bother your wife. It's only five minutes to nine, don't you see? What a crowd there is, to be sure. Mrs Lovett, you charmer, I hope you have ordered enough pies to be made tonight. You see what a lot of customers you have."

"Oh! there will be plenty."

"That's right. I say, don't push so; you'll be in time, I tell you; don't be pushing and driving in that sort of way—I've got ribs."

"And so have I. Last night I didn't get a pie at all, and my old woman is in a certain condition, you see, gentlemen, and won't fancy anything but one of Lovett's veal pies, so I've come all the way from Newington to get one for—"

"Hold your row, will you? And don't push."

"For to have the child marked with a pie on its—"

"Behind there, I say; don't be pushing a fellow as if it was half price at a theatre."

Each moment added some newcomers to the throng, and at last any strangers who had known nothing of the attractions of Mrs Lovett's pie-shop, and had walked down Bell Yard, would have been astonished at the throng of persons there assembled—a throng, that was each moment increasing in density, and becoming more and more urgent and clamorous.

* * *

One, two, three, four, five, six, seven, eight, nine! Yes, it is nine at last. It strikes by old St Dunstan's church clock, and in weaker strains the chronometrical machine at the pie-shop echoes the sound. What excitement there is now to get at the pies when they shall come! Mrs Lovett lets down the square, moveable platform that goes upon pulleys into the cellar; some machinery, which only requires a handle to be turned, brings up a hundred pies in a tray. These are eagerly seized by parties who have previously paid, and such a smacking of lips ensues as never was known.

Down goes the platform for the next hundred, and a gentlemanly man says:

"Let me work the handle, Mrs Lovett, if you please; it's too much for you, I'm sure."

"Sir, you are very kind, but I never allow anybody on this side of the counter but my own people, sir. I can turn the handle myself, sir, if you please, with the assistance of this girl. Keep your distance, sir, nobody wants your help."

How the waggish young lawyers' clerks laughed as they smacked their lips, and sucked in the golopshious gravy of the pies, which, by-the-by, appeared to be all delicious veal that time, and Mrs Lovett worked the handle of the machine all the more vigorously that she was a little angry with the officious stranger. What an unusual trouble it seemed to be to wind up those forthcoming hundred pies! How she toiled, and how the people waited; but at length there came up the savoury steam, and then the tops of the pies were visible.

They came up upon a large tray, about six feet square, and the moment Mrs Lovett ceased turning the handle, and let a catch fall that prevented the platform receding again, to the astonishment and terror of every one, away flew all the pies, tray and all, across the counter, and a man who was lying crouched down in an exceedingly flat state under the tray sprang to his feet.

Mrs Lovett shrieked, as well she might, and then she stood trembling, and looking as pale as death itself. It was the doomed cook from the cellars, who had adopted this mode of escape.

The throng of persons in the shop looked petrified, and after Mrs Lovett's shriek, there was an awful stillness for about a minute, and then the young man who officiated as cook spoke.

"Ladies and Gentlemen, I fear that what I am going to say will spoil your appetites; but the truth is beautiful at all times, and I have to state that Mrs Lovett's pies are made of *human flesh*!"

*　　*　　*

How the throng of persons recoiled—what a roar of agony and dismay there was! How frightfully sick about forty lawyers' clerks became all at once, and how they spat out the gelatinous clinging portions of the rich pies they had been devouring. "Good gracious!—oh, the pies!—confound it!"

"'Tis false!" screamed Mrs Lovett.

"You are my prisoner, madam," said the man who had so obligingly offered to turn the handle of the machine that wound up the pies, at the same time producing a constable's staff.

"Prisoner!"

"Yes, on a charge of aiding and abetting Sweeney Todd, now in custody, in the commission of many murders."

Mrs Lovett staggered back, and her complexion turned a livid colour.

"I am poisoned," she said. "Good God! I am poisoned," and she sank insensible to the floor.

There was now some confusion at the door of the shop, for three people were effecting an entrance. These consisted of Sir Richard Brown, Colonel Jeffery, and Johanna Oakley.

"Miss Oakley," said Sir Richard, "you objected to coming here, but I told you I had a particular reason for bringing you. This night, about half an hour since, I made an acquaintance I want to introduce you to."

"Who—oh, who?"

"There's an underground communication all the way from Sweeney Todd's cellar to the ovens of this pie-shop; and I found there Mrs Lovett's 'cook', with whom I arranged this little surprise for his mistress. Look at him, Miss Oakley, do you know him? Look up, Master Cook."

"Mark—Mark Ingestrie!" shrieked Johanna, the moment she glanced at the person alluded to.

"Johanna!"

In another moment she was in his arms, and clasped to his heart.

When Mrs Lovett was picked up by the officers, she was found to be dead. The poison which Sweeney Todd had put into the brandy she was accustomed to solace herself with, when the pangs of conscience troubled her, and of which she always took some before the evening batch of pies came up, had done its work.

That night Todd passed in Newgate, and in due time a swinging corpse was all that remained of the barber of Fleet Street.

The youths who visited Lovett's pie-shop, and there luxuriated upon those delicacies, are youths no longer. Indeed, the grave has closed over all but one, and he is very, very old, but even now, as he thinks of how many pies he ate, and how he enjoyed the flavour of the "veal", he shudders and has to take a drop of brandy.

Beneath the old church of St Dunstan were found the heads and bones of Todd's victims. As little as possible was said by the authorities about it; but it was supposed that some hundreds of persons must have perished in the frightful manner we have detailed.

8

VARNEY THE VAMPIRE

by James Malcolm Rymer

ANOTHER OF EDWARD LLOYD'S most prolific and popular authors was James Malcolm Rymer (1804–1882), whose work appeared under at least seven different pseudonyms and who himself was thought for some years to be a pen-name of Thomas Peckett Prest. Like Prest, his output was enormous, but unlike him he managed his working hours and finances with skill and died a wealthy man. (According to Louis James, at the height of his abilities Rymer was "writing ten serials simultaneously ... at his death his estate was £8,000".)

Born in the Scottish Highlands, Rymer trained as a civil engineer and surveyor and moved to London in the middle 1830s. Despite this trade, Rymer appears to have been captivated with the idea of being an author and when he met Lloyd at the Mechanics' Institute in London was easily persuaded by the astute publisher to write material for him. Shortly thereafter Rymer gave up engineering entirely and joined Lloyd as one of his editors. Determinedly though he strove to be a superior novelist, the young Scotsman realized that while he might excel in the field of lower-class literature, the achievements of those he admired—such as Leigh Hunt—were beyond him. So, grudgingly content with his lot, he gave the reading public a string of entertaining and successful Penny Dreadfuls including perhaps the most popular of the "later" Gothic novels, "The Black Monk" (1844), "The Mystery in Scarlet" (1884, the novel which so delighted

Robert Louis Stevenson), "The White Slave" (1844, a scathing attack on religious hypocrisy), and two of the most famous heroines in this area of fiction, "Ada, The Betrayed" (1845) and "Jane Brightwell" (1846), to whom we shall return in the next section. But it is as the author of Lloyd's "most ghoulish and goriest publication" (E. S. Turner) that Rymer is best remembered, "Varney the Vampire".

Perhaps the most famous penny-issue novel after the story of Sweeney Todd, "Varney" has been the subject of much discussion about its authorship. For some years it was believed to have been the work of Thomas Prest (I myself used an extract in an earlier anthology and supported this contention), but recent research by some of the foremost authorities now makes it seem as definite as we can ever hope to be that Rymer was the author. The famous collector of Penny Dreadfuls, Barry Ono, was one of the first to argue on Rymer's behalf, and he was soon after joined by the British Museum. The clinching evidence was then seemingly provided by the late Frank Algar who obtained a collection of Rymer's books and papers in which he had listed his works—and among them was "Varney the Vampire; or The Feast of Blood".

The story is everything that the image of a Penny Dreadful personifies: there are endless bloody adventures, scenes of horror and debauchery and a plot that meanders through situations bizarre, unspeakable and often highly unlikely. Rymer may well have drawn his inspiration from Dr William Polidori's pioneer vampire story, "The Vampyre", which was published in 1819 and at first wrongly attributed to Lord Byron, but certainly to this he added all the traditional elements of blood-lust which are now so much a part of vampire fiction. The story of Sir Francis Varney, the vampire, continues for 220 chapters over nearly 1,000 pages and is far too complex to be recounted here; but in the tradition of all good morality tales, the evil nobleman is brought to a terrible end in a volcano after many adventures.

There are several episodes which can well be extracted to

stand on their own, but I particularly liked the following narrative in which Varney joins with a group of five other vampires to revive a corpse on Hampstead Heath. It is evocative of the story as a whole, I think, and demonstrates that despite the passing of time, little has changed in the style and setting of tales about the un-dead.

The Resuscitation Of A Vampire

It is nearly half an hour to midnight. The sky is still cloudy, but glimpses of the moon can be got as occasionally the clouds slip from before her disc, and then what a glorious flood of silver light spreads itself over the landscape.

And a landscape in every respect more calculated to look beautiful and romantic under the chaste moon's ray, than that to which we would now invite attention, certainly could not have been found elsewhere, within many a mile of London. It is Hampstead Heath, that favoured spot where upon a small scale are collected some of the rarest landscape beauties that the most romantic mountainous counties of England can present to the gratified eye of the tourist.

Those who are familiar with London and its environs, of course, are well acquainted with every nook, glade, tree, and dell in that beautiful heath, where, at all and every time and season, there is much to recommend that semi-wild spot to notice. Indeed, if it were, as it ought to be, divested of its donkey-drivers and laundresses, a more delightful place of residence could scarcely be found than some of those suburban villas, that are dotted round the margin of this picturesque waste.

But it is midnight, nearly. That time is forthcoming, at which popular superstition trembles—that time, at which the voice of ignorance and of cant lowers to whispers, and when the poor of heart and timid of spirit imagine worlds of unknown terrors. On this occasion, though, it will be seen that there would have been some excuse if even the most bold had shrunk back appalled at what was taking place.

But we will not anticipate for truly in this instance might we say sufficient for the time are the horrors thereof.

If any one had stood on that portion of the high road which leads right over the heath and so on to Hendon or to Highgate, according as the left hand or the right hand route is taken, and after reaching the Castle Tavern, had looked across the wide expanse of heath to the west, they would have seen nothing for a while but the clustering bushes of heath blossom, and the picturesque fir trees, that there are to be beheld in great luxuriance. But, after a time, something of a more noticeable character would have presented itself.

At a quarter to twelve there rose up from a tangled mass of brushwood, which had partially concealed a deep cavernous place where sand had been dug, a human form, and there it stood in the calm still hour of night so motionless that it scarcely seemed to possess life, but presently another rose at a short distance.

And then there was a third, so that these three strange-looking beings stood like landmarks against the sky, and when the moon shone out from some clouds which had for a short time obscured her rays, they looked strange and tall, and superhuman.

One spoke.

" 'Tis time," he said, in a deep, hollow voice, that sounded as if it came from the tomb.

"Yes, time," said another.

"Time has come," said the third.

Then they moved, and by the gestures they used, it seemed as if an animated discussion was taking place among them, after which they moved along in perfect silence, and in a most stately manner, towards the village of Hampstead.

Before reaching it, however, they turned down some narrow shaded walks among garden walls, and the backs of stables, until they emerged close to the old churchyard, which stands on high ground, and which was not then—at least, the western portion of it—overlooked by any buildings. Those villas which now skirt it, are of recent elevation.

A dense mass of clouds had now been brought up by a south wind, and had swept over the face of the moon, so that at this juncture, and as twelve o'clock might be expected to strike, the night was darker than it had yet been since sunset. The circumstance was probably considered by the mysterious beings who sought the churchyard as favourable to them, and they got without difficulty within those sacred precincts devoted to the dead.

Scarcely had they found the way a dozen feet among the old tomb-stones, when from behind a large square monument, there appeared two more persons; and if the attorney, Mr Miller, had been there, he would probably have thought they bore such a strong resemblance to those whom he had seen in the park, he would have had but little hesitation in declaring that they were the same.

These two persons joined the other three, who manifested no surprise at seeing them, and then the whole five stood close to the wall of the church, so that they were quite secure from observation, and one of them spoke.

"Brothers," he said, "you who prey upon human nature by the law of your being, we have work to do tonight—that work which we never leave undone, and which we dare not neglect when we know that it is to do. One of our fraternity lies here."

"Yes," said the others, with the exception of one, and he spoke passionately.

"Why," he said, "when there were enough, and more than enough, to do the work, summon me?"

"Not more than enough, there are but five."

"And why should you not be summoned," said another, "you are one of us. You ought to do your part with us in setting a brother free from the clay that presses on his breast."

"I was engaged in my vocation. If the moon shine out in

The first issue of one of the most famous of all Penny Dreadfuls, James Malcolm Rymer's "Varney The Vampire" (1847).

all her lustre again, you will see that I am wan and wasted, and have need of—"

"Blood," said one.

"Blood, blood, blood," repeated the others. And then the first speaker said, to him who complained:

"You are one whom we are glad to have with us on a service of danger. You are strong and bold, your deeds are known, you have lived long, and are not yet crushed."

"I do not know our brother's name," said one of the others with an air of curiosity.

"I go by many."

"So do we all. But by what name may we know you best?"

"Slieghton, I was named in the reign of the third Edward. But many have known me as Varney, the Vampire!"

There was a visible sensation among those wretched beings

as these words were uttered, and one was about to say something, when Varney interrupted him.

"Come," he said, "I have been summoned here, and I have come to assist in the exhumation of a brother. It is one of the conditions of our being that we do so. Let the work be proceeded with then, at once, I have no time to spare. Let it be done with. Where lies the vampire? Who was he?"

"A man of good repute, Varney," said the first speaker. "A smooth, fair-spoken man, a religious man, so far as cant went, a proud, cowardly, haughty, worldly follower of religion. Ha, ha, ha!"

"And what made him one of us?"

"He dipped his hands in blood. There was a poor boy, a brother's only child, 'twas left an orphan. He slew the boy, and he is one of us."

"With a weapon."

"Yes, and a sharp one; the weapon of unkindness. The child was young and gentle, and harsh words, blows, and revilings placed him in his grave. He is in heaven, while the man will be a vampire."

" 'Tis well—dig him up."

They each produced from under the dark cloaks they wore, a short double-edged, broad, flat-bladed weapon, not unlike the swords worn by the Romans, and he who assumed the office of guide, led the way to a newly-made grave, and diligently, and with amazing rapidity and power, they commenced removing the earth.

It was something amazing to see the systematic manner in which they worked, and in ten minutes one of them struck the blade of his weapon upon the lid of a coffin, and said:

"It is here."

The lid was then partially raised in the direction of the moon, which, although now hidden, they could see would in a very short time show itself in some gaps of the clouds, that were rapidly approaching at great speed across the heavens.

They then desisted from their labour, and stood around the grave in silence for a time, until, as the moon was longer showing her fair face, they began to discourse in whispers.

"What shall become of him," said one, pointing to the grave. "Shall we aid him?"

"No," said Varney, "I have heard that of him which shall not induce me to lift hand or voice in his behalf. Let him fly, shrieking like a frightened ghost where he lists."

"Did you not once know some people named Bannerworth?"

"I did. You came to see me, I think, at an inn. They are all dead."

"Hush," said another, "look, the moon will soon be free from the vapours that sail between it and the green earth. Behold, she shines out fresh once more; there will be life in the coffin soon, and our work will be done."

It was so. The dark clouds passed over the face of the moon, and with a sudden burst of splendour, it shone out again as before.

* * *

A death-like stillness now was over the whole scene, and those who had partially exhumed the body stood as still as statues, waiting the event which they looked forward to as certain to ensue.

The clear beauty and intensity of the moonbeams increased each moment, and the whole surrounding landscape was lit up with a perfect flood of soft silvery light. The old church stood out in fine relief, and every tree, and every wild flower, and every blade of grass in the churchyard, could be seen in its finest and most delicate proportions and construction.

The lid of the coffin was wrenched up on one side to about six inches in height, and that side faced the moon, so that some rays, it was quite clearly to be seen, found their way into that sad receptacle for the dead. A quarter of an hour, however, passed away, and nothing happened.

"Are you certain he is one of us?" whispered Varney.

"Quite, I have known it years past. He had the mark upon him."

"Enough. Behold."

A deep and dreadful groan came from the grave, and yet it could hardly be called a groan; it was more like a howl, and the lid which was partially open, was visibly agitated.

"He comes," whispered one.

"Hush," said another, "hush; our duty will be done when he stands upon the level ground. Hush, let him near nothing, let him know nothing, since we will not aid him. Behold, behold."

They all looked down into the grave, but they betrayed no signs of emotion, and the sight they saw there was such as one would have supposed would have created emotion in the breast of any one at all capable of feeling. But then we must not reason upon these strange frightful existences as we reason upon human nature such as we usually know it.

The coffin lid was each moment more and more agitated. The deep frightful groans increased in number and sound, and then the corpse stretched out one ghastly hand from the open crevice and grasped despairingly and frantically at the damp earth that was around.

There was still towards one side of the coffin sufficient weight of mould that it would require some strength to turn it off, but as the dead man struggled within his narrow house it kept falling aside in lumps, so that his task of exhumation became each moment an easier one.

At length he uttered a strange wailing shriek, and by a great effort succeeded in throwing the coffin lid quite open, and then he sat up, looking so horrible and ghastly in the grave clothes, that even the vampires that were around the grave recoiled a little.

"Is it done?" said Varney.

"Not yet," said he who had summoned them to the fearful rite, and so assumed a sort of direction over them, "not yet;

we will not assist him, but we may not leave him before telling him who and what he is."

"Do so now."

The corpse stood up in the coffin and the moonlight fell full upon him.

"Vampire arise," said he who had just spoken to Varney. "Vampire arise, and do your work in the world until your doom shall be accomplished. Vampire arise—arise. Pursue your victims in the mansion and in the cottage. Be a terror and a desolation, go you where you may, and if the hand of death strike you down, the cold beams of the moon shall restore you to new life. Vampire arise, arise!"

"I come, I come!" shrieked the corpse.

In another moment the five vampires who had dug him from the grave were gone.

Moaning, shrieking, and groaning he made some further attempts to get out of the deep grave. He clutched at it in vain, the earth crumbled beneath him, and it was only at last by dint of reaching up and dragging in the displaced material that lay in a heap at the sides, so that in a few minutes it formed a mound for him to stand upon in the grave, that he was at length able to get out.

Then, although he sighed, and now and then uttered a wailing shriek as he went about the work, he with a strange kind of instinct, began to carefully fill up the grave from which he had but just emerged, nor did he cease from his occupation until he had finished it, and so carefully shaped the mound of mould and turf over it that no one would have thought it had been disturbed.

When this work was done a kind of madness seemed to seize him, and he walked to the gate of the graveyard, which opens upon Church Street, and placing his hands upon the sides of his mouth he produced such an appalling shriek that it must have awakened everybody in Hampstead.

Then, turning, he fled like a hunted hare in the other direction, and taking the first turning to the right ran up a lane called Frognal Lane, and which is parallel to the town, for a town Hampstead may be fairly called now, although it was not then.

By pursuing this lane, he got upon the outskirts of the heath, and then turning to the right again, for, with a strange pertinacity, he always kept, as far as he could, his face towards the light of the moon, he rushed down a deep hollow, where there was a cluster of little cottages, enjoying such repose that one would have thought the flutter of an awakened bird upon the wing would have been heard.

It was quite clear that the new vampyre had as yet no notion of what he was about, or where he was going, and that he was with mere frantic haste speeding along, from the first impulse of his frightful nature.

The place into which he had now plunged, is called the Vale of Health: now a place of very favourite resort, but then a mere collection of white faced cottages, with a couple of places that might be called villas. A watchman went his nightly rounds in that place. And it so happened that the guardian of the Vale had just roused himself up at this juncture, and made up his mind to make his walk of observation, when he saw the terrific figure of a man attired in grave clothes coming along with dreadful speed towards him, as if to take the Vale of Health by storm.

The watchman was so paralysed by fear that he could not find strength enough to spring his rattle, although he made the attempt, and held it out at arm's length, while his eyes glared with perfect ferocity, and his mouth was wide enough open to nourish the idea, that after all he had a hope of being able to swallow the spectre.

But, nothing heeding him, the vampire came wildly on.

Fain now would the petrified watchman have got out of the way, but he could not, and in another moment he was dashed down to the earth, and trodden on by the horrible existence that knew not what it did.

A cloud came over the moon, and the vampire sunk down, exhausted, by a garden-wall, and there lay as if dead, while the watchman, who had fairly fainted away, lay in a picturesque attitude on his back, not very far off.

Half an hour passed, and a slight mist-like rain began to fall.

The vampire slowly rose to his feet, and commenced wringing his hands and moaning, but his former violence of demeanour had passed away. That was but the first flush of new life, and now he seemed to be more fully aware of who and what he was.

He shivered as he tottered slowly on, until he came to where the watchman lay, and then he divested that guardian of the Vale of his greatcoat, his hat, and some other portions of his apparel, all of which he put on himself, still slightly moaning as he did so, and ever and anon stopping to make a gesture of despair.

When this operation was completed, he slunk off into a narrow path which led on to the heath again, and there he seemed to waver a little, whether he would go towards London, or the country. At length it seemed that he decided upon the former course, and he walked on at a rapid pace right through Hampstead, and down the hill towards London, the lights of which could be seen gleaming in the distance.

When the watchman did recover himself, the first thing he did was, to be kind enough to rouse everybody up from their sleep in the Vale of Health, by springing his rattle at a prodigious rate, and by the time he had roused up the whole neighbourhood, he felt almost ready to faint again at the bare recollection of the terrible apparition that had knocked him down.

The story in the morning was told all over the place, with many additions to it of course, and it was long afterwards before the inhabitants of the Vale could induce another watchman, for that one gave up the post, to run the risk of such a visitation.

And the oddest thing of all was, that the watchman declared that he caught a glance at the countenance, and that it was like that of a Mr Brooks, who had only been buried the day previous, that if he had not known that gentleman to be dead and buried, he should have thought it was he himself gone mad.

But there was the grave of Mr Brooks, with its circular mound of earth, all right enough; and then Mr B. was known to have been such a respectable man. He went to the city every day, and used to do so just for the purpose of granting audiences to ladies and gentlemen who might be labouring under any little pecuniary difficulties, and accommodating them. Kind Mr Brooks. He only took one hundred pounds per cent. Why should he be a Vampire? Bless him! Too severe, really!

There were people who called him a bloodsucker while he lived, and now he was one practically, and yet he had his own pew at church, and subscribed a whole guinea a year to a hospital—he did, although people did say it was in order that he might pack off any of his servants at once to it in case of illness. But then the world is so censorious.

And to this day the watchman's story of the apparition that visited the Vale of Health is still talked of by the old women who make what they call tea for Sunday parties at nine pence a head.

9

JESSIE, THE MORMON'S DAUGHTER

by Percy B. St John

JAMES MALCOLM RYMER's heroine, "Ada, The Betrayed" (1845), is today widely regarded as the most famous heroine in Penny Dreadful fiction. (Rymer himself was known to his associates as "Ada The Betrayed" because of the success of the work.) In this story—as in Rymer's other famous serial "Jane Brightwell"—the heroines have become changed in character from the delicate, swooning, incredibly naïve maidens of the Gothic novels, to young women actively seeking love and not entirely tied to the commands of home and parents. Now that reading material was finding its way into the hands of the poorest women, the voluminous and whimsical romances which had delighted earlier generations had little or no appeal. Certainly the new readers wanted taking out of their appalling circumstances, but their heroines had to have some basis in reality, rather than being the simpering offspring of aristocracy. They could by all means be of high birth, brought down or cheated out of their inheritance, but dramas played out against haunted castles and settings divorced from reality were far from acceptable. Rymer, in partnership with Lloyd, was one of the first to realize this change in mood and deservedly enjoyed the greatest success. But despite these new freedoms, one factor remained as constant as ever. Margaret Dalziel summarizes it succinctly when she writes, "but still no woman could ever be as clever as a clever man. What mattered above all else was the feeling heart." Perhaps the fact that this remained so constant is not to be wondered at when one realizes that very few of the penny-issue writers were women. Most female authors of this time were involved in much more prosaic work and, as we shall see in the next section, the number of ladies who did tackle these sensational serials were not large in number.

A skim through the pages of any catalogue of the period gives a clear enough picture of the kind of heroines readers sought: "Florence Graham; or, The Pirate's Daughter" (1847), "Adeline; or, The Grave of the Forsaken" (1850), "Harriet Stanton; or, Married and Starved for Money" (1860) and so on, not forgetting the works of G. W. M. Reynolds, Thomas Peckett Prest, *et al.* However, for me the strangest of all these heroines is "Jessie, The Mormon's Daughter" by Percy Bolingbroke St John (1821–1889), published in 1848. The crusading fervour against social ills did occasionally move some of the penny-issue writers as we have seen, but there can hardly have been a more bizarre subject for anyone to have taken up than the Mormons who, after a great many tribulations, had finally established a settlement at Salt Lake City in 1847. The author sets the tone of his work right from the beginning when he writes, "It is time that something was done to check their progress. In this work their own blasphemous account of their origin, their abominable fabrication of a Bible, their cunning mode of proselytism, their lustful adoption of polygamy, for which system of legalized infamy they alone have left the confines of civilization, are fearlessly exposed." Much of St John's tale is expressed in this same hysterical style and as such can only really cause amusement today. From any point of view, though, "Jessie" was a strange departure for him, for he was at that time the editor of the staid and respectable—not to say uncontroversial—*Mirror of Literature.*

Percy St John was the son of the historical writer, James Augustus St John, and in his youth travelled extensively with him in Europe and America. He is believed to have begun writing while still a teenager, and was particularly fired with an interest in America while visiting the country with his father who was writing a *Life of Sir Walter Raleigh*. He contributed first to newspapers and apparently on the side to several of the less scrupulous penny part publishers—and then became editor of the *Mirror of Literature* in 1846. In 1861 he joined the *London Herald* and also began translating as well as writing his own tales. His stories of American prairie life were much praised for their authenticity, and his "Blue Dwarf" (1869) remains as one of the best of all the fanciful novelizations of the life of Dick Turpin. In hindsight, it seems more than likely that St John was put up to writing "Jessie" during a period of financial embarrassment by one of his publishers, Edward Harrison, who was a renowned strict churchman despite the nature of his publications. It is a measure of his skill that despite the book's bias he keeps us constantly interested in the perilous adventures of our heroine on her unwilling journey to settle with the Mormons in America.

In the extract here, a reluctant young girl is to be forced into a Mormon marriage with a highly suspicious individual—but events are about to take a turn for the bloody...

Buried Alive!

The harem system, where eighty wives or more lived under one roof, or divan—the parent abode—had not, at the time of which we speak, been introduced. Mormonism, in its open defiance of the world, was not the hideous thing it is now—shameless, reckless, vile—beyond power of description. But even in its early days, when polygamy was restricted to two, or, at most, three wives, it was revolting enough.

A man may here keep a wife and concubine under the same roof, in the shape of a governess, or servant, or companion; but the woman knows it not; or even, if she suspects it, and, for her own dignity's sake, or the happiness of her children, declines to make a scandal of it, at least, she avows it not. Let us enter Dou's Creek, and see the picture it represents. It was a village of about thirty houses and tents, built without much regularity, but the doors always looking towards a common centre. There was always an affectation of Arcadian and patriarchal simplicity about the Mormons, which seems as suitable as might be with a congregated mass of London pickpockets and street-walkers.

In the centre were held the games, dancing, wrestling, running, and such like. There were several empty houses, which had belonged to Mormons, who had been forwarded to the upper settlement as they were ready.

It was now eight o'clock. Once again the altar of the false prophet had been erected to go through the blasphemous mockery of a marriage. All the chiefs of the Mormon camp were assembled and all the most contented of the women.

Walter de Vere was dressed out in a brave array. He had contrived to curb his drunken propensities for once, and stood on one side of the altar calm, collected, but very pale. Sarah Paulding was ghastly. Everybody whispered that they had never seen so unearthly-beautiful a pair. Both had a strange gleam in their eyes, which was, to a keen observer, perfectly Satanic. Nobody could make out, to see them, whether they were being united by great hate, or very great love. They stood about two feet asunder.

One of the Mormon elders took up the prayer-book and began to read its impressive "Form of Solemnization of Matrimony". He turned to Walter de Vere and asked him the usual question.

"Yes," was the ready reply.

"Wilt thou," continued the impostor priest, "have this man to be thy wedded husband, to live together after God's ordinance in the holy estate of matrimony? Wilt thou obey him, and serve him, love, honour, and keep him in sickness and in health; and forsaking all others, keep thee only unto him, so long as ye both shall live?"

"No!"

There were few more resourceful—or unusual—heroines in serial fiction than "Jessie, The Mormon's Daughter" by Percy B. St John (1848).

Had a thunderbolt fallen in among them, it could not have caused greater sensation than this single monosyllable.

"But Miss Paulding!" cried Walter de Vere paler still with rage.

"What is the meaning you will not have him?" asked the astonished priest.

"False and outcast minister of God!" she said, "do you think, I, the daughter of a real servant of the Lord, would wed a forger, and thief, who has already dragged two wretched beings into the mire?"

Walter de Vere fell back as if stunned. The blow was so fearfully sudden, the charge so unexpected, terrible, yet true.

"Who has been calumniating me?" he cried, amidst the suppressed jeers of his companions. They had all paid their bets. His discomfiture was amusing. But there were serious interests at stake, and to this it behoved them all first to look.

"No one here has said a word about you, except in your favour," replied Sarah, standing cool, collected, and firm, amid the excited mob.

"But what I say I know to be true, Mr Walter de Vere—alias Mr William Hicks, for whose apprehension I saw many bills about, when I was last in England."

"By heavens woman!" cried de Vere alias Hicks, savagely, "whether you like it or not, you shall be my wife. No one shall brave me with impunity."

"Proceed," said one of the elders.

"You dare not," cried Sarah, "you dare not violate the liberty of a poor woman. I will *not* wed this man, say or do what you will."

"Proceed," said the same nasal voice.

The ceremony proceeded, Sarah's two friends Lydia and Amy covering their faces with their hands, and weeping. Two strong men held Sarah by the wrists, and had the reckless audacity to announce to the assembly that Sarah had said "yes". The villain had money, which, on an occasion like the present, he used freely to lavish on his comrades.

Then Sarah was taken to a tent by four women. Lydia and Amy were sternly told to stop where they were.

"You had better mind what you are at," said Lydia, with a curl of the lip, which startled William Hicks.

"Why?"

"Two hours ago, a mounted messenger started to alarm her friends at the settlement," replied Lydia, with a triumphant smile.

"D—n!" shouted several of the Mormons.

"Who went?" said Harry sternly.

"You are angry. If you knew all, you would not be. Miss Paulding was an old and dear friend," answered Lydia.

"It matters not," said the young man, coldly. "The laws of the Saints must be obeyed."

"What mean you?"

"And those who aid and abet traitors must be punished," he continued. "Who was the messenger?"

"Jessie."

"By the foul fiend," cried William Hicks, "that girl will will be the ruin of us!"

Phineas Bristowe, an elder who hitherto had not said one word, groaned aloud.

"Let all the women return to their houses," said the elder, who had officiated as priest; "the Saints will enter into deliberation."

The women shuddered and obeyed. There was something in the tone of the man which terrified them. William Hicks hastened to the nuptial tent, turned out the women, and remained alone with his so-called wife. She was seated on a box.

"But dearest lady," he began in husky and constrained tones, "what is the meaning of this change?"

Silence.

"After all that passed this morning," he continued, in his old seductive tones, "surely you cannot have forgotten all that was understood."

"You are a Mormon."

"Well."

"Answer me."

"I do, for convenience sake, take that name in order to travel with the tribe."

"You have two other wives."

"Well, according to the ideas of the Saint I have, but in my own idea, I have only one wife, and that is you, my own, dear darling."

"You are William Hicks, the forger and embezzler—the man who would, if caught, suffer at the Old Bailey," she continued.

"Woman beware!" he cried, advancing closer to her, his eyes flashing, half with fury, half with passionate desire.

"Back!" she said.

As she spoke she rose, and showed a sharp knife, which hitherto, she had concealed up her sleeve. But William Hicks was nothing daunted by this display.

"Ah! ah! my Lady Macbeth. This acting will not do. Put down that knife, my dainty wife, or it will be the worse for you."

"Worse for you, felon!"

"Use that word again," he said, with sullen and lowering brow, "and you will repent it the longest day you live."

"Would you strike me, coward?" cried the exasperated girl.

A cold gleam of concentrated fury shot through his eyes, as, with a cry of frantic rage, he flew at her. She drew back, and, cold and firm, stabbed right at him. He fell to the ground, weltering in his blood, after giving one despairing cry for help.

"Murder—help!"

In they poured, to find her standing calm, resolute, firm, with the bloody knife held high above her head. Men, women, boys, came rushing and were scared by the sight before them. A man approached Hicks, while Sarah, without the slightest hesitation allowed herself to be disarmed.

"Is he dead?" she whispered.

"I know not, murderess—but dead or living, you shall die the death!" cried one of the elders.

"Anything better than his paramour," she replied.

"Bind her—let all leave but elders," continued the speaker, "remove the wounded man to his own waggon."

After some little difficulty and hesitation, this order was obeyed, and Sarah remained in the tent with the twelve elders. A brief conference was held, in low, hushed whispers, and then Sarah was seized, blindfolded, gagged and taken out into the open air.

She felt herself placed upon a horse; the clatter of other horses' hoofs could be heard around her, and then she was hurried away at a rapid rate. Presently they halted. They were in a dreary kind of dell, overshadowed by tall and wavy pine trees. They ungagged her, took off the bandage from her eyes, without untying her hands, and seated her on the grass. Two lanterns were placed upon the ground about seven feet apart. Then a pickaxe and two shovels were produced, and three men, casting off their coats, began to dig. Anyone could see at once that they were digging a grave.

Sarah shuddered. It was hard thus to die in her unrepented sin. She had acted in self-defence, but her hands were red with blood. It seemed a kind of retribution that she, too, should perish by a violent death. The idea of past happy days came over her, and the thought forced itself upon her, that she had been a wicked and ungrateful girl. Her uncle's character now appeared in a clear and vivid light—the light of truth and reason. How could she have so misjudged him? But these ideas availed her no longer. She was in the hands of men actuated by wild feelings of revenge. She knew that she was going to die.

It was strange, but she looked on at the preparations with a strange, odd, wild kind of curiosity. They were digging a mere hole in the earth; but then, what a hole. Not one spoke to her, reproached her, or alluded to the crime or the punishment. They were sullen, silent, and did not even speak among themselves. Whenever they glanced at the wretched girl, it was with looks of the most virulent hatred and scorn.

Up in the heavens not one of the starry lamps illumined the horrid, the fearful, and unparalleled scene. Sarah had been to a certain extent religiously educated, though a fond mother had nurtured her pride. She thought for a moment and then murmured a prayer. It was time.

Two of the men raised her and placed her in the deep hole, which was almost up to her beautiful cold neck. Then, while these two held her with the rigidity of bars of iron, the others began to shovel in the earth. Then the agonizing and maddening thought entered her brain that they were going to bury her alive! This was too much for her, and she burst forth with the most awful shrieks that female throat ever uttered.

"Silence!"

"Never! I will not be murdered. Let me have a fair trial. If you are men you will not thus ill use a poor girl."

"Gag her," said a sullen ruffian.

Again she gave a wild and horrible shriek. It resounded through the hills with fearful intensity. It was the agony of death. But then they gagged her. Then the men who were working did all they could, and in a few minutes the earth was up to her neck. She struggled fearfully, but it was of no avail.

"Hark! what noise is that?"

All listened. It was the trampling of horses.

"Mount and fly. Smother the hell cat some of you," shouted one of the Mormons.

She had forced off her gag and had given another fearful shriek.

"Kill—slay—burn!" shouted a maddened and infuriated voice. "No quarter to the bloody heathen!"

Every Mormon shuddered, and abandoning pickaxes, shovels and lanterns, they rushed to their horses, mounted and flew. Like a whirlwind, a body of mounted men sped by in chase. But two figures halted. One of them bounded to the grave, and casting himself flat on the ground, gazed in agony at the pale face of the girl.

"Dead, dead! my life, my soul, my own darling Sarah!" said a manly voice, in tones of fearful suffering.

"Not dead, but she has fainted," said Jessie, dismounting. "Dig away the earth—quick. I will support her head."

The young man did as he was told, working with the strength and vigour of a young Titanic giant. In a very brief space of time he had released her. A flask of brandy scattered over her face and pressed to her lips brought her to.

"Charles—dear Charles!" she said, clasping him round the neck and kissing his very lips, "was that a horrid dream? No! no! no! Take me away—I know I'm going to die—but take me home. Will you forgive me, Charley? I am very sorry—I wouldn't do it again. But you know that now. Let me die where aunt and uncle will be there to forgive me. I couldn't help it, he wanted to marry me—ah—I killed him!"

"Killed him!" gasped Jessie.

"Served him right!" said Charles, lifting her up in his arms; "but do not die—you shall not, will not die. You will live to be my happy, dear and honoured wife."

"You won't let them bury me alive?" said Sarah wildly.

"B—t 'em, no!" shrieked Charles, who saw that her head was slightly wandering.

He raised her quite up now, and placed her on a horse; Jessie mounted and he walked. In this way they reached their settlement, where none but women and children awaited them. The men were all out after the Mormons. At the entrance of the house Jessie paused.

"You will not go back?" said Charles, anxiously.

"I must."

"But not directly. Step and see how she is. Besides, if the people muster strong enough, not a Mormon will leave the country alive."

Jessie sighed and went in. They put Sarah to bed, and, under the judicious care of Mrs Paulding, she so far recovered in the morning as to be able to converse rationally.

She did not recollect all that passed except as a kind of fearful dream or nightmare. She got up to breakfast. The old man and Charles advanced to meet her with eager and sympathising looks.

"How do you feel, my child?" said the uncle, kindly.

"Like an erring child, seeking the pardon of her father," said Sarah, falling on her knees before the whole family.

"I will shrive you on one condition," said the old man.

"And that?" said Sarah, rising and taking a chair.

"It is that you become my daughter as soon as possible."

"Yes, Sarah—promise to be my wife, and all will be happy."

"If you are not afraid to take a weak, silly and vain girl to be your handmaiden, Charles, I shall be too proud to have won your honest heart," she replied.

"Though I am not a gentleman," said the delighted lover.

"Don't say that again. I had enough of that yesterday. Have you heard?" she said, with a shudder.

"The man is out of danger," replied Charles: "the miscreants who abducted you have fled far away, and the whole Mormon gang have left our state—or else—"

"No message for me," said Jessie, sadly.

"A letter," replied Charles; "but why, from a mistaken sense of duty, return to such infamous bondage?"

"I have promised."

"But such promises—surely you do not hold them binding?"

"All and every promise. Besides, those who love me are on the track. I know I am in no danger; give me the letter."

Jessie read it, but made no remark. She took her breakfast quietly, and then wishing them all farewell, left—after a solemn promise to call if she ever passed that way.

Such is a portion of a Mormon episode of every-day occurrence, and which only did not end in the usual disastrous manner, because the woman had both a bold and valiant heart, and a sympathising friend.

10

THE SHIPWRECKED STRANGER

by Hannah Maria Jones

IT IS PERHAPS not surprising in the light of their general content—and the position of women in society at this time—that there were not many female writers working specifically in the field of the Penny Dreadful. Many women did, of course, pour out romantic fiction which appeared in the main in the form of "three-decker" novels, but the requirements of blood, gore, death, torture and sensationalism which were the stock-in-trade of the penny-serial works seem to have been—probably by choice—beyond their range. This is not to say that there were no authoresses capable of these kind of tales; indeed Edward Lloyd is known to have had one or two writing some of the most bloodthirsty of his early publications. (One of these was his secretary, Elizabeth Caroline Grey, who also doubled as editor of several of the publications.) One authority has recorded a story of the female writer whose copy suddenly did not appear on time and when a messenger was sent to find out why, the lady was discovered to be in the middle of childbirth. Another writer then stepped in for two episodes, after which the new mother again took up her pen, "much chagrined by what had been developed in her absence".

Two women seem to have particularly succeeded in the field of the Penny Dreadful, although because of the anonymity of so many of these publications, there may be a few more whose lights will now never be revealed. (Even those who did leave enough clues for later identification did not help by references in their books to them being "the work of a young man of tender years".) The first was the unfortunate Miss Emma Robinson (1814–1890), the daughter of the famous bookseller, Joseph Robinson, who wrote numerous historical romances including "Whitefriars; or, The Days of Charles the Second" (1844), "Caesar Borgia", "The Gold Worshippers" and "The City Banker; or, Love and Money" which was begun in the *London Journal* by J. F. Smith and completed by Miss Robinson when he severed his connection with the periodical (see Extract 19). Through her prodigious output she appears to have driven herself insane and she eventually died in the London County Lunatic Asylum.

The other, and perhaps more gifted writer, was Miss Hannah Maria Jones (1796–1859) of whom Montague Summers has written: "Her popularity was enormous, and continued so, that until the end of the Nineteenth Century many of her romances were appearing in the cheapest guise with crudest woodcuts, generally without date or printer's name." Indeed throughout much of her writing career, Miss Jones suffered almost as much plagiarism and pirating of her works as Charles Dickens, and frequently complains in her introductions of the "cruel wrong" she has suffered from "pirates and robbers". She found immediate popularity with her first work, "Gretna Green", which appeared in 1820, and then showed the direction of her style with "Village Scandal; or, The Gossip's Tale" (1835), "The Gipsey Chief; or, The Haunted Oak" (1841), "The Ruined Cottage; or, The Farmer's Maid" (1846) and its best-selling sequel, "The Shipwrecked Stranger" (1848).

As a person Miss Jones appears to have been gentle and retiring—in complete contrast to the bloody and sensational nature of many of her stories, and after her marriage lived in Grosvenor Square, London, occasionally venturing out to attend the theatre or social functions. Towards the end of her life (1854) she endeavoured to counteract the publishers whose "unauthorized reprints and spurious editions of her work swarmed throughout her lifetime" (Summers), by selling her copyrights to the publisher John Lofts. Even he, though, was at a loss to stem the tide despite threat of legal action, and there can be little doubt that Miss Jones would have died an extremely wealthy woman if she had received her just rewards from the enormous sales of her work.

To represent her in this collection—and appearing as she does as its only female contributor—I have selected a short story which is taken from "The Shipwrecked Stranger", one of the many popular Penny Dreadful tales of the sea. I believe it is the equal of any other contribution in these pages for story-telling quality, drama and sensation.

The Life Of A Murderer

"A Murderer! God help me. Yes! Time was when I shrunk affrighted from the very sound—when the name was spoken in whispers. Little thought I then I should ever bear the name, or die ignominiously upon the scaffold.

"I was doomed in early life to lose both my parents. I was reared with more kindness than philosophy, by an aunt, for all said I was a spoilt child. I was an unruly boy, but never wanted affection. I was sent to a charity school, but mischief had more charms for me than learning; and the apple orchard in reality to that stamped in the reading lesson in my spelling book. Rebuke followed rebuke: chastisements without number were lavished upon me. I was the dunce of the school. Inspired by a sudden whim, I determined one night as I lay in my little cot to be so no longer—I would learn. For two years did I carry out this resolution, with a heat and impetuosity that characterized all my little proceedings; at the expiration of this time I was acknowledged to be the first scholar in the school. My time was up, and the parish apprenticed me to a carpenter: my master was a stern, cruel man: I worked hard, lived hard, and was treated badly. For some error that I committed, I was brutally punished and confined in a cellar below ground: for six and thirty hours was I confined there, and not a particle of nourishment passed my lips: I was famishing, and thought he had shut me there to die. Through that long dismal night, oh! the agony and fright that I suffered! I have often wondered since it did not turn my brain! Hideous visions, which nought but a crazed imagination could depict, arose before me: I shrieked with agony: and the drops of perspiration stood upon my brow, like beads. Young as I was, so bitter was that night, I dashed myself upon the ground and prayed for death. Morning came, and I was liberated; they said how pale and ill I looked. He cursed me for a sulky hound, and swore to kill me or my temper. I thought a few more nights in his dismal cellar would do both. That night I determined to run away. I had no money, and my aunt's house was a good twenty miles off. There was a small box in my room, in which my master kept his loose coin: at this time its contents were but a few shillings. The temptation was a strong one. I walked to and fro. God only knows the bitter struggle of good and bad within my breast. The latter triumphed; alas! that it did; for to that hour all my subsequent crimes, degradation, and death can be traced! I took one—one shilling! I crept softly down the stairs, and even went back again to replace the stolen property; but the fear of want (for I had bitterly experienced the pangs of hunger) prevailed, and I became a thief. With hushed breath and noiseless step, I crept stealthily away. On, on, I flew— but a thief. Had the coin been red hot, and seared and burnt me as I went, I could have borne it better than that rankling thought. Fifteen miles had I walked: I feared to go near house or human being, though my hunger and thirst was excessive. I felt as if my brow (Cain-like), had the crime written upon it. At length, wearied and fatigued—foot-sore and sick at heart, I crept into the hedge, and I suppose fell into a doze, for when I awoke, my cruel master, and the parish constable stood over me. I was terrified beyond

A tense episode from one of the few "bloods" by a woman—
Hannah Maria Jones' "The Shipwrecked Stranger" (1848).

measure. I threw myself at my master's feet, confessed the whole, sobbed out my contrition, and implored him for mercy's sake, to spare and forgive me. I have never forgotten his reply to this, or the laugh that accompanied it—it was spiteful, fiendish, beyond compare.

" 'Oh, oh, you took to thieving then, did you, my runaway apprentice. Well done! Mercy! oh, yes, after justice has been done, my lad—after justice. Constable, I charge this boy with robbery, and deliver him to your custody.'

"I begged he would kill me—anything but send me to prison. The very officer joined his entreaties to mine. 'You cannot mean this,' he said, 'damn the boy, thrash him— punish him in any way you like, but don't ruin him for life.' 'I give him into your custody, refuse to take him at your peril; he's a d—d young whining, thievish hypocrite, and it's a mercy it's no hanging matter now, for by God, if 'twas, not one word would I say to save him from swinging.' 'I can't refuse to take him,' said the constable, 'or I would, that's flat. I only say, and think it, and thanks be for it, that you may do as you like, but I would rather have my right hand chopped off, than the consequences of this sin resting on my soul, and troubling my conscience.' 'D—n your conscience,' said my master. 'With all my heart,' said the constable, 'some people seem to have no consciences to curse.' 'Yours is a clear one, no doubt,' he answered with a sneer. 'Come along,' he said to me, and he dug his nails so deeply into my arm that my shirt was stained with blood, and I cried out, the pain it caused me was so great. 'Loose the lad,' said the constable, sternly, 'he is my prisoner, and I'll charge you with an assault, if you lay another finger upon him—let him alone.' He turned to me, and I thought I saw a tear trembling on his eyelid as he spoke, for he was the father of a family, and bore a good name in the place, and said, 'Come, my poor boy.' He took me gently by the hand, and soothed me with kind words as he led me along, but when he left me it was within the dreary walls of the cage, or watchhouse. I threw myself upon the heap of straw and slept.

Sleep! with thoughts of death, and hideous forms and faces flitting to and fro! At morning dawn I was awakened; the gaoler entered my cell—it was the constable who had taken me. He bid me silence; and taking instruments fitting for the purpose, he sawed away, and two iron bars fell quickly to the ground. He stopped then, and said these words, 'If you was a boy of mine, and any ill came of this prosecution, I would have the villain's heart's blood; as 'tis, my poor lad, I pity you from my soul, and have risked my all to save you, for if they knew I aided in your escape I should lose my character, my place, and every means of livelihood. I have a young family dependent upon me, and cannot afford to do this; yet will I strain a nerve, and risk something to save you.' He pointed to the windows—'This act will be imputed to you. It will be your own fault if they ever catch you again; and if they do not, there are plenty of names beside your own you can adopt.'

"He opened the ponderous door. A horse and cart stood in waiting. He lifted me in, laid me at the bottom, covered me with a sack, and lashed the horse into a gallop. He checked it as we approached my native town, and jumping down, pulled me out, and thrusting some money into my hand, bid me run then for dear life. Panting and breathless, I reached my old home, and throwing myself at my aunt's feet, revealed all. 'God help us, child,' she said, 'they shall have both or none.' For three days I lay there secure and undiscovered; but at last I was found out. I was dragged before a magistrate and searched. The money I had given me was found upon me. They questioned who gave me such a sum; and my master said he had missed the like amount—the liar! What could I say—I could not betray my friend; and my varying countenance, they all said, during the examination, betokened guilt. So thought the recorder, I presume, for from his merciless lips came the merciless words, 'The sentence of the court is that you be confined in his majesty's gaol for twelve calendar months, and be twice privately whipped!' Oh, that it had ended here. The wretch had my poor old aunt at the bar, and preferred a charge against her for aiding and abetting in the escape of a felon. Charged *her* with a crime, whose kind, gentle heart never harboured wicked thought! She was too noble to ask pardon of such a wretch, and too much a christian to tell a lie. They sentenced her to be imprisoned for three months. God forgive them! She never came out alive. So great was the trouble that it snapped the fragile cords of life, and she had passed from this world into eternity ere her sentence was half completed. My young heart harboured thoughts of revenge, for I thought her a murdered woman.

"I came out, sadly altered for the worse. The consciousness of sin was gone, and I fancied I had suffered a martyrdom, instead of paying a just penalty for a sin. My former friends shrunk from me as though I had contracted a loathsome, infectious disease. Some few pitied the young villain, but more denounced. There was an old playmate of mine, who had been reared within a few doors from my aunt's cottage; she was a gentle, kind girl. One day I overtook her; I was, I well recollect, footsore and hungered: I laid my hand upon her arm—my tremulous voice, my tearful eyes betrayed how full my heart was, as I said 'And will you not speak to me Jane—not one parting word for him you may never see again?' 'They have threatened to beat me,' she replied timidly, 'if they ever knew I passed word with you again: but oh, Jim! I never went upon my knees, night or morning, but I prayed for you—prayed He would change your heart, and make you good and pure as I once knew you, and ever thought you, *even now*, for you are not guilty, Jim, are you?—you cannot be!' I buried my face in my hands, and wept bitterly. 'Did you, dear Jim, break from the watch-house?' 'No.' 'Have you been the naughty boy he said?' 'No.' 'You did not break your poor aunt's heart?' I was choking, and could not answer. 'You are no thief, Jim?' she continued, 'you did not rob your master?' I arose, and with uplifted hand, said, 'As I am a living sinner, never but of one shilling, so help me Heaven!' She dropped her hand, seemingly in despair, and moved away. 'Be not merciless,' I implored, 'have you no pity for a misguided boy?' 'Oh, yes,' she answered, 'my heart is full of pity for my dear unfortunate friend—but friendship for a thief, I have none!' My last friend had left me.

"Years flew by; I married, and had one child. I struggled with her to live honestly, but struggled to live in vain. We had walked many miles that day, with little or no refreshment, for the want of which my wife's milk had dried, and the child was foodless. He sucked her dry breast, and then, apparently in utter helplessness, looked into our faces and uttered the moaning cry of starvation. My God! my sufferings were naught compared to what I felt for my dear, patient, suffering wife, and my innocent, unhappy child. It almost drove me mad. I went to the overseer of the parish. I told him we were in the last stage of starvation—that my wife and child were dying by inches. He made me out an order for flour and potatoes. I asked him what I were to do with them, having no place to cook or prepare them. I wanted money to purchase medicine: potatoes were no food for a dying woman. He told me to leave his house—called me insolent, and threatened to commit me to prison. At that moment all the bad passions that ever raged in human breast, were struggling for the mastery in mine. I shook my clenched fist in the air, and my teeth gnashed together with rage. He drew back affrighted; and well he might, for had he known how near a dreadful death he stood, that haughty tone of his would have been humbled. I went back to my poor wife—she looked into my face—Great God! what a long tale of sorrow, suffering and privation was exhibited in that one gaze, and all borne without a murmur. Oh! I read in her pale face and sunken eye, the fatal inroads want had made upon her otherwise strong constitution, and cursed myself, in the bitterness of my agony, as the author of it all. I knew she was ill, but she was so patient—so resigned, I never had idea how much so. She never saw day again. When morning broke—oh, misery dire and dread! the partner of my bosom was cold and lifeless as the ground on which she lay. The only one in this dark world that ever had kind wish or thought for me, was dead! I had not tears—I rather thanked God he had removed my loved one from this place of torment, to a brighter sphere. The last link that bound me to nature, and kept the man from springing from his nature into a devil, was broken and dead. My orphan child yet lived, but I, its father, had become an inveterate drinker—the vilest of drunkards. I leagued myself with bad men, and became famous for villainy. To drown thought—to stifle all reproaches of conscience—all memory of the past—all dread of the future, I had recourse to drink—drink—drink! Some friend placed my poor child in the workhouse, and I was left to my fate. I had become, in reality now, a thief and robber. So notorious did I become, that a reward was offered for my apprehension, and I was eventually taken, and though convicted only of a trivial crime, (the greater ones could not be proved against me), I was sentenced to fourteen years transportation. I was sent to Van Dieman's Land. Now that I was debarred from the use of those cursed intoxicating drinks, I could think—and bitter agonizing thoughts perplexed me. My poor son was present to my imagination night and day; as though I had murdered him, was he before me. My time was almost up, and I determined for his sake, if possible, to reach England again.

"We were working in gangs, and in one of our expeditions to land a raft of logs, floating on the water, I, struggling with a load, more than my most strenuous exertions could support, stumbled and fell. Someone kindly assisted me to my feet again. I gazed in his face—Heavens above! it was my son; *he* that I had left a mere child in England fourteen years ago. So much agony, and so much joy was in the meeting, that I reeled and staggered like a drunken man. Happiness at meeting my son again, but bitter sorrow at meeting him there. He first found a tongue. 'Father, dear, listen,' he said, 'you think me guilty of sin, I read it in your face—but I swear,' and he raised his hands towards heaven as he spoke, 'I wear this degrading garb, but am as innocent of the crime imputed to me, and that doomed me to this fate, as a child unborn. Father, I have been falsely accused, and most unjustly punished. They swore to lies, and by lies was I convicted. I was accused of highway robbery, when, at the time stated, I was miles away, and had witnesses to prove it. But yet they condemned me. Oh! had they eyes to read the human countenance, they would have seen innocence in mine, and guilt in his by whose evidence I was condemned.'

"I asked his accuser's name; he said I could not know him, it was Baker, he lived at M——, in Kent. It was the same man that ruined me when young—had made me what I was! At this moment our keeper noticed we were conversing, he approached, and bid us, with a curse, 'get to work'. Night and day was his tale before me; sleeping and waking it was ever present. I heard our keeper whispering to another one day. He pointed to my son—'The doctor says that boy's in a deep decline—and I think he bears every sign of it; for that flushed face, too bright for health; that harassing, distressing cough; that hard drawn breath, as surely tells, as the sun-dial reveals the hour.'

"The man's words wrought such an effect upon me, that I threw myself at his feet, and begged of him, as though my boy's life lay in his hands, that he would recall those dreadful words. What more I said, or what he replied, I know not, for overpowered with excessive agony, I fainted at his feet. The shock I had received, threw me into a fever. I was delirious, frightfully so. My madness gave me strength; and in imagination I acted the bitter part in life I had fulfilled over and over again.

"I grew better, at length, daily; my son occasionally visited me, and then I watched the dreadful progress the blighting, incurable disease had made. At times when I noticed the bloom upon his cheeks, forgetting all, in a parent's deep love and pride, I would picture to myself, and tell him, what a fine, smart fellow he would be, and what happy days we would yet pass together in the old world. 'Or in a better,' he would add solemnly, though I little thought to what his words had reference then.

"Day by day he grew weaker. One morning a keeper came and, bidding me prepare for the worst, told me my boy was dead. Not a tear, sigh or groan escaped me. I bent over his lifeless body, and swore to have vengeance—bitter, bloody, terrible vengeance on his murderer. I nursed this thought as though it was the climax of all earthly bliss. Ha! kept it in my heart's core, to the exclusion of every other thought.

"A ship came into our port which had been dismasted in a storm, and many of its crew were drowned. My time was up, they gladly accepted my offer, and I worked my passage home to England. I set foot upon my native shore again with a heart full of dreadful thoughts. Actuated by these, I hastened, with all speed, towards the place where my old master (he who destroyed me, and murdered my poor son) resided.

"I have heard of men being possessed of a devil; I felt as if there was one gnawing at my heart, and urging me on to deeds of darkness and of blood. I went into a public-house; there were plenty there now, for the village had grown into a town. A party of men, who by their dress were of the lower order, were speaking of my enemy. One with glaring eyes and fearful words was telling the others how the old villain had distrained upon a neighbour of his, who had been long suffering; and from the effects of want of employment, and ill health, had been unable to pay his demands; and though an old servant of his persecutor, had been turned into the street, to die like a dog. The man's furious pretentions found an echo in my troubled breast. Another chiming in, said, 'He's as hard-hearted an old scoundrel as ever cussed mankind with his infernal life. Don't you recollect, mates, how he served poor Jim. He called it justice, but in my opinion, if ever a man in the world committed murder, he swore away the life of that poor boy.' He was referring to my son.

"Mastering the agitation which unnerved me, by a violent

effort, I turned to him, and said calmly, 'Were there any attempts made to prove his innocence?' 'Oh, yes,' answered the man, 'a cove named Curtis, Bob Curtis, swore he slept at his house the night in question, which was a good ten miles from the place where the old man said he was stopped and robbed; but Bob had been convicted once or twice of petty larcenies, so *his* oath wasn't taken; moreover, the old man swore point blank he was the man that robbed him. People mustn't speak about such things; but more than one, to my certain knowledge, thought the prosecution a persecution. I know *I* did for one, though I ain't over anxious any of you should say I said so.'

"I paid my reckoning and went out into the air. How opposite to the fierce passions that burnt and consumed me, was the placid scene that met my eye. The moon was at the full, and the spire of the old church, as it glittered in the solemn lustrous light, looked in good truth like a cross of grace! The very tombs in the quiet yard—those living records of the dead and withered past—looked more than usually awful in the silvery light. How many a tale of misery and crime—of sin and pain—lay hushed and silent there. Withered age, long suffering, and children early nipped, ere yet they had hardly entered into life. Sin and virtue, age and youth, the good and bad, the rich and poor, the morose and mirthful, the saint and sinner, the oppressor and the oppressed, the miser and the spendthrift, with all the various shades and form which human life presents, lay huddled side by side; all enmity stilled, all heart-burning hushed, in that one quiet bed. See yon pompous stone; that receptacle holds the ashes of one who in life was a powerful man; the manhood and the power, time's heavy hand has been at work upon, and all that remains is a heap of brown unwholesome bones.

"Death! thou mystery of mysteries, which every one must learn, yet no man, with all his mighty reasoning, in life, can imagine or fathom. One would have thought such a scene as this would have softened all the grosser, and called forth all the finer feelings of my debased nature. But, no; they only made the devil burn the more fierce! I went down to them, examined them minutely; traced letter after letter with my finger, in hope of discovering his name, the register of the death of a relative gone before him. I chuckled and rubbed my hands with demoniac joy at the thought of discovering a vacancy that I would soon fill up; of going there after he was dead, of treading down with my foot that mound under which his carcass lay rotting and festering! That is a fearful night for the memory to look back upon—a fearful one indeed! I thought of the difference in our situations. He had become a rich and powerful man—and look at me! I went to his house the next morning, under plea of requesting relief. I bound a handkerchief round my head to disguise myself; there was no need of that, time and care had disguised me enough. He asked me what I wanted, in a stern and unfeeling tone. I answered in a tone as harsh and haughty as his own, 'bread'. He told me 'I must earn it, such lazy villains as I was, if we had our deserts, would be in prison'. I answered him, until in his rage he called me an insolent dog, and struck me. One spring like a tiger, thirsting for blood, upon his prey, my hand was upon his throat. All my bitter thoughts came into action now. I pressed; his face grew purple; his tongue hung from his mouth, and his eyes seemed starting from their sockets; the clammy sweat of death bedewed his forehead. One minute more, and he would have known the secret of death, but the door was burst open, and the domestics, alarmed by the uproar, entered the room. To release my victim, draw a large Spanish knife from my pocket, and to bare its fearful blade, was the work of a moment. Alarmed by my fierce-glaring eyes, and the deadly weapon I carried, they drew back, and gave me free egress.

"Oh, how I laughed! He had suffered the pangs of death, but would suffer death itself the next time! I lingered about the neighbourhood for many months; still firmly bent upon carrying my damnable plot into execution. One day I was in a large unfrequented wood, a narrow path ran at my feet, and walking along with an enfeebled gait, and tottering steps, came that devoted old man, alone! With a shout of delight I strode before him, seized him by the collar, and dragged him into the recesses of the wood.

"I then released him. 'Listen,' said I, and I detailed to him who I was, and that I had purposely travelled hundreds of miles to execute justice upon the murderer of my son. With a face blanched with fear—with lips quivering from excessive agony, and pale and bloodless, he fell upon his knees, and, in tones that would have moved an iron heart to pity, begged I would not hurl him to the grave unprepared, and his past sins unrepented of, but that I would have mercy, and not bathe my hands in the blood of an old man! Would to God I had listened to his prayer!

"I drew forth the fatal knife—bared its hideous blade, and brandished it in the air! The old man shrieked with agony. My God! I can dwell upon this dread scene no longer. One fierce curse—one deadly thrust—one loud cry of despair and agony—a gush of thick life-blood—the deed was done—he lay at my feet, dead!

"Now, the hideous phantasy had left me, I would have given the world, ah, even my own life, to have healed that gaping wound, and to have put breath into those motionless nostrils. It was too late, alas! Cain's curse was upon me—I was a murderer!

"I was arrested, tried, condemned; in two days I shall suffer the dread death that is executed upon him who sheddeth the blood of a fellow man. God pardon me—my heart is full of grief—overflowing with repentance. Have mercy Heaven, upon him who was merciless. My kind friend, farewell. The blessing of a grateful heart, and of a dying, but repentant sinner, attend you. Farewell, until time verges into eternity! Then, I humbly hope, we shall meet in the promised land of bliss. Once again, farewell; and, oh, pray in your passage through life, tell the erring to take the path of rectitude, and forsake the path of death; and to the drunkard, speak—thousands beside myself have been untimely hurried into eternity by its instrumentality; tell them it is the high road to ruin, misery, crime and death. Farewell. The life of a murderer is finished, and in a few brief hours will be closed in frightful reality."

11

PAUL THE POACHER

by Thomas Frost

APART FROM THE tales of highwaymen, criminals, mariners and remarkable heroes and heroines—not forgetting the underside of London life—there was one further subject which proved very popular in the Penny Dreadfuls —the "Domestic Story". More than one authority has given this definition to a school of stories which embrace both town and country life, but pay more attention to romance and daily living than the other more exotic serials. Seduction is at the heart of many of these adventures, and villainous noblemen, squires and landlords seek the virginity of unsuspecting village maidens with fiendish lust. Madness, too, is frequently encountered as young girls become demented when losing their innocence, and the fathers of ruined daughters are never slow to take leave of their senses. A good many of these stories, which enjoyed their greatest popularity in the 1840s, are set in the English countryside, though later developments of the plot may take the leading characters into the big cities or even abroad. Most of the famous writers we have so far encountered—Reynolds, Prest and Rymer, to name but three—wrote serials around this framework, but perhaps none succeeded quite so well in terms of authenticity of setting and rural drama as Thomas Frost (1801–1879), the next contributor.

Frost made his name with a colourful history of the highwayman, "Sixteen String Jack" (1845), but earned most wide sales and attention with "Emmay Mayfield; or, The

Rector's Daughter" (1847) and "Paul The Poacher" (1850). Perhaps part of Frost's success must be attributed to the fact that, although his settings were rural and genteel enough, the passions that burned below the surface, and not infrequently burst into the open, were as sensational as anything else on the market. Indeed records indicate that he has the rare distinction of being one of the few authors who on occasions produced manuscripts that even Edward Lloyd considered too strong for his imprint. Louis James has aptly described Frost as a "realistic deviationist" and feels that he tried to model his style on the French writers of the day. "But", he writes, "his lighter touches fall flat and his salacious descriptions of sadism and vice may well have had a disturbing effect on minds already open to the temptations of city and factory life." Be that as it may, Frost was a writer of talent, though he may not always have put it to the best uses, and apart from his several bloody historical sagas—including "The Mysteries of Old Father Thames" (1848) and "The Black Mask" (1850)—he wrote a number of lascivious novels which appeared without author or publisher's name and also contributed to the scandal newspaper, *The Penny Punch*—"which nearly gained him a well-deserved ducking from his neighbours", according to one authority.

Although both "Emma Mayfield" and "Paul the Poacher" portray life in the West Country, they have numerous deviations to more familiar terrain, the first containing a superb vampire episode and the second a rape scene in a subterranean chamber which became a talking point throughout the country and quadrupled sales of subsequent issues of the publication. In time, it seems that Frost became disenchanted with his "sensational" writing and according to his autobiography, he devoted his declining years to writing for the Religious Tract Society. For this collection I have decided to reprint the abduction scene from "Paul the Poacher", not because it is sensational—indeed it is hardly more than mildly titillating in this day and age—

The Abduction

The sun was just sinking below the western horizon, and gilding, with its latest beams, the straw-roofed cot of penury as well as the palatial abode of rank and wealth, when Lucy Copsley and Emma Barnsley quitted the homestead of the latter's father, and walked across the fields to the lane, in which stood the cottage of Will Oliver, and that which had once been Lucy's home, but which was now untenanted and desolate.

"Then you like your situation at Sir Miles Robartes's, Lucy?" observed Emma, half interrogatively, as they entered the lane.

"Oh, yes! I have nothing to complain of, Emma," returned Lucy, "and had I no one to think of but myself, I should be quite happy. But the fate of my father often causes me a sigh, and I feel very anxious and uneasy about Robert. He has not written since he was here, and therefore I know not whether his fault, in leaving the regiment without leave of the colonel, was overlooked on account of the circumstances, or whether he has been punished."

"In the absence of any knowledge upon the subject, it is well to hope the best, while we prepare ourselves at the same time to hear the worst," observed Emma Barnsley.

"I have been much annoyed by an elderly gentleman lately," said Lucy, after a moment's pause. "He met me several times near the house, and spoke to me; but I did not like his looks and manners, and I behaved very distantly and cool. He would not be shaken off, however; and the other day he made me an insulting and dishonourable proposal. Then I answered him in a manner which his conduct merited, and I have not seen him since."

"Have you any idea who he is?" inquired Emma Barnsley.

"I do not know him," replied Lucy, "but I have described him to the cook, and she thinks he must be the Earl of Rona, who has a mansion at a few miles distance."

"Well, I must leave you now, Lucy," said the farmer's daughter, pausing at the top of the lane. "I dare say your elderly admirer will not trouble you any more, after the proper manner in which you have rejected his advances; and you must not be too much cast down about Robert, without knowing whether you have really any cause for anxiety."

"I cannot help thinking about him, Emma, for, whether he has been punished or not, I am sure he is not happy," returned Lucy. "But I appreciate your friendship and good intentions, and hope that your future will be as unclouded as the present is to you."

"I shall be so glad to see you smile again as you used to do," observed Emma. "You must strive to look forward, and not backward, dear. George Stapleton will, some day, make you amends for all. Good by, dear."

"Good by, Emma," returned Lucy, pressing her friend's hand warmly. "God bless you!"

Emma Barnsley then ran off down the lane, and Lucy proceeded on her way.

She had not gone far when she heard the sounds of wheels behind her, and, looking round, saw a light cart approaching, driven by a tall red-faced man, about fifty years of age, and clad in a clean white smock-frock. In another minute the cart came up, and the driver stopped the horse, looking attentively at Lucy as he did so.

"Don't you live at Sir Miles Robartes's, young woman?" said he.

"Yes," replied the maiden, pausing.

"I thought I had zeen you about there," said the man. "You have come vrom Varmer Barnsley's, beant you?"

"Yes, I have just left there," returned Lucy.

"Well, I be going within a mile of where you live, if you

The sensational scene from Thomas Frost's "Paul The Poacher" (1850) which quadrupled sales of the publication.

like to jump up," continued the man in the smock-frock. "I live near Sir Miles Robartes's, but I have been up to Riverdale to see a daughter of mine, that's in sarvice there."

Lucy had hesitated to accept the man's offer at first, for, though she had a long walk before her, and it was growing dark, she felt reluctant to trust herself with a stranger, but when she heard that he was a father, and had a daughter in service, she hesitated no longer, but got into the cart.

The man drove on at a steady pace, talking, at intervals, of his daughter, of the household of Sir Miles Robartes, the recent weather, and the appearance of the crops, and though it soon grew dark, Lucy knew that they were pursuing the right road. But at length the cart turned down a narrow lane, with fields on either side, dark hills in the distance, and not a single light glimmering from farm-house or cottage window which ever way she turned her eyes.

"Are we going the right way?" said she, as she looked around her, and became satisfied that she had never been down the lane before.

"Oh, yes," returned the man, "I won't take you out of the way, young woman. This is a near cut, that'll save us a mile or more."

Lucy's apprehensions were allayed by this reply, and the man continued to drive on. Presently the lane grew narrower and the hedges higher, increasing the murky obscurity, and she began to think that they were not making such a saving in the distance as the man had asserted. She was about to make some remark upon the length and dreariness of the lane, when the man all at once threw his left arm round her neck, and she shrieked involuntarily. But at the same instant the man thrust a piece of sponge into her mouth with his right hand, and not only stifled the cry of alarm to which she would have given utterance, but effectually gagged her.

She made an effort to rise, but the man threw his arms round her, and laid her down at the bottom of the cart upon some straw. She attempted to remove the sponge from her mouth in order to scream for assistance, but, before she could do so, the man seized her hands, and tied them together with a handkerchief. Then, while she yet struggled ineffectually at the bottom of the cart, he tied her legs together, just above the ankles with another handkerchief, and immediately drove on.

The unfortunate girl had now but a confused idea of whither she was being borne; the cart was driven on briskly for a little distance, and then it stopped, and the man got out. She heard him open a gate, and lead the horse through; and then he got into the cart, and drove on again over ground that seemed rough and uneven. Presently the cart stopped again, and the man stooped down, and first enveloping the head of the trembling girl in her shawl, he lifted her up in his arms, and leaped with her to the ground. He carried her a few yards over ground that seemed level, but uneven, and then she became aware that they were descending a flight of stone steps, on reaching the bottom of which he bore her a few yards, and then laid her down upon the ground.

Though the shawl, in whose folds her head was still muffled, somewhat deadened her perception of sounds, she now heard the man ignite a chemical match, and give vent to a half suppressed imprecation at not being able to find something which he sought. This object appeared to be a lamp, for in a few moments she became aware that there was a light, though her eyes strove in vain to pierce the folds of the shawl. Then she heard a sound as if a stone was being removed from its place, and immediately afterwards she was lifted from the ground, and borne down a flight of narrow stone steps; that they were narrow she knew from her feet touching the wall as they descended, and that they were of stone she judged from the sound of her abductor's footfalls.

At length they reached the bottom of this subterranean flight of stairs, and then she was borne along a narrow passage of considerable length, the footsteps of her ruffianly abductor raising dismal and prolonged echoes. Her brain began to reel before the appalling idea that she was being borne into the bowels of the earth, perhaps to be immured for life in some dungeon, where the atmosphere would be close and damp—where moisture would trickle down the green and slimy walls—where the toad and the newt would be her companions; or perhaps to be ruthlessly deprived of life, subjected to unheard of torments, or to the brutal lust of some miscreant whose crimes had made him shrink into gloomy vaults from the light of day and the outstretched arm of justice. But she was diverted from the appalling current of her thoughts by the discovery that the end of the long subterranean had been reached, and that she was now being borne up an ascent of stone steps, which relieved her of the dread with which she had a moment before been inspired, that she was to be confined in some horrible vault far below the surface of the earth.

The ascent was at first straight forward, but they soon came to a landing, and commenced the ascent of a flight steeper than the other, and apparently winding spirally round a perpendicular centre. Her bearer seemed to be getting fatigued with carrying her, for he twice set her down during this ascent, and rested for a few moments. At length the summit was reached, a door opened, and she was borne into a room, as she conjectured from the change of atmosphere of which she immediately became sensible, and from the circumstance of the man's footfalls emitting no sound, which seemed to show that the floor was covered with a soft and thick carpet. She was now laid down, and the man unbound her hands; she immediately raised them to remove the shawl from her head and the sponge from her mouth, but before she could do so she heard the door close, and when she threw off the enveloping shawl, and cast a glance of terror and apprehension around the place to which she had been brought, she was alone, and in darkness profound and impenetrable.

Almost frantically the unfortunate maiden tore the gag from her mouth, and, as her pent-up feelings found vent in a piercing shriek, she sank insensible upon the floor.

* * *

Half an hour after Lucy Copsley had thus been left to solitude, and the horrors which it might conjure up in her imagination, Captain Hector Fitzflash entered the drawing-room of the Earl of Rona, whom he found turning over some French lithographs, illustrating the amours of the deities of the Grecian mythology, and ever and anon applying himself to the wine and fruit which stood upon the table.

"Have you been successful?" was the eager question which the voluptuary put to his unprincipled satellite, the instant the drawing-room door closed behind him.

"The bird is safely caged, my lord, and awaits your pleasure in the matted chamber," replied Captain Fitzflash, taking a seat at the table.

"Beautiful! beautiful!" exclaimed the Earl of Rona, rubbing his hands, while his sallow countenance became radiant with satisfaction. "Well done, thou good and faithful servant! Help yourself to the wine, captain; pray do not stand upon ceremony. Does she seem quiet and resigned, or is she violent?"

"Oh, not at all violent, my lord, but rather frightened," returned Fitzflash. "As I pulled the spring door after me, and descended the stairs, I heard faintly—that of course—a shriek, and I expect that, if she has not yet recovered, your lordship would find her at this moment prostrate and insensible upon the floor."

"Here is a cheque for the promised amount," said the Earl of Rona, giving it to the captain as he spoke. "I knew that the faithful Fitzflash would not disappoint me of the gratification that I have been so eagerly anticipating, and, therefore, drew it last night. I do not like transacting pecuniary matters on the Sabbath, captain. But how did you manage? —tell me how you caught the pretty flutterer in your toils."

"As easily as possible, my lord," returned Captain Fitzflash, consigning the cheque to his pocket-book. "I assumed for the occasion the smock-frock of a rustic, and, borrowing a light cart, drove to Riverdale, arranged so as to overtake her soon after she turned out of the lane leading to the farm-house, and representing myself as a steady old file who had been to see his daughter, she did not hesitate to trust herself to my protection, and accept a ride home. The rest was easy enough; gagged and bound, and laid down upon the straw at the bottom of the cart, she was powerless as could be wished and escape was out of the question."

"Beautiful creature!" ejaculated the earl. "How I long to clasp her in my arms."

"Well, I wish your lordship all imaginable success and felicity," observed Captain Fitzflash, and he then took his departure.

* * *

How long Lucy Copsley laid in that insensibility which came upon her when she found herself alone, and in utter darkness, in the place to which she had been borne, bound and gagged, along that interminable subterranean and up and down those underground stairs, she had no means of ascertaining; but at length, consciousness returned to the bewildered maiden by slow degrees, and, raising herself to a sitting posture, she strove to collect her thoughts. Back from the memory-cells of her brain came the recollection of her riding from Riverdale in the cart of the pretended rustic, of his treatment of her in the lane, and then of the echoing subterraneans through which she had been borne to the dark chamber in which she now found herself.

Where was she—and for what purpose had she been brought there? These were the questions which she vainly asked herself as she untied the handkerchief with which Fitzflash had secured her legs, and which that vile miscreant had not removed when he quitted the room. With regard to the first question, she could not form the most faint conjecture. She had never before been down the lane in which Fitzflash had gagged and bound her, and had not even the slightest knowledge as to where it led. She shuddered involuntarily as she asked herself the second question, for the thought suggested itself that the purpose for which she had been brought there could only be an evil one; and how black, she thought, must be the degree of the criminality that hid itself from the light of day, and required so many precautions to veil it in mystery impenetrable and profound!

She rose from the floor, which was covered with a carpet so soft and thick that her footsteps fell noiselessly upon it, and groping with her hands to avoid coming in contact with any projecting article of furniture, she made a few cautious steps in the direction of the door, by which she had been borne into the room by her abductor, but, to her surprise, her hands encountered a padded matting with which the wall was covered, and no tangible indications of a door were there. She moved her hands slowly and carefully to the right and left, but no door could she discover; and she groped along all that side of the room, from one angle to the other, with no better result.

She now thought that she must have erred in her supposition that the door was on that side of the room, and accordingly groped her way along the wall; but though she made the circuit of the room, she could discover no indications of either a door or a window, the thick matting covering the wall on every side, nor was there a single article of furniture in the room. She stood still in the centre of the room, and listened; but not a sound from without met her ears—the silence was so profound that she could hear even the beating of her heart. And as she stood there, with upheaved bosom and bated breath, a fear-fraught idea suddenly flashed like an inspiration upon her mind, and she pressed her hand upon her throbbing brow, as if her brain reeled before it.

The thickly carpeted floor, the matted walls, the secret door, the darkness that seemed palpable, all must be parts of some infernal contrivance to shroud in secrecy and mystery some diabolical outrage, from the contemplation of the probable nature of which she shrank in horror. Through that concealed door which she could not discover, but which she yet knew to exist, the perpetrator would enter—those matted walls would shut in every sound, and deaden every shriek—that palpable darkness would veil the crime, and guard from the chance of future recognition the criminal! It was dreadful for one so innocent and so defenceless to stand there alone, enveloped in darkness, anticipating all that was horrible and revolting to her pure mind, and fearfully conscious of her utter powerlessness to evade her impending doom.

She clasped her hands, and, though in darkness, her eyes wandered round the room, and could any one have seen her countenance at that moment, it would have been seen pale and impressed with an aspect of mingled wildness and despair. A new thought suddenly struck her, and partly stilled the tumult of her mind; she would pray—it was impossible, she thought, that God would forsake her, if she prayed to Him for succour and deliverance. In obedience to this impulse, she knelt down upon the thick carpet, and prayed long and fervently that He whose name was Love, and whose attributes were Power, Wisdom, Justice, and Mercy, would deliver her from the doom which was impending over her, whether that doom was a violent death, or dishonouring outrage, which she dreaded most. This act of devotion exercised a tranquillizing influence over her mind, and she rose from her knees considerably comforted and strengthened.

At that very moment she heard a clicking sound, as if emanating from the wall on the opposite side of the room to that on which she supposed the door to be situated by which she had been brought in by Fitzflash, and turning her eyes in that direction she perceived a vertical line of light upon the wall, a portion of which appeared to be opening like a door, the light widening and increasing as it did so, until she beheld before her a man well-dressed, and evidently past the prime of life, but whose features were concealed by a black mask, and who carried in his hand a small bronze lamp.

The man entered, and the mysterious door rolled back

into the wall, of which it then appeared to form a part. Lucy stood still, with her left hand pressed upon her bosom to repress the wild beating of her heart, and she could see, as the man held up his lamp so as to throw its light full upon her lovely countenance and Peri-like form, that his eyes gleamed through the holes of his mask with the expression of those of a satyr springing with libidinous intent upon a wood-nymph of classic story.

"I do not know who you are, sir," said Lucy, in a trembling voice, "but you appear to be what the world calls a gentleman, and I appeal to you as such, whether the treatment to which I have been subjected, in being brought here against my will, and with brutal violence, is consistent with your apparent character."

"We will not discuss that point, if you please," said the Earl of Rona, for he was the intruder, as the reader has probably conjectured. "I am afraid we shall not be able to settle it to our mutual satisfaction. Let it suffice that I admire you, my beauty of the moors, and that I am determined that you shall be mine. It is for you to decide whether you will surrender upon terms which will make your future life one of luxury and ease, which I am ready to propose, should you be pleased to signify your willingness, or whether you will compel me to carry the fortress of your chastity by assault."

"I am in your power, sir," returned Lucy, after a moment's pause, "but I beg of you, for your own sake, for the sake of your immortal soul, to pause before you commit an outrage which you would probably regret until your dying hour, and which, if unrepented, will peril your eternal salvation."

"Upon my word, it is a pity, for your sake, that the Church of England does not admit female preachers," returned the Earl of Rona. "But you have not made your decision, my charmer."

"For the love of heaven, spare me!" exclaimed Lucy, throwing herself upon her knees in despair, and raising her clasped hands and pallid countenance to implore the voluptuary's forbearance.

"Silly girl!" said he, setting down the lamp, and approaching her, "you compel me to take by force what I would fain owe to your good sense, if not to mutual inclination."

A frantic shriek burst from the maiden's lips as the earl seized her in his arms, and then she fell insensible upon the floor, overpowered by the intensity of her highly wrought feelings. Her unconsciousness did not prevent the voluptuary from executing the purpose for which he had caused her to be ensnared, and her insensibility enabled him to accomplish its perpetration without hindrance or resistance.

Sad was the awakening of poor Lucy Copsley from the swoon which bound up every faculty while the Earl of Rona made her the victim of his brutal sensuality—terrible were the thoughts that first flitted through her bewildered brain when consciousness returned, and with it the sense of the deep and unatonable wrong which she had suffered. With the crimson blushes of mingled shame and outraged modesty glowing upon her cheeks, she veiled her lovely countenance in her hands, and the pearly tears gushed between her white and tapered fingers.

What sad considerations were involved in the incident of that night—what mournful thoughts were evoked by her present situation. Not only had she been despoiled of her chastity by rude and lawless violence; she knew how long she might be immured in that diabolically constructed chamber, how often the outrage of which she had been the victim might be perpetrated, without her being able to prevent it, and even if she could succeed in effecting her escape, her reputation would be damaged, for who would believe the strange tale of mystery and crime which she would have to tell?

THE MERRY WIVES OF LONDON

by James Lindridge

IT IS PERHAPS not surprising in hindsight to see how, with the increasing popularity of the Penny Dreadfuls, the major publishers began to try and outdo each other with new sensations and horrors. Public attention was notoriously fickle and not only had the drama to be kept up in each issue, but new gimmicks must if possible be introduced to prevent sales flagging. Sex, as distinct from love and passion, was not long in appearing on the stage. Obscene and indecent publications were, of course, nothing new and there has always been a flourishing underground trade in what each age has termed "pornography". The 18th century had been particularly rich in licentious pamphlets and books and not a few small publishers were reprinting these in penny editions in the 1830s. William Dugdale (who employed Thomas Frost for a time) was just one of several who were frequently in and out of prison for selling this kind of material, and among the many famous publications of the time, reference must be made to the *Memoirs of Harriet Wilson*, the story of a London madam which, when it was first published in weekly parts in 1825 by John Joseph Stockdale, created such a demand that barriers had to be erected in Stockdale's shop to control the crowds demanding copies. In this climate it was not long before explicit sex—or what passed for it—appeared in the Penny Dreadful.

A writer in *Blackwood's Magazine* noted in 1834: "It is not generally known to our readers out of the metropolis, what immense manufactories of infidelity and exciting sensuality there exist, and to what extent they are diffused in the cheapest form throughout the great towns of the empire. The great part of these publications profess to deal with the intrigues and devices of the aristocracy, illustrated, of course, by appropriate cuts and innuendoes ... all for the edification of the footmen and *femmes de chambre* of London, and the numerous class which the Schoolmaster has trained to mental activity in the metropolis." It comes as no surprise to the researcher to find that the vast body of these publications have completely disappeared; few survive in even the biggest of our libraries or the major private collections. In the light of what we know of them, this is perhaps not to be regretted; but one serial work which does still exist in perhaps no more than two or three copies is "The Merry Wives of London" by James Lindridge (1820–1891). Montague Summers dismisses the work—published in 1850—as "pseudo-pornography" but I doubt very much whether he can have read it, for the story is well-constructed, written in a light and engrossing prose style and shows real insight and understanding of the prevailing sexual morality. Perhaps his opinion was too easily formed by the striking and very biased description of the work on its cover: "A picture of life, high and low; from the refined sensuality of the rich to the coarse and depraved debauchery of the poor". What in fact the author has done is drawn together a whole series of stories about wayward wives, sensual playboys and beautiful serving girls with an eye to the main chance, which culminate in the exposure of the corruption of leading noblemen and a half-hearted attempt by the authorities to curb vice in the capital city. It is a timeless story, really, and the modern reader is soon struck by how little vice has changed in 150 years.

Author James Lindridge (sometimes spelled Lenbridge) was another of those larger-than-life characters who populate the history of penny-issue publications. Of his background we know very little except that he was a well-known figure around the taverns and sporting houses of London, and earned his living from contributing to newspapers and writing the occasional "fake" Restoration pornographic novel, and producing a variety of widely differing Penny Dreadfuls including "Tales of Shipwreck" (1846), the very popular "Jack Rann; alias Sixteen String Jack" (1850) and a bizarre novel of working class struggle, "The Socialist Girl" (1849). He wrote "The Merry Wives of London" for the firm of Vickers, a concern which had been started by a London newsagent, George Vickers, who later left his mark on publishing in a rather more distinguished way by founding the *Illustrated London News* which still runs today.

As an example of the style of the work, I have selected an episode which details the activities of a bizarre society for the roués of London. I should perhaps add that in a footnote to his book, Lindridge writes, "the intelligent reader will no doubt observe that the word 'merry' is used in the title and throughout the narrative in the sense in which it is employed by the renowned Othello".

The Episode Of The Knights Of The Round Table

The gentlemen who constituted the society distinguished by the ancient and chivalric title of the "Knights of the Round Table", were a singular set of beings; for, although as loyal as Britons are expected to be, they would persist in throwing the mantle of secrecy around all their proceedings. They feared not the light, but preferred that the business of their incorporation should be conducted in private. Having this characteristic, it will not excite much surprise that their meetings were held amid many precautionary ceremonies, and accompanied by several almost masonic solemnities. The locality selected was the classic one of Covent Garden Market, where, as if by common consent, the last faint lines of West End decency terminate, and those of eastern squalor and filth commence. The street was a respectable one, and the public-house in it the largest in the whole region of

An old roué with his "playgirls" from James Lindridge's "The Merry Wives of London" (1850).

Bedfordiana. Imagine the hour to be nine o'clock in the evening, and that a couple of apparently gentlemanly-looking men are emerging from the snug bar-parlour, and, preceded by a hoary-headed confidential waiter, ascend a long flight of stairs, until they arrive at the third floor, where they pause, and then, by means of a house-key open a substantial iron-bound door, which, moving inwards, noiselessly discloses a neatly-furnished ante-room, in which the two gentlemen, after ordering brandy-and-water, seat themselves. Presently others, garbed as if belonging to the well-to-do classes, arrive, and, after many whisperings and exchanges of passwords, are allowed to pass through another iron-bound door, which admitted them into the brilliantly-lighted hall of the Knights of the Round Table. This room was a circular one, painted in gold and black; but surely the artist must have had large amatory organs; for on the panels was every species of display of the perfections of woman, and the modes in which man can render them serviceable to his devouring propensities. At one end of the room was a beautiful scroll, which contained the following sentence, in raised golden letters:

"Eat, drink, and love—the rest's not worth a straw."

Underneath this, resting on a pedestal on the floor, was a statue of the Venus de Medici, and at the other end of the room was a gigantic one of Bacchus. At intervals round were several busts, chiefly of men distinguished in literature and for latitudinarianism in morals. Among them was George IV, Charles James Fox, Sheridan, Mirabeau, Duncombe, Handsome Jack (a notorious *protégé* of a distinguished actress), Edmund Kean, *cum multis aliis.* In the centre of the room was a large oval table, around which were armed and well-cushioned chairs, bearing on their backs numbers ranging from one to fifty. As the members entered, each took possession of one of these seats, and at ten o'clock they were all filled, except one, from the piece of black crape bound round the arms of which, it might have been inferred that its former occupant had departed to the unknown realm, where the good and the bad have to render a true and just account of themselves. Dr Wriggles—who, by the way, had left Walter in the ante-room—presided; and, after taking a preliminary glance round the table, struck it two or three sharp blows with the hammer which lay before him. At this intimation every voice was hushed, and the members adjusted themselves in their seats, so as to face the chair.

"No. 45," said the president, "read the minutes."

No. 45, a hawk-eyed, wiry little man, of about forty years of age, opened a large book before him, and read as follows:

"Since our last meeting I regret to have to announce the loss of No. 49, the oldest member of the order, with the exception of your venerable self. He died full of years, and in the firm persuasion that, as he had never violated a single law of nature, he had nothing to fear, either for his memory or that future which is such a bugbear to the imaginations of the vulgar. On this point it may be interesting to record his last observations. 'The immortality of the soul,' said he, 'is one of those consoling beliefs which it would be impolitic to destroy. It is the highest and last hope of man, and must exercise a beneficial influence over his mental faculties, restraining some and encouraging and developing others. The idea of an individual immortality is absurd, but that of a general one is correct; but to support the latter the former is indispensable, for few among us have the courage to recognize only the general immutable principles of nature. We make others to meet our individual wants and aspirations. The only immortality worth anything to man is the Egyptian one of the resuscitation of the body, afterwards adopted by the early Christians, under the fanciful conception of the complete resurrection of the body after its total annihilation, and the mingling of its elements with the common original ones from which they sprang.' These were his last words," continued No. 45, "and soon after he died as placidly as a child falling to sleep."

The president tapped in approval of so dignified a termination to a life of gaiety; each member, with the same object in view, gently inclined his head, and No. 45 proceeded:

"The affairs of the order continue in the same prosperous condition, but I regret to have to report several grave cases, which call for immediate attention. The first is that of No. 7, who has been charged by one of his late servants with having caused her present pregnancy. No. 7 does not object to afford the girl pecuniary assistance as a matter of charity, for none of us can be too liberal to women in that respect; but he does object to being made the victim of extortion. He asks the advice and counsel of the order."

"No. 7," said the president, "in what private relation did this girl stand to you?"

No. 7, a bald-headed, unwieldly, plethoric man of seventy, rose, and gravely replied:

"She was my servant, and sometimes lay with me to keep my extremities warm; but I declare, on the honour of a knight of this table, that I never was carnally acquainted with her. I regret to say the capability has disappeared. My valet, I suspect, is the author of the woman's condition, but I will do as you advise in the matter."

"Then I would propose," said the president, "that No. 45 be instructed to give the girl a ten-pound note, and settle the affair. Your incapacity did not extend to manipulations of the girl's body, and your valet only completed what you began. Gentlemen, do you approve of my proposal?" None spoke. "Carried," and down went the president's hammer.

"The next case," resumed No. 45, "is that of No. 30. He has had an action brought against him by a peer of the realm, for criminal conversation with his wife, the Lady Tyrone, formerly known as Peggy Johnson, the most lascivious actress on the Irish stage. He admits the fact, but submits that, as the lady has notoriously been guilty of amours with other men since her marriage, he would be justified in defending the action, with the view of either obtaining a verdict, or reducing the damages to a nominal amount. He confesses that the case perplexes him, for, should the judgment be adverse, it would prejudice him in the proceedings he is about to institute with respect to his wife, whom he strongly suspects."

"What say you, No. 30?" inquired the president.

No. 30, who was the readers' old acquaintance, Mr

Smythe, the banker, rose, and said he had nothing to add to the statement of the secretary; all he wished to know was, whether resistance or a compromise would be preferable.

"I know something of the facts of this case," said the president; "both the lady and her husband, it is true, are adventurers: he lives upon her want of chastity, and would starve if he divorced her; but then No. 30, who has a charge against his wife—from statements already made, I fear a true one—should go into court with clean hands. I strongly advise a compromise, and will gladly lend my assistance. I know the lady's brothers—the O'Blazes—and a whisper from me into one of their ears would be sufficient. I undertake to settle the affair for a thousand pounds."

No. 30 gladly accepted the offer.

"This being a compromise, the money will have to come entirely out of your own pocket," said the president.

No. 30 bowed his acquiescence, and No. 45 continued:

"The next case is that of No. 48, who has been sued for loss of services, by the father of the girl who accuses him of having been her seducer."

"No. 48," said the president, "answer upon your honour: did the girl willingly and cheerfully submit to your embraces?"

"She did," replied No. 48, standing up and presenting the commanding appearance of a dark, handsome man of about thirty.

"Did you make any promise of marriage?"

"I did not."

"Then she was as willing as yourself?"

"Quite. The occasion was inviting. I placed her gently on her back, and she lay as quiet as a lamb."

"Has the connection been repeated?"

"Innumerable times."

"And pregnancy has ensued?"

"It has."

"A clear case," said the president. "I move that No. 45

be instructed to either compromise or defend the case. Any amendment? No: then it is carried."

No. 45 proceeded:

"The next case is that of No. 5. He has been accused of being the father of a male child, to which his servant, a girl of seventeen, lately gave birth. He admits the fact of connection, but denies that of paternity."

No. 5, a spare old man, with a profusion of white hair, here nodded his acquiescence, and the president rather briskly said:

"The admission damns the denial. He must pay; besides, it is well known that a man is never too old to get a woman with child. Many instances are on record of men being fathers at 120, and even 140 years of age. I move that No. 45 be instructed to compromise the affair, and be allowed for that purpose five pounds out of the funds."

Several members here suggested that the amount should be ten pounds, which was ultimately agreed to; No. 5 being advised to keep a complying male servant, on whom for the future he could safely throw the onus of all such responsibilities.

"The last case," said No. 45, "is the gravest of the whole. It refers to No. 29, who has been accused of a criminal assault upon the person of a married woman. He has been prosecuted, and is now out on bail."

"Stand up 29," said the president, severely.

No. 29 did so. He was a hale, stalwart, middle-aged man, with a jovial, pleasant countenance.

"Are you guilty or not guilty?" demanded the president.

"Not guilty of the assault, most decidedly," replied No. 29, with a laugh; "if there is any charge at all against me it is that of rape."

"Explain yourself."

"Being a bachelor I have no establishment of my own, but live in apartments in Park Lane. My landlady, a merry, pleasant creature, of about thirty, plump and pretty, with a large roguish eye, that follows you wherever you go, deigned for several weeks to listen to my idle nonsense, and at last suffered me to embrace her warm waist, and kiss her moist lips. I saw immediately that she would, and she would not. Her husband I found out was a jealous Turk, and she was afraid of him. A few evenings ago she came into my sitting-room to make some inquiry, when I invited her to take a glass of wine with me. She did so, and I began to pull her about. At first she was angry, but soon cooled down, and went off into another kind of heat, which, I perceiving, became more ardent in my advances, and after a good deal of struggling—for at the critical moment she got horridly afraid of venturing—I had my way. She then began to cry, and who should then walk in but the monster, her husband, to whom she complained that I had assaulted her, with intent, &c. She was obliged to say something, for her clothes and hair were in great disorder, and so she put the most charitable construction on the affair, and assured her husband that, villain as I was, she had resisted so stoutly, that she was still his pure, true, and lawful wife. I was dragged to the station-house, and next morning committed, but liberated on bail."

"A narrow escape for you, 29," said the president; "but you could not have displeased the woman, or you would at this moment have been in Newgate. Will any member make a proposition?"

It was promptly moved, seconded, and carried, that No. 29 should be defended at the expense of the order, and that the president should admonish him upon his indiscretions, this being the third of the kind of which he had been guilty within the last three years.

"No. 29," said the president, with great gravity, "for a man of your years, being now—"

"Forty-five last birthday," said the secretary.

"Being now forty-five years old," continued the president, "this amour of yours is positively an offence; and you must be cautious for the future, or you may meet with a spiteful woman, who will not hesitate to prefer the graver charge of violation. But your conduct amazes me. Until this moment I had always believed that every Knight of the Round Table was too much a man of the world to risk his liberty for the sake of possessing an unwilling woman, when, by a little diligence, scores might be found who would not make the slightest objection. The man who uses violence to a woman is a recreant knight (hear, hear) and dangerous companion. Love, like honey, must be gathered with caution. Even in plucking the rose it is necessary to avoid the thorn by its side; and how much more necessary it is, in gathering the fairest flowers of the earth, that we should use circumspection, and that gentleness which protects the tender plants from injury either by accident or design. Unless we mingle refinement with our pleasures they soon pall upon the senses; and if we pursue them further, it is only in the degenerated form of mere animals. To a knight of your experience, and established reputation for kindness of disposition and purpose, I need say no more. Be warned in time, and refrain from setting our younger members so vicious an example."

No. 29 returned thanks for the consideration shown towards him, and promised to be more discreet in his future commerce with the fair sex.

The secretary, No. 45, then read the remainder of the minutes.

"All the children of the order are in good health. Two of them—boys—with the consent and approbation of their parents, have been apprenticed to good trades. Three girls, having completed their education, have been received into most respectable families as governesses. Those approaching the age when they should mingle with the busy world, have been sedulously attended to, and the governess of the institution reports very favourably of their progress. It is perhaps scarcely necessary to repeat, that all the children are being most carefully trained under the rules of the system of education of which our venerated president is the author; and that when they leave school, they do so with a thorough knowledge of their duties, responsibilities, and passions, as men and women. It is not left to them to acquire knowledge through the channels of vice or sad experience, but are taught everything that it is proper a human being should know, and which, when unwisely withheld from them, they are sure inevitably to obtain surreptitiously." (Hear, hear.)

No. 45 closed his books, and sat down. The president then tapped three times very significantly, and every member simultaneously began writing something on a slip of paper, which he passed to those seated near the centre of the table, who deposited it in a beautiful urn standing before them. Presently the president said:

"No. 25, ring the bell."

The member so requested pulled a bell-handle, which rested in a groove in the table, and in a moment the part of the table whereon the urn stood opened, and when it closed again the urn had disappeared.

The members then indulged in a general and unrestrained conversation, which continued until the compartment in the table again opened, and closed again, but this time bearing upon its surface not only the urn, but a little army of well-filled decanters, jugs of hot water, wine-glasses, goblets, tumblers, lemons, cigars, tobacco, pipes, and all the etceteras indispensable in convivial hours. As soon as each member had filled his glass, and selected his pipe or cigar, the president again tapped, and there was again the most profound silence.

"I declare the Good and Welfare opened!" cried the president—and up sprang every man to his feet—"and give you the loyal and constitutional toast of our order—'MERRY GIRLS, MERRY WIVES, AND PLENTY OF THEM'."

This sentiment was received with uproarious applause, and then each member in the drinking department did as he liked. Harmony, in the shape of song, jest, and anecdote, then commenced, and at the end of an hour the hammer again sounded, and, as before, there was a dead silence.

"Gentlemen," said the president, before whom stood a steaming tumbler of brandy-and-water, "we will once more proceed to business, if you please. The only address I have to make to you, is one of congratulation. We are in a prosperous condition, and every one of us as moral as the state of society and our own peculiar organizations will allow us. But I must, nevertheless, recommend to you moderation in all your enjoyments. The true end of life is to live as long as possible, and at the same time be as happy as possible. This cannot be attained without temperance—no true epicurist is intemperate. Therefore I warn you, in the language of the poet, to—

> 'Beware the poison in the cup of gold,
> The asp among the flowers.'

In the shape of information I have only to communicate that a royal commission has been appointed to inquire into our marriage laws, and, from the elevated rank which many of you hold, I have no doubt you will be called upon to give evidence as to their operation among the higher grades of society. I entertain not the slightest doubt that you will denounce their stringency as oppressive and vicious, and show that, as far as morality is concerned, they are wholly inoperative. Adultery should not be the sole ground of divorce, as some of you, perhaps to your sorrow, can too well advance. But this is delicate ground, and each member must, if called upon, act as a true knight and a man of experience and common sense. The bill legalizing marriages with a deceased wife's sister, will be again introduced, and it will be for the interest and welfare of legitimate children that those among you who are legislators should give it your earnest and undivided support. On general grounds it is entitled to—it demands—our cordial support and sympathy, for, not trenching upon the objection as to affinity of blood, it does not tend to promote any deterioration of race, to guard against which is one of the true ends of marriage; if it were not so, the necessity for the enactment of laws at all would be obviated, and, like the lower animals, we ought only to obey the impulses of instinct. As to the moral features, nothing novel is introduced: sexual connection between husbands and their wives' sisters has been practised from the earliest ages, and the opinion of the multitude does not condemn the union as repulsive. Legalize such marriages, and you at once put an end to the majority of illicit connections between husbands and their deceased wives' sisters, for few women, unless intoxicated by desire, will voluntarily throw an obstacle in the way of marriage with the man with whom she is pleased; and, as you all know, surrender of person without the sanction of the body is rarely followed by the man performing either his given or implied promise. But this also is a question for your own private judgments, and to that tribunal I confidently commit it. It now becomes my duty to receive the propositions members may make."

No one spoke; indeed, there rather seemed to be a prevailing disposition to be more hilarious than methodical; but the president arose, and announced that he had a new member to propose in the room of their lately deceased one. This aroused the attention of every one, and the president commenced:

"Gentlemen, my new member, or rather candidate, is a gentleman and a soldier. Like us all, he worships more at the shrine of Venus and Bacchus than those more sacred ones which we are pledged to respect. He is in every respect a man of honour, and one in whom we may place the utmost reliance. He graduated at Cambridge, where perhaps he won more hearts than academic laurels; but, as a soldier, he acquired imperishable renown in those hard-fought battles on the north-west frontier of India, which perhaps, more than any other modern ones, have served to consolidate the power of Britain in that interesting and remarkable portion of the globe. His valour was so distinguished that, unsolicited, it obtained for him a captain's commission in her Majesty's Guards; and in that celebrated corps he established, or, I should say, confirmed, his reputation as an officer and a gentleman. Among the ladies he is an universal favourite; and, from an intimate knowledge of his career and conduct, I can confidently say that I do not know of an instance in which he has behaved with the slightest heartlessness, or been guilty of the least want of principle. He is a gay man, but a chivalric one; and a recent exhibition of his spirit on behalf of a persecuted maiden, enables me to announce his name—Captain Morris. He is now, as you are aware, owing to his duel, in a kind of abeyance, or prudent retirement; but, wishing to have him amongst us, and aware that I could safely trust both you and him, I have brought him with me tonight. I now, therefore, beg to propose him as a member of our order."

A dozen rose to second the nomination, and the election by ballot was ordered to be proceeded with. While it was going on Wriggles drew Smythe into a corner, and, after a brief, but emphatic conversation, extracted from him a promise not to oppose the election by throwing in his black ball. When the box was examined it was found that Walter had been unanimously elected, and the result was received with loud applause. Order having been restored, the president tapped, and a slip of paper being transmitted to the regions below, through the medium of the urn, the gas-lights in the room were suddenly lowered, so as to veil it in comparative darkness.

"Tilers, admit the applicant at the door," cried the president. And Walter in a few seconds was conducted to where his proposer stood ready to receive him.

"Captain Morris," said the president, "I have the honour to announce to you that you have been unanimously elected a member of this order; but to complete your success it is necessary that you should answer a few questions, and enter into an engagement, as a man of honour, to preserve our secrets inviolable. We do not ask for oaths, because we are convinced of their inefficacy, compared with the plighted word of a gentleman, and more especially one who has carried arms in the service of his country. As a preliminary,

I must request you to listen to the general rules, which our secretary will recite to you. No. 45, inform Captain Morris of the nature of our general laws."

No. 45 then recited the following, as glibly as a well-conned lesson:

"Our motto is, the greatest amount of pleasure with the least amount of pain; and the objects of our association are, mutual assistance in cases of distress, and the promotion of enjoyment in all its phases. To carry out these views, we have acknowledged, and do abide by, the following maxims and rules, namely, that—

"Love is the keenest, noblest, and most glorious of all earthly pleasures: it is the spring from whence bubbles the pure waters of hope, and the sunbeam that gives them light and beauty. All nature acknowledges its sovereign sway; therefore, it is one of the lords of the universe. Difficulties, however, attend the gratification of its impulses, and to overcome them men often subject themselves to the gravest accusations, and plunge into dilemmas from which they can only be extricated by the charity and forbearance of their fellow-men. To afford this assistance, and, at the same time, to refine the passions of mankind, is the primary regulation of this society. And to develop the intention in its full integrity, we have adopted eight cardinal sentiments, upon which we base our laws:

"1. Love is a physical pleasure, out of which—from association and mutual agreement of organization—proceed the spiritualities that endear a man to a woman, and a woman to a man, independent of the sexual connection.

"2. The sensual estimate of woman is the natural one, but with civilized races it is refined by marriage and other conventional necessities; therefore, it is proper to respect all the moral and social laws which have been enacted for the control and subjection of the appetites to salutary restraint.

"3. Mere coition is not love, but, being necessary to the health of the body, is, when enjoyed in moderation, a fundamental necessity.

"4. Man having the life-giving power, polygamy does not outrage any natural law or sentiment of the human mind; but in the densely-populated countries the institution, for political purposes, is disallowed; and hence are formed illicit connections, which no human laws can repress; and the responsibilities attached to them being thrown upon the parties concerned, it follows that too much discretion, prudence and generosity, cannot be associated with these indulgences.

"5. The union of the sexes being indispensable to the propagation of the species, regulations placing obstacles in its way are illegal and repugnant to nature.

"6. Promiscuous intercourse is a brutish and abominable outrage upon health and decency, therefore a woman should only enjoy the society of the man to whom she is engaged, either for life or a limited term. But as extraordinary emergencies will arise, such as physical incapacity in the man, or such a bankruptcy of conduct that he is no longer worthy of her favours: then the woman, whether married by law or promise, is at liberty to choose another mate.

"7. As society, as at present constituted, is imperfect, and human beings are not all formed alike, all errors should be viewed as mildly and extenuatingly as possible; and those of woman, owing to her inefficient training, more so than those of the stronger animal, man.

"8. Drunkenness, gluttony, and excesses in love are positive crimes.

"With these views, and believing them to be correct, we have formed ourselves into a society for the promotion of the gratification of all our propensities and faculties, and their confinement within the bounds of reason, propriety, and social convenience. To develop our objects, we have pledged ourselves to be bound by the following regulations:

"1. To meet once a fortnight. 2. To contribute rateably to the pecuniary necessities of the order; but the amount subscribed within one year not to exceed 100*l.* 3. To keep the secrets of the order. 4. To abstain from the discussion of theological or political subjects. 5. Each member in turn to deliver a lecture on the philosophy of the Epicureans. 6. To defend each other from the slanders of the world. 7. To promote the education of the illegitimate children of the members of the order. 8. To contribute by general vote towards the damages and costs which any member may have sustained in his commerce with women. 9. To obey the mandate of the chair."

No. 45 ceased, and the president then said:

"Captain Morris, you have heard the rules of our order—are you willing to subscribe to them?"

"I am."

"Will you promise, on your honour as a gentleman, not to divulge any of its secrets?"

"I do."

"Will you, at all times and at all hazards, protect women, whether young or old, from outrage or injury?"

"I will."

"Then, Captain Morris, I have to announce your complete election to our vacant number, by which you will only henceforth be recognized here; and long and worthily may you enjoy it. After you have passed your noviciate, you will be still further initiated into the mysteries of our order; but before that time shall have elapsed, you will have discovered that we are no anchorites, but that our motto is the right royal one: 'Eat, drink and love; the rest's not worth a straw.' A health, gentlemen, to the new Knight of the Round Table."

The lights shot up and blazed brilliantly, and Walter, amid uproarious cheers, was conducted to his seat, from the arms of which, at the same time, the sign of mourning for its late occupant was removed. Merriment then became the order of the evening, and, amid flashes of wit and floods of eloquence from lips, the names of whose owners are treasured by the multitude, Walter yielded to the charm of the excitement, and soon became one of the gayest of the gay. At midnight the member whose turn it was to deliver a lecture, read a paper on the worship by the ancients of idols, symbolizing the creed of the obscene god Priapus; and at its conclusion there was held an animated but lascivious conversation, interspersed and enlivened by songs and jests. At four in the morning the president rose, and, as a hint to break up, gave the standing toast of the order—"Merry girls, merry wives, and plenty of them".

13

SISTER ANNE

by Paul de Kock

TO THIS POINT in our study we have concentrated solely on the Penny Dreadfuls published in Britain; but a similar form of publication was flourishing in both Europe and America and, as we shall see, there was a good deal of cross-fertilization, not to mention much outrageous plagiarism and double-dealing on the part of publishers in the various countries. Up until the 1830s much of English literature had been influenced by Germany—in particular the Gothic novels and *Schauerromane*—but from this date America, and France in particular, were to take over the dominance. As Louis James has written, "The way was now open for a flood of literature... French and American authors expressed a democratic culture and brought the work of vivid imaginations to a reading public seeking novelty and sensation." Although it has been claimed that the American influence was felt first, it best suits our purpose here to begin by considering France.

Despite the fact that the Napoleonic wars were not long over, English people were already visiting France in ever-increasing numbers and many workmen also crossed the Channel to find employment. There was a great interest, too, on the part of both nations in each other's literature, and almost simultaneously we find the development of the serial work in Britain and *le roman feuilleton* in France. The French writers who were drawn into producing these weekly instalment stories included some of the nation's most famous authors, including Dumas *père*, Honoré de Balzac, George Sand, Victor Hugo, etcetera—just as their famous counterparts were doing in England. From the late 1830s onwards, serials running in France were appearing in translation in English only weeks later and vice versa. Short stories, too, proved grist to the mill and many of the leading English periodicals drew heavily on the French to fill their columns. Plagiarism was commonplace and worked equally in both directions—though occasionally the pirates did come unstuck if a serial was suddenly discontinued through the failure of the original author or publisher.

Popular though many of the famous French authors were in England, one now almost forgotten writer stood head and shoulders above the others in the 1830s, Paul de Kock (1809–1891). In the light of what we learned in the previous extract about the public's enjoyment of sensuality and vice, de Kock's popularity is perhaps more easy to understand. For, though no great craftsman, he was—to quote Thackeray—"the delight of the lower classes ... they certainly give his tales of debauchery a most hearty welcome". The notorious William Dugdale was one of the first English publishers to translate his work (including "The Barber of Paris" and "Jean") and we find early reviews referring to him as "a gross and indecent caricaturist". Certainly much of his work was coarse and lacking human sentiment, but at his best—as Louis James has said—"he offers an irreverent mockery of all life in the tradition of Rabelais, if on an inferior level".

De Kock was an incredibly prolific and inventive writer— he claimed to have written over 400 books—and shares with Thomas Frost the distinction of having been one of the few writers to be expurgated by his publishers. In later life, with the emergence of the romantic fiction written by such as Hugo and Dumas, he began to tone down his style, but in doing this much of his inventiveness and exuberance seems to have diminished and his popularity waned sharply.

The great George Reynolds was responsible for the translation of several of de Kock's best works into English and claimed, in introducing one, that "he enjoys more celebrity than any living writer". He was, said Reynolds, read by everyone, from the highest lady in her luxurious *boudoir* to the poorest *grisette* in her miserable attic; from the statesman who mounts the tribune in the Chamber of Deputies, to the copying clerk in the attorney's office. "A new novel by Paul de Kock creates a more powerful sensation than the speech of the King himself," he claimed in introducing his translation of "Sister Anne", one of the Frenchman's finest works. It was not until some years later, when he used the entire text of "Sister Anne" as an episode to pad out his serial *The Empress Eugénie's Boudoir*, that Reynolds admitted that he had made his translation of this story of a dumb peasant girl who is seduced and then abandoned by a young nobleman "with much expurgation".

It is certainly a gruelling tale, with the speechless girl and her illegitimate child trekking across France in search of her lover who has by now married into his own class. They are beset by all manner of disasters—including rape—until Sister Anne is finally taken into the home of her former lover, Frederick, by his wife—who of course, knows nothing of the seduction. The dénouement, which is reprinted below, is de Kock in the form which riveted hundreds of thousands of readers over a century ago.

Sister Anne and her son continued to reside in the pavilion. The poor mute seldom ventured to walk in the garden; and when she did quit her abode for a moment, she chose those paths that were nearest to it. She never approached the house; for she was fearful of meeting Frederick, although her heart was still as deeply attached to him as ever. But Frederick himself dared not venture near the pavilion. The conduct of his wife, since the day when he pressed Sister Anne in his arms did not leave a doubt in his mind that the cry which he heard had issued from her lips. If Constance had seen him at the feet of his mistress, what faith could she put in his promises? She probably imagined now that she was not loved alone! Often was he inclined to throw himself at her feet, and assure her that he loved her still: but he would be obliged to confess that he had broken his promise; and if she were not already acquainted with the fact, he would thus betray it. In this state of incertitude, he held his peace, hoping that he should eventually be able to dissipate all jealous suspicions from the mind of his wife.

Constance did not leave the house: she did not even walk in the garden. Her countenance was changed, her cheeks lost the glow of health: vainly did she endeavour to smile—the sorrow that undermined her, manifested itself in all her actions. She was as amiable and gentle as ever; she was deeply sensible of the attentions of her husband; and, perceiving that he scrupulously avoided all visits to the garden, she begged him to continue his walks there as usual.

"Why should I leave you?" asked Frederick: "can I be better elsewhere than with you?"

Constance pressed his hand tenderly, and averted her head to conceal her tears. She could not dismiss from her mind the scene which she had witnessed in the arbour: she saw Sister Anne in the arms of her husband, in her dreams at night; she believed that his heart was no longer hers, and that he regretted his absence from the young mute: and she fancied his present conduct was only a sacrifice he made to her peace. These cruel thoughts tormented her by day and night—and vainly did she essay to hide her sorrows.

"Things cannot last thus much longer," said Dubourg to Frederick from time to time. "Your wife is dying by inches—and the poor mute is broken hearted. If those two women continue to dwell together, they will both fall into a consumption."

"What can I do?" asked Frederick. "Sister Anne's fate is in the hands of Constance. When I speak to my wife concerning her, she closes my mouth, or declares that the poor creature shall not depart!"

An abduction scene from Paul de Kock's notorious serial, "Jean", which was published in England by William Dugdale.

"It is certainly a very embarrassing situation," observed Ménard; "and if I were in Frederick's place, I know very well what I should do!"

"What would you do?" exclaimed Dubourg. "Speak!"

"Why," returned the old tutor, "I should do as he does—not know what plan to adopt!"

An event which now took place, was calculated to work considerable changes in the house where sorrow and grief prevailed. One morning the Count de Montreville, whom the gout had at length abandoned, arrived at his son's country residence. Dubourg, although unaware that the Count was acquainted with Sister Anne, was pleased with the arrival of that nobleman, because he hoped that his presence would compel Frederick to adopt some decided measure. The young man was exceedingly troubled by his father's visit, the Count being as yet ignorant of all that had lately occurred. Should he tell his sire the whole truth? Should he inform him that Sister Anne was an inmate of that pavilion? But before he met his father Constance had implored him not to mention the subject to the Count; for she fondly believed that his lordship was ignorant of his son's fault, and she did not wish him to be acquainted with it. On his side, the Count de Montreville had been for a long time enquiring concerning the dumb woman who had saved his life. The last messenger he had despatched to the farm-house, informed him that she had left that dwelling to repair to Paris; and the Count, finding that she did not make her appearance at his mansion, caused the most vigorous searches to be made after her.

On his arrival at his son's house, the Count de Montreville was struck by the sorrow and affliction which were depicted on the features of Constance. He anxiously inquired the reason of this change; and the young lady avoided further interrogation, by pretending that she had only just recovered from a severe indisposition. The old nobleman was however a shrewd observer; and he saw that some secret was withheld from him. His son was embarrassed in his presence— M. Ménard avoided him as if he were again fearful of receiving a reprimand—Dubourg alone was charmed by his arrival. Everything seemed to denote a mystery of an extraordinary nature in the house.

Constance was aware that the Count de Montreville was in the habit, during his occasional stay at Montmorenci, of repairing to the pavilion to read : she accordingly hastened to inform him that a young woman and her son were resident in that retreat. The Count did not ask any more questions; he was very far from suspecting that he was so near the object of his long search; nor was it at the house of his son, that he hoped to find her.

On the morning after his arrival, the Count, according to his custom, rose early and went into the garden. It was only when he was close to the pavilion, that he recollected what Constance had told him on the preceding evening, he accordingly turned into another path, and advanced towards the terrace. But scarcely had he walked a few paces, when a child ran out of the pavilion and hurried up to him; and in another moment a young woman was at his feet, covering his hands with kisses. What was the surprise of his lordship when he recognized the dumb girl and her son?

Sister Anne had perceived the Count from the window of the pavilion, and had immediately recognized him. The features of her benefactor were engraven upon her memory, and she had hastened to throw herself at his feet as he turned away from the pavilion. She testified as well as she was able all the pleasure she experienced at seeing him again; but the Count was a considerable time before he could recover from his astonishment.

"What! you are here!" at length exclaimed the old nobleman: "and who received you? Do you not know that you are in the house of your seducer? and are you ignorant that the lady who has granted you an asylum is Frederick's wife?"

Sister Anne made signs to intimate that she was well acquainted with those facts—that she had seen Frederick—and that Constance had urged her to continue to reside in the pavilion. The surprise of the Count augmented every moment. Not being able to obtain from the dumb girl all the information he required, he longed to seek his son.

"Return into the pavilion," said he to Sister Anne; "you shall speedily see me again. Already you have been here too long! But I will not abandon you!"

Sister Anne withdrew to the pavilion; but before she left the Count, his lordship embraced her son tenderly.

Frederick suspected that an interview of this kind would take place. He was therefore on his way to seek his father and confess the entire truth, when he met the Count, whose severe look made him aware that the meeting had already occurred.

"I have just seen the person who dwells in the pavilion," said the Count; "and I am no longer astonished at the altered appearance of your wife, whose manners are entirely changed. Unhappy young man! behold the recompense of so much love and of such exalted virtues! You allow the woman whom you have seduced, to dwell in the same house with your wife—"

"I am not guilty, my lord," returned Frederick: and he recounted to his father all that had taken place during his absence—how his wife had charitably granted an asylum to the poor mute—and how she daily became more attached to her and her son. The old nobleman listened to his son's narrative in silence.

"It is thus," said his lordship, after a long pause, "that your wife knows all! She is aware that you are the seducer of that young woman, and the father of her child: and yet she permits Sister Anne to inhabit the pavilion!"

"Her intention," resumed Frederick, "was at first to send her to one of our estates, and install her in a house which she would have had fitted up for her. The day of departure was fixed—I know not what could have made her change her resolution—but she will not now suffer Sister Anne to leave this place!"

"And you cannot guess the motive?" exclaimed the Count. "My dear son, this behaviour on her part is too remarkable not to be the result of some secret reason! The nature of a woman, who loves and adores her husband, will not suffer her to dwell in the close vicinity of a late rival, and of one who may be a rival still, without some extraordinary motive or design. But Constance possesses a soul capable of making every sacrifice to your happiness: she would immolate herself to procure you a single day of enjoyment! Can you permit her thus to languish? do you not see the change which has taken place in her? She conceals her tears from you—but she cannot hide the deadly pallor of her cheeks, nor the effects of sorrow upon her lovely countenance! Every moment of the day she remembers that you are in the neighbourhood of the mother of your son—that you may speak to her—see her—"

"Oh! my dear father!" exclaimed Frederick: "I swear—"

"I believe all you told me, Frederick," interrupted the Count; "but you must confess that the position of your wife is cruel in the extreme. From tomorrow Sister Anne must cease to dwell in this pavilion!"

"What, my lord?" cried the young man.

"Do you blame my resolution?" demanded his father.

"I—Oh, no!" returned Frederick. "I feel all that I owe you—I need not recommend that unfortunate creature to your care—and—my son—"

"No—I will take such measures that they shall both be happy," continued M. de Montreville. "The excellent intentions of your wife shall be fulfilled. Do you think that the young woman and her child are objects of no interest to me? Because I no longer experience the turbulent passions of youth, do not suppose that my heart is made of ice! Allow me to be the means of restoring peace to yourself and wife; and do you make it your care to recall the bloom to her cheeks by redoubling your kindness and attention to one who is so worthy of all your esteem! It is thus, Frederick, that you may efface the memory of your fault, and reward me for all I intend to do for Sister Anne and her son."

Frederick covered the hand of the worthy old nobleman with his tears; and the Count hastened to rejoin Constance. He did not utter a word concerning the poor mute; but as he contemplated his daughter-in-law, he could not repress his admiration, and he felt that he loved her more dearly than ever. Constance knew not to what to attribute those symptoms of increased attachment upon the part of her father-in-law, who was usually cold to all around him; and she still fondly believed that the Count was ignorant of his son's guilt.

The Count despatched his valet to Paris, with orders to return on the following morning with the travelling carriage, and a pair of excellent horses, and to conduct the equipage to the back-gate of the garden, near the terrace, as he himself resolved upon accompanying Sister Anne to the place whither he intended she should proceed. In the meantime he hastened to the pavilion to inform the poor mute of his arrangements. The movements of the Count backwards and forwards in the house made Dubourg imagine that his lordship had already contemplated certain plans in reference to Sister Anne.

"There will be some changes here soon," said Dubourg to Ménard: "God grant that they may restore happiness and tranquillity to this abode!"

"I admit that for some time past we have not been very gay," exclaimed Ménard. "Her ladyship sighs—my pupil is pensive—the poor mute does not say a word to a soul—and you yourself, my dear Dubourg, are totally changed."

"How would you have me gay, when those whom I love are wretched?" demanded Dubourg. "In spite of my philosophy, I am not indifferent to the sorrows of others."

"You are just like me in this respect," returned the tutor: "I think of nothing but the position of Frederick and his wife all day long."

"And yet it does not deprive you of your appetite."

"Do you suppose that if I were to make myself ill, I should restore them to gaiety?"

"You certainly do not look like a man who is inclined to be ill," answered Dubourg: "you are as stout as a barrel."

"The cook gives us capital dinners," observed Ménard; "and how can I prevent myself from getting fat?"

"I calculate much upon the arrival of Frederick's father,"

said Dubourg, after a short pause. "He has been to the pavilion—he has seen Sister Anne—and I am sure that a change will shortly be introduced—"

"What!" interrupted the old tutor; "do you think that we shall not have such good dinners in future?"

"Really, M. Ménard, you were not born to live in France; you should go and live in Switzerland, where people eat all day long."

"I was born to dwell anywhere, sir; and when you played *Baron Potoski* with us, you were quite an adept at getting rid of the money with your three courses at dinner. And by the bye, talking of appetite reminds me that I was obliged to give you a hint yesterday that you had eaten all the turbot, and when I applied for some more, there was none."

"Turbot, M. Ménard, is very heavy," said Dubourg. "It is not good for you."

"I beg you not to interfere with my health, sir," returned the old tutor, "and to leave me some turbot when that fish next appears upon table. You ought to know that at my age I may be allowed to give myself an indigestion if I choose."

While every one throughout the house was a prey to his conjectures, the Count hastened to the pavilion. Sister Anne dwelt on the first floor; and it was already night when the Count de Montreville resolved upon making her aware of his intentions. He however stopped a moment at the foot of the stairs, before he sought the presence of the young woman who had saved his life.

"Poor creature!" thought he; "I am about to afflict you deeply! I must separate you from Frederick—separate you for ever from your lover! But it is a duty which I cannot omit—and your soul is too pure not to feel convinced that it is necessary to restore peace, tranquillity, and new life to her who saved you and your son from the horrors of want, and who overwhelmed you with kindness."

The old nobleman at length ascended the stairs, and entered the mute's apartment. Sister Anne, the moment she recognized the Count, rose and hastened to meet him; and her eyes expressed the attachment she felt towards him. He was affected: he contemplated her for some time in silence; but he was aware that it was his duty to inform her of his intentions, so that she might be ready on the following morning.

"My dear child," said he, "as I told you this morning, it is impossible for you to remain any longer in this house: your presence would inflict a mortal blow upon her who received you here. Constance loves her husband tenderly—and I am certain you would not wish to deprive her of repose and happiness for ever. She conceals the torments she experiences; but I have read the secret at the bottom of her heart. You would not wish to send to the grave her who saved you from it!"

Sister Anne intimated by a significant gesture, that she was ready to sacrifice herself for Constance.

"You must depart then," continued the Count: "you must leave this place. Tomorrow, at daybreak—without even seeing your benefactress, you must depart! I will undertake to assure her of your eternal gratitude and love. Nor will it be possible for you to take leave of Frederick. I am convinced it is scarcely necessary to inform you how strictly you must avoid all interview with him!"

Sister Anne was unnerved by these injunctions. To depart so suddenly, without being prepared—and without being allowed to say farewell to Frederick—Oh! this was more than her courage could support. She felt her strength failing her—and her tears flowed copiously. The Count approached her, and took her hand, saying, "Poor creature, this sudden determination on my part afflicts you; but in your position, every moment of delay is a crime! I tear you away from this abode, it is true: I am nevertheless compelled to be severe. Courage, Anne—courage! It is the father of Frederick, whom you saved from the dagger of the banditti—it is he who now demands this sacrifice in order to secure the happiness of his son!"

These words produced upon the young mother the effect

which the Count had anticipated. The moment she learnt that he was the father of her lover, she fell at his feet, and her hands were joined together as if to implore his pardon.

"Rise—rise!" said the Count, depositing a kiss upon her forehead. "Unfortunate girl—why cannot I make you happy? All I can do is to ensure a comfortable subsistence for yourself and your son. I shall conduct you to a beautiful farm which I intend to bestow upon you: a pretty house is attached to it—and there you will reside, surrounded by faithful dependants who will love and respect you. There also you will rear your child. I shall frequently visit you in your peaceful retreat; and I sincerely hope that tranquillity may become your guest."

Sister Anne listened to the Count, and was resolved to obey him. She felt that happiness could never again exist for her; but she seemed to say to him, through the medium of her signs, "Dispose of me as you will—I am ready to follow your slightest inclinations."

"Tomorrow, then," said the Count, "at daybreak I will come and fetch you. We will depart before any one shall be awake in the house. Prepare everything for your son: you need not take much apparel with you, for all that you require shall be provided for you at your future abode. Adieu for the present, Anne. At daybreak I will be with you."

The Count departed from the pavilion—Sister Anne was again alone—and her son slept. It was night—the last night which she was destined to pass near Frederick! She was to leave him—leave him for ever! The idea was maddening—and the poor creature remained motionless upon a chair near the cradle of her child! One thought alone occupied her mind; and this was the necessity and the certainty of her departure from the vicinity of one whom she had found with such difficulty, and whom she had loved so tenderly! She must leave him who in the arbour had appeared to love her still! The peace, and perhaps the life of her benefactress, demanded this great sacrifice!

The last few hours which she was to pass in the pavilion

seemed to glide away with unusual rapidity. A prey to her thoughts, she did not remember that it was necessary to prepare for her departure. Midnight was announced by the village clock; and the mute was still seated near her child's cradle, and in the situation in which the Count left her. The monotonous sound of the clock aroused her from her reverie. She rose—prepared a small bundle of necessaries—and, when her arrangements were completed, several hours of the night still remained to be passed away. Should she deliver herself up to repose? No—she knew that any attempt to woo the approach of slumber would be a vain one. But what sentiment occupied her mind? Every one slept in the house: —might she not profit by that opportunity to cast one last glance upon him she loved so well? She would not arouse him—she felt that were she to seek an interview with him, she should be guilty of ingratitude towards her benefactress and to the Count! But, unknown to Frederick, she might bid him an eternal adieu : she knew which were the windows of his apartment—she could contemplate the room in which he slept—and she fancied that she might then depart less unhappily, and that in his sleep Frederick would hear her farewell.

Sister Anne did not hesitate any longer. She placed upon a chair the bundle of necessaries she had just wrapped up, and then put the candle in the grate. Her son slept tranquilly in his cradle, upon which she shed many tears—for she remembered that he was shortly to be for ever separated from his father! No noise was heard—she issued gently from the pavilion; the night was dark—but she was acquainted with the turnings of the paths in the garden—and her feet scarcely touched the ground. Like a volatile shadow, she flew rapidly along the gravel-walks towards the house. Frederick's room was on the right hand, on the first floor : she fell upon her knees beneath the windows—she stretched out her arms towards the apartment—she addressed her last adieu to her lover! Bathed in tears—supporting her head upon one of her hands—and still reluctant to avert her eyes from the spot which she knew he inhabited, Sister Anne gave herself up to all the wildness of her despair, to her love, and to her regret; —she was some time absent from the pavilion—the moments passed rapidly away—she could not tear herself from the place—and yet she was compelled to leave it!

The unfortunate girl made a last effort. She rose—she withdrew, heart-broken and in despair—she staggered as she threaded the alleys of the garden—and her bosom gave vent to the most violent sobs. Suddenly a strong light illuminated the garden. Sister Anne raised her eyes—she could not conceive whence emanated that unusual brilliancy. She advanced towards the pavilion—the lustre gradually increased —the obscurity of night had yielded to a terrific glare—and broad red flames streamed from the garden into the air. Seized by a sudden alarm, Sister Anne walked no longer: she ran—she flew towards the pavilion—volumes of fire issued from the windows of the first floor. A terrible cry escaped the lips of Sister Anne; for she thought of her son— her child, whom she had left in the apartment whence emanated the flames of the appalling element!

In her despair she recovered strength and courage at the same time. She reached the pavilion—a thick cloud of smoke enveloped the staircase—but a mother knows not the meaning of danger! She must save her child, and boldly did she rush through the dense mists that obscured even the glare of the flames. She could not find the door of her apartment— the smoke hid it from her view—and her trembling hands sought it in vain! At length the fire burst forth with fearful fury—and its light, for a moment dispelling the smoke, guided the almost heart-broken mother. She penetrated into the room—it was enveloped in flames! Her bundle of clothes had rolled from the chair, and had caught the fire which so rapidly communicated itself to all objects near. Sister Anne rushed to the cradle which contained her son—she caught him in her arms—she sought the door—but she saw not the direction it was necessary for her to take. The flames already hemmed her in on all sides—her strength was gradually failing her—she endeavoured to call for help—she felt that she must summon her vocal power to her aid, or die! At that moment, her voice, yielding to the force of a new effort of nature, broke the bonds which enchained it—and the poor girl fell to the floor, exclaiming distinctly, *"Frederick—hasten and save your son!"*

In the meantime the flames, which enveloped the pavilion, were perceived by the inmates of the house, two or three of whom had not been able to retire to rest. Frederick, yielding to his terror, rushed from his room, calling for assistance. Every one rose and hastened to render prompt aid where it was so much required.

"The pavilion is on fire!" was the general cry.

Thither ran the inmates of the house—but Frederick was the first to gain the dangerous spot. He braved death to succour Sister Anne, and penetrated into her apartment a few moments after she had fainted. With one arm he raised her—in the other he held her son; he traversed the flames—he was once more in the garden—he had saved them both!

Every one had followed Frederick to the terrible scene; and Constance was not the last in the traces of her husband. She received Sister Anne in her arms, and transported her to her own apartment. The young mother was speedily surrounded by every soul that dwelt in the house—her body exhibited the marks of the fire—but her son had not experienced the slightest effects from the danger in which he had been enveloped. Her recovery was anxiously awaited by all present, in order to present her son to the unhappy mother. At length a profound sigh escaped her bosom; her eyes opened slowly, and Constance placed her child in her arms.

"My son! my son!" exclaimed Sister Anne; and she covered the child with kisses.

These words threw all present into the most unfeigned astonishment. They listened attentively—they gazed upon Sister Anne—they were uncertain if they had heard rightly.

"O God!" cried the young mother; "it is not then a dream! You have restored to me the power of speech! O

Frederick, I can now tell you how much—how deeply I have loved you! And you—his tender, his affectionate wife—forgive me! I feel that I shall not long enjoy the blessing which is bestowed upon me. All that I have this day suffered has prostrated my strength! I am about to die—but my son is saved!—Oh! do not deplore my fate!"

The poor young mother had made a violent effort in order to pronounce these words: her eyes became glazed—her hand grew cold—and a fearful pallor already overspread her visage. Frederick had fallen upon his knees by her side, and bathed with tears the hand which she abandoned to him. The Count was overwhelmed with grief; and Constance endeavoured to recall her back to life by imploring her to gaze upon her child. Every one took some part in that distressing scene; and Dubourg—who had never shed tears before, wept bitterly, as he sustained the head of Sister Anne.

"Wherefore do you mourn for me?" she said, making a last effort: "I could not have hoped for happiness in this world—but I die in peace! Take care of my child, Constance—he is so well in your arms! You will be his mother! Adieu, Frederick! And you, my lord—Oh! forgive me for having loved your son so tenderly and so well!"

Sister Anne cast a look towards Constance who held the innocent child in her arms; and, as she smiled upon her son, the young mother closed her eyes for ever!

* * *

In the cemetery of Perre la Chaise, there is a marble tomb, of simple architecture—plain, but elegant: and on it are inscribed naught but these words: "SISTER ANNE".

14

THE RAFT OF DEATH

by Eugène Sue

IF PAUL DE KOCK was the most popular of the *feuilleton* writers in the 1830s, he was totally overshadowed —as indeed were most other French writers, whichever section of the reading public they served—by the emergence in the 1840s of a former naval surgeon, turned novelist, Eugène Sue (1804–1857). His impact on the reading public on both sides of the Channel was immediate and amazing— his "Mysteries of Paris" (1843) was to prove the inspiration of a whole host of rambling sagas about capital cities around the world by many and varied pens, and "The Wandering Jew" which appeared a year later was so popular that no fewer than nine English publishers were issuing it simultaneously in one form or another. (There were also numerous plagiarisms—one at least published by Edward Lloyd— which trudged along heavily in the wake of the original or occasionally darted ahead when the action slowed down.) One anonymous English reviewer said Sue was "far more talented than A. Dumas" and there is certainly no denying that he outsold his more distinguished contemporaries with ease.

Born the son of a naval physician, he had gone to sea himself as a young man and taken to writing in his spare time. With the almost immediate acceptance of his work, he returned to France and poured forth a stream of naval romances, portraits of the seamy side of city life and historical dramas of all periods. At first he was greeted as the man who had lifted French fiction "from the reproach which the Paul de Kock school has thrown upon it", but he was unable to resist a penchant for scenes of sadism and brutality, and the only saving grace of some was the moral purpose which gradually emerged within the story.

Only once during the height of his popularity as a writer was Sue seriously challenged—and that by a work unashamedly imitating his "Mysteries of Paris". This was "Mysteries of London" (1847) written by Paul Ferval, which had been specially commissioned by a Parisian journal in an attempt to wrest some readers from Sue. The success of the serial in both France and England—"it has, I believe, made a huge sensation", Charles Dickens wrote in a letter to a friend—was all the more remarkable when one learns that Ferval had never even been to London. (When he did later visit the English capital, Ferval "expressed satisfaction that the place was exactly as he had described it", to quote a news report.)

Even this work, however, could not topple Sue from his pedestal: it remained for him to do that himself. Because of his enormous following and his championing of the socialist cause, he was elected a Republican deputy, but then outraged the authorities with his brutal and savage novel "The Mysteries of the People" which was published in 1849. Even his popularity could not save him when the book was condemned as immoral and seditious, and he was driven into exile, where he remained until his death in 1857.

Just as Sue's later work offended his own countrymen, so in England it was held up as the leading example of a school of novels that "demoralize those weak minds who have little depths of experience". It was perhaps fortunate for the continuing literary *entente* between the two nations that the adventures and romances of Dumas and Hugo were available to quickly take the public fancy.

In selecting an example of Sue's work for this book I have had to bear in mind that several of his works are still easily available, and consequently I have decided on reproducing one of his few short stories, "The Raft", which seems to demonstrate the many facets of his talent. The story is extracted from *Dicks' English Library*, a publication by John Dicks, the London printer who made his fortune issuing many of the works of George Reynolds, and—in the tradition of several others—when he had made his money, attempted to conceal his beginnings by changing the titles of his more sensational journals. (Because of the necessary brevity of this section, the reader interested in this period is also directed to the works of Frédéric Soulié, Jules Janin, Eugène Scribe and the remarkable Marie Aycard and her "Curé Buonaparte" published in 1845.)

The Raft

How beautiful is the pale light of the silvery moon, when its rays are reflected upon the pure and transparent waters of a lake! But when its chaste beams are frequently concealed by dark and rapidly flying clouds, and when it appears at long intervals red and ominous like a meteor, Oh! how truly consistent is its funereal gleam with a night of storm and of despair!

And what a terrible night was that! The boiling billows, high and impetuous, and covered with white foam, commingled together in one vast whirlpool; and if at times the tempest lowered its voice of thunder, and murmured only through the hollows formed by the waves, it seemed to recover fresh vigour from that momentary repose. And then a sharp and long whistling rent the air; and that was succeeded by a hoarse and rumbling din which appeared to emanate from the very entrails of the earth—and upon these conflicting noises would break short and plaintive sounds which resembled the cries of human agony.

And with every wave the raft experienced a new shock; and it spun round upon the uneven surface of that tremendous sea, for it had neither helm, nor mast, nor oars to guide

THE FEMALE BLUEBEARD:

OR

The Adventurer.

BY EUGENE SUE.

CHAP. I. THE UNICORN.

TOWARDS the end of May, 1690, the ship Unicorn left la Rochelle for the island of Martinique. Capt. Daniel commanded the vessel, which was armed with twelve nine-pounders—a defensive precaution exceedingly necessary, for not only were we at war with England, but the Spanish pirates cruised constantly to leeward of the West Indies, despite the strenuous efforts of our privateers. Among the few passengers of the Unicorn, the Rev. Father Griffon was the most remarkable. He was returning to Martinique, to take renewed charge of the parish of Macouba, of which he had the cure during several years, to the great satisfaction of the inhabitants and slaves of the locality. The very

The first issue of one of Eugène Sue's most bizarre penny serials, "The Female Bluebeard".

it. But as the principles of its construction were such that it offered no resistance to the fury of the angry main, it would not sink: it merely succumbed beneath the force of every billow which broke over it; and, while it was submerged for a moment, its platform was completely swept by the raging torrents.

And for five days that terrible storm had lasted! Thus, it was no longer the gay and gallant crew of the once lively *Salamandre* that now occupied the frail raft: it was a troop of ghastly and miserable objects! It was a number of beings without names—discoloured, cadaverous, their garments wet through and through, their long hair hanging over their shoulders, their eyes wild and glaring, their bleeding and cracked lips wreathed in hideous and mocking smiles—for during five days those emaciated creatures had experienced the horrors of famine! They were a prey to all the imperious nature of their wants—beyond their vital instinct, all with them was as with the dead! Hunger gnawed their entrails, thirst burnt their throats: their wounds, red and painful, were rendered the more galling by the salt of the ocean that dashed over them—rage was in their breasts, curses upon their tongues. And still they clung to life—to that life, with all its agony! Arrived at such a pitch, with them suicide was impossible; for suicide is the effect of a reasoning faculty, and that faculty was lost to them!

Moreover, suicide is but little in vogue where misery and privation abound. Suicide requires sumptuous and intoxicating repasts—perfumes and women—flowers and costly wines. Suicide must concentrate in one single joy all other pleasures known or dreamt of, and fill its jewelled cup with the essence of every bliss; and then, having drained the goblet to the dregs, suicide must exclaim, "The bowl is empty. Adieu!" Then only can existence disgust, because it has brimmed over on every side.

But in the midst of miseries the most horrible—when scarcely a spark of life remains—oh! how that flickering light is cherished—watched—and cared for, as if it were the last ember of a fire which we would not wish altogether extinguished. Thus, on board the raft, did those wretched beings cling to existence; although, to support the thirty people that survived, there were only three pounds of biscuit and a small barrel of wine.

With one accord the unhappy creatures could have put an end to that horrible state of agony. But, no—they must live—live in tears, in hatred, in torture, and in crime. And, what matter how they lived? They did live!

And amongst them no longer existed the distinctions of father and son—officers and subordinates—women and girls. On that miserable raft were beings who were devoured with hunger, and who in order to eat, would attempt everything. Good luck to the strong; misery to the weak!

One man alone, however, appeared to be above the pinching wants which oppressed the others; this was Szaffie. He was still the same—calm, unmoved, and cold. Standing near the stump of the broken jury-mast, on which he leant with one hand, he tranquilly observed all that was passing around him.

At every shock occasioned by the waves, some bent their heads upon their breast, others endeavoured to oppose the force of the billows with a feeble plank, and a few, lying on their backs in a species of lethargic indifference, with their glassy and listless eyes wide open, gnawed a piece of rope, or a glove, which hazard had thrown in their way. Some, whose legs were caught between the planks of the raft and were nearly shattered in their concussions with the waves, laughed wildly, reckless of pain. Grief and hunger had made them mad. The greater portion, standing, and huddled together in the centre of the raft, obeyed, like an inanimate mass, the oscillation of the frail platform which separated them from eternity. On one side were Paul, his father, the old Doctor Garnier, who loved the crew as if they were his own children, Alice and her aunt, and Szaffie.

A remnant of subordination had hitherto left the officers in command of the little food which was yet upon the raft.

The lieutenant supported himself upon the cask of wine, and watched his son Paul, who in his turn was gazing upon Alice.

Alice, seated upon the raft with her head supported upon her emaciated arms, never took her eyes off Szaffie. Madame de Blêne saw nothing, felt nothing—she was inert.

The tempest now seemed to redouble its violence; and the raft, floating upon the mighty waves, which hurled it up to heaven and then dashed it fifty feet into an abyss beneath, was sometimes almost perpendicular in that chaos of storm and danger. It was in vain that the officers endeavoured to give the men certain orders which would enable them to resist the shocks thus occasioned by the motion of the raft. They were not listened to.

At this terrible crisis, the sailors, fancying themselves to be in danger of death, and after a few words exchanged amongst them, advanced towards the place where their superiors were standing.

"We want wine!" cried La Joie, the boatswain, brandishing an axe: "we want wine, that we may die in peace!"

Pierre Huet rose suddenly from his recumbent position over the cask, and, presenting a pistol at the head of the ringleader, exclaimed, "Wretch—it is our only resource. We must economise it to the utmost of our power!"

"Ah! ha!" cried La Joie, knocking down the muzzle of the pistol. "It will not harm any one here—the powder is wet. Wine! wine!"

"Wine! wine!" shouted the sailors. "Give us the wine—or die!"

"You dare revolt!" exclaimed the lieutenant, looking round for a cutlass.

"There are no longer any officers here!" was the reply. "We are the stronger—give us the wine!"

"Never!" said the lieutenant.

"We will have it!" rejoined La Joie, advancing in a menacing way towards Pierre Huet.

Paul rushed upon him to protect his father; but the boatswain knocked the youth down with the axe; and Pierre, in an attempt to avenge his son, was wounded also. Then, covered with blood, furious, and not knowing what they did, both father and son, supported by the doctor and two faithful sailors, endeavoured to oppose the designs of the mutinous crew; but they were beaten back, and forced to succumb.

In the midst of that infernal tumult, Madame de Blêne, carried by the crowd of mutinous sailors towards the edge of the raft, fell into the sea, and was borne away by the waves, vainly extending her hands to Alice for assistance. But Alice saw her aunt disappear without being able to succour her; for she was compelled to hold by an iron ring in one of the planks to prevent herself from sharing the same fate.

"Wine! wine!" shouted La Joie, with one hand upon the cask, and the other flourishing a tin cup over his head.

"Wine! wine!" exclaimed the others. "Let us drink our last stoup, and die drunk!"

And they rushed with one accord upon the cask, which was immediately broken open and speedily emptied. Intoxication soon worked its baneful effects upon those brains which had been attenuated by want and privation; and, amidst the howling of the tempest and the roaring of the infuriate sea, they began to chant strange glees in hoarse voices; and their song resembled the hymn of a madman! By the reddish light of the portentous moon some endeavoured to dance upon the raft, but they tottered at every step, and then, blinded by ebriety, fell upon the spars, rolled here and there for some moments, and at length disappeared in the surrounding billows without uttering a single cry!

The Parisian—such was the nick-name given to one of the sailors by his comrades—suddenly espied Alice crouched up by the empty barrel, and desperately clinging with one hand to the iron ring, while with the other she supported her once lovely head.

"There—drink," cried the Parisian, who was thoroughly intoxicated: "drink—I say!"—and he placed the tin cup to the lips of the young girl.

Alice drank with avidity every drop that remained in the

cup; and her countenance became flushed with a sudden glow.

"You begin to look pretty again," cried the Parisian. "So for my trouble you may as well permit me—"

And the inebriate wretch with his foul lips imprinted a kiss upon the mouth of Alice; and the young girl, as she scarcely pushed him aside, exclaimed, "Oh; that wine has done me so much good! I am still thirsty: give me more—oh! give me more!"

"Paul," said Szaffie, "look there!"—and he pointed towards Alice and the sailor. "Do you see that?"—then, leaning towards the unhappy youth, who was suffering with the blow inflicted by La Joie, he added, "It is as I thought. Such is human nature! Dost thou now believe in innate virtue—in innate modesty? Oh, no—rest assured that subordination, chastity, devotion, love—and all the fine feelings that concrete in the breast of man—all, all yield to the irresistible influence of hunger and thirst. Noble sentiments, which depend upon such ignoble wants!"

Paul did not hear all that Szaffie whispered to him: he was absorbed in his own misfortunes, and those of his father.

"Oh! you shall hear me—you shall not swoon away before I have done speaking!" cried Szaffie, with a demoniac smile; and he poured some cordial, which he had about him, into the youth's mouth.

"Oh! pity me—pity me—add not fresh horrors to this already too terrible scene!" exclaimed Paul, recovering his senses.

"I am your saviour, child!" said Szaffie. "Eat—eat!" and, having cautiously opened the red portfolio, which he had brought with him from the wreck, and which was supposed to contain papers, he took from thence a piece of solid meat-substance, and gave it to Paul.

Paul carried it greedily to his lips: then, after a moment of sublime reflection, he stopped, broke it into three little pieces, and dragged himself towards his father. Alice was too far off—he had not strength enough to crawl up to her.

THE RAFT OF DEATH

Two days after the tempest was entirely calmed.

The sky was blue—the air pure—and the sun rose gorgeously from his palace in the eastern main.

The wine was all gone—the biscuit crushed under foot or spoilt by the salt water—and the miserable creatures upon the raft were fain to crush hats, shoes, and ropes. Some had, in their ebriate madness, drank the salt water with avidity. Others put nails and little pieces of lead into their mouths, with the hope that the metallic moisture would abrogate a portion of their thirst. A sailor was slain in a dispute relative to a leathern waistband which each wanted to possess. The old Doctor Garnier was killed to supply food for the famished crew: he died in cursing those whom he used to call his children. The Parisian was drawn in a lottery to decide who should be the next victim! But this execrable food only served to abridge the existence of those who partook of it.

With difficulty could two or three sailors, besides Szaffie, maintain themselves upon their feet. They kept their eyes intently fixed upon the horizon, and watched its vapoury boundary with the most painful anxiety.

"A sail! a sail!" was the feeble cry that suddenly issued from the lips of those wretched men.

Szaffie in particular watched the spot where the sail appeared with the utmost attention; for he himself began to entertain the most dire apprehensions. At the moment when the *Salamandre* struck, he had provided himself with his writing-case, in which he placed a substance exceedingly nourishing, and concentrated in a very small space.* Up to this moment he had therefore escaped the tortures of hunger: but his means of existence diminished; and he lost all hope of seeing the raft cast upon the African coast by the currents, for the wind had impelled it afar from land. It was

*Venison, mashed into a paste, and dried with sugar. The Indians, in their long hunting excursions, carry no other food. An ounce a day is sufficient for a man even in a robust state of health.

therefore with an expression of joy that he exclaimed, "A sail! a sail!"

That magic word—"A sail!"—was echoed by even the lips of the dying. Glazing eyes recovered a gleam of lost fire —the wounded rose with difficulty—and every glance was directed towards the spot indicated by Szaffie. Others joined their hands together—many burst out into loud and wild shouts of laughter—and a few were so happy as to shed tears in profusion! For a moment grief was dumb—hunger appeased—and thirst quenched! Hope eradicated every sentiment of hatred; and all unkind feelings were banished by the thought that succour was at hand. And then those men, lately so fierce—so cruel—so terrible, rushed into each other's arms, shook each other's hands, and gave vent to the most unfeigned joy.

Paul and his father exchanged a significant glance, and indulged in a long and fervent embrace. And Alice, poor girl! sat dozing near the ring which it was not any longer necessary for her to hold, as the sea was now calm; but she understood not the meaning of the joyous shout, "A sail!" Alas—poor child!

And the sail gradually became more distinct; and at length a large frigate was discernible in the horizon, its white canvass reflecting the rays of the effulgent sun. Oh! how delicious was that moment—when all doubt disappeared— and when that sign of safety was welcomed by the enfeebled voices of the suffering crew!

The sailors, who had before mutinied and blasphemed, now felt a species of religious gratitude steal into their breasts: their lacerated hearts could not contain so exceeding a joy; and they experienced the necessity of pouring forth their souls in prayer and thanksgiving.

Their burning eyes were moistened with tears:—it was a sublime picture, those men—pale—emaciated—and suffering—joining their hands together to thank God for so unexpected a relief! And the frigate drew nearer—and nearer towards the raft.

"We shall leave the raft in the manner prescribed by the articles of war in cases of shipwreck," said the lieutenant, mechanically resuming the reins of discipline.

"Yes—yes, lieutenant!" said the sailors with one joyous accord.

"The lady first," continued Pierre Huet—"then the cabin-boys—thirdly, the midshipman and the passengers—next the sailors—and lastly, myself and my son."

"You never will be able to climb on board without the help of the accommodation-ladder," said Paul to his father with a cunning smile.

"My dear child," returned the fond parent, "I know not what secret voice told me that we should not be separated yet awhile. And in sooth! heaven could not part us; for I employed its aid often enough for thee, my boy—Oh! I prayed for thy safety night and day! And heaven never abandons those who pray with sincerity; as this unlooked-for aid must prove to you."

"My mother has often said the same," replied the affectionate young man, kissing his father's cheek with tenderness and reliance on all he had affirmed.

"Heavens!" cried Szaffie at this moment, in a tone of deep emotion and alarm: "what does that mean?" he added —as he pointed out the frigate to a sailor who was occupied in preparations for a speedy departure from the raft.

"She can't bear down upon us, Sir," replied the man; "but as the tide will—Oh!—no—no."

And the man screamed like an infant disappointed in its desire to possess some toy.

"Rage—hell—damnation!" ejaculated Szaffie, suddenly stamping his foot with violence upon the planks beneath him.

"What is the matter?" demanded Pierre Huet.

"She has not seen us," returned Szaffie, in a voice of thunder, his eyes flashing fire, and his teeth grinding against each other. "Ah! ha! my fine singer of psalms—heaven never deserts those who pray—eh?"—and the irony of that man pierced like a dagger to every heart.

"Oh! it is impossible!" cried the lieutenant.

It was, however, too true. The frigate luffed, and was speedily out of sight. So long as even the faintest outline of its sails were perceptible upon the horizon, the occupants of the raft would not give up all hope: they could not—dared not believe that destiny, or fate, or heaven could have prepared for them so atrocious a mockery!

But when the vessel had entirely disappeared—when nothing but the sun glanced on the waters of the Mediterranean, calm and deserted—Oh! it was then that the horrors of their situation were felt in all their acuteness—all their poignancy! And, as is the case in all moral and physical reactions, a state of torpor—of feebleness—of incapacity, succeeded to that predicament of exaltation and of joy.

This prostration of the nerves lasted some minutes; that length of time appeared to be necessary for those wretched men to precipitate themselves from the eminence of sanguine hope to the depths of the darkest despair.

When the horrors of their situation were again felt in all their intenseness—when they once more saw themselves face to face with the most awful of deaths—and when (the sky, the sea, and the horizon being without a speck) these terrible convictions rushed to the heart of each, cold and piercing like the bite of a dying man,—oh! then what a dread commingling of oaths and prayers, blasphemies and supplications, and cries of rage and of death, ascended to that heaven which a few minutes before had been so sincerely invoked by all!

And then, also, those, who ere now had embraced each other, felt the sentiments of hatred, and the pangs of hunger, more acutely than before; and the wretched mortals, to avenge their miseries, as it were, upon each other, rushed in wild tumult together, and fought with exasperation and frenzy.

Szaffie also uttered a terrible cry, which was wrung from him by an acute pain, and fell senseless upon the raft. For one of the famished creatures was endeavouring to cut a morsel of flesh from his leg!

On the following morning, this access of frenzied rage had passed away—and hunger had once more stifled every other feeling. Pierre and his son were lying close to each other—their tottering reason seemed to be ready to abandon them—everything appeared to turn round, as if they were under the influence of wine.

"Paul," said Pierre, in a faint and hollow voice, "I am very hungry. Have you no more of that meat which you gave me yesterday morning?"

"It was Szaffie's," returned Paul.

"Has he any more?" demanded the lieutenant.

"I think he must have," was the reply.

"Let us take it from him by force," said Pierre.

And they both dragged themselves towards Szaffie, who appeared to be motionless. Pierre placed one knee upon his stomach and held a dagger to his throat, while Paul rifled his pockets. The red box was speedily found, and opened.

"Give it to me," cried the father to his son.

"Wait a moment," exclaimed Paul.

"No—no—give it to me," persisted the famished sire.

"It is mine," said the son to the father, breaking off a piece of the small remaining portion of the comestible, and carrying it to his lips.

"I will have it—or—"

And Pierre rushed upon his offspring with a wild howl and a savage look.

A terrible struggle ensued, and Szaffie recovered from his swoon.

"Oh! you have robbed me and you wished to assassinate me!" cried Szaffie, in a feeble voice. "You see, Paul," he added, as the father and son continued to wrestle together, "that the poniard must decide between you two. Now— parricide—now, infanticide—and all for a mouthful of food! Ha! ha!"

The night soon put an end to that scene of horror; and

on the following morning Szaffie, awakening out of a heavy and deep sleep, fancied that he had been under the influence of a nightmare.

It was mid-day. The vertical sun darted his hot rays upon the placid waters of the Mediterranean, on which the raft was almost motionless. The fragile ramparts of barrels, casks, and netting had been broken; and the actual platform alone remained upon that ocean which was now smooth and polished as a mirror. Here and there floated the remnants of garments, of cordage, and of planks, on which the sun shone gaily and gorgeously. The sailors, who survived, were all stretched upon the raft, their eyes brilliant, their lips red, their countenance flushed, animated, and resplendent. Only, instead of that soft and penetrating heat which their external appearance seemed to indicate, they were bathed in a cold sweat, and their members were stiff and iced. Except this phenomenon and a nervous *tic* which gave a singular and awful expression to every countenance, nothing bespoke the long torture to which they had been exposed. For some began to arrange their jackets, pull down their shirt sleeves, and tie their cravats, and exclaimed, "The lieutenant is going to commence the inspection: we must be decent and clean!" Others fancied that they saw in the distance a city resplendent with gold, and marble, and verdure; and they said, "That is Smyrna!"

"We have arrived, then," observed one. "O God! how lovely is that prospect. There are the domes—and the harbour—and the orange-trees; and there are fair women who beckon to us."

And then they who laboured under this delusion, took each other's arms to advance towards the city, and falling from the raft into the sea, they sank to rise no more, save as disfigured and inanimate corpses. The waters rippled for a moment—and the ocean became still and tranquil as before.

Similar delusions continued with those who were left. Some commenced a gay waltz to celebrate their near approach to land: alas! the dance was commenced upon the raft and finished in the waters. Others fancied that they were in the cottages where they were born, surrounded by their wives and children, and all that was dear to them. And they melted into tears—and they blessed their offspring—and promised their wives to tempt the dangers of the ocean no more!

But all this was done with a smile upon the lips, or with tears in their eyes, as circumstances seemed to suggest: it was an illusion which was expressed by voices so convincing and so natural, that a blind man would have taken those aberrations of fever for undoubted realities!

At the sight of this horrible drama, Szaffie was stupefied with silent horror. He and Paul were now the only two that retained their faculties unimpaired. And therefore was it with the most terrible emotion that they perceived Alice rise with an almost supernatural force from the place where she had hitherto remained seated. She was emaciated and haggard; but her eyes shone with supernatural lustre—her cheeks were suffused in a scarlet hue—and her lips were red as if they were dyed with gore.

She advanced towards Szaffie: Paul concealed his face in his hands.

"O Szaffie," said Alice in a tender and touching tone of voice, "you are mine—my lover—my adored one!"

Paul endeavoured to withdraw to another part of the raft: but his feet and hands refused to aid him to drag himself away.

"I thought I loved Paul, poor fellow," continued Alice: "but I only looked upon him as a brother—that was all! But you—oh! you, Szaffie—you are my lover," she continued with pride; "and every look of yours is for me a pleasure and a torment at the same time. Oh! your caresses—since that day, when almost in the very face of death, I gave myself entirely up to thee—those caresses have made too deep an impression upon me ever to be abrogated! From that day my life has been one long—long pleasure; for your kisses—they are still upon my lips!"

"Oh! let me die," ejaculated Paul in a tone of voice that pierced to the very heart of those who heard him, madmen as they were.

"Who speaks of death?" cried Alice, gazing wildly around her. "To live with you, Szaffie—to live with you, is my only hope. Come, Szaffie, come—my aunt is dead as well as my father and my mother—as well as all the rest of the world for me! Come, then, I am thine, Szaffie. This is our blue curtain," she continued, pointing to the sky; "that is my white bed," she added, indicating the ocean; "and on every side are the flowers that you love! Come, my love—for I am thine—and thou art mine. What matters the scorn of the world to me? I can say to thee, without asking the permission of a soul, 'Thou art mine!' For thou art my world, Szaffie."

The eyes of Szaffie sparkled as she spoke.

"Now let my long hair float wildly upon the winds," continued the unfortunate girl, pretending to disengage her tresses from the large comb which confined them. "That long hair, Szaffie, which you loved so much—that long dark hair —Oh! let it float over my shoulders. And now, my love— my Szaffie—come—hasten—I go before thee—and shall wait in the bridal chamber. Oh, come!"

And the poor girl beckoned Szaffie to follow her—and she hastened towards the edge of the raft, as if she would endeavour to walk upon the surface of the sea—and she sank in the deep abyss of waters below.

Paul gave vent to a terrible cry, and stretched out his hands, as if that useless movement would save her.

"Monster!" he exclaimed. "Not one single effort to recover her!"

Her last word was "Szaffie!"

"She dies happy in her illusions," said that individual in a hoarse voice, while a tear stood upon his eye-lash.

"Alice! Alice! My father—father—Alice!" cried Paul, wringing his hands, a prey to the most acute agony.

15

THE MAD WOLF

by Ned Buntline

ON THE OTHER side of the Atlantic in America cheap periodicals were similarly booming in the 1830s with adventures of frontier life and the War of Independence enjoying the greatest popularity. There was not the same tradition of penny-issue works as in Europe, but many full-length novels made simultaneous appearances in both bound and paper editions. Anonymity cloaked most of the writers in the sensational school, but there is little doubt that two men, E. Z. C. Judson and J. H. Ingraham, enjoyed the widest sales and both were held in almost similar esteem to the great James Fennimore Cooper, then the most popular American novelist. To draw a parallel, Judson—who wrote under the pen-name Ned Buntline—and Ingraham were the American equivalent of Rymer and Prest in England, and de Kock and Sue in France. They were prodigious writers, gifted with extraordinary imaginations, and pursued the most incredible life-styles. Their work was invariably pirated throughout Europe—perhaps the greatest compliment that could be paid to any writer in these days before effective copyright protection—just as the new American publishers were quick to extract what they wanted from across the Atlantic. English and European publications of the time are replete with stories by American authors—rarely attributed —and Washington Irving, Edgar Allan Poe and Nathaniel Hawthorne suffered as much as any from this pirating.

It has been maintained by some critics that the worst American fiction was so crudely sensational and morally unpleasant that it had a detrimental effect on English taste, but I think in the light of what we have already seen of publications in both Britain and France that this is perhaps a piece of nationalistic jingoism. Undoubtedly, though, the tales of prairie and frontier life did add a new dimension to modern fiction and should be regarded as the most important element in the American contribution.

After Fennimore Cooper, the writer to exploit this area most was Edward Zane Carroll Judson (1823–1866) whose life was as dramatic and eventful as that of any Penny Dreadful hero. Born in Stamford, New York, he displayed a penchant for adventure from his earliest days and ran away to sea when barely in his teens. He quickly rose to become an apprentice and then, for a remarkable display of heroism in 1838 when a boat capsized, he was made a midshipman. His career at sea continued for several more years, and of these *The New York Times* has noted, "as in strength, activity and capacity for mischief he was already the equivalent of his weight in wild-cats, his nautical days were correspondingly eventful". His restless nature, however, was not long satisfied at sea, and in 1842 he resigned from the navy and took himself off for two years into the American wilds where he is believed to have soldiered in the Seminole Wars and then worked for a fur company in the Yellowstone region.

In 1844 he began to develop his other natural ability—as a writer—and because of the drama and authenticity of his stories was eagerly accepted by publishers. He had already adopted the pen-name Ned Buntline for his work and sensing his popularity, founded the first of several publications bearing his name. This also did not satisfy him for long, however, and he was soon off to Kentucky where he set out single-handedly to capture three men wanted for murder. He brought in two of them, collected a bounty of $600, and used this to start his second magazine, *Ned Buntline's Own* in Nashville. By all accounts this was a "scandal sheet", and in 1846, Judson was himself involved in trouble again when he shot and fatally wounded a certain Robert Porterfield, with whose wife he had been carrying on an affair. Arrested, he was brought before the local court and underwent an experience that was straight out of the pages of a Penny Dreadful. As he stood in the witness box, one of Porterfield's brothers opened fire on him from the back of the court and he was forced to flee from the room in a hail of bullets. Returned to the jail, he was seized by a mob during the night and hanged in the nearby square. Amazingly his neck was not broken, and a friend cut down his "corpse" and smuggled him back to the jail again where he was revived. Following this remarkable escape, the Grand Jury failed to convict him on the charges and he wisely decided to move to New York. Here he briefly revived *Ned Buntline's Own*, but the wanderlust was still in him and the next few years saw him serving in the Mexican war, leading political demonstrations and generally following a riotous career. As a public figure Judson was by now widely known, and in 1850—after a year in prison for disorderly conduct—formed the "Know Nothing" Party. Unfortunately, however, because of his criminal record he could not stand for office, and without his presence the group collapsed in 1856.

Throughout all this activity, Judson had continued to write sensational fiction with a predominantly American background which became widely popular. As the *Dictionary of American Biography* has put it, "He was in fact the first of the dime novelists, having invented the technique and brought it to perfection some twelve years before the firm of Beadle and Adams popularized the form". He was frequently the hero of his own tales and drew heavily on his personal experience. His popularity—always high—soared still further and in time he became extremely wealthy, living in a huge mansion and keeping a steam yacht on the Hudson River. Still, life had one more fling of adventure to offer him. In 1862 he joined the army, but so discreditable was his conduct that in 1864 he was reduced to the ranks and then discharged completely. During this period he had become friendly with a certain William Frederick Cody who, like him, had enjoyed a colourful life in the old west. Renaming him "Buffalo Bill", Judson began a whole series of adventures featuring this retired hunter, and quickly turned him into a household name. Shortly thereafter, however, the two men parted company when Cody began to feel that his partner was taking more than his share of their proceeds.

For the remainder of his life, the now ageing Judson lived in retirement in New York, turning out a steady stream of highly readable novels dealing with pirates, "The King of the Sea"; city life, "The Mysteries and Miseries of New York", after the style of Sue and Reynolds; Indians, "Thayendanegea the Scourge; or The War Eagle of the Mohawks"; and the wild west, "Life in the Saddle; or The Cavalry Scout". It has been reported that he spent his last years in some pain due to the several unextracted bullets still lodged in his body from his earlier roistering life.

To represent Judson—Ned Buntline to be correct—I have selected a typical short story from his pen, replete with drama, suspense and no little bloodshed.

The Mad Wolf

In the month of October 1833, I was on my return from a trapping tour on Green River, the Grand Colorado of the West, in company with three companions, one named Alexandre, a half-breed, Verboncœur, a Frenchman, and an American named Worthington. After a long day's tramp, we halted in a nest of timber, upon a tributary of the Colorado, immediately bordering upon a wide-spreading prairie; and, having pitched our tent, and tied the animals, we started out to reconnoitre the neighbourhood surrounding the camp-ground.

The country we had been travelling over all day lay

The title-page illustration for Ned Buntline's short story, "The Mad Wolf".

immediately in the path of the roving bands of Arapaho and Crow Indians, and the former tribe was the white man's inveterate foe. Caution, therefore, counselled us to examine the track imprinted around us before we resigned ourselves to security and repose.

Having mounted a willow-covered ridge near the encampment, I descended into a small valley on our right, and had not proceded far before I descried smoke issuing from the covert. Carefully approaching the spot, I soon discovered a numerous war party encampment of Crows; and, as they were friendly to the company I belonged to, without hesitation I entered the circle seated around the fire. All seized their weapons, with a general exclamation of "how!" when, informing them, in their own language, that I was Little Wolf—a name conferred upon by me an old chief of the tribe while I was sojourning at their village—they immediately remembered me, and all signs of hostilities were stayed between us. After a friendly shaking of hands, and a short smoke of the calumet, I obtained all the information I needed relative to the Arapahoes, and with pleasure learned that the war parties of the Crows had driven them far from the southern hunting grounds. The chief of the party, and a number of his braves, accompanied me a short distance on my return, and, when we parted, it was with mutual expressions of friendship.

On arriving at camp, I found my companions awaiting my coming. Each reported his observations, and the information which I imparted was received with general satisfaction. It also confirmed their several reports, all declaring their search yielded no signs of hostile footsteps.

Every preparation was now made for a night of uninterrupted repose, and everything promised the luxury. Our wearied march, with the unceasing watchfulness necessary for safety, had worn us down, until a night of unbroken sleep was looked forward to as the greatest boon circumstances could confer upon us. A foe would not approach us in the position we occupied, with our friends, the Crows, posted in such close proximity—they were nearly within hail, certainly within sound of our guns. A final examination of the *lariat* ropes which confined our animals, and then a short smoke— the trapper's greatest luxury—was indulged in; after which, spreading the buffalo robes, we dropped off into a sound slumber that needed no artificial aids to prolong its soundness.

How long we had lain in sleep I know not; but, all at once, with a suddenness which started repose into flight, I felt myself jerked from the robe on which I was resting. My first thought was, that Indians had attacked us; but the light of the fire disclosed my antagonist to be a wolf, which had seized and still held me fast by the left hand. I had no weapon within my reach, so, without hesitation, I struck him with my shut fist, and, delivering the blow upon his grinning muzzle with all my force, I broke his hold, but, in doing so, lacerated my thumb against his tusk. The whole was but the work of a moment. Alexandre, who lay nearest to me, aroused himself, and no sooner was I released from the infuriated beast, than it seized him by the cheek. He choked it off, when, by this time, Verboncœur and Worthington having secured their knives, they rushed upon the animal. Each inflicted wounds upon him; but both were bitten. With a howl that curdled the hearer's blood, our assailant fled and disappeared in the darkness.

This sudden and violent interruption to our slumbers was not endured with Christian meekness, nor commented on in those choice epithets which bespeak a delightful surprise. On the contrary, we indulged in a few bitter expletives against this nocturnal visitor; and, having thus in a measure appeased the wrath within us, we hastily bound up the wounds we had received, and once more forgot our dangers in the oblivion of sleep.

When morning broke, all sallied forth in different directions, filled with revengeful purposes against the wolf, believing that he would lurk in our neighbourhood. But, after an extended search, we were forced to forego the promised revenge, and vent our anger in declarations of what we would have done if chance had only placed him within gun-shot. On my return I again encountered the Crow party, the chief of which informed me that a *mad wolf* had visited their camp the night previous. He had been driven off, however, before he had bitten any of their party. This intelligence chilled my blood with a horrid apprehension; and when he added that the animal fled in the direction of our camp, I felt assured. he had been our fierce visitor. With gloomy forebodings of coming ill, I returned to my companions, who were preparing for a start.

Everything being in readiness, we departed from the camping ground, and, holding our way down the valley, came upon the great Crow trace, where, discovering the tracks of a large party of white men, we followed it up, and fell in with a trapping party of the North American Company.

From them I obtained some whisky and salt, which I applied to my wounds, and, advising my companions to take the same precaution, I intimated that the animal which bit us might be rabid. They laughed at my fears; but after, as I thought, sufficiently amusing themselves about my "womanish" dread of a wolf-bite, I checked their mirth by imparting to them the intelligence I had gained from the Crows. Having, however, commenced amusing themselves at the expense of my fears, in a spirit of bravado they continued. I was awed by a presentiment of coming evil, and exhibited it, no doubt, in my countenance. Moreover, between dread of the wounds I had received, and chagrin at their ill-timed merriment, I was influenced to drink freely of the liquor. My stolid air of indifference, together with my continued libations, alarmed them, for I was habitually temperate as regarded drink, but the reverse in passion. An outburst of anger on my part would have been natural, and have amused them; but my troubled countenance, coupled with the quiet despair of my actions, made them uneasy, and they watched me with interest.

The liquor first made keen my sensibilities, then imparted a reckless indifference, which was followed by a stupor of deep intoxication; and, wrapped in its attendant robe of oblivion, I forgot the previous night's encounter. The songs and adventures related around the camp fire on that night were unheard by me, and both companies were prepared to separate in the morning before they aroused me from my deep sleep. All the painful feelings of intoxication awoke with me, and, stupid and sick, I made my way to the halting-ground, and laved my head and body in its cooling waters. Here Worthington, one of my companions, separated from us, and joined the other company. Bidding him and the party adieu, we turned our horses' heads, and again took up the line of march for the Laramie river. We were in a region where danger lurked in every bush, and where the footsteps of human beings brought hostility, almost as surely as the clouds betoken rain. Thus far through the whole season of trapping we had escaped unhurt, and were returning, richly laden with spoils.

But while successfully avoiding the savage foe, a hidden one was at work in our midst, more terrible than the painted warriors of the wild desert—more appalling in its promised fatality than the torturing knife of the ruthless red man. *Hydrophobia*, in all its horrid panoply of terrors, looked out from the eyes that surrounded me, and I thought the madness was reflected back from my own.

On the day we crossed *Cache-à-la-Poudre*, a colt, on which we had strapped some light articles, betrayed symptoms of the malady, and for the first time we found out he had been bitten. Alexandre and Verboncœur had fastened their guns upon his back, to relieve themselves of the burthen while climbing the river banks, and now with dismay they observed him break loose from the mule to which he was tied, and with a yell of terror fly from the stream we had just crossed, the foam gathering around his mouth, indicating with certainty the cause of his frantic actions. The arms he bore away were necessary for our protection. I, therefore, started in pursuit, but the mad animal being lightly laden, soon left my jaded mule far behind, and dashing over a ledge to our left, ere I reached the promontory he was entirely lost to view. Misfortune appeared to have thrown her mantle over us, and to a dread of the disease which threatened us was now added the loss of weapons.

Continuing our course down the borders of the Laramie, which became frozen over by the continued cold weather, we approached the North Fork of the Platte, and while in its immediate neighbourhood, fancied we observed the colt quietly grazing in a plain before us. Leaving Alexandre, who complained of being ill, in the tent, Verboncœur and myself started in pursuit. A flicker of hope stole about our hearts that this might indeed be the runaway animal, free from hydrophobia, which had fled, started by the close proximity of a beast of prey, or had been only stung to momentary madness by some venomous insect. As we neared the animal, all hopes fled; distance and our ardent wishes had converted the hump of a buffalo into the semblance of a pack, which, on nearer approach, resolved itself into its real character, and cast us back again into a state of despondency. At this moment, a cry from my companion, who was pointing towards the camp, directed my attention thitherward, and the next moment I beheld our tent on fire, and the half-breed flourishing around his head a burning faggot. We instantly turned our horses' heads, and rode with all speed towards him; as we approached, he started off the pack-mules with his brand, and when we reached the spot all our worst fears were confirmed—he was a howling *madman*!

After a violent struggle, in which he inflicted severe blows upon us both, we succeeded in securing his arms, and, having bound him upon a pallet of skins, we drove stakes into the frozen ground and there tied him. While he raved and howled, all the savage in his nature made predominant by his malady, Verboncœur and myself sat weighed down with horrid dread, and were contemplating each other with fear. I fancied I beheld a wild expression in his eyes, and no doubt he observed the same in mine. Alexandre, in the meantime, recovered from his convulsion, and, in tones of earnest supplication, besought us to end his torture, by sending a bullet through his brain. His supplications but echoed the thoughts which were coursing through my mind—I was meditating suicide with all the coolness of a wretch whose cup of despair is full, and the tide of which but lingers on the brim. Another, and another convulsion followed the progress of the disease upon our poor Alexandre. In his terrible paroxysms he tore one arm loose from the cords, and, with a howl, began to rend it with his teeth. When we secured the limb he tried to seize his shoulder; this we prevented by placing a strap across his forehead, and fastening it on each side with stakes. He now bit his lips with fury, and the blood and foam gathered about them in his agony, while the pupil of his dark eye shot fire, and the ball, which, a few days previous, was white as the snow upon the hills, assumed a hue as red as blood. All other dangers vanished before this one—the savage foe no longer inspired fear; indeed, he would have been welcomed to a conflict which promised for us certain death. As the sun of that day of sorrow went down, the half-breed's paroxysms became more violent, and, seating ourselves beside his rude mountain couch, we watched him through the gloom of night. Morning at length dawned, and we were rejoiced that, with its first blush, the spirit of our comrade fled, leaving his tortured body to its long sleep.

Alexandre's knife had been carried off by the colt, with the guns; and the amount of arms between Verboncœur and myself was one rifle, two knives, and a pistol; of these my companion had but a knife as his share, and I felt selfishly glad, for he was an athletic man, who, armed, in madness, would slay me in a moment; I, therefore, clutched the weapons I possessed with an eager gripe, and watched my comrade's motions with painful vigilance. We could not bury Alexandre's body, the earth being so frozen it was impossible to dig it with our knives; we, therefore, started down to the river, with the intention of cutting a hole through the ice, and depositing it in the stream, out of reach of the wolves. Verboncœur first commenced cutting, but had not succeeded in making a crevice before he snapped his knife-blade off about midway. This accident, at any time while in the mountains, would have been looked upon as a great misfortune. In our situation it was viewed as a frightful calamity— a loss which rendered us weak and helpless in defence, and which it was impossible to replace; and yet, paradox as it may seem, while I grieved I rejoiced, for, while it diminished the number of our weapons, it robbed my companion of the only dangerous one he had left, and one I had looked upon with dread, represented to him the necessity of carefully preserving the other knife, and he assented; we, therefore, concluded not to risk it in the ice, but, folding up the remains of our dead companion in a buffalo robe, left it upon the prairie without sepulture, with the winds alone to murmur his dirge. So perished the first victim of the mad wolf!

When we again started, my companion asked me for the pistol in my belt, and the knife in my sheath, which he argued would be a fair division of the weapons, and I had no good reason for refusing him, other than my wakeful fears; but I put him off with an excuse that I wished to place them in proper order before I resigned them. He smiled, and we journeyed on. After observing his countenance for some time, I began to grow reassured—he looked calm and undisturbed, and his step displayed a firmness and decision which I believe could only belong to health in body and mind. While thus growing in hope and confidence, and when on the very eve of yielding up a weapon to him, a wolf howled in our immediate neighbourhood, and I could see him shudder, the muscles of his face contract, and his eye assume an unusual lustre, while a low groan broke from his heaving chest. I hugged the weapons in my possession with increased eagerness, and clung to them with a tenacity founded on absolute fear, for I conjectured, and rightly, that the seeds of the dread malady which carried off our half-breed companion were making themselves manifest in Verboncœur. In crossing a small branch which emptied into the Laramie, I again watched his features, and all the symptoms of hydrophobia burst forth in a paroxysm, unmistakeable in its character. He instantly rushed upon me, when with the heavy barrel of my rifle I felled him senseless—my fears had made me a Hercules in strength—and then leaping upon his insensible body I bound him with a *larsat* rope so tightly that in vain he struggled for freedom. I sat down beside him with my teeth clenched, and listened unmoved to his ravings and prayers for death—he, like Alexandre, besought me to despatch him—but finding his supplications moved me not, he broke into horrid imprecations and threats, in which he swore that he would kill me—that he would tear me with his teeth, and, bound as he was, he rolled his body towards me. I held him down to the earth, and he again relapsed into dreadful convulsions. My despair had now no lower depth. I looked upon my remaining comrade and shared in his agony, for I expected that, inevitable as fate, my turn would come next; and yet, with this belief preying at my heart, some unknown power of the human will held back my hand when I would have yielded to my comrade's entreaties for death.

At times the resolution to despatch him, and follow it with my own death, was on the very eve of being consummated, when a whisper of hope would bid me firmly to suffer on. Worn out nature could bear up no longer without repose, and so wearied was I in mind and body, that almost unconsciously I sunk into slumber. While the fire at my feet grew more and more dim, my senses wandered away in a delightful dream to the fireside of my old home, and the wildness of the trapper's life, its many perils and hardships, melted away in the soft sunlight of an autumn sky, which appeared to throw its golden beams over my far-off home. There the settler smoked his pipe in security, his household slumbered in peace, and the morning sun awoke him to enjoyment instead of fear. My dream had taken the hue of my hopes and wishes.

While my senses were thus wrapt, the report of fire-arms dispelled the vision, and not knowing for a moment whether it was a dream or reality, I sprung to my feet and felt for my pistol—it was gone! I stood for a moment collecting my thoughts, and partly waiting to feel the effects of a wound; but no sensation of pain manifesting itself, I seized a brand from the smouldering fire, and held it over my bound companion. All was solved at a glance—he had in his struggle released one arm, and a lucid fit intervening, poor Verboncœur had drawn the pistol from my belt while I slept, and ended his agony by his own hand.

I was now alone—far in the wilderness—a dreadful apprehension of the poison being in my veins ever present to my thoughts—and, thus seated in darkness by my dead companion, my heart bowed down, and my mind cheerless as the gloom surrounding me, I yielded to the feelings which were preying upon my manhood, and wept like a child. Morning at length dawned, and folding my dead companion up, as we together had previously bestowed the first victim, I mounted a mule, and, with the pack animals, pursued my solitary way. My march was now one of indifference, and, with a kind of foolish daring, I plunged through every stream impeding my progress, inviting, as it were, the madness I was sure would come. My progress was tedious, difficult, laborious, and full of hardships; but at length, almost worn down, I arrived at our trading post on the North Fork of the Platte. When I presented myself to the commander of the post, he did not recognize my gaunt form and seared visage. Suffering, both of body and mind, had so stamped my features, that I looked like some escaped maniac, and the uneasy appearance of my sunken eyes made old friends look upon me with suspicion—they thought I was crazed.

When I told my story, and showed the wounds upon my hands, inflicted by the rabid wolf, and related the death of my comrades, they shook their heads with doubt, and I could hear it whispered among them that some dreadful affray had occurred between us, resulting in their death. Others suggested that the savages had slain my companions, and that, through suffering alone in the wilderness, I had become insane. All these doubts worked upon my troubled mind until reason did indeed begin to totter upon its throne. A few days after my arrival at the North Fork post, an express rider arrived, who had passed a night in the camp of the American trapping party our companion, Worthington, had joined, and he not only had heard our encounter with the mad wolf related, but the fact of his having the malady dreadfully confirmed in the death of Worthington, who perished in their camp, under all the certain symptoms of hydrophobia. My story being thus confirmed, and painful suspicions removed, I felt a change in the tone of my mind; fears which had harboured there began to diminish in intensity, and no symptom of the much-dreaded malady appearing, hope grew strong within me. This produced a corresponding improvement in health, until gradually the marks of my dreadful march disappeared from both form and feature.

I have often since endeavoured to assign a cause for my escape, and have as frequently been led to attribute it to my free use of liquor and salt, at our meeting with the north-western trappers—combined, they nullified the poison. Thirteen years have passed since the adventure, and with a thankful heart I chronicle the fact, that no vestige of its effects remain, except the vivid recollection of our night encounter with the mad wolf of the prairies.

16

THE LEAGUE OF "THE THIRTY"

by J. H. Ingraham

SHARING EQUAL POPULARITY with Ned Buntline among American readers of sensational fiction, was another ex-seaman turned writer, Joseph Holt Ingraham (1809–1860). According to Louis James he "was one of the most prolific writers of his time and comes second only to Fennimore Cooper in the number of lower-class editions of his works". Unlike Cooper and Ned Buntline, however, he did not draw as extensively on personal experience, but was more concerned about social conditions and the abuse of morality, in the style of Reynolds in England and Sue in France. His life gives us some clues as to the formation of his viewpoint.

He was born in Portland, the grandson of one of the city's chief benefactors, a wealthy shipper, and perhaps not surprisingly went to sea in his youth. As a man he took up teaching and when installed in his first post in Washington, Mississippi, began to write the serials which were to make his name a household word. An early product, reflecting his interest in the sea, was "Lafitte" (1836) about the pirates of the gulf, which the *Dictionary of American Biography* says is "typical of his work in that it makes of an impossible series of events pegs on which to hang a luxurious fabric of Spanish treasure troves and Byronic ravings". During the middle 1830s and the late 1840s he wrote so much and so rapidly that all attempts to compile a full bibliography have failed.

An insight into Ingraham at this time has, however, been left to us by W. H. Longfellow who wrote in 1846 of a meeting with him. "He says he has written eighty novels, and of these twenty during the last year; till it has grown to be merely mechanical with him." This enormous production indicates how he was earning the then princely sum of $3,000 a year and living in either the north or the south of the country as the fancy took him. This movement is reflected in the titles of some of his works, such as "Scarlet Feather; or The Young Chief of the Abenaquies" (1843), and "Frank Rivers; or The Dangers of the Town" (1845), and in his growing concern for morality. This concern, which was to eventually direct him into abandoning authorship to enter the Church, can be strikingly contrasted to some of his books of the time such as "The Unhappy Bride; or The Grave of the Forsaken" (1847) which has been described as "licentious in the extreme". Nonetheless, in 1849 he married and two years later became a deacon in Natchez. He was not entirely finished with writing, however, and for the next few years devoted "the midnight hours stolen from parochial duties" to write three enormous religious romances which "aided in popularizing the novel form in America" (*Dictionary of American Biography*)—"The Prince of the House of David" (1855), "The Pillar of Fire" (1859) and "The Throne of David" (1860).

According to his grandson, Ingraham thereafter tried desperately to live down the popularity of his sensational works. "The income from his religious novels was used largely to buy up and destroy the copyrights of some of his early romances," the younger man tells us. Ingraham's life was to end tragically when he accidentally let off his own gun in the vestry of his church in Holly Springs, Mississippi, killing himself almost instantly.

Because of his dislike of them, many of Ingraham's earlier books have disappeared for ever, but I have been able to trace the following story set in the years just after the French Revolution which clearly illustrates his views on morality and the aristocracy. It is also, I believe, a horror story the equal of Ingraham's contemporary and fellow countryman, Edgar Allan Poe. (Perhaps before closing this small section devoted to America, I should mention the work of George Lippard (1823–1854), another sensational writer whose "The Quaker City; or The Monks of Monk Hall" (1844) ran into twenty-seven editions and put him for a time in the front ranks of the American popularity stakes along with Mrs Emma Southworth (1819–1899), a one-time Washington schoolmistress who wrote over sixty serial novels which had a wide readership on both sides of the Atlantic. Space has precluded either being represented here, but both repay study by the reader.)

The League Of "The Thirty"

If the reader has ever been in Paris, and rambled in that quarter of this vast moral maelstrom of France, which is known as Rue de Maitre, he will recall to mind a remarkable row of houses that arrest the eye, both from their apparent antiquity and their fantastic style of architecture.

The street in which they are situated commences at the Seine, and penetrates, like a winding snake, into a dark abysm of wretched habitations, occupied by the lowest population of the metropolis. But the row of old houses to which we are directing the notice of the reader is but a third of the way down this narrow passage, which only at noon enjoys the light of the sun, so lofty are the buildings, and so far towards each other lean over the projecting stories. There is no sidewalk in the street, and scarcely room for the *voiture* to pass through it, without grazing the doorway with the wheels of his vehicle.

One evening, about half an hour before the sun set on the Boulevards, but while it was already deep dusk in Rue de Maitre, a person entered the close from the river, and began carefully and vigilantly to traverse its dingy way. He was

The conspirators meet in J. H. Ingraham's "The League of 'The Thirty' ".

a gentleman by his bearing, and wore a short cloak, such as were in vogue in the first society in Paris. He walked on until he came near the Maison Negre de Louis, or the Black House, which we have alluded to; and well did it deserve its appellation. Time had covered its plaistered walls with a moist dark mould, which in some places, particularly about the mullions of the windows and niches of the doors, was of inky blackness. This sombre hue, together with the low and obscure situation of the house; its heavy, cumbrous style of structure, which dated back three or four centuries; its numerous turrets, some of them in ruins, with the general decay stamped upon the whole exterior, impressed beholders with awe, while at the same time it awakened their curiosity.

The building was long and rambling like a congeries of several ill-matched tenements huddled together to make one; for originally it had been a single structure, erected for a single family; though at the time of our story it was converted into a score of contracted habitations for as many households, whose modes of livelihood puzzled even a Parisian police.

The whole of the Maison Negre was not, however, taken up by lodgings. The person whom we have seen approach it stopped in front of a large arched door, the principal *porte cochere* of the edifice. It was level with the street, so that a carriage might enter, but long years had passed since the gilded coach of a French noble had rolled beneath the carved gateway, which still supported his sculptured arms, graven deep on a stone shield—arms known no longer in the land.

The man took from his pocket a key, which admitted him into the court of the old mansion. He closed the heavy door, and secured it with a short iron bar affixed to it for the purpose. If it had been dusk before in the street, it was the deep obscurity of night where he now stood. He felt his way with the confidence of one who knew the place—and finding a staircase against the wall on the left, he began to mount it. It led him to a sort of open gallery or corridor, which was comparatively light. He crossed its broken marble pavement, and came to a doorway set between two columns that supported half the weight of the groined roof of the hall of the corridor.

He struck this door thrice with the key which he carried in his hand. It returned a ringing sound. He listened, and a footstep was heard within; a turning of a strong bolt followed, and the door was carefully opened a few inches, but no one was visible.

"The word!" said a voice from within, in a quick, stern tone.

"Mort!"

"Bien! Enter, comrade!" was the response of the door-keeper, who could not see the face of the stranger.

The door was freely thrown back, and another, standing near, grasped the newcomer by the hand, in a peculiar manner, which sign was reciprocated by a similar movement and pressure of the fingers upon the palm. He closed the door upon his guest, and, locking it, preceded him through an empty ante-chamber to a large richer apartment, with a lofty ceiling, an elaborately carved cornice, and large panels, on which were painted gorgeous pictures, now much abused by neglect, and defaced by decay. The floor of this room, which had once been the banqueting hall of the chateau, in its lordly days, was elegantly paved with coloured marbles; and on one side of the hall stood a double row of marble columns, supporting an architecture of the most elegant design. But time, with his cobwebs, and dust, and moisture, had obscured all the richness of these things; and the same gloomy, desolate character, which had given the name of "The Black House" to the chateau, pervaded the room.

But the most extraordinary object of attention in the room was a group of men, comprising about thirty in number, who were standing together in the centre of the hall, around a circular table, upon which stood a pair of tall silver candlesticks, in which burned wax candles. Upon the entrance of the stranger, there was a general movement of the eyes towards him, with the quick, active, wary glance of a party of conspirators, jealously scanning every intruder.

"Grace de Dieu! It is l'Anglais!" was the unanimous exclamation of a score of deep voices, in accents of surprise and joy, as he advanced into the hall, and dropped his cloak from before his face. His features could now be seen to advantage, and truly noble they were, so far as physical outline could stamp them so. But it was the noble and grand beauty of a fallen angel. His fine dark eye was full of evil light, as if from it blazed forth the fires of a lost soul. His lofty brow was the throne of pride, and hatred and defiance of his kind curled his chiselled lip. His person was tall and commanding, and the perfection of manly elegance.

He was dressed in black, and beneath the cloak glittered the hilt of a sword. As he advanced towards the group about the table, they all fell back. He stepped before a large book that lay upon it, and placing his right hand upon the open page and the left hand upon his heart, he read aloud what he saw written:

"I, Pierre Robert, do swear to obey all the laws of this Society of Thirty, on the pain of suffering the penalties hereto annexed."

"Accursed be he who shrinks from his oath!" responded every man in the hall, in a startling bass tone, as it were one voice.

"Now, messieurs," said Pierre Robert, lifting his hand from the book, "having renewed my oath, as each one is bound to do at every meeting. I trust you will be convinced that I am still a worthy member of this confraternity."

"You will best prove that, monsieur," said a man who was leader among them, "by recording the success of your mission."

"These are the evidences of it," he answered, laying upon the table, before all eyes a dazzling coronet.

The man who had spoken took it up, and glaring over it, turned to the rest, while his face manifested great pleasure—

"Our brother has acquitted himself. It bears the marks of blood!"

"Aye, blood!—that never lies!" was the response of several, in tones of deep satisfaction.

All the men were clad in long surtouts, of a claret colour, with black trousers, and wore small red velvet caps, with visors. This seemed to be their uniforms.

"It speaks the truth here!" said Pierre Robert. "The head that wore that coronet is food for worms."

"Vive l'Anglais! mort a tyrannie!" cried they all in tones of menace.

"Come, Monsieur l'Anglais! we will seat ourselves, and listen to the account of this good deed you have done," said the first speaker. "Messieurs, be seated."

The thirty, without confusion, placed themselves on benches, arranged around the table. Pierre Robert, having removed his cloak, showed that he also wore beneath it the claret-coloured surtout; he then placed a red cap upon his head, distinguished from the other caps by an embroidered cross supporting a sword—the mark of his dignity as chief of the thirty. He who had spoken with him had also the cross upon his cap, as the insignia of his rank as second in authority; but his cap wanted the sword.

The circle of men around the table presented an extraordinary spectacle. They were all of them young men, under thirty years of age, most of them with an aristocratic bearing. There was an expression upon their faces of a singularly enthusiastic character. It was bold, superstitious, evil; and altogether fearful to contemplate. They looked like a community of murderers. While they eagerly listened to the report being given of their long-absent chief, of some enterprise that had been entrusted to him by the society, we will unfold the mysteries of this secret conclave:

The French revolution had left the elements of society in France in a state of the wildest disorganization. The blood of the nobles had flowed like water to appease the sanguinary thirst of Robespierre. The proud nobles of the realm—the influential families that traced their descent from the knights of Charlemagne's chivalric court, had been swallowed up in the citizen; a war between castes had destroyed all caste, and with the king perished the supporters of his throne, the peers of the realm.

But the war of vengeance had been all on one side. France was divided into two great parties—the hunter and the hunted—the slayer and the victim. But with the overthrow of that blood-stained fiend, Robespierre, the victim became the avenger; but there were few left of the nobles to take up the sword of vengeance against those who had well-nigh exterminated their class. Besides, political wisdom suggested other steps, and circumstances brought about modifying measures.

But there was one young man, who belonged to one of the oldest and noblest houses of France. He could trace his lineage to the Teutonic kings, and his family was old when Charlemagne came to the throne. The family of this young noble had been visited with the deepest hostility of the national assassin. His father and mother, two lovely sisters, and a beloved brother, had fallen beneath the axe of the tireless guillotine. He escaped through the agency alone of a young, humble girl, who risked her life to secure his safety.

After the revolution had passed, this young noble appeared from his concealment, and returned to Paris, his bosom torn with indignant grief for the fate of those dear to him, and his spirit burning to avenge them and all other victims. He had lost his patrimony! He came back to Paris poor. Vengeance day and night burned in his heart. At length he resolved that it should find its vent; that he would avenge kingly France, so far as one man could do it, of the wrongs she had received at the hands of the rabble.

He found one young noble, and then another, to whom he made known his purpose, and gradually unfolded his plan. They were suitable materials to work upon. Their souls were burning, like his, with the wrongs they felt only blood could avenge. At length, one night twelve nobles, young men who had survived the guillotine by assuming the lowest disguises, by concealment, by flight, assembled together in the very hall in which we have seen the thirty meet. This hall was one of the chateaux of the young noble, their leader.

In this hall, with closed doors, and in the profoundest secrecy, they pledged themselves, by the most solemn and fearful oaths, that for every noble that fell by the axe of Robespierre, a Frenchman should die. They pledged themselves to slay one citizen every day, and if a day passed without the life of a man offered by each to the shades of their fathers, the delinquent should die by crucifixion in the hall!

In no land but France could such a society have been formed; or, having been formed, could have existed a week.

Bound together by their oaths and their wrongs, these desperate avengers of blood commenced, on Christmas day, their sacrifices. At night, when silence and darkness reigned, they sought, one by one, their rendezvous, and reported the day's doings.

Seventy-one victims to their revenge had fallen by their knives!—in proof of this, seventy-one human ears were cast into a heap upon the table. Their victims were from the canaille of the streets. In but three instances had the assassins received wounds in their attacks; and but one man had escaped who had been struck and wounded; but his ear had been taken. Such was their report, which was not long in being confirmed by the public outcry of horror and alarm. The Morgue could not contain a fifth part of the dead that were brought to it from every street and faubourg and quarter of Paris. And, what was remarkable, every man was killed with a blow through the heart, with an instrument as fine as a needle; for scarcely a wound was visible, and an ear was wanting to every head.

The subject caused the most intense excitement, from its singularity; for death by violence had nothing in it to astonish the Parisians. But the number, the nature of the wounds, all in the heart, and all made, as it apeared, with the same weapon, and each victim having lost an ear, threw all the metropolis into the most intense agitation. It was the subject of conversation in the coffee-houses and restaurants, on the Boulevards and Champs de Mars, in the palace of the Tuileries, and the hovel of the lowest citizens. Another singularity connected with the murders, was, that they were all men of the humble class—the Bourgeois of the city.

By night, the people had left the matter to the care of the police, and forgot the events of the day in the gaieties of the night. The police, however, resolved to search the mystery to the bottom. Their pride of profession was at stake. That the most vigilant police in the world should be at fault, should never be said. But their inquiries only served to mystify them, and increase their astonishment. They could find no one who had seen even one of the men slain; yet they were found dead in the most thronged places, as well as in the most out of the way spots; but all they could learn was that they were picked up dead. That one man could have slain, in one day, all these victims, seemed to them impossible; yet the fact that they were all struck through the heart, and with a sharp needle-like instrument, and were deprived of an ear, cut off, precisely in the same way, as if with scissors made for the purpose, almost rendered it necessary that they should believe it. But who could he be? Could he be a human being, or a demon? for so far as they had yet learned he was invisible; for no one had been found who saw a blow struck.

At length, just at night, a Bourgeois entered the office of the Prefect of Police with his breast open, and his ear bound up.

"Monsieur Prefect," he said, "I was yesterday afternoon going through Rue de Poitier, and was going into a cafe, when a man dressed in a black surcoat passed me, and, as he went by, touched the side of my head. I heard a clicking sound, like a knife snapped into a box, felt a sharp pain, and was crying out, when I felt something prick me in the bosom. The pain in my ear made me spring back and roar out, and the man disappeared in the crowd. On feeling my head I found my ear gone; and upon looking at my breast I found it bleeding from the little wound. I thought the devil had been at me, especially when I couldn't find my ear on the ground. I have been at home all day, fearing to go out; but when first I heard how many had been killed, and lost an ear, and the police were at work, I thought I would tell you what had been done to me."

Here the man showed the bleeding stump of his ear, and exhibited a minute orifice in the fleshy part of his breast. It was plain he had saved his life by the start caused by the sudden loss of his ear. Soon afterwards two other men came, and each reported that he had seen a man in black pass two of the men who had been killed in their quarter the moment they were seen to fall dead, and to hurry away.

The Prefect had now gained something. Whoever committed the murders, simultaneously clipped the ear and struck at the heart, and was dressed wholly in black, a costume, common as it is in England, little in use in France, save among the clergy. Moreover, the assassin used a sharp wire. But here was the difficulty. Could the one man in black, to have been seen by three different persons, have done all these murders? It was possible; but it appeared more likely to the experienced mind of the Police Chief, to have been done by several persons; a combination of assassins similarly armed and attired. To ferret out such a society, if such existed, he resolved to direct all his energies and power.

The next morning the Morgue was again filled with fresh victims, and almost every five minutes men came bearing dead men, with one ear gone; and a small wound in the heart as before. The number was eighty-five, an increase upon that of the day before. These men had all been slain in the night, too, the first having perished by broad day. The Prefect saw in this, that whoever was the author of these horrible murders, he or they had taken alarm at the vigilance which had been around throughout the city, and performed their deeds of blood under cover of night. This second wholesale assassination fairly took Paris by surprise. The police were abroad everywhere, most active. Men in black were arrested whenever found, and brought before the tribunal to answer for themselves and to pass an ordeal of search. Black became a banned colour. In twelve hours not a black coat was to be found in Paris. The greatest terror prevailed among the Bourgeois, for the last batch of victims, like the first, had been of this class—from the *sans culottes*—who had followed at the feet of Robespierre, and lapped up the blood of the brave and beautiful of the land like dogs. These classes now feared to step abroad, or went out fully armed and took the middle of the street.

The third morning one hundred and one dead men lay stretched out on the blood-stained pavements of Paris. If it were possible to have increased the alarm and excitement that prevailed the day before in all parts of the metropolis, this fact was well calculated to do it. All was consternation and horror. Men avoided each other in the street, as if their breath exhaled the plague. A bulletin from the police tribunal was issued, forbidding citizens to appear out of their houses after sunset, on pain of imprisonment; while a reward of ten thousand francs was proclaimed to whomsoever should discover or recognize the perpetrator of these mysterious assassinations.

This command was rigidly enforced and obeyed; and save the armed police, from sunset to sunrise, no person walked abroad in all Paris. But who can describe the consternation that chilled every bosom, when the astounding rumour flew through the city that one hundred and thirty persons had been found murdered in their beds in various parts of Paris, one of their ears gone, and a needle-like wound in the heart. This intelligence, confirmed by the dead-book at the Morgue, and by the bulletins of the police, brought confusion to its height. Consternation, suspicion, horror reigned. Every house from which a body had been brought to the Morgue, whether unrecognized or well known (for such was the order of the Prefect in reference to these cases), was visited in person by the Chef de Police, accompanied by the Minister of State. But nothing could be learned from the inmates, save the victims were found dead in the morning, though some had lain with those who had escaped the fate of their fellows. In no instance had a female been assassinated, nor a child, nor a very aged person. The young and robust of the Bourgeois were the victims. So wonderful was the whole affair, so unaccountable, and so mysteriously and systematically carried on, that the Prefect would have felt himself justified in referring the whole affair to a supernatural agency, save that there were in many of the houses visible proofs of the bodily entrance of human beings. Locks were picked, hinges unscrewed, windows removed from the sash-panes, and in some instances panes from the sashes. In one such case, an arm had been thrust in where a man lay upon a bed, with his head near the window, and the death-blow given, and the ear severed and taken away, with the unerring certainty which marked all these extraordinary murders.

Men began to be superstitious. The terrified revolutionists among the *sans culottes* openly asserted that they believed these deaths were done by the upraised spirits of the guillotined nobles; and one man made an oath before the police, that he had met coming out of a cafe, in which a murdered man was a few minutes afterwards found, a nobleman he himself had seen guillotined. But the Bourgeois had taken Pierre Robert for his father. This declaration, though in itself treated lightly by the Prefect and the investigating committee which had been called for the purpose of aiding his researches, gave birth to a hint which brought them near the truth. The idea struck the Prefect that the whole work of blood might be the act of some of the survivors of the nobles. This opinion was strengthened by the fact that nearly all who had perished had been actively engaged in the work of death under Robespierre. No sooner had this idea fastened itself on the mind of Monsieur le Prefect, who was a man of great judgment and courage, and equal to the emergency, if any man could be, than he issued an order, by the authority vested in him, commanding every nobleman in Paris to register his name and lodging within four-and-twenty hours, on pain of the severest punishment. No one suspected the motive, for the Prefect kept his suspicions in his own breast. The same night the police guard was quadrupled all over the city; and every person commanded to stay within and keep a light burning wherever men slept.

"You see, messieurs," said Pierre Robert, the young noble who had conceived and carried forward in a manner so remarkable his plan of sanguinary vengeance, addressing his companions on the fourth morning after the outset of their enterprise of blood; "you see what order the Prefect has issued. We must tonight for the fourth time change our disguise. Tonight we shall work as policemen. We have need of circumspection. You have done well all, and you have your reward. Your skill, courage and coolness have mystified Paris. But our task is not yet done. Today I shall add to our numbers five more nobles."

"And I, two!" said another of the twelve.

"And I, one!" cried a third.

"Can you trust them?"

"With our lives! They all lost parents under the axe of the Bourgeois."

"Then they may be trusted. We will receive them as confreres!"

The next morning Paris was moved as if an earthquake had shaken it to its centre. Every man was appalled, and trembled for himself. The intelligence flew like wildfire from lip to lip that forty-four policemen had been murdered by the same mysterious persons, in the same manner; yet all the police force made oath, man by man, that they had not seen in the streets during the night only their own comrades.

The Prefect was now at his wits' end to divine the fearful mystery. He was half inclined to refer the whole to the machinations of the Evil One. But he had knowledge enough of human iniquity to lead him to put it down to mortal agency, until he could prove it supernatural.

At length he took such a vigilant course by making one half of Paris keep watch on the other half, that the avengers of blood, unless they had been in truth supernatural, could no longer pursue their work. Paris, therefore, for some weeks remained quiet. The events which had passed were in a measure obliterated by others, and "the murders of the three nights", as they were called, were left to silence and mystery.

In the meanwhile the young noble had increased his number to thirty, all young men of like spirit. But their sentiments partook now of modification. Some of the more enthusiastic proposed that they should, as pastime, till it was safe once more to strike their mortal foes, the Bourgeois, unite to punish with death every bad man whose character was notorious for oppression and cruelty. This idea was at once seized upon by them; and, from becoming murderers of the revolutionists, they became zealous for the oppressed, whether rich or poor, peasant or prince.

Having formed their plan, they dispersed to meet that day three months. All France was soon thrown into commotion by the rumoured murders in every department, from the Pyrennees to Calais; and in the manner of these murders was identified, in part, the hand of the assassin or assassins of the "Three Nights".

The needle-like stiletto had perforated the heart, but the ears of the dead were intact. There was another difference also. In every instance, the murdered men were men of property, and were noted for their oppression and vices. And what confirmed the Prefect at Paris in his opinion, that the murders in the city were the work of nobles, was the fact that every man who was secretly murdered in all the departments during a period of three months, occupied the estate of some executed nobleman.

All attempts to discover the perpetrators of these acts failed, as they had done the authors of the murders in Paris. The thirty re-assembled at the expiration of the period of absence, and not one man was wanting at the hour and place. They reported nine hundred deaths of usurpers of the nobles and of oppressors of mankind.

The project of once more dipping their hands in the lives of the Bourgeois was again proposed, but rejected. Many other wild schemes and stranger projects were suggested and abandoned. A new idea was started at length by one of the most influential. He proposed that a certain prince, Henri ———, who had been born a peasant, should be taken, and his crown be brought before them, in attestation of the deed;

and he who performed it should bind the whole thirty to himself, to do his will in everything.

The attempt was made, a certain time being set in which to effect it by each one, but it failed. Pierre Robert undertook it last of all, and returned, after fourteen days' absence —the time given being twenty-four days—and, as we have seen, laid before them the crown of the murdered prince and tyrant.

This assassination filled all Europe with amazement; not because it was a new thing for a prince to be murdered, but because the hand that gave the blow was recognized as that of the author of "the Murders of the Three Nights" at Paris. The prince had been pierced to the heart with a slender weapon, as fine as a needle, which scarcely left a visible wound, and his *right ear was clipped off* precisely as those of the victims at Paris.

Speculation was now rife as to the mysterious agency of these crimes. The authors of them seemed to bear a charmed life, to be invisible, and to be possessed of ubiquity. The murder of the prince had been perpetrated thirteen hundred miles from Paris, the scene of the former deeds. All Europe was in amazement. Every means was set on foot to discover the invisible band. Every man watched his fellow, and was watched in his turn by the police. The strictest vigilance in the passport system was enforced, and France became Argus-eyed. The conclave of Thirty, finding that their impunity was likely to be invaded, broke up to meet, by command of him who was now their master, one year and a day from that night, and in the Wood de Boulogne, at a tree called Louis's Oak. Each one, by his command, pledged himself by a solemn oath (for so much had blood become their sustenance) to put some one to death ere midnight to the full of the moon of every month, whether that one were friend or foe. This pledge given and secured in its performance by a most fearful penalty, these men of blood parted, one by one, each to seek his own fortune, and sworn to the hatred of their race. Familiarity with blood had made them demons. The noble and commanding figure of their chief, Pierre Robert, as he stood up among them to receive their adieus, his handsome dark face and nobly expanded eye, seemed a second Lucifer, or his impersonation in the body, well fitted to rule them by his iron will. Revenge for the blood of his fathers had brought with it upon his heart the fearful curse of blood-thirstiness and hatred of mankind.

At the end of a year and a day, there was a midnight meeting held in the Bois de Boulogne. There were but twenty-seven out of the "Thirty" present. Each of these latter had performed his allotted task, in obedience to the will to which he had, by his own oath, sold his hand and muderous steel.

"You have done well, confreres," said Pierre Robert. "Now, who can give me information of Jean de Loraine, Racine Vinet, and Lascelles? Loraine is the youngest noble of the society; where is he?"

"No one has seen either of them, monsieur," was the response.

"I fear they are slain. They were the last to join us, and have had no experience. I fear they have had some misfortune come to them. Now, my friends, there is no need that we meet so frequently, as peril attends our steps. In seven years from this hour meet me, as many of you as are living, beneath this oak, or, if it stand then, in my father's old hall, in Rue de Maitre."

"We will be there!" was the unanimous reply of the dark group of young men, who had, by their deeds of blood, shaken Europe to its centre, and made the fair fields of France a Golgotha, and its gorgeous capital a crimsoned Aceldema.

At that moment the tramp of many feet reached their ears. They beheld moving towards them from all sides masses of troops, encircling them as the Indians surround and concentrate forces upon the hunted lion and tiger.

"We are betrayed!" cried Pierre Robert. "The traitor is

Jean de Loraine! Behold him in the advance. He dies by my hand. Save your own lives, or sell them dearly!"

There was a hurried drawing of swords, and muttering of deep oaths, and an attempt to form a point of defence about the tree. The troops, a regiment, one thousand strong, with one hundred cavalry, rushed in upon them at the bayonet's point, shouting—

"A bas les assassins! Mort a les diables."

They rushed on like the waves of the sea. In vain did the assassins display the most extraordinary valour in a desperate defence. They were cut down and overrun with a resistless tide of vengeance, and not a prisoner, save their chief, was captured. He was taken in the very act of attacking the young noble, Jean de Loraine, who led the soldiers to the rendezvous. But Loraine, who had proved himself true to his country, though false to its foes, with great skill and courage disarmed and secured him, like a lion taken in the toils.

Thus terminated the existence of the most extraordinary society ever known on earth; and for its destruction humanity was indebted to the brave Jean de Loraine, who joined it by initiation; but when he learned the horrible character of the combination, and discovered in these men the assassins who appalled France and astonished Europe by the boldness, extent, mystery, and sanguinary nature of their deeds, he resolved to betray them to the police. He did so the very night after their separation. But before they could all be arrested, it was necessary to wait patiently till the year and day expired, when they would be again found assembled together in the wood of Boulogne.

The result is known to the reader, whom we have been entertaining with no wild fiction, but presented before him a narrative founded on facts which are recorded on the police records of Paris. It will also be seen there that Pierre Robert was tried and guillotined the third day after his arrest, meeting his fate with firmness, expressing his wish that the Bourgeois of Paris had but one head, and that it could be laid on the scaffold, underneath the axe, by the side of his own.

Jean de Loraine was rewarded by the government with the rich estate of his noble ancestors, and the fair hand of Antoinette d'Angouleme, one of the fairest high-born maidens of the realm of France.

But the fate of Racine Vinet and Lascelles, two more of the absent confreres, who shall narrate the cause of their absence at the Louis's Oak?

A manuscript, filed in the archives of the Prefect's palace at Paris, unfolds the cause, and, at the same time, reveals one of the most touching and terrible circumstances which the imagination can conceive to have been the offspring of so terrible a society as that of the Thirty Confreres. It may be the subject of a future story.

17

THE PEOPLE'S PERIODICAL

Edward Lloyd, Publisher

SENSATIONAL SERIALS IN weekly parts were not the only fare available to English readers in the 1840s—their precious pennies could also be spent on weekly periodicals and journals which not only contained lengthy instalments of blood and thunder, but short stories, articles of instruction, essays on current topics (of the more unsavoury kind) and letters dealing with readers' problems. The impetus for these journals had been provided in 1840 when the *Sunday Times* had begun to serialize "The History of a Royal Rake" by William Blanchard Rede. The paper apologized for the inclusion of this "novelty" but pointed out that "in these stirring times men scarcely find leisure for the perusal of volumes". The success of this venture was immediate and sales of the *Sunday Times* soared. But it cost the princely sum of seven pence per issue and as soon as the cheap publishers sensed this new trend they were busy undercutting each other with rival papers. At the head of the vanguard—not surprisingly—was that impresario of the Penny Dreadful, Edward Lloyd, who produced the *Penny Sunday Times and People's Police Gazette* which consisted of serials and faked police cases. It soon had dozens of rivals, and Lloyd was so delighted with his success that he shortly thereafter introduced *The Companion to Lloyd's Sunday Times*. Lloyd went on to add to his stable the *Penny Weekly Miscellany*, *The Entertaining Journal* and perhaps the most wide-ranging in scope of all, *The People's Periodical and*

Family Library. This last named got much of Lloyd's personal attention, and in it he ran the serial which gave the world a new figure of horror, Sweeney Todd, in "The String of Pearls" by Thomas Prest. He also bought the *Clerkenwell News* and spent a fortune in establishing it as a daily newspaper under the name of the *Daily Chronicle*. With the growth of his fortune and the respectability of his periodicals, Lloyd tried to cover up the fame he had achieved as a publisher of Penny Dreadfuls and indeed sent agents around the London coffee shops and circulating libraries to buy up the stocks and destroy them.

Although he had been attacked for "diffusing a moral miasma through the land", Lloyd did have certain standards and claimed in one editorial in *The People's Periodical and Family Library* that all his stories were constructed to show that the "wild turbulence of vice will bring nothing but evil fruits and deep vexation of spirit". Of course, his guard slipped on occasions, so prodigious was his output and so widely did the opinions of his associates differ on what was acceptable, that the occasional appalling publication did emerge. Certainly, though, he was little involved with the publications which led to the making of the Obscene Publications Bill in 1857, and if the establishment had any qualms about him they were not obvious when he was elected to be a member of the political committee of the Reform Club. The only stain on his character must, however, be the pecuniary way in which he treated many of his writers, and how on occasions he was not above using child labour in the composing room of his printing plant.

One man who did well out of his association with Lloyd was James Rymer, whom we have already met; another was E. P. Hingston (1805–1882) who wrote a number of Penny Dreadfuls including "Helen Porter; or The Mysteries of the Sewers of London" (1847) and "Amy; or Love and Madness" (1849), but perhaps contributed most as the author of short stories for Lloyd's periodicals. He was a notably fast writer and it is said that he could produce enough copy in a week to be able to spend the next fortnight abroad in his favourite haunt, Paris. (And remember that Lloyd's rates were in the region of fifty pence for an eight-page penny instalment or the equivalent number of columns in a periodical.)

As much of the material in these publications was anonymous, it has been extremely difficult to substantiate authorship in most cases, but several authorities are in agreement with me that this tale, "Confessions Of A Deformed Lunatic" bears all the hallmarks of Hingston's work. It appeared in *The People's Periodical* dated 17 April 1847 and well serves to emphasize the comment made about the publication by E. S. Turner in *Boys Will Be Boys* that, "Despite the extreme thinness of the paper and the trying type-face, the stories sent new joyous waves of horripilation through the families who read it".

Confessions Of A Deformed Lunatic
by E. P. Hingston

The reader will be surprised at my confessing the imputation under which I labour. Alas! it forms one of my severest horrors. I have thought there are times when I am mad. I will endeavour to describe some of my sensations, and also several little incidents in my life, by which may be seen that if I am no lunatic—it is not because I have not suffered enough to make me so. Listen to my adventures, dear reader. Amid the many who raise their claims to excite your mirth, or amuse your fancy with soft pictures of ideal bliss, let me speak my melancholy thoughts, my dark and brooding imaginations. Even as I write a tenderness rises in my bosom, and I would weep, but that I am accustomed to restrain my feelings, and act with an apparent callousness which is far from my real state of mind. Before I proceed further, I must explain a theory of mine, accounting for the different degrees of happiness allotted to human beings. I do not believe

An illustration for "The Haunted Studio", a short story from one of Edward Lloyd's numerous publications, *Lloyd's Weekly Volume* (1847).

prosperity is measured out in equal parts, any more than peculiarities of personal appearance. Of these the world presents a never-ceasing variety. Look around on your fellow-creatures, and see how they are formed. What prodigies meet your eye—giants, dwarfs, skeletons, and creatures of unwieldly bulk—a thousand kinds of beauty and ugliness. The same accidental reckless distribution of blessings and curses is observable in the minds, characters, tastes, and dispositions of those about us. Dunces and geniuses, persons of slow or quick apprehension, cold-hearted, enthusiastic, noble and brave, cowardly and mean, are all mingled together. Who shall assert these are equal?

This diversity may be perceived in human happiness. To say that all are equally contented, or even that they ought to be, takes away the stimulus from industry, perseverance, and virtue. Why shall one labour to obtain an object, if the accomplishment of his purpose adds nothing to his happiness? Or if his design be good, and could make him happier, how often may he strive without effecting it, while others succeed? The dogma, I know, is consoling to the wretched. They cling in anguish to their imaginary claim upon fate, and amuse themselves with the prospect of expected bliss, till death cuts short their ideal enjoyments. My opinion is, that there are unlucky ages for certain characters to be born in; when their capacities for happiness lie idle, in consequence of the state of the surrounding circumstances, and in the great mass of human events there are layers, if I may so speak, of misfortunes, in the influences of which a man may be born, and through which he may run his whole career, thwarted in all his desires. In the light phraseology of the day, these might be termed unlucky men, but this tendency sometimes takes a bolder course. Perhaps a simile, which has often struck my mind, may illustrate my meaning more clearly to the reader. It seems to me, then, that human beings are floating on a vast stream, crossed with ten thousand intersecting tides, some of which lead along limpid and silver waters, and by pleasant summer shores, while others lapse, with silent but resistless sway, into the deep, dark passages and caverns of misery and guilt, bearing their shuddering victim on and on, away from light and innocence for ever. Few indeed are those waves which glide altogether through peaceful scenes. The vast majority are varied with joy and sorrow; but some conduct with heavy rolling billows, in gloomy directions, with a power which no intrinsic intellect or virtue can altogether resist. On these sluggish and loathsome currents, float the scowling forms of guilt and anguish. With the dash of the sullen waves are mingled shrieks and execrations. Mothers howl over their dead children; murderers wave their reeking blades; dreadful sounds of woe, wail and moan for ever, and despair flits across the scene, rendering visible its fathomable recesses with the light of her lurid torch. At the outset of life, the writer of this mournful sketch fell into the influence of such a stream; and although sometimes in its sinuous channel, it has wound so near the regions of human joy that I listened to the laughter of sweet voices, and inhaled the wandering fragrance of the balmy air, yet this temporary indulgence only rendered my contracted journey more repulsive, and heightened the torture of my soul. It is for believing this that men call me a lunatic. Ah, may experience never teach them their error; may it never teach them that it is the wretched who read the book of truth—that the mad are the happy.

The fates made me sensible of their unfriendly designs concerning me, by sending me into the world marked by a deformity, of just sufficient importance to make me frequently an object of ridicule or disgust, without being one of sympathy. The next among their gifts, which contained the germs of much mortification and misery, were an acute sensibility and pride, and a strange ambition. In early youth these were added to a wavering constitution, which sometimes led me to the brink of the grave, unfitting me for any active duties, and rendering me a burden to my friends. I do really believe, so fatally predominant were my faults and ugliness over those feelings of an attractive nature, which, by being uncalled for, were nearly concealed in my own bosom, that at the age of sixteen, when my disease began to assume a serious appearance, there was not in the wide, wide world, any single being who would really have regretted my death. This may be accounted for, partially, by my peevish habits and ill temper, arising from the continually wounded state of my mind. No one imagined my susceptibility to ridicule, or they must have pitied and excused me. I found it often undisguised, and sometimes, doubtless, thought I saw it in mere ordinary conversation. Yet it was the same to me. I have felt a casual remark like an adder's sting, and a curled lip has haunted me for a month.

Among my other evils was poverty. This compelled me frequently to do things which disgusted me, and sometimes to submit to insult. Gorgeous dreams of wealth have floated through my mind, all tinged with the golden hue of fancy, but I turned from them ever to slavish occupations—to a state of harrowing perplexities and care—to privation—scorn —solitude and anguish. I recollect having once thought that I could be happy—perfectly happy—(I was lying on a sunny-green bank on a summer morning on the verge of a forest) if there were no other human being in the world.

At this time, in the country village where I resided, there came to board a lady with her little son. She was not rich, nor of high rank, but very beautiful, and of a temper not unlike what I fancy my own might have been, had fortune blessed me with a happier lot. Her sensibilities were keen; her mind clear and intelligent; and I never knew any one with a disposition altogether so amiable and affectionate, tempered with so admirable a sense of propriety, and such uniform, all-pervading good sense. Her person was an emblem of her character. It was while looking on her face that the first gleam of rapture I ever knew struck upon my soul! I was—(why should I conceal it now?)—occupying a menial situation in the house where she was residing that summer. Everybody scoffed at me. I had no means of resistance, and flight would have conducted me only to new scenes of insult and pain. One morning, a person possessing some authority in the house arraigned me for an offence, (I do not even yet distinctly know what it was) I hurled back the accusation on his own head, with furious execrations. Dog, wretch, brute, were the words most usual in his mouth to me, and those with which at present he greeted me, till his rage grew so ungovernable that he seized a large stick, and was in the act of inflicting a blow upon me, when I rushed on him in a rage as fierce as his own and prostrated him at full length on the floor. When Mr B——, the master of the family returned, I was accused anew before him, and my foe appealed to the lady who had been accidentally present. I turned upon her scowling and then looked down on the ground, muttering to myself "they are all leagued against me", and expecting, as usual, to hear myself represented as a guilty and noisome reptile, altogether in the wrong.

If the veins of any lover of music ever thrilled at a rare passage, so did mine as I listened to her reply. She expressed in a few words, the most graceful, the most endearing I had ever heard—exactly the truth. She explained my situation and feelings, which I had never been able to do. She represented my conduct as natural, and my anger at the accusation as proper. She spoke of me as a lonely and unhappy being, who had many good qualities, if people would but use me well; and conveyed a rebuke so touching and tremulous against the unfeeling cruelty of my foe—so precisely what I would have said if I had possessed the power—that when I turned my eyes on her lovely face, to thank her with a look, I was so blinded with tears as to be unable to distinguish any object. That simple office of kindness bound me to her for ever. I was always afterwards more kindly treated in the house; even my foe came to me, gave his hand, and said he was sorry for what had happened. The feelings of gratitude which rose in my heart became absolutely painful. Gratitude did I say? It was love—hopeless love.

I have omitted until now to describe the young boy, her son. He was a miniature of herself. Gleamings of her face were perpetually flashing over his features. His society to me became a source of the strangest fascination. I am naturally ardent, and there is something in the innocent brightness of the child that charms me perfectly. It is no wonder that our Redeemer blessed little children. Nature has formed nothing more fresh, pure and winning. So far from having any desire of evil, they cannot comprehend it. They are better beings than we. Guilt and woe to them are unintelligible things, and their thought is perpetual sunshine, varied by shadows more fleeting than summer clouds.

My attachment to this little fellow was strengthened by my feelings towards his mother. I loved her. Yet I knew that even she must have smiled had she known it. In her presence, therefore, I was by no means at ease. But he acted on me like a spell which called up all the new delight I owed to her, without the awe which she inspired.

If the innumerable and continually recurring charms of this child's manner impressed me so powerfully, the reader can form some idea of the affectionate solicitude with which he was regarded by his mother. I never saw an interest so strong as that with which she watched his growing beauties; and I trembled to reflect upon the chances of a life which to me had been so dark and wretched. I, too, had been once the idol of a mother who turned not away from the repulsive marks which angry nature had stamped on my countenance. She, too, had suffered fears and woven hopes of my future career, and dreamed that Providence might compensate for my defects of person, by shedding the light of prosperity on my path. Alas! her forehead is in the dust and my course has ever been wild, dark and lonely. No hope has cheered my steps—no love has soothed my sorrow. What other men make a merit of bearing, even with the added charms of friendship and affection, I have endured alone. By alone, I do not mean the solitude of the desert, but of the heart. Why may not this boy though his face beams with radiant happiness, though grace and beauty are shed upon him like a light—why may he not also feel the miseries as dreadful as those which had afflicted me? Under my uncouth exterior I cherished a tender heart, which misery had rendered at once sympathetic and melancholy, and I shuddered to watch that exquisitely graceful communion between the mother and child, which in sincerity, disinterestedness, and heavenly purity, passes all other human feelings.

I am writing these lines in the cell of a madhouse. It overlooks a lovely scene of hill and dale and velvet meadow; white buildings are peeping from under heavy masses of foliage. I can just distinguish their angles, their chimneys, and ever and anon, the gleaming of their snowy fences through the trees. In the distance a river spreads its golden waves. The sun is setting, and the air is full of crimson light.

How like a cold iron into my inward soul goes the thought, that I am regarding this scene through a grated window. Whatever may be the cause, I am touched; and the recollection of the incident which I am about narrating, moistens my eyes and makes my heart tremble and recoil.

One day, even such a time as the present, a glowing, mellow afternoon in summer, I found the child alone playing in the garden. I had an errand to execute at the distance of half a mile, and, yielding to the pleasure I derived from his companionship (if companionship it may be called—the temporary relation between one bright and blessed as a creature of Heaven, and one blessed like a perturbed and fallen spirit), I took him with me. Our way wound along green woods and undulated meadows. We passed by vines and flowers and through quiet valleys, till we came to a lake of extraordinary depth, and celebrated through the surrounding country for the richness of its wooded shores, and the transparency of its limpid waters. On one side were picturesque rocks, overhung with heavy foliage, on the other a snowy beach encircled it; and here and there a field of verdant grass ran so close to the edge of the stream that the high tide washed the fresh turf. In the circle of this little lake or pond, rose a rock, three sides of which were perpendicular, and the fourth a very steep acclivity. It was, perhaps, only large enough to hold fifteen or twenty persons. One stinted cedar grew in a cleft; and beneath, on the slender stack of soil which had accidentally accumulated on its summit, a few wild flowers, by their brilliant leaves of white and blue could be discerned from the shore, where we stood. That beautiful scene and rich hour! will they never leave my recollection? We stood on a rock, the child took off his shoes and bathed his little naked feet in the water. At his side lay a fairy-looking green boat, so small and light that it swayed gently in the waves. To spring in and row across to the small island was but a natural impulse, and with the delighted child I landed on it, and clambered to the top. I well remember the laugh of music with which he reached the height, and commenced plucking the flowers for his mother. At that moment, a demon took possession of my heart; for only some wandering spirit of evil could have whispered me to an act which is as surprising to me as to all the world. It struck me that I would play off a jest upon him, and amuse myself with his surprise; and accordingly, while he was absorbed with his employment, and while the words of silver sound were dropping from his lips, I stole down noiselessly into the boat, pushed off, and had reached the shore before he suspected my absence. On discovering it, however, his presence of mind instantly deserted him, and his manner underwent a change, which surprised and alarmed me. He screamed, he raised his little hands to me, and approached so near the brink, on the abrupt side of the rock, as actually to hang over it. I could not swim and the boat which I had left unmoored parted from the shore, and glided away out of my reach. Horror seized me. I had no power to move. Remorse for what I had done, terror at his peril struck me for a moment into the inanimation of a statue. My apathy was interrupted by a plunge. I saw the bleak rock deserted. A faint cry was smothered in the bubbling wave; then the struggling and splashing ceased, the long circling ripples came gently to the shore, my head reeled, and I fell to the ground. When I awoke to consciousness, the sun had set, and the moon was shining. I had no distinct knowledge of what had happened, and sat down on a broken rock to recall my scattered senses. While thus sitting my attention was attracted by an object floating near the shore, and sparkling in the pale light. Memory rushed on me like a torrent, and I fled into the woods. What happened to me I have not sufficient interest in now to relate. I know one absorbing thought haunted me—the dread of that mother's look. I had rather die at the stake, than meet it even yet. They say she is dead, and I have been tried for murder.

Now I am here for a madman. If I were not mad before, this is enough to make me so. Such looks as I have caught from some around me. Such scenes as I have beheld. Sometimes I am awakened at midnight by shrieks and groans, and to the cry of murderer. Heavens! how it rings through these silent halls. Yesterday I saw a party passing through the grounds. This boy whom they say I killed, was with them. He has grown much, and is very noble-looking. It is a tyranny by which I am immured here; and I heard last night the mother's voice screaming, because the keeper was beating her. They conceal her son's escape from her, and that has made her mad. She waved her handkerchief to me yesterday through the grate, but some brutal wretch dragged her away.

REYNOLDS' MISCELLANY

G. W. M. Reynolds, Publisher

JUST AS EDWARD LLOYD and George Reynolds had been rivals in the Penny Dreadful market, so they became again when both had their own weekly journals. Reynolds, as we saw in Extract 6, had been first a journalist and then latterly an author, starting the unsuccessful *London and Paris Courier* with his inheritance in 1835, and then returning to London where he was first a contributor to *Bentley's Miscellany* and the *Monthly Magazine* before becoming the editor of the *London Journal* (to which we shall return in the next extract) and finally founding *Reynolds' Miscellany of Romance, General Literature, Science and Art* in 1846. Reynolds saw the rôle of these new penny weeklies as a means of enlightenment as well as entertainment, and tried to mix the two without the strong layer of the gruesome which Lloyd believed to be so necessary. Aware of his own popularity, Reynolds commenced straight away with a thrilling serial of his own, "Wagner: the Wehrwolf", and used his columns to review other published fiction (mainly his own—"The Mysteries of London" was selling 40,000 copies a week at the time), expose inequality in society (he was a strong Chartist supporter) and give advice on etiquette in all walks of life. Although, as has been noted, Reynolds was certainly a prodigious writer, more than one authority has claimed that he trained several ghost writers to ensure that none of the serials in the *Miscellany* ever fell behind. (It has been estimated that between 1841 and 1856 he wrote over thirty novels and a multitude of short items, not to mention the marathon "Mysteries of the Court of London" which ran to well over four million words.) He undoubtedly played an important rôle in "purifying" the penny press, and while publications for all tastes—even the lowest—were to be a continuing part of the English scene, it was the work of men like Reynolds, his paper, and others such as the *London Journal* which raised the standard of working-class literature.

Montague Summers is just one of many authorities who consider him the most popular writer of his day—though he does feel he might possibly have been rivalled by J. F. Smith (see Extract 19). Politics played an increasingly important rôle in his later life and he also founded *Reynolds Weekly Newspaper* which was to last until quite recent times. His wife, Susannah Frances Reynolds, was also a writer of some distinction, and the author of a popular weekly serial, "Gretna Green; or All for Love" published in 1847–8.

In examining copies of *Reynolds' Miscellany* we find that the proprietor was somewhat more generous with credits than his rivals and many short stories appear in his pages beneath their author's by-line. By far the most consistent and popular contributor—after Reynolds himself, of course, —was Edwin F. Roberts (1802–1854). Roberts was another of the amazing group who turned out popular fiction at great speed and among his better works can be numbered: "The Road to Transportation in Six Steps" (1848)—he wrote on several other topics "in Six Steps"—, "The Vampyre Bride" (1850), "The Forgotten Troth-Plight" (1851), and numerous biographies and dramas. He was also deeply interested in history and the occult and one of the best tales I have come across from his pen is this item dealing with supernatural events. It has much of the story-telling skill which one finds in the works of George Reynolds and it comes as no surprise to learn that the two were close friends and contributed much in the way of ideas and suggestions to each other during their long and fruitful association.

The Rosicrucian
by Edwin F. Roberts

Among the numerous secret societies, the elaboration of the middle ages, which political agitation, the thirst of revenge, or the desire of knowledge, called into existence, none became more powerful and renowned than that body of men designated the Illuminati, who sought to pierce into the deepest secrets of nature—nay, far beyond into the sphere of the spiritual world: men who led a lonely and almost desolate life; men whose thin, pallid cheeks, and sunken eyes, which, however, shone at times with an almost unnatural brilliancy, white marble forehead, and altogether attenuated frame, gave indication of a student-life of that ardent, abstracted, enthusiastic kind, which wears away the vital spark of life, even as the oil in the lamp is devoured by the flame. Bright flashes and coruscations are occasionally struck out; but, on the whole, the light is calm, equable, and lucid, till when towards the last, the source of light and life is exhausted and becomes dim; so the worn soul, turning itself wearily from the world, perhaps in disappointment, disappears at last, and all that remains is dust and darkness.

Among the many branches of that noble and philanthropic brotherhood of freemasonry so widely extended throughout the world, is one known as the "Rosicrucians", though at the present day, they have little or nothing of the elements of their mysterious and profoundly erudite predecessors, save what tradition chooses to invest them with.

We may add, too, that the pursuits, employment, study, and course of life of the past and the present Rosicrucians, are as different as darkness from light. The one sought to unravel the mysteries of the invisible world, while the other is a good citizen in the tea line, deals in eggs and butter, or manufactures the chairs on which you sit—no whit the worse man, though less the scholar perhaps—for all that.

The stars which trace the destiny of each living human

George Reynolds wrote many of the serials for his *Miscellany* including the shipwreck tale, "The Coral Island; or, The Hereditary Curse" (1848).

soul are not always to the sensible eye. Either the burning radiance which denotes their place or orbit, kindles up when life first dawns upon the world, or the lucid urns do not give forth their Promethean fire till the spiritual influence by attractive concord illumines it, or else it is shaded in the depths of an impenetrable darkness, which requires the fiat of unseen intelligence to make it palpable to us.

The great secret of the art is at first to acquire a knowledge which is in reality the star of the individual's destiny. By watching that shining oracle, then, in all its phases, the book of life becomes a mystery no longer; the future indicates itself whether in paths of danger or safety, in happiness or misery. Its dimming or its splendour denote the predominance of the good or the evil genius.

Few even with the most intense study can attain to this knowledge; many waste away life in the pursuit, and find they have been following a chimera; others again acquire this in an eminent degree; and among the numbers was one Count Arman, of the Rosegeberge, the representative of a noble house in the province of Suabia. The secrets of alchemy and magic, that other wondrous life which lies beneath the veil, was also known to him.

Quitting the court, and resisting the impulses of ambition, turning from the path which led to fame, honour, and wealth, he entered as member of a college in the old town of Nurnburg, where, in the secret fastnesses of an almost impenetrable tower, he passed away his youth, poring over those theurgic pages, in which erudition he became profoundly skilled.

He gave himself up to the amazing enchantments which he gleaned from the pages of Cornelius Agrippa and of Lilly; the bold empiricism of Paracelsus; the mysticism of Plato and Robert Fludd; or the more scientific, though loosely connected treatises of Sandivogius on mineralogy in particular. From those pages he learned that the elements of the philosopher's stone are sulphur, mercury, and salt; but in the method of their combination arose the difficulty. He found that air bears the seeds of all things, while water is the conveyancer, that fire is the germinator, and earth is the matrix: therefore the Sagani, or the spirits of the four elements, became the objects of his more daring pursuit; and the seven presiding intelligencies of Zoroaster were evoked, from time to time, but evoked vainly. He had not attained the grand secret; he stood as yet upon the threshold, though his advancing foot would soon lead him into the circle of mysteries, which it requires patience, study, and perseverance to reach.

He was still young, and it was rumoured that it was not alone the attraction of alchemy or magic that had led him into this unsocial path at the outset; but disappointment in the love he bore for a noble and beautiful lady, whose pride contemned his worship. He devoted himself to the wooing of the loftier powers, and learned to care no longer for the world that no longer could afford him aught but dim and saddening glimpses of an earthly happiness lost for ever. Let us, then, see in what manner his dark, stern studies repayed him.

Undismayed by the difficulties in the way of reaching the indescribable object for which he panted with all the powers of a great soul, now wholly roused, he still pressed on. In one of his rambles he met a tall, bearded man, whose majestic port and noble air awed him, and whose Armenian garment was marked all over with singular cabalistic figures. Without a word the man offered him a curiously bound folio, fastened with brazen clasps. The moon was up at the time, and the stars were out. Arman was so intensely occupied with the stranger and his wondrous book, that he looked not to the broad page that was unrolled sublimely above; for, had he done so, he would have found that his natal star was no longer visible among the shining sybils. He therefore took the book, when offered him the third time, and the unknown individual quickly turned away without breaking the silence, and vanished in the forest; and the count hastened back to devour the occult pages.

The windows of his tower were turned to that point of the heavens where the stars dawn first; and day and night he proceeded with his enraptured study, though he observed that each page he turned over, his star twinkled but faintly, and even when, at some tremendous revelation, its obscure glimmerings were almost totally lost, Count Arman persevered in his dark and awful task.

One night, when the moon was at the full, he went forth an hour before midnight, and in a neighbouring churchyard plucked up a quantity of certain herbs whose virtues, used under certain planetary aspects, had a Thessalian power. From thence he returned to his lonely chamber, and taking out a huge oak press, a number of ingredients, some liquid, some calcined, and others in a crude state, he kindled a fire in his crucible; and throwing in the materials waited patiently while their combustion went on.

The moon rose up to the meridian; a calm glory shone throughout the whole ocean of azure, while stars dotted it, like islands of light; but the count, as he glanced through the open casement, beheld not his own. Above, all was beautiful —below, all was black and murky; the streets, as seen from the tower, were like huge and yawning sepulchres. It was just on the stroke of midnight, the magical volume lay open, and Arman, gathering the herbs, flung them with muttered and inaudible words into the crucible. A thick smoke followed which filled the room, and, from the midst of the fuliginous cloud, there stretched forth a lean, terrible hand, clenched in menace. It bore a scroll on which were written some unutterable words. A pause ensued, during which Arman read them and he felt the blood curdling at his heart as their tremendous import became known to him.

"Show me thy face, dread being," said Arman at last plucking up his courage: "if I have summoned thee, I must not be daunted, nor shall mine eyes be daunted with a sight that might perchance turn other hearts than mine to stone. Appear!"

As he spoke, the clouds began to writhe and twist into

shapes that were both ludicrous and horrible, till in the centre, a lambent blue flame began to broaden and spread out, then, as suddenly extinguished, and in its place there appeared the head of a dreadful being, so sublimely terrible, with its meteoric hair, dark brows, livid cheeks, and eyes where living fires flashed out with an intolerable blinding lustre. Arman shuddered, veiled his eyes with his hand, and said in a voice less bold than before, "Spirit of fire, what can'st thou offer me if I will worship thee as thou demandest?"

"The mysteries that surround the world to thee shall be revealed," was the answer, while the muffled thunder pealed with a sound of doom into the concave of heaven, as if in disapprobation of the Rosicrucian's unhallowed rites.

"I have the power already to call thee," was the reply; "and I can force thee to give me answers unconditionally: 'tis not sufficient—my soul is priceless, and if I serve thee, thou must give me more."

"The gold of the sunless mine, the gems in the unseen caves, the jewels now elaborating in the crystallizing fires," continued the terrible being.

"My art can transmute lead into gold, and I can crystallize the waters into starry masses," replied Arman.

"Choose powers like those of eastern monarchs, and innumerable armies shall obey thee," pursued the phantom.

"Man should be free and unfettered," returned the count, growing bolder as he saw that the fearful eyes calmed their lurid fires. "I will rule no slaves."

"Wilt thou dwell in ancient cities, now all dead and silent? I will replace the stupendous temples and the marble and granite palaces shall be restored. The hundred-gated Thebes shall pour its thousands out to meet thee, roused from the slumber of centuries."

The count made an impatient gesture. "No—no," he said, "of all the fleeting things this feverish world can give, there was but one—"

"Behold that one!" interrupted the phantom; and then a

singular change ensued, which shook the soul of the count, even as a reed is shaken by the wind.

Gradually and insensibly the fluent vapour assumed the forms of pillars, walls, ceiling, pictures, and furniture. It was the interior of a splendid chamber fraught with elegance and luxury. Seated on a couch was a young maiden of such a haughty and commanding beauty, that while gazing upon the magnificent face, the heart of Arman beat fast.

"It is she—it is Herminia!" he murmured, while tears came into his eyes. "Spirit, why show me this? She is betrothed—nay, wedded to another: she loved me not. Thinkest thou, I had left the flowers and the sun, for these grim walls, if her smiles had but lightened up my path?"

"Thou did'st see greater beauty in those old tomes than in Herminia's face," retorted the spirit, "or neither thou nor I had been here."

"False—false!" shouted Arman. "I loved, but did not then seek to hold communion with the beings of your kind; but it was not till her eyes darkened upon me that I turned to these pages," and he pointed to the formidable folios scattered about his chamber.

"Would'st thou be revenged on him who robbed thee of thy prize?" demanded the frowning phantom.

"No!" answered Arman; "and if I would, is not my arm as strong, my hand as powerful, my dagger as sharp as his? If I would thus heal up the bleeding wounds in my own heart, it is not to thee that I would turn for help."

"I can give her to thee," whispered the spirit.

"Hah!" ejaculated the count as he drew in his breath between his set teeth, and gazed upon the reclining figure so exquisitely lovely. "Let me possess her and I am thine."

The strong walls rocked; the towers shook as he spoke, while the sound of rushing winds swept by the window, and in the whirling clouds which he beheld were innumerable shapes floating here and there, some brightly beautiful, while others were as hideously ugly, until at last a scene of such unutterable horror broke upon his vision, that with a great cry he sank to the floor.

* * *

After this, Count Arman became still more absorbed, melancholy, even morose. His books were shunned and the unrevealed secrets of the massive volume were still bound up within its brazen clasps. He dreamed of Herminia, and thought not of the sublime secrets which his science taught him. Months passed away and he scarcely stirred from his old tower. He heard that Herminia was wedded long ago, and he did not demand the phantom to fulfil his part of the compact: but all this while his natal star shone out with all its wonted purity.

All at once it happened that one day, he suddenly started forth from some impulse he could neither comprehend or control, and unnoticed by any quitted the tower and the city, and striking boldly into the country, as if guided by his star alone, pursued with unfaltering limbs his dreary route till he arrived in the neighbourhood of an old castle belonging to his family.

It so happened that Herminia, with her husband, and two bright children, the fruit of their union, together with a group of their friends, were holding the anniversary of their wedding-day beneath the shade of the trees on a spreading lawn. The laughing eyes, the twinkling feet, the sound of the lute and the merriment of young and old, spoke of the happiness that pervaded every heart.

The husband of Herminia was a frank and loyal-hearted knight, who had wooed and won her hand. He had known the count as a moody, and as he thought, misanthropic man some years before, but their acquaintance was a slight one. He also knew of Arman's passion for Herminia, and when he gazed upon her face, he smilingly admitted, "that it was no great marvel, for she was beautiful enough to bewitch anyone"; and with no pang of jealousy he lived contentedly, adoring his wife, and fondly loving his children.

Rumours only of Count Arman's studies reached them. It was stated that he pursued alchemy, magic, and the profounder secrets of the Rosicrucians—and it was spoken truly; but more than this was not known. He had severed himself from the world and from mankind, with whom his communion was distant, cold and constrained. No one thought for a moment that in the bosom of the magician there burned the fires of a wild and fervid love, unchecked by time, distance, or coldness on *her* part; that his bosom glowed with all the delirious, headlong impulses of youth; that he had entered into a terrible compact to possess her.

When the mirth of the gay party was at the highest, their attention was suddenly called by one of their number uttering an ejaculation of surprise and fear; and turning their gaze in the direction, they beheld the figure of a man emerging out of the wood, with folded arms and imperious gait advancing towards them, and then, on perceiving them, suddenly halting. Herminia instantly recognized the count.

Count Arman seemed to have grown suddenly old after that fearful night. His form, naturally tall and majestic, appeared to be crushed; for no trace of decay was visible upon it, and his seeming age shrouded him like some tremendous mantle, whose ponderous weight clung to limbs of iron. His physiognomy, grave, handsome, and commanding, had an aspect at once grim and full of sorrow. The cap he wore, with its studded gems, gave it an appearance of barbaric splendour; and the dark mustachios, the flowing beard, the stormy ragged hair, together with the almost supernatural brilliancy of his eye, made him look like the being of another world, wilder, worse, and yet nobler than the world of man. His scathed brow was like the brow of a ruined archangel.

"It is Count Arman," whispered the almost appalled Herminia to her husband.

"He looks as if he had made misery his companion for ever," observed her husband in reply. "Let the children go and welcome him—invite him to share our sports, and partake of food and wine."

Arman was dreadfully agitated when he found himself thus abruptly cast into the presence of a woman whom he worshipped, witnessing the joy with which she gazed upon her husband, her children, her friends, while for him there were affrighted gestures and timid looks. His presence had damped the mirth of the party. He was evidently an unwelcome guest.

As these bitter feelings forced themselves upon him, rage and anger took in turn possession of his mind. Seeing the young children advancing towards him and guessing their errand, some emotion more human softened the ruggedness of his nature; but he dared not trust himself in the midst of the group, and abruptly turning upon his heel, with a proud and lofty step he vanished from their view; and having arrived at a spot, the gloom and horror of which was heightened by savage rocks, while the trees that clung to them were twisted and tortured into a thousand fantastically hideous shapes, the heavens above being obscured by a pall of inky blackness, the Rosicrucian tossed his arms aloft, and cried, "Spirit of good or evil! phantom which my art hath raised! I call upon thee now—bring Herminia to my castle, but let her come willingly!" At this moment the sound of heavy wings fell sullenly upon the ear, as if some huge being were winnowing the air—and a voice replied:

"She is a wife, hath plighted faith to her husband, and willingly she may not come."

"Hast thou, then, no power to rule her will?" demanded Arman.

"She is a mother," said the phantom. "Other spiritual essences are bound to her own spirit, by ties that no power can break."

"Steep her senses in forgetfulness," cried the count. "Let some of thy potent essences work on her as they have worked on me. Dreams and images of fancy, hast thou no phantasies locked up in secret caverns, that can blind her for a space?"

and the tortured man stamped in renewed rage and disappointment on the ground.

"It is All-souls' Eve," returned the phantom, whose form was unseen, but whose lurid eyes, like dying fires of some extinguished universe, cast a spectral light through the profound gloom. "It is All-souls' Eve; and brighter, purer spirits, though not more powerful than myself, are abroad. This night belongs to gentler influences. It is the turn of the enthusiastic worshipper of the mother of heaven to dream of the beatitudes of the blest, to behold in visions some apocalyptic glimpses, like those of the wrapt Ezekiel—"

"Juggling fiend," shouted Arman, "dost thou fool me to the brink of eternal ruin, and yet show me what I have lost? Fulfil thy compact, or, accursed one, depart for ever from me."

"I dare not the first this night," was the answer, "and the latter I may not; *for thou wilt not let me*;" and with a low, bitter laugh the phantom departed, leaving the Rosicrucian almost stupified. Casting his eyes upward he beheld his radiant star shining through the trees; and as he crossed his arms upon his chest and gazed longingly upon it, he felt moved. Sadly and sorrowfully he moved away.

* * *

Ere the moon rose there went an alarm throughout the old castle that lights had been seen and sounds heard in the Count Arman's room, and that the retainers had fled in horror and affright from the spot. The news had rapidly spread abroad, and the father confessor who dwelt in the castle, conquering his fear and mastering his doubt, while devoutly crossing himself, boldly entered into the apartment, and found the count moaning upon his pallet.

"What, in heaven's name! is the matter with you, my son?" demanded the monk, grasping his crucifix.

"Little or naught, good father," replied Arman collectedly, though the fever drops were oozing from his brow. "I am about to expiate the tremendous secret that my studies have taught me."

"Alas!" said the monk, "I fear your knowledge is as unholy as it is profitless."

"Not so, father," replied the count, quickly; "else why this passionate anguish of the soul to know?—why this diseased thirst for communion with the subtler spirits that people the element of fire and air, of earth and water?—why these devouring desires to be partakers of secrets locked from all human eyes, but to those who dare to lift the veil at any cost?"

"At any cost, indeed, my son," echoed the monk. "Think of the peril of thy soul, and pray for aid in time."

"I do," groaned the man; "but, look—behold!"

Dilating, broadening, spreading into a gigantic and colossal vastness, stood the evil spirit of the Rosicrucian in the air. Between him and the moon, between him and the holy stars; between him and the awful face of God, the features of the threatening phantom came.

"Awful shape what wantest thou?" demanded the monk.

"Ask him who bade me come," was the reply, in tones that made the flesh of the monk crawl upon his bones.

"I called thee not," said Arman. "False spirit, thou hast sought to juggle me out my soul; but thou wilt fail. Thou hast not kept thy promise, and so the bond is broken."

"Hope till the morrow," said the spirit, frowningly: "again my power returns, and still Herminia shall be thine."

"Herminia!" ejaculated the monk, a suspicion flashing across his mind.

"Avaunt with thy dark sorcery," cried the count, rising up on his pallet, his features darkening in wrath. "Avaunt! I defy thee!"

"Thou art mine," muttered the phantom, with a ghastly laugh.

"Thou liest, spirit of evil, I am not; and yet," he added, as he sank back, "it may be so; but we shall see anon." While he spoke the phantom vanished, and all was bright again.

"Father," said the Rosicrucian, "send to the Lady Herminia and her noble husband. Say to them that a dying man would see them and crave pardon of them."

"Dying," repeated the monk in amazement.

"Aye, father, dying. If in the night you hear sounds that may harrow up the soul, the rocking of the earth, the tolling of passing bells by unseen hands in the steeples, or shrieks in the air—but I am wandering. Will you do my bidding?"

"I will," replied the monk, cowering, and quitted the place.

Not long after there stood around the dying man's bed the lovely lady, radiant as light, and her loyal husband. A change had come across the Rosicrucian at last, and on his haggard cheeks there wandered a quiet smile.

The wide window opened to a tranquil and lovely scene without. Streams murmured along the plains in the distance; the cottages peeped forth out of the trees; the far-off mountains were clothed in a soft and delicious haze of purple, and the breeze which passed with gentle sighings, rising and sinking, as breaths of air came in fresh vibrations through the Æolian strings, bearing some winged harmony palpable to the adept alone, who listened to it for a time in silent rapture. At last, turning his face to Herminia, he took her hand and said: "Lady, forgive me: I loved you mightily, and I have wronged you, though you have been protected. Ere midnight goeth, I shall pass hence away."

"Behold yon starry sky!" said Herminia, softly; "you who have so often read its pages can trace upon the restless surface some footprints of the past and future. Has it never struck you that your science has one fatal error in it?"

"What is it that?" demanded the count, turning his bright and powerful eyes in surprise upon her charming face.

"You forget the *present* in following the future, and therefore have *no life*. You live by anticipation, and know not the season of the flowers, nor the joyous festival-time, when the snows are on the mountains, and the frost lies on the ground. You seek shadows of joys, and all your happiness is evanescent."

The Rosicrucian groaned. "True," said he, "true, in part only; for you know not the sublime attractions of the science I have sacrificed all for; but all is vain now. What see you out there?" he suddenly asked. "Cover your face, avert your eyes, you may not gaze upon the dread shape."

"What shape?" inquired Herminia's husband, approaching the bed. "Compose yourself: there is nothing to be seen."

"Be not too sure of that. You imagine those masses of fleece are cloudlets passing beneath the moon, do you not?" and he indicated with his hand the spot in the heavens he meant.

"I see naught—the sky is clear as a fountain!" was the answer.

The Rosicrucian shook his head. "Your eyes are sealed," he replied: "I heard the sounds of worlds rushing through the blue void; I see the restless orbs passing like shuttles to and fro; I behold the living fires traverse the blue ocean, and through the whole there streams sad melodies, with dirge-like accents;—still, I say, do you behold naught there?" and he pointed with his finger across the fulgid landscape towards a cluster of bright stars that shone far beyond Orion. One in particular gave forth a radiant light as if it were diffused from the centre of a lucid globe, so clear and soft it was.

"My star shines forth," again he shouted. "My natal star, without a spot to soil its purity; but now, ah! now! What darkens it?"

From the distant plains, from bog, and fen, and marsh, meteors tossing among murky vapours appeared to rise, to assume shape and form, till the whole took the aspect of the same terrible head which the Rosicrucian had called to life by the aid of his wondrous book with the brazen clasps. Wild, majestic, lightning-struck, but horribly vast, that head, filling up the whole space appeared, and fold upon fold, in gigantic masses trailed away behind it in the infinite distance, while the eyes flashed with a demoniac lustre upon the dying man.

His hands were clasped together, and his lips moved; but no word passed them. The features of the phantom writhed with hideous convulsions, it gnashed its teeth, it was infuriated—its doomed prey was escaping. Suddenly a blinding ray seemed to dart from Arman's star, and pierce the spectre in the forehead. In an instant the whole phantasma vanished, the starshine was dawning down again, the plains were lovely as ever, and the count was lying dead on the pillow with a radiant smile upon his thin lips.

When they examined his room in the mystic tower at Nurnburg, the book with the brazen clasps had vanished, and the whole of the remainder were burnt.

19

THE LONDON JOURNAL

George Stiff, Publisher

GEORGE REYNOLDS WAS, as I have indicated, the first editor of the *London Journal*, the publication which was to play an important rôle in what has been called the "purification of the penny press". Margaret Dalziel says, "What periodicals like the *London Journal* did was to combine the merits and avoid the defects of such really cheap publications as had so far appeared. Avoiding the sober realism of *Chamber's Journal*, they yet attained a certain degree of respectability; avoiding the sordid realism of Salisbury Square fiction they achieved an equal degree of excitement."

The *London Journal* began its life as nothing more than a business speculation by an out-of-work engraver, George Stiff, who managed to sustain his venture through its teething problems by getting himself into debt with his paper supplier so that the unfortunate man had no alternative but to subsidize him until the publication was successful. His choice of George Reynolds as the first editor was just one of several excellent moves, for the young man obviously had the feel of the public pulse and—aided by his fine stories which appeared in serial form—quickly moved the circulation up to 450,000 per week by early 1846. Later that year Stiff and Reynolds quarrelled over business matters (not for the last time—see Appendix 3) and the writer left to set up his own publication, the *Miscellany*.

Stiff again displayed his ability to pick the right man for

the job and obtained the services of one John Frederick Smith (1803–1890), who in time was to challenge Reynolds at the top of the popularity stakes. He, too, contributed immensely long and popular serials to the *Journal* and could literally add 50,000 copies to the sales when one of these was drawing to a close. (It appears that while the earlier instalments were under way, many readers would wait to borrow a copy, but when the end neared the tension had been screwed up to such a pitch by the author that their patience was difficult to maintain.) The popularity of Smith caught the eye of another publisher, John Cassell, who in time enticed him away to the columns of his *Illustrated Family Paper*.

Still the ingenious Mr Stiff was not at a loss. Smith's editorial chair was swiftly filled with none other than the renowned Pierce Egan Jnr. Perhaps feeling that his luck might not hold out indefinitely, Stiff later sold the *Journal* for a handsome £24,000—and it continued to run successfully until 1912, less of a pioneer in "pure" fiction than it had been, but still "exhibiting a morality not quite diabolical, sentiments not incurably depraved and characters much above the gross personages of the 'Penny Sunday Times' ", to quote Hepworth Dixon's famous attack on popular literature of this period.

But to return to J. F. Smith who is the contributor of our next extract. He was the son of the manager of the Norwich theatre circuit and his absorption with the stage was such that by his teens he was busy writing plays, one or two of which may well have been performed. In his twenties he travelled in Europe and lived for a time in Rome, gaining further education from the Jesuits, and returned to London in the 1830s claiming (with no means of substantiation) that he had been made a papal count by Gregory XVI, for services as a secret agent. After his early experience with drama, he turned easily to writing serials and stories and probably contributed quite substantially to Edward Lloyd's publications. Descriptions of him at this time picture him as a "pure Bohemian", living in a small boarding house in Bloomsbury, socializing with other writers and keeping up a prodigious outflow of words. It is said that he often wrote in the offices of his printers, locking himself in a room with a bottle of port until he had composed the next instalment of his serial. He was, as I noted earlier, recruited first for the *London Journal* and then Cassell's *Illustrated Family Paper*, but it was the one-time newsagent, George Vickers, who had bought the copyright in much of his material, who benefited most when his popularity really soared. What fees he did earn seem to have been quickly used up, for his generosity to those less well off was legendary. About 1880 he decided to move to New York—where his work was already well known—and the closing years of his life seem to have been mainly devoted to the re-publication of his stories in a series, *J. F. Smith's Celebrated Novels*, selling at one dollar each. Montague Summers believes he may well have written some further stories, but sadly "passed away in obscurity, if not actual want".

Smith's works cover a multitude of subjects, but he achieved his greatest success writing historical serials, of which "Stanfield Hall", which appeared in the *London Journal* (1849-50), is undoubtedly the best. This huge saga, later reprinted numberless times in three and more volumes, traces the fortunes of the Stanfield family from the Middle Ages to the Restoration. A great many actual figures of history appear in the story (though not always in context or quite the right generation), but it is the inventiveness of the author which makes the work so outstanding. Among the several amazingly prophetic items that he introduces are gas bombs, electrolysis, a silver screen which throws up pictures in the manner of a cinema and—more surprisingly still—a primitive form of plastic surgery. It is the section dealing with this last idea which I have selected, and I think it ideally represents what Louis James has so admirably paraphrased in his study of literature at this time: "Inventions like this are quite unlike anything in previous fiction: they are a sign

Stanfield Hall
by J. F. Smith

In a vaulted chamber in the house of Abram the Jew, the entrance to which was so cunningly concealed as to defy detection, sat, or rather was bound, in an iron chair, the gaunt form of Robert of Artois. The wound which Rachel had inflicted was more dangerous in appearance than in reality, and the skill of her father had quickly caused it to heal. During his progress to convalescence the old man had treated him with the tender solicitude of a parent. He had preserved him, not for love, but vengeance; for as soon as the cure was complete he had removed him, whilst in a deep sleep, by the aid of Ezra, from the apartment above, and securely bound him in his seat of torture. The room in which the victim was confined was a low, arched vault, built of unhewn stone, and lighted by an iron cresset, suspended from the ceiling.

The first idea of Robert, on recovering from the stupor in which he had been plunged, was that he was dead, and the gloomy cell his assigned place of punishment; for, before him was an object well calculated to strike terror to a soul more firm than his. The Jewess, embalmed by her father's skill, was seated on a species of tribune before him—her dark hair, as when living, glittering with gems—her eyes, glazed by death, fixed with a stony glare upon him. Vainly he sought to shut out that fearful image; if he closed his eyes it presented itself but more vividly to his mental sight—there was a species of fascination from which he could not fly. Memory presented her as he first beheld her—young and unpolluted, innocent and happy, till, like a serpent, he had left the trail of his destroying passions on her young heart and

A vivid scene from J. F. Smith's enormously successful and inventive *London Journal* series, "Stanfield Hall" (1849-50).

blighted its existence. There was something too horrible for reason in this silent commune between the living and the dead; his mind began to wander; at times he would entreat her to forgive him, then revile and curse her. Still the impassible accuser gazed upon him, unmoved alike by imprecaution or by prayer. The countenance of Robert of Artois gradually became distorted by passion and terror; Rachel's retained the cold expression of the dead. It is impossible to say how long the guilty man could have remained in this frightful solitude and lived, his ravings already began to be incoherent, when Abram, with a case of instruments under his arm, entered the chamber of death.

"Dog!" exclaimed the indignant noble, as soon as he beheld him, relieved from the worst apprehensions that he was dead. "What sorcery is this? Why am I bound like a thing for sacrifice in this dark cavern, and what means this carrion here?"

"It means," exclaimed the old man, with a passionate burst of grief, "that she was my child, and thou wert her destroyer. It means that she was betrayed, and that I am her avenger."

"Beware!" shouted the captive, writhing with impotent rage; "beware how thou attemptest my life. My uncle, the prior, will soon return to claim me; his wrath will light a fire that will consume thee."

"He will return no more," calmly replied the Jew; "he hath seen thee, as he believes, dead. Brantone, thy esquire, witnessed thy interment in the neighbouring church from which I have released thee, for not e'en the grave could shield thee from a hate like mine."

"What wilt thou do?" demanded Robert, blanched with terror, when he saw how completely he was in the speaker's power.

"I'll tell thee," said Abram; "I will not take thy life, for that were mercy, not revenge; but I will so change thee, that e'en thy mother could not, were she living, recognize her child. A premature old age shall replace thy manly strength —a gift thou hast so oft abused; the muscles of thy scornful brow and haughty cheek I will dissect away, till not one lineament remain of Robert of Artois. I'll change thy raven hair to grey, and pluck thy beard from off thy living face. Then, when thou art deformed in person as well as mind, when not one trace remains for men to know thee by, I'll send thee into the world to beg, to rot, to starve, to be the scoff of those who lately licked the dust from off thy feet. What thinkest thou, Christian—shall I not be revenged?"

"Horrible!" shrieked his prisoner. "Mercy! Mercy!"

"Ay," continued the old man, drawing a scalpel from his case of instruments, "such mercy as thou showedst to her. Writhe on, serpent," he added, "thou canst not escape me."

A groan of anguish broke from the unhappy man, as Abram plunged the instrument into his cheek, and began to remove the skin. Cries and supplications, mingled with threats and curses, were repeated, as with a firm hand and unmoved heart the avenger pursued his fearful task within the vault—the only witness the cold and passionless dead.

Day after day he returned to his victim, and relentlessly pursued his vengeance. By some corrosive preparation the beard was utterly destroyed, and the deep brown clustering hair thinned almost to baldness. As the Jew foretold, agony and terror turned it grey. At last, when the transformation was entirely accomplished, when the once haughty features of Robert of Artois, seared by a thousand minute cicatrices, were no longer to be recognized either by the eye of love or hate, Abram resolved to release him from his seat of pain; the preparations for his own departure from England had long been secretly made. Again the powerful narcotic was administered, and the disfigured tyrant found himself, when he awoke from his deep slumber, reclining beneath a tree, not far from the castle of Ormsby, once his own domain; he was clothed in rags, an oaken staff and wallet were on the ground beside him. Slowly he dragged his enfeebled steps towards the porch, where several men-at-arms were amusing themselves with Brantone, discussing the late siege of Filby Hold; not an eye recognized in the wretched object before them their once haughty lord, and one, a fellow more surly than the rest, asked why he came prowling round the manor.

"Do you not know me?" he demanded, in a trembling voice.

"Know thee!" exclaimed Brantone. "No, fellow, the servitors of the prior of the Dominicans keep better company. Get thee to the convent. The reverend father bestows no alms here."

"The prior! Do I dream?" said Robert. "Methought this manor belonged to his once powerful nephew."

"Did belong," replied the men; "but since our young lord's death, it hath been granted to his uncle."

A low groan was the unhappy man's only reply to the announcement.

"Lost!" he murmured to himself—"lost for ever. The accursed Jew spoke truly. My own menials spurn me from my door."

As this moment an old hound, which had long been useless for the hunt, but which had once been his companion in many a gallant chase, approached, and began to whine and sniff the air uneasily around him.

"Look!" observed Brantone, "if old Rollo does not seem to recognize him."

"Because," said Robert, dashing aside the indignant tear which the faithful animal's recognition had caused him to shed, "he is more faithful in his instinct than thou art in thy reason. Changed as I am, he knows his wretched master, Robert of Artois."

A shout of laughter followed the announcement.

"Master," said one, "ha, ha, ha! The noble knight returned from Purgatory! Ha, ha, ha!"

"From a worse place," observed another, pointing to his scarred face. "Satan has left the mark of his claws; he must have battled stoutly to have got back again."

"Peace," cried Brantone; "don't you see the poor wretch is mad? There," he added, throwing a small copper coin, "there is a mite for thee; stoop for it, and begone."

The o'erfraught heart of his quondam master swelled bitterly at this last insult. Alms to be offered him at his own gate, by one of his own creatures, a thing whom but a few days before he could have crushed, was more than his haughty spirit could endure.

"Slave!" he exclaimed, "it was not thus thou didst promise to me when my mistaken pity saved thee from the gibbet to which thy life was forfeit, for plundering the abbey at Lisieux; hast thou forgot thine oath of gratitude?"

The loud laugh of the men, to whom the tale was imperfectly known, roused the anger of the esquire almost to madness, and catching up a quarterstaff which was near him, he would have felled the seeming beggar to the ground, had not the faithful hound sprung from his, by all but him, forgotten master's side, and pulled him to the ground. In an instant a dozen weapons were raised, and the brains of the faithful animal dashed out upon the spot.

"Villains! you shall dearly pay for this!" exclaimed the excited Robert. "Deeply shall my poor hound's death be revenged!"

"Begone!" cried Brantone, rising from the earth. "I am a fool to listen or be angered at a madman's ravings. Use your staves," he added, sternly, to the men, "and drive the beggar forth."

The men-at-arms, eager to recover the good graces of the esquire, who was known to be high in favour with their new master, eagerly obeyed his commands, and, despite his curses and imprecations, drove the wanderer from the gate.

"God!" exclaimed Robert, as soon he was alone, "can this be real? Is it not some hideous dream? Rachel," he added, as the horror of his position flashed upon him in its bitter reality, "thou art fearfully avenged!"

Then commenced the real punishment of Robert of Artois.

BOYS OF ENGLAND

Edwin Brett, Publisher

AS THE 1850S PROGRESSED and writers like Reynolds and Smith and publications such as the *London Journal* set new standards of literacy, the Penny Dreadful began to decline in popularity as adult reading, and the remaining publishers in the field (the likes of Edward Lloyd had now gone "respectable") fixed their sights more specifically on the juvenile market. Working-class readers, thanks to the emergence of the radical and educational movements, were now more interested in "news" papers and serial fiction became regarded as "children's stuff". The clearest indication of this shift is instanced by the sudden upsurge of stories with boy heroes: those serials which had any pretentions towards respectability presented their lads as pirates, soldiers, apprentices or youngsters who had been cruelly wronged; the less concerned dealt with the likes of "The Wild Boys of London" and "Charley Wag, the Boy Burgler", larding in helpings of violence, rape and sexual indulgence. As might be expected, just as the emergence of the Penny Dreadful had produced a new group of publishers, so the development of the new "juvenile" serials gave rise to a new generation of printer's devils.

One of the first of these was Edwin J. Brett (1819–1895) who in 1866 gave the youth of Britain the first Penny Dreadful weekly journal, *Boys of England*. Like Lloyd before him, Brett had founded his business on serial works of great violence and dubious value, but sought better things with the new publication which he claimed was "aimed to enthrall you by wild and wonderful but healthy fiction". Brett early displayed a talent for finding the right authors and among those he recruited were Lord Lytton (for a short time); Robert Justin Lambe "a most prolific writer of historical London romances", to quote John James Wilson; Henry Whyte, author of the long running "Sons of Foes"; and Bracebridge, Hemyng, creator of the immortal Jack Harkaway, to whom we shall return in the final extract. Brett embraced all the traditional figures of the serial era in his stories: criminals, highwaymen, pirates, and historical figures from all ages, particularly ancient Rome and Greece. Indeed, as E. S. Turner has commented, "Often these stories did not greatly differ from the story put out as 'Penny Dreadfuls'. They were written as often as not, in the short-breath, short-sentence style. Gothic influences were by no means extinct, and the tales were still bloodthirsty to a degree."

Brett was not long in attracting imitators, of course, and though the battles for circulation were often protracted and frequently unscrupulously fought—every publisher invariably claimed the "only original, best and genuine version" of any historical tale—he seems to have had by far the most successful publications. Among the other titles he added to *Boys of England* were *Young Men of Great Britain* (1868), *Boys of the Empire* (1888) and the *Boys' Comic Journal* (1883) which was "noticeably more sensational than comic" (E. S. Turner).

Much of Brett's early success was undoubtedly due to his chief editor, Charles Stevens, of whom we know very little except that he was a prolific journalist, conducted the pioneer *Boys of England* to its dazzling success, and wrote perhaps its most popular serial after Jack Harkaway, "Jack Rushton; Or, Alone In The Pirates' Lair". This work is typical in style of much that the Stevens–Brett partnership published, but I think the extract I have selected is interesting in that it concerns the "confessions" of a pirate to his young prisoner, Jack Rushton, and draws on all the traditional elements of plot that made pirate stories such popular Penny Dreadfuls.

Jack Rushton: Or, Alone In The Pirates Lair
by Charles Stevens

Jack Rushton was conducted by the English pirate into a large vault-like chamber in the rocks.

Ambrose had dismissed his companions, and taking the link in his hand, had moodily and silently preceded our hero.

Jack looked around him with a look of curiosity and interest.

The place presented a peculiar aspect.

On one side there was a niche in the wall, occupied by a figure of the Madonna, rudely carved in stone, and on all sides were many strange inscriptions cut in the living rock.

A hammock was slung across the chamber, and the place was furnished with a beautifully inlaid table, evidently the spoil from some plundered vessel; a log of wood and one empty cask served for seats.

The cavern was lighted by a flaring oil lamp, depending by a chain from the roof, and throwing its lurid, fitful light on trophies of sheeny steel weapons and finely-mounted firearms, arranged around the walls with much tastefulness.

A gilded couch stood in a corner, to which Ambrose pointed.

"You are weary, my boy," said he, in a gruff but kindly voice; "rest yourself."

Our hero, who was exhausted with pain and excitement, made no other answer than by a grateful smile, and stretched his weary limbs upon the soft cushioned sofa.

Ambrose trimmed the lamp, drew his pistols from his belt, took off his sword from his side, and hung the weapons on a nail in the wall.

Then he retired into a little cell at the far end of the vault, and after a while returned with a bottle of wine, some biscuits, and a piece of roasted meat, which he spread out upon a table, upon which he had previously set a couple of richly-chased silver goblets.

"Come, lad," he said, with a faint smile, "since I am to be your gaoler, whatever happens you shall not starve while in my keeping."

One of the earliest and most popular serials specifically for boys and featuring a youthful hero, "Jack Rushton; or, Alone In The Pirates' Lair" by Charles Stevens (1866).

The exciting events of the day had not spoiled Jack's appetite.

He rose, and murmuring his thanks, seated himself at the table.

"Shake hands, little messmate," said the pirate, extending his hard palm.

Our hero turned pale, and recoiled, shuddering.

The pirate frowned.

He got up from the barrel, and moodily paced through the cavern.

"Why don't you eat?" he said, after a pause, folding his arms, and casting a peculiar look upon his prisoner.

"I will. I thank you with all my heart for your kindness," returned Jack, in a quivering tone.

He made an attack upon the viands before him, and partook moderately of the wine, which he found to be of a rare good quality.

The pirate seated himself on the couch, and watched the boy with strange interest.

Still the thunder growled without, and the waves kept up their fierce and hollow roar.

From time to time Jack cast a furtive glance at the pirate, who seemed lost in deep thought.

At length having finished his supper, Jack removed the log of wood which served for a seat, to some distance from the table, and looked inquiringly at the pirate.

The man remained silent, his arms tightly folded across his broad breast, and his eyes fixed sullenly on the ground.

At length he started up, and, drawing a deep sigh, advanced to the boy, and once more held out his hand.

"Shake hands," he said.

"Do not think me ungrateful," said Jack, lowering his glance, "but, indeed, I would rather not."

"And why?"

"Because—because," stammered Jack, "your hand is stained with the blood of my poor shipmates."

"As you please," returned the pirate, with a sickly smile; "my hands are not clean, I know."

He passed his brown fingers through his raven black hair, and, as if stung by remorse and passion, clenching his teeth, he hissed forth some unintelligible mutterings.

Jack looked at him with awe.

His dark eyes were fixed on vacancy, and his face worked with ill-suppressed emotion.

"I fear you will consider me thankless," said Jack, softly;

"but I assure you that I feel very, very grateful for the protection you have afforded me. The life you have saved is yours; I would gladly lay it down to serve you. But my mother has taught me," and here poor Jack's voice grew faint, and the tears sprang to his bright blue eyes, "that I should not shake hands with those whom I cannot esteem. She wished me to be sincere in my dealings with everybody, and so I tell you frankly that, though I would do anything in my power in return for your kindness to myself, I cannot forget your treatment of my poor captain and messmates."

Jack paused, as if aghast at the bold impulse which had prompted him to make this rash speech.

The pirate stared at the boy.

He grimly smiled.

"You may say what you like, you will not offend me."

"I—I trust not," rejoined Jack, with genuine fervour. "I hope my motive is not misunderstood."

"No," sighed the pirate; "there was a time when I should have refused to have taken a hand stained with blood. Blood! pah! I have come to look on the shedding of blood with as much indifference as the pouring out of water. Custom reconciles one to anything."

"How terrible!" gasped Jack; "but yet you saved my life—"

"And tried to save the lives of your shipmates."

"Is that true?"

"True! Lying is a coward's vice, and, at least, I am not a coward," returned the pirate, gloomily. "Harkye, little cherry, I was not of the boarding party; I knew by her bunting that your vessel was English, and I tried to dissuade the senor from attacking her; but all in vain. So come, your honest hand will not be polluted by grasping my guilty one. I have never injured you: I will use all my influence to protect you from harm. Come, will you shake hands now?"

"Yes," said Jack, getting up.

The pirate took hold of both his hands, and gripped them strongly, fixing a steady look upon the boy's frank face.

"So, that's hearty," he said, in a tone of pleasure; "you are a fine lad. You spoke of your mother?"

"God for ever bless her!" cried Jack, unable to repress his tears. "Oh, how I rejoice when I think that she does not know of my situation; she would kill herself with grief."

"And is your father living?"

"No; my mother is a widow; I am her only child."

"Poor soul," rejoined the pirate. "It is well, as you say, that she does not know what has befallen you; the senor would contaminate a saint; if he takes a fancy to you, he will scoff away all your good principles, and in a month you will become as bad as the rest."

"Never!" returned Jack, vehemently.

"And what is your name?"

"Jack Rushton."

"And mine is Mark Ambrose; and so we know each other, and are friends."

There was a pause.

"Talk," said Ambrose, simply, at length breaking the silence. "I like to hear you talk; your English accent is music in my ears, for, though the senor, the negro Matanza, and several others of the band, speak our language, they talk as foreigners. I have not heard the voice of an Englishman for two years."

"Then you have not boarded an English ship lately?"

"No; there is a compact between me and the senor, by virtue of which I am excused from waging war with my own countrymen, unless in defence of the band. But tell me, lad, what port do you hail from?"

"From Plymouth, where I was born," answered our hero.

A dark shade overcast the pirate's face.

He appeared to be greatly moved by this simple reply.

"From Plymouth!" he gasped. "Did you ever hear of Sir Richard Varney of that town?"

"Oh, yes; the captain of the *Fearless*, poor Captain Transom, knew him well; when we lay off the old place, he came aboard with his lady."

"Ha! and you saw her then?" asked the pirate, quickly.

"A very beautiful lady," rejoined our hero, "though she looks sad and timid, and seems to be much afraid of that surly old commodore, Sir Richard. Oh, I remember her well; I was in the captain's gig when she was put ashore from our ship. I have heard that her father was but a poor man, a channel pilot; but, to judge by her appearance, one would take her to be a lady born, her manners are so refined, so gentle."

"Avast!" growled the pirate, "do not praise her. The curse of my heart cleave to her and blight her! She was my ruin!"

"Lady Varney!"

"Marion Leigh; and she is still beautiful, eh?"

"The loveliest lady that ever I beheld," rejoined our hero, warmly.

"Lovely!" hissed the seaman through his gnashing teeth; "aye, the sea is 'lovely' when it slumbers in fair weather, and sparkles in the sunlight, but there's treachery in its smile; these tropic isles are 'lovely', but they are nests for the serpent and the scorpion, and lairs for the fierce pirate. Ah, boy, you are young, your heart is free; you know nothing of those storms of the soul, the passions! Lovely! aye—false— false!"

Ambrose hid his face in his hands, and groaned bitterly.

Then, as if unable to bear his agonizing thoughts, he leaped up. Backwards and forwards he paced, his head bent on his breast and his arms folded.

Jack gazed at him wonderingly.

He stopped in his walk, laughed harshly, and again nervously passed his fingers through his crisp, black locks.

"Lovely!" he muttered. "Aye, she *was* lovely—there was the curse!"

"I suppose she was your sweetheart?" said Jack, bluntly.

The pirate made no answer.

He kept his measured pace, tramping through the cavern chamber with folded arms and downcast eyes.

Suddenly he walked to our hero's side, who was now seated on the couch, and clutched his arm.

"Harkye, lad! but no—you are tired—some other time."

"You are going to tell me why you turned pirate," cried Jack, with animation.

"It will ease my heart," said the pirate; "but I will not tell you now; it is almost daybreak; you require sleep."

"Aye; but I can't sleep till I have heard your story," returned Jack, with a boyish smile.

"Well, then, I will twist the yarn, and you shall judge whether I deserve pity or not. Yet, how can I excuse myself? I am a vile pirate, and those whom I destroy never wronged me; while *he*—*he* escapes. Oh! shall I never know the joy of wreaking my vengeance on him? Some day I will go to England and seek him out. I will not die till I have had my revenge!"

"'Vengeance is mine!' the Creator has said," returned Jack, seriously; "besides, we live but a little while, and there is justice hereafter."

"Your mother taught you that," sneered the pirate. "She is a woman, and women are less vindictive than men. If she had suffered the same kind of wrong that I have, she would not preach patience, I'll be sworn. I open my heart to you, boy, I know not why; perhaps because you come from my native place, because you are frank, and bold, and loveable; however, you shall hear my story."

Again the pirate rose, and tramped about the chamber, speaking rapidly.

"I must begin at the beginning, then. I was born to the sea; my father was the master of a coasting vessel; my mother, too, came of a seafaring family. At sixteen I entered on the books of the *Martha*, a merchant barque, bound for the river Plate, or, as I should say now, since I have had so much commerce with Spaniards, the Rio de la Plata; that was my first voyage. When I returned I was nearly nineteen. But I should have told you that the father of Marion Leigh rented a cottage adjoining my father's—they had been shipmates together—and that I and Marion were playmates from childhood."

The pirate paused, and an expression of fond and poignant regret passed over his face.

"Old Alan Leigh was poor; he had been damaged by the fall of some block or spar, which struck upon his head, and injured his brain, for often his wits were quite unsettled, and at all times he was a poor, shambling, helpless, grumbling creature.

"When I returned from sea, I asked for Marion, and found that she had removed to a neighbouring village, having been adopted by a kind old vicar, who had sent her to school, from which she had but lately returned a fine lady.

"I did not half relish this news, especially as I was told by the neighbour folk that old Leigh had sworn that his daughter should marry none but a gentleman; and, with mad cunning, set up a story that he himself was descended from a good family; and the crazy old man would often point to a chest, in which he pretended were locked up deeds and papers to prove this assertion.

"However, I went to see my lass.

"It was then that I first knew how much I loved her; she was a being so bright and beautiful, that the passion she inspired in my wild heart was not a feeling of common affection and respect, but the blind adoration of a devotee for his idol.

"Ah, God! how I loved her!"

Ambrose turned aside his head.

Our hero could not see his face, but could tell by the heaving of his breast and the twitching of his fingers what a tempest was raging in the strong man's heart.

"Avast! 'tis the old story. You will weary of it."

"No," replied Jack; "I am much interested; pray go on."

"She drove me mad!

"She was so kind and gentle, but as cold and impassible as an iceberg.

"I acted like a fool and a brute, and in the frenzy of my despair, reviled her.

"She did not return me one evil word, but listened meekly to my wild upbraidings; but her father had wrung from her a promise to reject me.

"I extorted from her a half promise not to marry till my return from sea, for I was about to sail in a ship outward bound for the Bermudas.

"I had entered for a term of two years.

"I tore myself away from her."

"And did she break her vows?" asked Jack.

"You shall hear. I had a prosperous voyage, made a good haul of rhino, had been promoted to the rank of second mate, and was homeward-bound.

"In the mid Atlantic our brig was overhauled by an infernal man-o'-war cutter; the lieutenant in command picked out the best hands of our crew, myself among them, and pressed us into the king's service."

"What a shame!" cried Jack, indignantly.

"Aye, mate; imagine my feelings when the *Wyvern*, the name of the man-of-war on which I was a slave and a prisoner, lay off my own town, within sight of the very cottage where my beloved one dwelt, and I forced to keep my weary watch, and do my irksome duty, while almost frantic with disappointment and impatience, and thinking every moment that I must fling myself over the bulwarks, and risk my life to get to land."

"What, wouldn't they let you go ashore?"

"Not the pressed men; we were detained for fear we might desert."

"And did you see your sweetheart no more?"

"Listen. After we had lain at anchor for some days, orders were given to man the side to receive the captain; salutes were fired, and the flags run up. He came aboard, and proved to be a sour, severe-looking old ruffian; in fact, Sir Richard Varney."

"And did he come alone?"

"No; he brought his bride with him," gasped the excited pirate. "I happened to be stationed at the gangway, and offered my hand to help her over the side; she touched me; I turned. Oh, that I had fallen dead at her feet! It was she—my loved, loved Marion!"

"And did she recognize you?"

"Why, lad, I had her in my grip," returned the pirate, with the touching simplicity of deep grief, his face working with agonizing passion. "She shrieked and fainted in my arms; and there stood I, clasping her in my tight embrace, and glaring my hatred upon the hoary old dotard who called himself her husband."

"I think she must have loved you, Ambrose, after all," said Jack, with a sigh.

"Well, there is one thing, though, that I must say for her. The first mate of the merchantman from which I had been pressed—a mean, sneakish hound, who always bore a grudge against me for being an abler seaman and a man more liked than himself—either from spite, or bribed by the titled villain who robbed me of my love, spread a report that I had died on the voyage."

"The scoundrel!"

"Marion was torn from my clasp, and borne below; I was instantly seized, the quarter-master was sent for, I was put into irons, and confined in the hold. Days passed; how, I know not, for time stood still with me. The ship sailed, and I was tried by my officers for insolence and insubordination."

"And was Sir Richard your judge?"

"Aye, mate; and it was from his lips I received my sentence."

"What villainy and injustice!"

"I was lashed to the gratings, and my back torn by the bo'swain's cat; but they might as well have lashed the mainmast as my insensible body; my brain was in flames, my heart rent by harpies; I was insensible to mere bodily suffering."

"I suppose you had a hard time of it under your jealous captain?"

"I was stung to death with gnat stings," hissed the pirate. "Do what they would, they could find no fault with my seamanship or my performace of duty; but they brow-beat, baited, and badgered me till one night I got out of my hammock and stole to the magazine, and should have fired it, and blown the ship off the face of the waters, but on my way I met one of the ship's boys reading a letter from his mother, and then my heart failed me."

"But how did you escape?"

"For months I brooded over my wrongs; time brought no alleviation to my grief and rage. I was again flogged for not saluting the captain as he passed me, and then recked of nothing but how to compass my revenge.

"One day, as the captain stood bullying a poor, trembling lad in the gunroom, the devil was roused in my heart; I lost all presence of mind, all care for my own life; I seized a marlinspike, and, rushing upon the tyrant, stretched him senseless at my feet.

"Ah! the delirious joy of that moment. I stamped my foot upon the prostrate tyrant, and yelled my defiance at the officers, who stood round, calling upon them to hack me to pieces; and I doubt not they would have taken me at my word, and have gashed me to death with their drawn dirks, but for the first lieutenant, who interposed to save me; but I had not killed the villainous captain—my revenge remains to be completed.

"Of course you were again arrested?"

"Aye, mate; and for weeks I gnawed my chains in the dark hold, two sentries keeping watch over me with loaded firelocks."

"And with the prospect of death before you," rejoined our hero; "for, of course, had you been brought to trial, you must have been sentenced and swung off at the yard-arm."

"There was my comfort. All that life had of peace or pleasure was lost for me. Ah! how I wish I had submitted to my fall, and had escaped what followed. A mutinous spirit had broken out amongst the pressed men, and they looked upon my conduct rather with pity and approval than with abhorrence; and it was whispered in the forecastle that the only thing I deserved hanging for was the not striking hard enough.

"One of the sentries was a young fellow to whom I had done some service—what it was I forget now—but for which he was very grateful. He connived at my escape; a messmate brought me a file, with the aid of which I got free from my shackles. At dark I crawled out of the hold, and getting out through a port in the orlop deck, I dropped into the sea and escaped to this island, abreast of which the king's ship was anchored.

"For days I lay hid in the woods, narrowly escaping the boat's crew sent in pursuit of me.

"About a month elapsed, and more than once boats from passing vessels put in shore for water and provisions; but I was afraid to reveal myself to any of them, for fear they should discover the real state of my case, and give me up to a man-of-war.

"At length a schooner appeared off the coast, and a motley crew of fellows landed. They were pirates under the command of our present captain, Don Pablo Parades.

"I told my story to the Spanish skipper, showed him my fetter marks, and the weals and scars on my shoulders. He offered me a command on board his vessel, of which I have now the honour to be first-lieutenant."

"An honour, indeed!" cried Jack, contemptuously.

Ambrose smiled faintly.

"Belay," he said, rising, "I am not sorry that I have told you my story—a weight seems lifted from my heart; but it is time you went to rest. I shall turn in for a few hours only, but you can sleep as long as you please, or until the senor sends for you. I will take care that you shall not be needlessly disturbed."

Jack Rushton expressed his thanks in a tone of exhaustion,

for he was terribly shaken by the wild events of the day, and felt faint and dizzy.

He threw off his jacket and shoes.

Ambrose arranged the couch for Jack to sleep upon, piling it with rich velvet cushions, and when our hero had stretched his stiffened limbs upon the downy bed, drew a gauze curtain over him to screen him from the stings of the mosquitoes.

He then got into his hammock.

The lamp was left burning.

Weary as he was, Jack felt too much excited for sleep.

A whirl of strange recollections confused his brain; it seemed that he had lived a century since he first found himself alone in the Pirates' Lair.

The incidents in the story, which he had listened to with such interest, seemed presented before his eyes with painful vividness, and he was for some time wide awake listening to the beating of the waves as they rushed up the beach and washed into the echoing caves along the coast, and to the fitful growling of the distant thunder.

At last he slept.

But his slumbers were broken by hideous visions. Again he was struggling in the fiery fight,—then hunted by the yelling Malay savages,—was then bound to the rocks, the cruel, satanic face of the pirate chief glaring over him, and the red-hot irons being thrust into his scorching eye-balls! He uttered a loud cry and started up.

"What cheer, lad?" cried Ambrose, springing from his hammock. "What ails ye,—what has frightened ye?"

"Oh!—nothing—" moaned poor Jack. "A dream—a horrible dream!"

21

CARACTACUS, CHAMPION OF THE ARENA

George Emmett and Harcourt Burrage

EDWIN BRETT'S GREAT rival for the pennies of young boys was W. L. Emmett, who can be seen in hindsight as something of a plagiarist and imitator. Like Brett, he emerged as a publisher of dubious serial works and, hard on the success of *Boys of England*, launched his own *Young Gentleman's Journal* in 1867. A year later Brett published *Young Men of Great Britain* and Emmett countered with the almost identical *Young Gentlemen of Britain*. In examining these, and other journals from the two houses, the similarity is striking and one wonders how readers distinguished one from another; if indeed they bothered. The animosity between these two publishers was not only conducted through the columns of their publications: both would revile each other if they should meet in Fleet Street where they had their offices. As there were five Emmetts connected with the magazines, poor Brett must have suffered the most, but undoubtedly gained satisfaction from the greater success of his products.

Apart from W. L. Emmett, one of his sons, George, was to make quite a mark as publisher and editor, though as a writer he has become somewhat discredited because of the number of works he published under his own name which were subsequently shown to have been the work of others. He was, nonetheless, a versatile writer, ranging from school yarns to army tales, and one should mention "The Boys of

Bircham School", "The King's Hussars", "Shaw The Lifeguardsman" and "Death or Glory".

One writer whose work Emmett seems to have purloined more than most was E. Harcourt Burrage, who was popularly called "the boy's Charles Dickens". He wrote literally hundreds of serials for the various journals, of which the "Ching-Ching" series ("a sort of juvenile Charlie Chan", E. S. Turner) and the "Tom Wildrake" tales were the most popular. This latter series had apparently been started by George Emmett who then "got on the rocks" and called in Burrage to complete the work. A particularly popular aspect of the stories was the introduction of a character called "Old Dabbler", a supposed friend of Nelson, whose appearance sky-rocketed sales (shades of Dickens and Sam Weller). Burrage was also unique among his contemporaries in that his schoolboys were never beaten by their masters. "It is to be wondered at", he wrote in "The Island School", "that the old style of punishment has been tolerated so long." He was certainly ahead of his time with statements like this and earned respect not only from his readers, but the press as well—who, though they thought his writing was "somewhat sensational", nevertheless "carefully avoided all that tends to immorality" (*Morning Advertiser*).

I have examined several of his novels—including a number of nautical tales like "Sheet Anchor Jack" and "The Pirate's Isle" which are credited on the title pages to Emmett —but believe the most intriguing and suitable for this collection to be "Caractacus, Champion of the Arena". It is doubly interesting in that it is a typical example of a popular serial from this period dealing with ancient history, and may also have been partly the work of Emmett and Burrage. In the episode I have selected, the British slave, Caractacus, who has already proved his valour as a gladiator, is about to take part in a special event being staged for the Emperor Nero. At stake is freedom from slavery—or his life.

The Arena Of Blood

The vast amphitheatre rang round with the loud ceaseless hum of the mighty multitude.

The slant beams of the morning sun flooded the stupendous building with a dazzling glare, save where the canvas awnings threw their square crisply-defined shadows, by dusky bluish patches, upon the wavering yet densely-packed field of faces.

The clear, brilliant sunlight glistened on the fair silvery sand in the arena, so soon to be imprinted with the footsteps of wretches engaged in the death struggle, and to be soddened and stained by the crimson flow from many a gallant heart.

The sunshine glistened, too, upon the rich dresses and ornaments of gold and jewels along the gay equestrian benches, where the nobles of the empire were ranged.

It bleached the lily robes, long and sweeping, of the cold, demure vestal virgins—those chaste nuns of Paganism—in their parted stall.

It glared and sparkled with a rich golden glow upon the pulpit or tribunal of imperial Cæsar.

Claudius himself was already present.

His chair was distinguished by a canopy of velvet.

On his right hand were seated his wife, Agrippina, with her son, Nero, while around the royal group were arranged the nobles, courtiers, eunuchs, slaves, and other attendants.

Cæsar, a bloated mass of infirmities, wrapped in Tyrian purple and blazing gold, lolled in his chair, and rolled his eyes about him with a stolid slumberous glare.

He appeared to take little notice of what was going on, but shuffled about with an air of discomfort, as though he would much rather have been at home, sprawling upon a downy couch in his own splendid palace.

Agrippina did not design to cast a single glance at him.

She sat, her arm leaning on the ivory arm of her chair,

less brilliantly white than the moulded limb that rested on it.

Her black, fearless eyes rolled round with a dull wonder, and dazed delight upon the multitudinous faces that packed the amphitheatre.

Two bronze vases, filled with incense, burnt on either side of her throne.

All was now ready for the entertainment to begin.

The sound of trumpets rang out.

The multitude rent the air with a prolonged shout.

Then came another flourish of trumpets and the clash of cymbals.

Then a folding-door on the right hand of the arena was thrown wide open, and a single trumpet sounded.

The gladiators marched in with slow step, a long and seemingly interminable file.

Each man naked, except that he was girt with a cloth about his loins.

Each bore on his left arm a small buckler, and had a short straight sword suspended by a cord about his neck.

They marched slowly and steadily, so that the whole assembly had full leisure to contemplate the forms of the men, and form an estimate of their chances of being victorious.

They made the circuit of the arena three times, and then forming in a double line before the tribunal of Cæsar, they raised their voices in a loud solemn chant.

"*Ave, Cæsar, morituri te salutant.* Hail, Cæsar, those about to die salute thee."

But let us quit the arena a while, and seek out our brave Caractacus and his two comrades, who were arming to do battle with their three foemen.

They were gathered together in a stone room under the podium or gallery—Caractacus, Manlius, and Lycaon, with their lanista, Ventidius.

The three gladiators, though feverishly excited, were buoyant and eager for the fray.

Not so Ventidius.

Another widely successful serial, "Caractacus" (1868) from the publisher and author, George Emmett.

His face was flushed, and his brow gloomed with doubt and anxiety.

He nevertheless assumed to be in high spirits, like a good general as he was, knowing that his lads would take their tone from him.

Three slaves acted as esquires to the three gladiators, and assisted them in buckling on their armour and so forth.

"What cheer, my sons?" cried Ventidius. "Look well to your accoutrements, and here's a choice of swords. You will conquer, boys, for never had I such a brave triplet of thorough-bred war-hounds in leash. Here, Manlius, drink from this cup of Cæcuban, and may it fire your heart! Pass it on to your comrades."

Then, turning to Caractacus, he went on:

"Why are you fussing with that buckler? It don't suit you—I see why; the arm brace is too tight. Take another; so, look here, just your size and weight."

The lanista slipped on a shield, and threw himself into a fighting attitude, and moved his left arm about to show that it was in working order.

"Thanks, lanista," answered Caractacus, "I will take your advice."

Then Ventidius glanced at Lycaon, and asked him with some sternness:

"What is that piece of frippery you wear in your helmet?"

Lycaon turned red, and laughed rather bashfully.

" 'Tis a riband the Lady Julia gave me, and bade me wear it as her token."

Ventidius frowned and shook his head.

"I like it not," he said. "It has happened more than once in my experience that gladiators decking themselves in such womanish frippery have come to grief. Take my word, lad, it is not a good omen."

"Fear not, my master," answered Lycaon. "I shall fight the better for wearing it."

"Why, then, do as you please," answered Ventidius. "Yet

I wish you may not have cause to be sorry that you did not heed my warning."

He then addressed himself to the Briton:

"Hey, Caractacus! you are in splendid form," he said, smiling and clapping our hero on the shoulders. "But be on your guard against a too great eagerness to pick out and to vanquish Caius Licinius."

Caractacus stared in surprise.

"Yet is it not against Licinius that I am specially matched?" he asked.

"Not especially, mark you that," returned the lanista. "You three will be matched against the three trained men under Phorbus, to fight them indiscriminately, to kill whichever of them you can, and then to aid your comrades in destroying the rest. Which of the two parties kills the first will stand the best chance, because that party will be fighting with the odds on its side—three to two."

"I will remember," said Caractacus. "Nor will I permit any private motive of revenge to injure our general interest."

"Very well. When you are paired I will set Lycaon against Licinius," said Ventidius. "Make quick work with him, Lycaon, and, by my head, half the battle is won."

Lycaon appeared delighted.

"You do me too much honour, worthy lanista," answered Lycaon, gleefully. "I shall fight with the better will. The Lady Julia is devoted to her mistress Agrippina, whose enemies she hates—none more than Narcissus and his partisans, amongst whom is Licinius."

"To Hades with the Lady Julia!" growled Ventidius. "Put not your trust in Venus, but in Mars. Think only of the man you must kill, and not of the women you would live for. Put your soul in your sword, or you are a lost man."

Then, once more turning to Caractacus, he looked him heedfully in the face.

"If you do not like this arrangement say so, and speak out boldly," urged the lanista.

"I am sorry that Licinius should escape me, but I consent to your proposal, on one condition," replied the Briton.

"Name it."

"That you will oppose me to that traitor Arvirargus, who betrayed me to the Romans."

Ventidius grinned.

"Your countryman! Trust me. Such was my intention," he replied. "Do I not know that no foes are so bitter against each other, or contend so fiercely, as domestic foes?"

"Then I am satisfied," return Caractacus.

"And now, my lads," added Ventidius, cheerfully, "fight like Trojans. Remember what you have at stake—your lives and liberties! May you all come off with slight damage. Each survivor earns his manumission and a purse of gold. Remember, freedom! Fight hard for freedom!"

An officer now came to inform them that it was their turn to appear in the ring.

They waved their swords, and answered with a:

"Pluto, befriend thine own!"

There was a little delay in the passage that led to the gate of death.

Here Phorbus was awaiting with his three men—Licinius, Telamon, and Arvirargus.

Arvirargus took an opportunity, while the two training masters were conferring together, to steal near to our hero.

The Brigantian was a very handsome fellow, two or three years older than our hero, and, though not quite so tall, was stouter built.

He was finely proportioned, and had blue eyes, and fair hair like Caractacus, but he was neither so graceful nor stately as our hero, and his beauty was of a coarser and less noble type.

"So, Idris-ap-Caradoc," he whispered, "we meet again."

"Yes, Arvirargus, son of Alvan, and we meet for the last time," retorted our hero sternly.

"We meet as equals here," hissed his rival; "we are both slaves."

"True, but I fell into this condition by the chance of war," replied Caractacus; "you by that treacherous nature that betrays itself. When you and your accursed tribe sold your country to the invader, you should at least have kept faith with him. But no! in turn you would have betrayed your patrons."

"I did but avenge my wrongs."

"Mine remain to be avenged," answered Caractacus.

Ventidius interfered between them.

He saw by their glaring eyes that they were likely to fall foul with each other before the proper time.

It was near at hand.

The doors were thrown open, and in martial array the two parties, each headed by its lanista, marched into the vast arena.

A shout of loud applause rent the air as they came in.

After making the usual salutation to the emperor, they formed themselves in two opposing lines, and in this array—

Our hero was opposed to Arvirargus, Lycaon to Licinius, Manlius to Telamon.

The lanistæ retired.

Then the signal for the conflict to begin was given by the blast of a trumpet.

Now came the shock.

Clashing their swords against their shields the combatants rushed upon each other.

Above all the noise, loud rose the battle-cry of the impetuous Britons.

The two men were fighting with the fury and savagery of their Celtic blood, and our hero had already forgotten the sage counsels of his lanista, Ventidius, for he seemed to forget the presence of his comrades, and to think only of his individual adversary.

Their swords clashed together and their countenances blazed with sheer wrath and thirst for blood.

Caractacus seemed transformed, and drove his foe before him with blows that shocked Ventidius by their wild impetuosity—not that they were at all unskilful, but were so reckless.

"He forgets himself, and only thinks of his man," the lanista muttered to himself. "Too rash, though Phorbus' novice stands a poor chance. I was a fool not to match the Briton against the Roman after all; still, perhaps this will be over quickest."

He was right in that.

Caractacus beat his British foeman to his knee, and then, with one swift swish of his sword, struck off his head, and sent it, the long yellow hair in streams, rolling on the sand.

The assembled multitude seemed to have gone mad with excitement.

"Caractacus! Caractacus!" they yelled.

Meantime, how fared it with the others?

Calmly and skilfully they fought together, but the combat was scientific, in regard of the devil's master-art—fencing.

Manlius and Telamon thrust and parried, but as yet had not even touched each other, but Licinius had wounded Lycaon on the sword-arm.

Truth to say, the poor Greek's attention had been called off for one fatal instant by a waving scarf from the empress's stall—a signal waved by the Lady Julia.

Still he fought well, though under a disadvantage, for his arm grew weaker and weaker.

Caractacus stood for a moment with the air of a man who had made a fool of himself.

But Lycaon fell.

Then our hero engaged Licinius, and the fencing was cool and perfect.

Their attitudes were most graceful, and their magnificent style won universal admiration.

As they fought on, Licinius seemed to gain confidence, and held Caractacus at bay with wondrous skill and intrepidity.

Manlius had always been reckoned to be the second swordsman in the "family" of Ventidius, poor Lycaon being the first until the matchless Briton came to eclipse them all; and now he was exasperated to find that Telamon was more than his master.

It is true that, so far, not one drop of blood had been drawn, but Manlius had attacked him furiously, striving for the honour of being the first to kill his man, while Telamon had acted simply on the defensive.

But now came the tug of war.

Telamon, having made sure of his power, dashed at Manlius so savagely and swiftly that the Roman was struck to the ground, the blood gushing from his shoulder.

Then, with a joyous cry, he turned his sword against Caractacus, eager to gain renown by slaying such a famous challenger.

The Briton sprang back and stood at bay, and so majestic and lion-like was his look that the amphitheatre rang with applause, and his two opponents looked at him in wonder.

Caractacus stood undaunted.

His right foot rested on the body of Arvirargus, his keen steadfast eyes watching for the first hostile movement on the part of Licinius and Telamon.

The latter made a savage lunge at Caractacus, but our hero caught the point of the sword on the boss of his shield, and in the same moment parried a thrust from Licinius.

The young hero prolonged the contest with desperate valour.

In the midst of this, Manlius, though desperately wounded, raised himself from the ground, and made a feeble attempt to renew his combat with Telamon. But his strength was gone.

After tottering a few paces he fell, and lay helpless, while a stifled groan escaped him.

Telamon, leaving our hero and the young patrician to settle their difference between themselves, flew upon Manlius to despatch him.

In the same moment Licinius received our hero's sword

in the shoulder, and faint with pain and loss of blood, fell to the earth.

Thus released, the Briton hasted to the rescue of his comrade Manlius.

Telamon had levelled his sword at the breast of his wounded and disabled antagonist, and was about to strike home when Caractacus interposed his shield and stopped the blow.

Telamon abandoned his intention of slaying Manlius, and immediately attacked the Briton, and desperate was the fight between them to decide which of the two should survive—sole victor and Champion of the Arena.

They practised every ward, feint, and lunge with the most admirable skill and swiftness, but it was evident to the eyes of the more experienced spectators that Caractacus was the better swordsman.

Soon and fatally their judgment was confirmed. With a masterly thrust Caractacus broke down the guard of Telamon and ran his sword through his body, the hilt striking against the breastbone.

Caractacus stood alone, erect and triumphant. He shook back his golden locks, waved his dripping sword above his head, and uttered his British war-cry:

"Iero!"

But Licinius was not slain.

Burning with hatred and thirst for vengeance he crawled on his hands and knees towards Caractacus, with the purpose of stabbing him in the back.

Our hero turned upon him, and was about to plunge his sword into his heart when he felt himself dragged back, and found himself struggling in the arms of the three lanistæ—Ventidius, Phorbus, and Antipas.

"Hold, good lad, enough has been done," cried Ventidius. "You are to spare the life of Licinius; such is the express command of Cæsar."

"I obey," returned Caractacus, sheathing his sword. "He

is wounded already. I bear him no further malice; my honour is satisfied."

The victor of this bloody fight received quite an ovation.

He was borne round the ring upon the shoulders of his rejoicing comrades belonging to the "family" of Ventidius; he was crowned with garlands, and presented with the rudis, a wooden foil with a silver hilt, in token that he was emancipated and that henceforward he would not be called upon to risk his life upon that field of blood and guilt—the Roman arena.

GUY FAWKES
OR, GUNPOWDER, TREASON AND PLOT

by G. A. Sala

THE THIRD PROPRIETOR who was to enjoy great success during the boom in juvenile Penny Dreadfuls was Charles Fox who ran his publishing empire just around the corner from Fleet Street in Shoe Lane. Fox appears to have had far less scruples than either Brett or Emmett—not the most scrupulous of men, certainly—and his publications are almost unrelentingly devoted to historical characters involved in crime and violence. His penny-issue works were indisputably less inventive than either of the other two men, but his weekly journals did show the first glimmerings of concern for the problems of young boys, which were to be so successfully utilized by the *Boys' Own Paper* and other later periodicals which took a strongly Christian and moral viewpoint on all youth issues. Among Fox's more successful titles can be listed the *Boys' Standard* (which appeared in 1875 and ran for twenty years)—although he did publish a number of popular serials which harked back to the old Gothic themes of demented noblemen and haunted castles. It seems likely that he took over a number of Edward Lloyd's old titles when the latter became too proud to own such things, and re-edited the original texts for a new readership. He certainly made great use of the Sweeney Todd legend, first publishing a revised 48-part penny version under the title which is now most usually associated with the story,

"Sweeney Todd, the Demon Barber of Fleet Street" (1878), and then utilizing the character to pep up a serial entitled "The Link Boys of London" which began in the *Boys' Standard* in 1883.

Montague Summers informs us that the illustrator and writer George Augustus Henry Sala (1828–1895) was most likely the re-writer of Prest's story, although Sala indignantly denied it in later years. Sala, in fact, features once or twice in the history of the Penny Dreadful although later biographies have made little mention of this. Born in London of Italian ancestry, he studied art at school and was then apprenticed to a certain Mr Calvert who "cut" the illustrations for most of Lloyd's serial works. There is a well documented story in Thomas Frost's "Recollections" of Sala receiving a letter from Lloyd in which he was requested to put more blood in the illustrations—"much more blood, spouting blood in fact, and more prominent eyes to show devouring lust". A study of some of the publications which he is believed to have illustrated at a later date confirm that he followed these instructions to the letter. Sala of course went on in 1851 to become a contributor to *Household Words*, and thereafter the *Illustrated London News* and *Temple Bar* which he founded and edited from 1860–6—not forgetting his periods as a foreign correspondent for the *Daily Telegraph*—but there seems little doubt that he produced a number of serials for the "juvenile" publishers of the 1860s. It has proved extremely difficult to authenticate Sala's authorship of such works, particularly those like "Charlie Wag, the New Jack Sheppard" and "The Woman with the Yellow Hair", because of his determined attempts in later life to conceal all details of his early writings. What has made experts believe he *did* write these two books is not only their style, but the title page by-line of "By G. A. Savage". For they are Sala's own initials and we know that he was a prominent member of the Savage Club in London.

Another similarly vivid and dramatic story credited to his

pen is "Guy Fawkes; or, Gunpowder, Treason and Plot", which was published by Charles Fox. Our evidence here other than style is that Fox was a known associate of Sala, and both men shared a strong interest in parliamentary history, making it comparatively easy for the writer to have turned his hand—albeit anonymously—to a saga based on Fawkes and his exploits. Although making no absolute claim about its authorship, the extract from the work which follows would certainly do Sala some credit for its almost timeless quality. For here is the moment of capture of a hero working outside the law, his confrontation with torture to make him reveal all, and his amazing rescue by an enamoured lady. Is this not exactly the formula which has made the modern stories of James Bond so universally popular?

The Vault Of Death

Guy Fawkes instinctively looked around the gloomy cell, into which he was thrust by his captors, for some means of escape.

A pale, ghastly light was feebly burning, and there were two hideous men, with sacks over their heads, which formed a grotesquely ugly point at the top. Two large holes were made through which their eyes sparkled redly, and close by stood a strange, weird-looking instrument.

Horror! It was the rack!

His cheek, in spite of himself, became ashen white, he felt the blood running coldly through his veins, and the horror of bodily torture triumphed for the moment over the native fearlessness of his character.

"Time presses," said the masked cavalier, in the same cold tone; "shall I bid the rack-wheel turn or not?"

"What would you have?" inquired Guy Fawkes, scarcely able to conceal the tortuous thoughts which racked his agitated bosom.

A desperate situation for Guy Fawkes in G. A. Sala's serial published by Charles Fox.

"The letter containing the secret instructions of the power ye serve."

"I have it not," returned Guy Fawkes, openly. "Search me if ye will, and prove the truth of my words."

"What have you done with it, then?"

"It has been delivered to whom it was addressed."

"It boots not," returned the cavalier, impatiently, "since of a surety ye must know its contents ye can e'en tell us by word o' mouth."

"Think ye I would stain my manhood by an act so base as to surreptitiously acquaint myself with the contents of a missive entrusted to me in all good faith for its safe deliverance, or betray the confidence of those to whom I am bound by no ordinary tie. It is evident ye little know me, Sir Cavalier!" cried Guy Fawkes, with passionate vehemence.

"This is trifling," said the nobleman, sternly; "and the moth that flutters round the paper flame has as much wisdom as he who trifles by the side of the rack. Speak out. This is no place to employ the slippery arts of the wily Papist priests ye serve, and whose blind, besotted tool ye are!"

"Ye have had my answer," said Guy Fawkes, firmly and defiantly.

"Ah! you refuse then—"

"To betray the councils of our sacred league I do!"

The swarthy features of the disguised nobleman glowed.

He started to his feet, but suddenly checking himself almost in the act of giving a hasty command to his ready satellites, exclaimed, excitedly:

"You are tampering with more than life—with more than death pangs—it will leave your body blasted—a curse on your miserable existence. On that iron bed," he continued, pointing to the rack, "your bold mien will change to yells of agony—you will leave it with disjointed limbs—with a body incurably distorted, that will make life a curse and torment to you! Mark me, young sir. It may be that woman's love is dear to thee. Her heart loves heroism, but not in a palsied body. She will pity the helpless cripple, but her bright eyes will wander to him whose soul, although less noble, is better housed."

Guy Fawkes's thoughts instantly reverted to Violet, and he shuddered visibly.

"I wish to spare you," went on the cavalier; "but, believe me, from no kindness towards yourself. I could crush you like a worm, nor think once again on your lingering agony. But I wish to spare ye, because your sufferings would serve me less than your enforced aid might do.

"The king, did he but know, would buy the knowledge of the contents of the despatch in question with his fairest province. Gold has been lavished to discover it, but in vain.

"The secret is now within these walls—locked, indeed, in your bosom. But there"—and he again pointed towards the rack—"there is a key of iron that will open it."

Guy Fawkes was silent—stunned and overwhelmed with conflicting thoughts.

"You still hesitate," resumed the crafty nobleman, watching him narrowly. "It may be that your honour pricks you, but will it render you insensible to torment? The madness of enthusiasm itself is quelled by one turn of that grim wheel!

"There is nothing to stir the blood, nothing to dare, here. It is no battle front, no crossing of blades, no conflict with your kind; one look of the strong man's agony, one shriek of he whose fearless soul would have confronted death unmoved, would tell you that here you have not even the exultation of despair."

He waited, but still Guy Fawkes replied not.

"And whom do you betray?" pursued the masked tyrant, sternly.

"A faithless priest, a base deluder of his misguided followers—an ambitious knave, that masks guile under the purple robe, a very villain, although the head of the Church, that—"

"It is false!" cried Guy Fawkes, fiercely; "base heretic. You lie! you—"

"To the rack with him!" yelled the indignant noble, in a voice of fury.

Quick as the words were uttered Guy Fawkes was seized. He made a desperate resistance, but all in vain.

His foes were too many for him. He was forcibly dragged to the rack and bound firmly hand and foot upon it.

"Proceed with the torture," cried the noble, passionately.

The grim executioners immediately thrust their iron-tipped levers into the rollers of the rack and gave them a turn.

Another moment and Guy Fawkes's limbs would have been torn from their sockets.

At this critical juncture, however, a wild scream rang out loudly in the vaulted cell, and the frenzied face of a girl appeared, though unseen, at the grated window.

Simultaneously came a stunning shock, a wild, roaring sound, like the peal of a hundred cannon.

The stone walls shook and trembled, and the very earth seemed moving.

The tapers and torches fell down and were extinguished. The air was charged with fumes that made the breathers gasp.

Captive and captors, prisoner and judge, stood in the darkness and ruin, aghast and panic stricken.

Then instantaneously a thick sulphuric vapour filled the place.

Guy Fawkes heard one of the ruffians near him mutter in a hurried, terrified whisper:

"There is treason in the camp. We have been betrayed by one of our own people."

They all stood in trembling expectancy of something still more fearful to follow.

Presently, however, the sounds of angry voices without broke upon them, among which were the excited tones of a female voice, which Guy Fawkes fancied he recognized as belonging to Evelyn, the dancing-girl.

The stout door was open again, and a ruffian trooper entered, pale and agitated bearing a torch.

The fellow addressed a few words to the masked nobleman, who burst into a torrent of angry imprecations.

"Release yon stubborn idiot from the rack, but leave him firmly bound; then follow me."

Seeing that the men faithfully obeyed his orders, they quitted the cell in company of their tyrant lord: whilst Guy Fawkes was left a prisoner in the bolted and barred chamber, in utter darkness, and with no companion—but the rack.

Deepest silence followed their departure.

The sulphurous odour still remained and made the damp air oppressive, but the stillness around him was perfect and unbroken.

He became convinced that a powder magazine had blown up, and his heart throbbed with a sudden hope that it might lead to his escape.

He could not guess where he was, but knew enough to be confident that he was immured in one of the secret strongholds which in those days abounded on various parts of the river-side, originally prepared for the purposes of contraband merchandise and the spoils of piracy, but now and then applied to purposes of State.

"They must mean to destroy me," muttered Guy Fawkes, "so here I must remain, with powerless limbs, a helpless and a hopeless prisoner, until death relieves me of my misery."

He seated himself by the side of the rack. Both arms were painfully fastened, and his temples throbbed feverishly.

He thought of Violet and his hopeless passion for her—he thought, too, of his rival, Harold Rookby, whose condition he compared with his own; yet never once did he think of betraying the agents of the cause he served, and of which he deemed himself the chosen of heaven.

Then he remembered the scream he had heard immediately

before the explosion, and the evident dismay of the ruffian who rushed in with the torch.

Thus his wandering thoughts ran on until his brain grew dizzy and his wearied mind sank into a kind of stupor.

It was not sleep—nature has a species of lethargy which is not repose.

With his tired head resting against the oaken post, his eyes shut, and his features wearing their accustomed melancholy expression Guy Fawkes lay, unconscious of time.

From this state, after a long interval, he was suddenly aroused.

He felt a soft hand laid gently upon his shoulder.

On opening his eyes the graceful form of a woman stood before him, with a small lamp in her hand.

Guy Fawkes uttered an ejaculation of surprise, for his visitor was none other than Evelyn, the dancing-girl.

She was pale as marble, but the expression on her beautiful countenance was earnest and full of life.

Her gaze met his, but only for a moment.

Making a signal of imploring silence, she drew a bright keen knife from her girdle, and with trembling hands cut the cords that bound Guy Fawkes's stiffened arms.

Then, raising the lamp again, and repeating the signal of silence, the dancing-girl beckoned him to follow her.

She led the way with the utmost caution to a narrow iron door immediately behind the rack, which had hitherto escaped Guy Fawkes's attention, and proceeded with noiseless steps to an apartment in which two rough, seafaring men were standing, as if waiting for him.

Not a word was spoken by anyone, and here he was again compelled to have his eyes bound.

After passing, or being led, through what seemed to him a detour of similar passages, he felt the cool refreshing breeze of the river once more playing on his face.

He could now hear the lapping of the tide, and, from the swaying motion, knew that he was entering a boat.

The next moment it glided from the shore.

Guy Fawkes breathed freer, and the spirit of adventure again rose strong within him.

Still uncertain whither he was going, he was about to tear the bandage from his eyes when he felt his hand gently seized.

The soft fingers that clasped it, however, told him that it was no unfriendly grasp, and a sweet, earnest voice, whispered:

"If you uncover your eyes we are lost."

"Then be it as it is," replied Guy Fawkes, the buoyancy of his spirits returning. "I care not how far I sail since I travel with such a companion."

"Peace—peace! for heaven's sake, peace!" said Evelyn, in an imploring whisper, suddenly withdrawing her hand.

On they rowed in silence.

But Guy Fawkes found with increasing uneasiness that the boat, instead of returning towards Southwark, was running down the river.

He began to fear that he was to be put on board some outgoing foreign vessel, which would utterly prevent him carrying out, at least for a time, the great purpose he had in view.

He heard the Greenwich clock strike four, and the hail of vessels on the river, to which, however, no answer was made.

After a considerable time Guy Fawkes worked up to a high pitch of desperation, tore the bandage from his eyes, resolving, if need were, to plunge into the stream and swim to the shore.

A muttered curse and a long steel pistol—the bright barrel of which glittered in the moonlight—pointed towards his head now greeted him.

Evelyn suddenly interposed, and, addressing the man in Romany with a fluency which rendered her words unintelligible to Guy Fawes, stayed his arm, while the rowers rested on their oars.

The man put the pistol sullenly into his belt, and, giving

a sharp and angry word of command, the light boat bounded on again.

Guy Fawkes had now leisure to notice this person, who seemed to be the commander of the boat.

He was not, as he had at first anticipated, the former companion of the dancing-girl, but a person of older appearance, though still in the prime of manhood.

He wore the dress of a sailor—richly, even gaudily embroidered—his thick curling hair and bushy moustache were black, and his small bright eyes of the same colour.

His aspect was reckless and sensual, indicative of the indulgence of passion. Without being dignified he was commanding.

"Whither are you taking me?" demanded Guy Fawkes, who felt a sudden repugnance, he knew not why, against the individual who commanded the boat.

The question was unheeded by the party addressed, but the girl answered:

"You will be landed anon."

Guy Fawkes, on the impulse of the moment, took the dancing-girl's cold hand in his, and pressed it to his lips.

Again the hand of the sailor crept to his pistol hilt, and Guy Fawkes saw he had changed countenance.

The girl covered her face with her hands, and her long fair hair fell over her shapely arms like a veil, baring her beautiful white neck, the rich ringlets resting on her knees.

Guy Fawkes looked on her with undisguised admiration.

Her extreme loveliness, her devotion to himself, and the rude companions with whom her lot seemed to be cast, awakened in his breast an interest of the most intense and passionate character.

23

JACK HARKAWAY

by Bracebridge Hemyng

JUST AS THE early penny serial works had produced their own super-hero in Robin Hood, so too were the new Penny Dreadfuls for boys to have their most important character—in the person of one Jack Harkaway. Unlike any previous creation in literature, Harkaway was to delight generations of readers in both Europe and America with his adventures from schooldays to old age and give rise to a veritable host of youthful imitators. (Later tales in fact gave him a son and a grandson before the series was finally completed.) The stories embraced a variety of elements, adventure, humour, sentiment, exotic locations, out-of-the-way knowledge, religion, the occasional love interest, and not a little violence and sadism. As E. S. Turner has written in *Boys Will Be Boys*: "There can hardly have been a character as hard-boiled as this idol of the youth of the seventies, eighties and nineties ... the truth is there are few publishers of juvenile fiction today who would care to print unexpurgated some of the episodes in the strenuous career of Harkaway."

This resourceful lad was the creation of Bracebridge Hemyng (1829–1904) the son of the Registrar of the Supreme Court of Calcutta, who was raised and educated to follow in his father's footsteps at the Bar. However, once established as a barrister in the Middle Temple, he decided to fill in his time between briefs—which were not as plentiful as he had hoped—by writing fiction. He proved a swift and dramatic writer and apart from contributing numerous long serials to the *London Journal*, wrote several novels including "Curious Crimes", "Secrets of the Turf" and his best-seller "Called to the Bar", not to mention a few "yellow backs" such as "A Stock Exchange Romance" and "The Man of the Period". (He is also believed to have collaborated with Henry Mayhew in compiling *London Labour and the London Poor*.)

It was in 1871 that he found his most enduring fame when he began writing the Jack Harkaway serials for Edwin Brett's *Boys of England*. This one character probably did more than anything to ensure the success of the magazine and make Brett's ultimate fortune—and it is said that at the height of Harkaway's popularity, newsagents fought with each other in the street outside the publisher's offices to get their copies, so great was the demand by readers. The stories were almost immediately pirated in America by the publisher Frank Leslie; who, perhaps suffering from a quirk of conscience at the enormous success he thereafter derived, invited Hemyng to move to America and continue his series from there. This Hemyng did, and the huge circulation of the adventures kept him in affluence in a palatial residence on Staten Island.

In 1877, however, he decided to return to England, and for a time even took up the practice of the law again. He continued to write Harkaway stories for Leslie and Brett until the English publisher's death in 1895, and thereafter produced tales of the Harkaway offspring for George Emmett until his own passing.

The variety of his work is indicated by just a sample of the titles in the series: "Jack Harkaway's Adventures Round the World", "Jack Harkaway on the Prairie", "Jack Harkaway and his Son's Adventures in China", "Jack Harkaway in the Transvaal", etcetera. He is also believed to have written numerous other serials for boys—several of which appeared in penny-parts—including the well-known

"Scapegrace" stories, "Fatherless Bob" and "Mischievous Mat"; but none matched the popularity of Harkaway.

To conclude this collection, then, I have selected an episode from the first tale in the series, "Jack Harkaway's Schooldays" which presages not only the young man's ability to fall inevitably into adventure and rely on his own resources to extricate himself, but sets him on the course which was to change juvenile fiction once and for all. E. S. Turner sums up the event superbly: "There was nothing Gothic about the Harkaway stories. There may have been a strong smell of blood, but not of the charnel-house. There may have been some uncommonly ruthless characters, but there were no secret, black and midnight hags. Here, at last, were stories which were free from the aura of the *Newgate Calendar*."

The Road To Adventure

It may be as well to state that in running away from school our hero had no defined plan.

He was merely goaded into an act that had very little to defend it but the harsh treatment he received from the headmaster.

His wish was to get away, at all hazards, from the tyranny under which he groaned, and when we remember that he was friendless and persecuted, perhaps some excuse can be made for him.

Let us not be misunderstood. We are no advocates for running away; boys who run away from their schools generally turn out scamps in after life.

They show an independence of action and a strong self-will, in which it is very injurious for the young to indulge.

It was dark and cold; rain began to fall from the heavily-charged clouds, and a more cheerless November night could not have been found upon which to dare the unknown perils of the outside world.

Pulling his cap over his eyes, and drawing up his coat

collar, Jack trudged along manfully, going along a road which led he knew not where.

In his pocket he had a few shillings, which he thought would get him a bed and breakfast at some roadside inn, or, failing in that, he could lie down under a haystack, a dry ditch at that time of the year being out of the question.

For a couple of hours he went on at a jog-trot before he ventured to stop.

He reckoned that he had travelled about six or seven miles.

The road was lonely, and it was a relief to see, on the right, some lights shining from the windows of a large house.

A clock over some stables struck the hour of eleven.

Tired and weary in brain and body, he got through a gap in the hedge, hoping to find a place of shelter in some outbuilding, where he could rest until morning.

A shed, in which were some agricultural implements, invited entrance.

A few trusses of straw in one corner afforded prospect of a bed.

Crawling in, Jack laid himself down on the straw, into which he sank till he was nearly covered.

As usual, he said his prayers, and with a sense of relief at his good luck, turned over on his side in the fresh clean straw to go to sleep.

It was now raining steadily outside, but he was not very wet, and soon began to feel warm.

While half asleep and half awake, he fancied he heard voices in the shed.

Opening his eyes, he could see nothing; but he felt that he was not alone.

His heart beat violently, but he breathed as gently as he could, and listened.

Suddenly a man spoke in a hoarse whisper.

"I say, Jem, just give a look outside, and see if there is a light still in the butler's pantry. That's the way we mean to get in, and it won't do to let old Blocks have a shot at us with his blunderbuss."

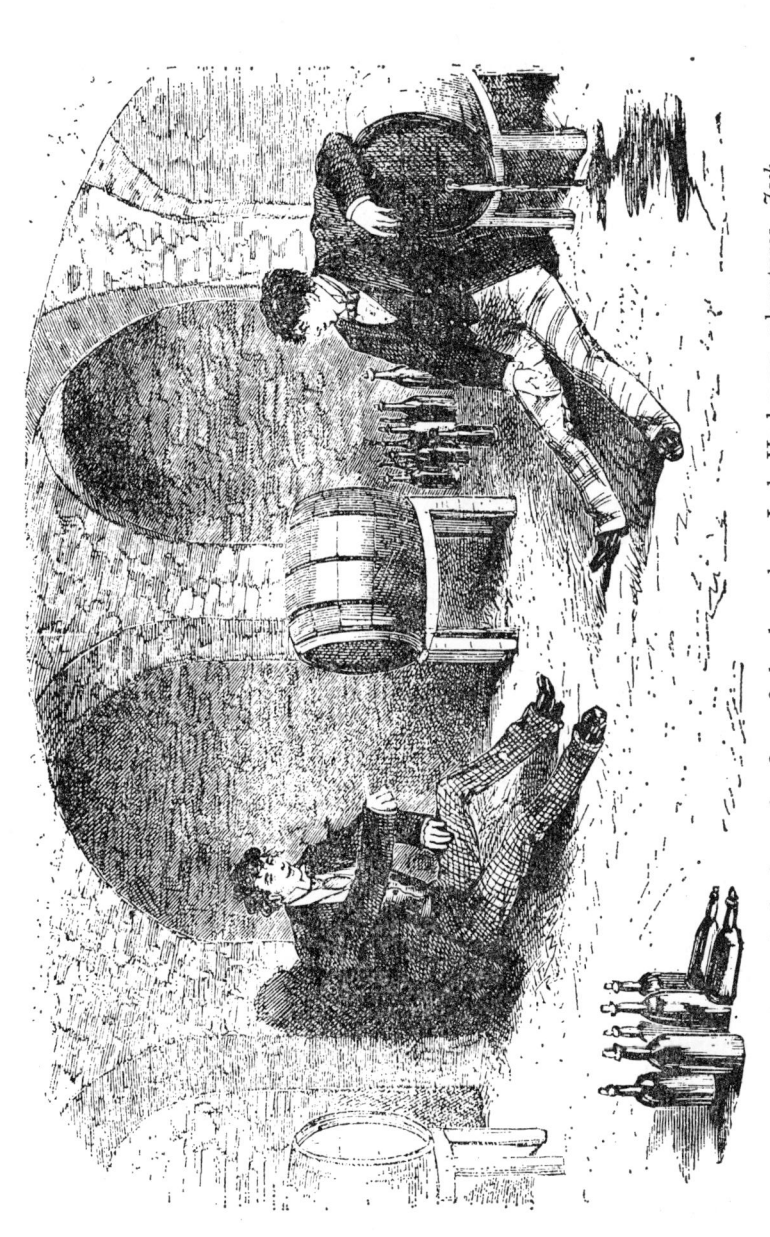

A carousing episode from the first of the legendary Jack Harkaway adventures, *Jack Harkaway's Schooldays* by Bracebridge Hemyng (1871).

"Right you are, mate. I'll just take a squint," replied the other.

In an instant Jack comprehended that these men intended burglary at the big house in which he had seen lights as he had come along the road.

Perhaps by crawling into that shed he might be the means of preventing robbery and even murder.

Who could tell?

But how to do it?—that was the question.

For the present all he could do was to lie still and listen.

He feared to make the least sound or movement, lest the desperate men in whose company he was should hear and kill him.

It was a terrible position for so young a boy to be placed in, and he had need of all his courage and self-possession.

But he was a boy of ready resource and his nerves were strong.

Jack was no coward, as he had proved already on more than one occasion.

Presently Jem returned and said in a half whisper:

"He's doused the glim, Tony, but we'll have to bide a bit. It won't do to risk the job."

"No, no! If we crack this crib proper," returned the one addressed as Tony, "the swag will make us for life."

"You're right," replied Jem, "we're made then, and I for one shall step it over to 'Stralia and try my hand at farming in the bush. I'm tired of this country, where a poor man can't get a living unless he takes what isn't his'n."

"And when he's cotched he's sent to prison," laughed Tony.

"Lor'! what a number er times I've been fullied (i.e. fully committed)! There isn't a prison in Lunnon as I haven't been inside of, and I know most of the gaols in the home counties."

"Same here, but I don't want no more on it," Tony exclaimed.

"Have you got the bottle of liquor?" asked Jem.

"It's here."

"Give us a toothful. I feel as if a drop would keep the rheumatics out of one's bones this cussed weather."

"It's lovely weather for our job though, dark as pitch, with a nice blinding rain."

"Yes; that's what a cracksman wants," answered Jem, who put the bottle to his lips.

A low gurgling sound, followed by a sigh of satisfaction, told him that he had taken a good draught.

"That's the stuff to warm a chap," he said, approvingly. "Give me brandy to do work upon on a cold night."

"Right you are. Give it here. I'll do ditto," replied Tony.

"Have you got the tools safe?"

"In the bag."

As he spoke, Tony rattled a green baize bag containing jemmy, centrebit, dark lantern, silent matches, and the varied stock-in-trade of an experienced burglar.

Jack would have given the world to be able to crawl out at some hole in the corner of the shed, and alarm the inmates of the big house.

But he was afraid to move lest he should call the attention of the burglars to himself.

That they were burglars there could not be the shadow of a shade of doubt.

So he remained as still as a mouse, every minute seeming an age.

At last the stable clock struck the hour of twelve.

Carefully he counted the strokes.

Midnight!

The hour when ghosts are supposed to walk, and graves give up their dead.

A time more suitable for desperate deeds that will not bear the light of day than any other.

"Time's up," said Tony.

"Right lad," replied his companion.

"Business, Jem."

"I'm your man. I suppose we'd better make for the pantry winder."

"That's the ticket," said Tony.

"I hope there ain't any plagey dogs about. I can't abear dogs; they do yelp and bark so. But we've some poisoned meat if so be as they give tongue."

"They bite, too, cuss 'em. I had a bit taken out o' the carf of my leg once, when I was doing a bit of work down at Edmonton, and I don't know which hollered most, the dorg or me, for I got the dorg's tongue in my hand, and pulled it every night out. That job got me lagged, it did, and I've hated dorgs ever since like steam, I have."

Presently the burglars vacated the shed, and Jack heard their footsteps retreating as they went towards the house.

"Now's my time," he thought.

Rising quickly, he crept out of his warm bed of straw, and got into the open air, which was heavily charged with moisture.

The rain descended steadily, and it was evidently going to be a wet night.

It was useless to go to the back, as that was the direction taken by the burglars.

So Jack determined to make his way to the front door, and either by ringing the bell, or knocking as a last resource, to disturb the inmates, and put them on their guard against the robbers.

*   *   *

It was with some difficulty that Jack, in the dark, found the front door of the house, which, from its size, appeared to belong to some rich landowner.

It was not of the farm order at all.

The architecture, the elegant flower beds, the luxuriant laurels, and other shrubs, betokening taste and wealth.

There was no light to be seen.

All the inmates had presumably gone to bed, which increased the difficulties Jack had to contend with.

Having found a bell, he pulled it at first gently, and again with more violence.

His object was not to disturb the burglars at their work, for should they take the alarm and go away, the people of the house would not believe his tale.

Probably they would take him for a thief, and drive him with threats from the door, if they did not give him in charge of the police.

To his great satisfaction, after the second ring, he heard footsteps approaching across the hall; a key grated in the lock, and the door was opened cautiously.

"Who's that?" cried a man's voice.

"A friend, who wants to speak to you on most important business," answered Jack.

"To me? Do you know who I am?" said the man.

"No; it is enough for me that you are an inmate of this house."

"I'm Mr Blocks, the butler, and was just turning into my bed. Am I the person? No humbug, now."

"Yes—yes; you'll do as well as anybody else. For goodness sake don't waste any more time. Open the door," cried Jack.

"I don't know whether I ought to," said Mr Blocks, in a tone of reflection. "It's past twelve. I'm the only one up in the house, and it seems to me that you haven't told me who you are, or what your business is."

"Do you want to lose your plate, and perhaps be murdered in the bargain?"

"Oh, Lord! he says he'll murder me. Where's my blunderbuss?" cried the butler.

"You've nothing to fear from me," rejoined Jack, in despair at his thickheadedness. "I've come to put you on your guard."

"Oh! You're not after the plate?"

"No. Is it likely I should come here and talk to you if I had any such intention?"

"Well, on consideration, it isn't."

"Open the door, then. I am only a boy, and surely a man like you isn't afraid of a lad."

"Only a boy? Why didn't you say so before? Only a boy? I ain't afraid of no boys," replied Mr Blocks, in a tone of contempt.

He opened the door a little wider.

"I say," he exclaimed, as a new thought struck him.

"Well, what now?"

"Have you got anyone with you? No tricks upon travellers, you know. I've got a loaded blunderbuss, and I ain't particular to blowing a man's brains out if—"

"But I'm not a man," answered Jack, impatiently.

"Ah! I forgot that. Now, then; what's all the row about?"

The butler flung open the door as he spoke, and stood revealed, a little, stumpy, fat man, with a white cotton nightcap on, shivering in his shirtsleeves and trousers, and holding in his hand a candle which flickered and sputtered in the wind and rain.

Jack stepped quickly inside and closed the door, rather to the alarm of the butler, who retreated towards the domestic offices, which were reached by a passage to the rear, leading from the hall.

"I will tell you all in a few words," said Jack. "I am, or rather was, at school near here."

"Crawcour's," said the butler.

"Yes. Do you know it?"

"Never mind; go on," Mr Blocks replied, with a sagacious nod which would have done credit to a magistrate on the bench.

"This evening, I ran away and walked till I came here. Feeling tired, I crept into your shed at the back."

"Rogue and vagabond," muttered Mr Blocks, suspiciously.

"While on some straw in the shed, two men came in, who I am convinced were burglars from their conversation. Their object was to break into your pantry, and steal all they could lay their hands on."

"Bless us and save us!" cried the butler, raising his hands.

"There are two of them. How can we catch them?"

"Two of 'em!"

"Yes; are you the only man in the house?"

"Stop a bit. There's the coachman and some grooms over the stable, and the gardener, he's got a gun. Will you stop here? I feel I can trust you, young gentleman. I'll go and rouse them; stand close by the door, and when you hear three taps with the knuckles open softly."

"Shall I go instead of you?" asked Jack.

"It's no use; you don't know the way, and we have no time to lose."

"All right," said Jack.

Mr Blocks, owing to the imminence of the danger, had awakened to a sense of activity, which as a general rule, was quite foreign to his character.

Putting on a coat which was hanging up in the hall, he sallied forth into the wind and rain, and Jack was left alone.

More than once during his brief vigil he fancied he heard the centrebit at work filing away the iron bars, which had to be removed ere the burglars could effect an entry into the house.

His heart throbbed proudly, for he felt he was the hero of an adventure for which he would receive the thanks of those whom he was protecting.

One, two, three.

Mr Blocks was tapping at the door; gladly Jack opened it, and two men entered.

"This is the coachman," explained Mr Blocks, "the gardener and two men have gone round to the back. We mean to have the rascals."

"I think they have already got in; the grinding noise I heard has stopped," said Jack.

"All the better," remarked the coachman, who was armed with an iron bar, heavy enough, when wielded by strong arms, to fell an ox.

In a side room was the blunderbuss, which belonged to

the butler. He took it up, looked to the lock, and the men followed by Jack, stole on tiptoe along the passage.

The candle was left in the hall.

A lantern was carried by the coachman and its light concealed by a fold of his coat which was thrown over it.

When the pantry was reached a light was seen under the door.

The thieves were at work.

Quickly turning the key, Blocks threw the door open.

Jem made his lantern dark immediately, but the coachman turned his light on.

The plate-chest was broken open, and the costly articles it contained were thrown about on the floor ready to be packed up for removal.

Tony made a rush for the window, and fell into the arms of the gardener, who struck him a blow which rendered him senseless, and he was made a prisoner, being strongly bound with ropes, provided by the groom.

Jem drew a revolver which he presented at the butler, who however was too quick for him.

He discharged his blunderbuss and shot the villain, who fell to the ground with a prolonged groan.

"Oh! Lord have mercy upon me! I'm done for this journey," he cried.

"And serve you right too, you thieving rascal," answered the butler.

The coachman proceeded to fasten him securely, regardless of the pain of his wound.

"Are there any more of them?" he asked.

"No," said Mr Blocks, "one inside one out, that's the lot."

The wounded man's hurt was staunched as well as could be done, and the burglars were placed on the floor of the pantry, while a mounted groom was sent off for the attendance of the police, and surgical assistance.

"Well," said Jack, who had been an attentive but silent spectator of what had taken place, "now you have settled your little affair, I suppose you can dispense with my services, and will allow me to return to my bed and my straw."

"Begging your pardon, sir," replied Blocks, "you will do nothing of the sort."

"What shall I do, then? Will you give me a shakedown?"

"Will I? Of course I will; after the service you have rendered to this establishment, you have a right to a bed."

"Will you let me go in the morning?" asked Jack dubiously.

"Will I let you go? Go where?"

"I am not quite clear about that; but go somewhere I must and will. I don't want to be sent to my school, and I have told you that I ran away."

"You may stop a month if you like," said Blocks.

"Who does this house belong to?"

"Lady Mordenfield."

"Indeed!" Jack said, with surprise. "Is this Willow Copse?"

"That's the name, and our young master is at your school."

"I know him well; but I wish I had come to any other house. However, I will accept your offer of a bed, and we can talk tomorrow morning," replied Jack.

The butler pressed him to have something to eat, which he did not refuse, and when his wants were satisfied, he was shown into a spare bed-room.

It was too late to rouse the housekeeper for sheets, and he was sufficiently tired to turn into the blankets, between which he slept soundly.

* * *

When Jack woke in the morning, he found his boots nicely cleaned, and a shirt spread out on a chair for him, showing that someone had cared for him while he slept.

His night's rest had done him good.

The morning was bright and clear, and no sign of the storm of the night before remained.

When dressed he rang the bell and Blocks came up.

"Morning, sir. How did you sleep?" asked Blocks.

"First rate, thank you," answered Jack.

"Her ladyship sends her compliments, sir, and will be glad to see you at breakfast."

"Is she down?"

"Just come, sir."

"All right. Lead the way," Jack said.

The butler ushered our hero into the breakfast-room, which was very handsomely furnished.

Standing near the window was a lady.

She turned as Jack entered, and advancing towards him, offered her hand.

"How do you do?" she said. "I am glad to make the acquaintance of one who, I hear from my servant, knows my own little boy."

"We were at school together," replied Jack.

"Why do you say you *were*?" she asked.

"Because I have run away."

"Indeed, that is very wrong, is it not? May I inquire why you have left your school, without seeming rudely inquisitive?"

"I was so badly treated," replied Jack.

"If so, could you not write to your friends?"

"I have none."

"None at all?"

"My mother and father I never knew, and my guardian is not at all kind," Jack said.

"What is your guardian's name?"

"Mr Scratchley, of Highgate."

Her ladyship started and seemed much astonished and perturbed.

"Scratchley?" she repeated, abstractedly.

"Do you know him?" asked Jack.

"The name seemed familiar to me?" she answered. "And you are—?"

"John Harkaway!"

Recovering herself from her momentary confusion, by the exertion of a violent effort she said:

"Sit down, and have some breakfast. We must be great friends. I have to thank you for preventing my house from being robbed last night."

"I am very happy, my lady, to think that I was so lucky as to be able to be of service to you."

Jack made an excellent breakfast, and his spirits rose, but he was in reality ill at ease, for he scarcely knew what to do.

"Now," continued her ladyship, "I am going to ask you to let me drive you back to your school."

"Oh, no, I cannot go back," he replied.

"I will make Mr Crawcour promise to let you off this time," she said, smiling.

"I don't believe he would keep such a promise if he made it. He is dreadfully strict," replied Jack.

"What do you think of doing?" Lady Mordenfield inquired, regarding him curiously.

"Schoolboys have only one resource when they run away," Jack replied, laughing.

"And that resource is—?" said Lady Mordenfield.

"To go to sea."

"So you think of going to sea?"

"Yes, I shall try and make my way to the coast. I should have gone by train if I had had money enough."

"A sailor's life is a hard one," she replied.

"I am strong, and young, and hardy. Beside, it is a life of adventure, and what can be more delightful?" Jack said, his face flushing with pleasure, at the thought of the prospect before him.

"Will you stay with me?"

"Thank you very much, but I must make a start in the world some time or other, and I may as well begin at once."

"Have you no ambition?" Lady Mordenfield, queried.

"As to what?"

"A profession. Would you not like to be a great soldier, or a barrister, doctor, or something of that sort?"

"If I had the chance," replied Jack, adding, "you forget that nobody cares for me."

Her ladyship rose and kissed him tenderly on the forehead.

"You are mistaken, my dear boy, *I* care for you, I will be your friend," she said.

Jack was surprised at this unexpected exhibition of affection, and his eyes filled with tears.

"Will you but stay with me?" she urged.

"I cannot. I must be doing something!" he answered, reluctantly.

Her ladyship seemed disappointed.

"Will you promise me one thing?" she asked.

"Certainly. You have only to name it."

"Give me your word of honour that you will write to me when you reach the coast and tell me all about yourself and your plans."

"With pleasure," replied Jack.

Lady Mordenfield was obliged to be content with this reply.

She gave Jack a sovereign, which she with difficulty made him accept, and he trudged away manfully on the road.

APPENDIX 1

"Penny Packets Of Poison"
by James Greenwood

THIS ARTICLE APPEARED in Greenwood's collection of essays *The Wilds of London* published by Chatto & Windus in 1874. The author was a noted journalist who wrote on many contemporary social issues and said it was his delight to do "my humble endeavour towards exposing and extirpating social abuses and those hole-in-the-corner evils which afflict society".

* * *

There is a plague that is striking its upas roots deeper and deeper into English soil—chiefly metropolitan—week by week, and flourishing broader and higher, and yielding great crops of fruit that quickly fall, rotten-ripe, strewing highway and by-way, tempting the ignorant and unwary, and breeding death and misery unspeakable. Were it possible to keep a record of the wreck and ruin the plague in question engenders, and to officially publish it as the cholera and cattle plague returns were published, a very considerable sensation would undoubtedly be the result; but since its baleful influence is—as is generally supposed—confined almost entirely to the vulgar ground it is indigenous to, and there is little fear of its spreading beyond certain well-defined and ascertained limits easy to avoid; since it is not, according to the popular acceptation of the term, "catching", and one need labour under no alarm lest it come on the wings of the wind in at our pleasant chamber window, and street cabs are not likely to be impregnated with it, nor omnibuses, nor theatres, nor halls of public assembly, why—why, there's an end of it.

It is, however, a plague not included in the ordinary category that is the subject of this paper—the plague of poisonous literature.

Before me I have twelve penny packets of the poison, gathered at random out of a choice of at least twice as many offered me at the little shop—one of a thousand—devoted to its propagation. It was not on account of their unpromising titles that the remaining pen'orths of poison were not secured. There was "The Boy Bandit", "The Black Monk's Curse", "Blueskin", "Claude Duval, the Dashing Highwayman", "The Vampire's Bride", "The Boy Jockey", "The Wild Boys of London", and many more, of the names of which I have not a distinct recollection. The dozen I received in return for my shilling are entitled, "The Boy King of the Highwaymen", "The Skeleton Crew", "Roving Jack, the Pirate Hunter", "Tyburn Dick", "Spring Heel'd Jack", "Admiral Tom, the King of the Boy Buccaneers", "Starlight Nell", "Hounslow Heath, or the Moonlight Riders", "Red Wolf, the Pirate", "The Knight of the Road", "The Adventures of an Actress", and "The Pretty Girls of London".

Nasty-feeling, nasty-looking packets are every one of them, and, considering the virulent nature of their contents, their most admirable feature is their extremely limited size. Satisfactory as this may be from one point of view, however, it is woefully significant of the irresistibly seductive nature of the bane with which each shabby little square of paper is spread. I have been at the pains to weigh them, and I find that the weight of each pen'orth is but a fraction more than *a quarter of an ounce*. The "Leisure Hour" weighs nearly eight times as much, so do the "Family Herald" and one or two other penny publications of a decent sort. It is the infinitesimal quantity of trash that may be palmed off for a penny that serves as the carrion bait to attract towards it the blow-flies of the book trade. They are enabled to hold out strong inducements to the needy shopkeepers of poor neighbourhoods. The ordinary discount to the trade on ordinary publications is 25 per cent., but the worthy publishers of "Alone in the Pirates' Lair" and "The Skeleton Crew" can afford to allow double that, and more. Wholesale you may buy the precious pen'orths at the rate of fivepence a dozen, and there is no risk to the dealer, since all unsold copies from last week are changed for a similar number of the day's date. This is the lure that tempts the tobacconist and the sweetstuff vendor and the keeper of the small chandlery, and induces these worthy tradesmen to give to this pernicious, though profitable, class of goods all the publicity of which their shop window is capable. No doubt that many of these retailers engage in the business utterly unconscious of the sin and shame they are aiding and abetting. It was at a chandler's shop where I purchased *my* twelve pen'orth, and quite a wholesome, matronly woman, with a baby in her arms, served me.

"To be sure, sir," said she, "you are quite right. 'Tyburn Dick' and 'The Pretty Girls' just make the dozen"; and made up the parcel with as much indifference as though it were sugar or biscuits. She would have been mightily astonished, and not improbably indignant, had she been informed that this branch of her trade was as injurious to public morality as if she had kept a repository for stolen goods. It would have been no more than true had she been so informed, however; and if she and other sellers of poison for the minds of girls and boys should happen to read this, and take it to heart, why, so much the better.

A delectable company appears to be foremost of the gang whose profit is the dissemination of impure literature; but there are many rivals in the field—some bearing the printer's or publisher's name and address, others without either—and each vies with his neighbour in the decoction of the pen'orths of muck, endeavouring to outshine him. One and all of the poison packets are illustrated on the outside, and we will give a glance at each, both inside and out, as the fairest method of testing its quality. It may be mentioned that this may be done no less fairly by a weekly instalment of eight pages than by a review of the completed story. There is no such thing as "plot" in this sort of literature. Such an arrangement would only embarrass the publisher, whose sole and single aim is to go on supplying his public with "The Red Wolf" or the "The Skeleton Crew" just so long as they will swallow it. One pen'orth of my collection—"Black Bess; or, The Knights of the Road"—is *a hundred and eighty-four weeks old*, and is quite as vigorous now as at the first week of its birth.

"Spring Heel'd Jack, the Terror of London", is the first on the list. Picture: Jack—with the spring visible at his heels, punching savagely at a policeman's face, and dashing his head against the wall. Summary of contents: Jack indecently assaults a maiden lady, drags her about her bed-chamber by her bed-gown, which is pulled over her head, and finally thrusts her into another bedroom to pass the night with an elderly bachelor gentleman. Somebody springs a rattle, neighbours rouse, bachelor's door forced, bachelor in night garment exposed, and maiden lady dragged nude from beneath bachelor's bed. Next chapter: the loves of a policeman and a maid-of-all-work, and a "spicy" scene of the pair in the shadow of a tomb in a churchyard at midnight.

"Says the policeman: 'You lets them catamarans (the girl's mistresses) frighten you from doing your duty, you does.' 'My duty?' 'Yes.' 'What duty?' 'What duty, Peggy? Can you look me in the face and ask the question?' 'I don't know what you mean.' 'You don't?' 'No.' 'I do.' 'What is it?' Bristles placed his hand beneath his belt, and heaved a deep sigh. 'Don't you tumble?' he asked. 'No.' 'Then you is green.' 'What do you mean, Mr Bristles?' asked the girl, in surprise. 'Mean? Oh! Dull of comprehension!' 'I know I am.' 'You are.' 'But 'tain't my fault.' 'Not yours; no, no, not at all; but part—but part,' said Bristles, shaking his head sadly. 'Oh! do explain,' said the girl, in a pleading and half terrified tone. 'What can I do? What do you want me to do? What do you ask?'"

And, in reply, Mr Bristles, makes a joke disgusting enough to provoke the ghost of Lord Campbell, and so the story is left "to be continued in our next".

"Tyburn Dick" is the next. Picture: A young gentleman, presumably the King of Highwaymen himself, with lace and ruffles, cocked hat, jack-boots, and a splendid jewelled star extending across his chest by way of denoting his rank, sword in hand, on a lonely heath at midnight, defiantly receiving the "warning of doom". (Doom being represented by a hideous spectre rising in flames out of the grass.) Summary of contents of part: "Dick in Newgate—The gaoler trapped into Dick's cell—'Give me the keys, or with my manacle, will I scatter your recreant brains against the slimy wall!'— Newgate on fire: the cell growing red-hot—'Give me the keys!' 'Ha! ha! never!'

"Dick was exasperated to madness. Putting his two hands together, he grasped the long links, and, poising them straight and firm, dashed them into the gaoler's exultant face. The iron ring joining them struck him between the temples, the two long links dashed into his eyes. He uttered a fearful groan, and fell blind, stunned, and bleeding. 'It grows frightfully hot,' he muttered, as the hot beads of sweat rolled down his face. 'The cell is like an oven. There must be a furnace outside. Am I doomed to perish here? Confusion! why don't they batter down the walls? Ho, there! Help! help! I am here, chained to a wall, amidst the flames!'"

However, it is all right. A friend of Dick's has gone on a visit to the incarcerated highwayman's mother, who is a countess. There is a ball at the countess's, to which all the bloated aristocracy of the kingdom have been invited. However, hearing that she is wanted, the countess hastens down to the parlour, where Claud (the friend) is waiting, and is thus addressed by that gentleman:

" 'Be not alarmed! I am not come to taunt you with the

wrongs you have done me, though they have seared my brain, I am come, unnatural and adulterous mother, to warn you of your persecution of that poor boy, against whom you have steeled your bosom—forgetting that he first drew his sustenance from it. You have hurled him from these halls, which are rightfully his, and have driven him to a life of roadside robbery, and even now have hounded him to a prison, whose walls he may only quit to go forth to a felon's doom. We shall free him this time, but I warn you, fair-faced devil!—cold, callous, unwomanly demon!—I warn you that if the bitter death you desire befalls him—if a hangman's accursed hand crushes out his young life—you shall pay the penalty, and the penalty shall be death, though I myself tear your infamous heart from your unnatural breast!'"

And since, so far as the story goes, the lady shows no signs of relenting, the reader is justified in his expectation of getting a very fair pen'orth next week.

No. 3. "The Skeleton Crew." Picture: A pair of ghostly, bodyless legs advancing towards a cavalier who has an affrighted lady under his protection, and, who, with hair on end, stands with his rapier advanced to receive the goblin remnant. Since the typographical part of the number makes no allusion to this mystery, it may be assumed that it was accounted for in the last pen'orth, or will be in the next. From what can be gathered in the eight pages, the "Skeleton Crew" are a band of decayed robbers risen from their tombs, and still continuing the nefarious pursuits that was their bent while in the flesh. They, however, retain an appetite for the substantials of life, and rob and murder wholesale and retail. Death-wing is the chief, and here is a specimen of his everyday employments:

Old Redgill had two ships on their way from the Indies, laden with gold, spices, and silks. In consideration of receiving half of the cargo, Death-wing and his infamous crew resolved to waylay these two ships and attack them when about fifty miles from the Land's End. This was done. The crews of both ships were murdered in cold blood. This system of villany was repeated more than once, but as Philip's father's ships did not arrive in port except at intervals of many months, the villanous young man frequently found his money running short. "Bloodshed to him was quite a usual thing." So he murdered his father's cashier, and made merry with the money. However, the detectives are on his track, and unless his friends the skeletons assist him, he may look out for squalls. Humorous fellows are these fleshless ones, and the number is agreeably lightened by a droll account of how they hanged half a dozen innocent men in a belfry.

Pen'orth number four is entitled "Hounslow Heath". Picture: A poor wretch undergoing some frightful torture. He is extended on the ground, a waggon wheel is lying atop of him, and by his side are various instruments of torment, consisting in a knife, two flaming torches, a glue-pot, and a spoke-shave. Gloating over his agony stand two ruffians with highwaymen's masks on. Dick Turpin figures in this story. Our number opens with an account of how he was hard beset by the officers of the law, how he blew out the brains of a Jew and sliced up others with his sword; but, overpowered by numbers, is about to yield, when in the nick of time he is rescued by some old friends who "suddenly appear on the scene". Then Dick stops a stage-coach single-handed, and robs the passengers in his customary polite and graceful manner. Further on, it seems that the band of which Mr Turpin is the captain capture a person whom they suspect of planning to place them in the hands of justice. So they proceed to torture him as the picture on the front page faintly foretells.

"Firstly, they fastened him securely round the ankles with some stout cords. Then they passed two more ropes through these thongs, and dexterously enough hauled him up to the roof of the cave, where he was allowed to hang head downwards. In this unpleasant predicament they put him through such a course of novel tortures that a tribe of North American Indians might have picked up a wrinkle there. And they made merry while he was in the greatest agony. The more he shrieked with pain, the louder grew their shrieks of laughter. They probed him with their swords and burnt the tip of his nose with a red-hot poker, while one of his torturers held back his arms. A huge, square block of stone was brought and tied across with stout cords, the ends of which were made into a noose, and slung around Toby Marks's neck. No rack ever known could create such awful torture as this."

After a while, however, they released the victim from the weight of the stone. "Toby Marks dangled now a dead weight by his legs; the two robbers saw the thick and deep-coloured blood roll sluggishly from his nostrils. Then it burst in a torrent from his ears and mouth, and soon his face presented a horrible spectacle to look upon. The blood had completely saturated his hair, until he looked as though he had been newly scalped. The torture was over. The traitorous wretch could bear no more in safety, and so they cut him down. And thus did they avenge the sad end of the gallant Tom King!"

"The Pretty Girls of London" has, as its title was doubtless calculated to imply, more to do with the tender passions than with the bravery of masculine adventure. The illustration on the outer page depicts a hideous lady administering the Russian knout to three young women, who are naked to the waist and gracefully writhing in agony. A young lady named May would appear to be the heroine of the tale, and we find her immured in a convent over which the Rev. Mr Blinker has authority. An interview between this person and May occupies a considerable portion of the part.

" 'I tell you I want to be your friend; come with me quietly,' says the Rev. Mr Blinker. 'And if I don't?' 'I shall take you by force.' May shuddered. 'Come along then.' As he spoke he gently drew her a few steps. She followed him mechanically out of the room door and into the passage. What did his conduct mean? She trembled and recoiled from him in terror. He held her hand tighter and drew her into a room, the door of which was locked when May tried it. He seated her on a couch and himself beside her. 'Listen to me,' he said in a thick whisper, while his eyes had a strange wolfish glare in them which made May shiver and flush deeply beneath his devouring gaze. 'I do not wish to harm you or get you into trouble. Will you leave this house with me quietly, or stay till your persecutor returns? you know your doom if you stay.' 'I will not go with you,' said May firmly. 'Then I shall take you.' She gave a violent start, although his words were more than half expected by her. She endeavoured to disengage herself from the encircling arm which he stole round her waist. She pushed back the hideous face which he thrust close to hers. She was like a child in his arms; her struggles were without avail. With loosened hair, flushed face, and disordered apparel, she struggled madly in the monster's arms. His hot and hateful breath upon her face, his dry lips glued to hers so red and moist. She felt her last remaining strength fast failing away, and soon nothing could save her from the clutches of this odious ruffian. But in her desperate striving to free herself from this monster's embraces, her hand fell upon some hard substance in her pocket; she recollected a little knife she always carried about her. With a desperate effort she tore herself from his arms, and to open the knife was the work of a moment. She plunged the tiny weapon into the man's face. He started back from her with a sharp cry of agony, and staggered away a yard or two, the blood streaming down from his wound."

The pestilence in question is old enough to be grey—as one of its earliest promoters is alive to attest. It is now nearly a quarter of a century since the "Mysteries of the Court" and similar works from the same talented pen appeared to poison the minds of boys and girls; and at the present writing I have before me a "penny number", by the author of the "Mysteries of the Court", and I am bound to state that a cursory glance through it convinces me that it lacks none of the ancient fire—and brimstone. It is, therefore, quite a mistake to suppose that the literary ape is an animal of recent birth—a mistake the less excusable, because for a very long time past he has been at no pains to conceal his existence. Any day within the past ten years he may have been seen in his most hideous complexion staring bold-eyed from a hundred shop windows in and about London, alluring the unwary by means of pictures so revoltingly disgusting and indecent that modest eyes unexpectedly encountering them tingled in shame, and of which as much of the text pertaining as was exposed to view was the faithful echo. Possibly this ape, turned romancist—this "old man in the cloak"— has grown bolder of late. It is not unlikely that by dint of patient wallowing and groping in muck he has contrived to scrape together a considerable sum of money, and his terrors of a sentence of fine or imprisonment have consequently decreased, while it has enabled him to push the sale of his contagious trash by means of millions of handbills and advertisements in the few nasty newspapers remaining open to him. Anyway, it is certain that for a shameful length of time he has dared to bring his wares to the public market openly and unblushingly, and with the cool assurance of an honest man; and it is not a little curious that the lynx-eyed guardians of public morality have not ere this joined hands to catch and crush him.

It is always better, if possible, to show what a thing is in its own shape and colour than to endeavour to describe it. Half the abuses and miseries that, as a civilized nation, disgrace us, might be cured if the public could be brought to view them with its own eyes instead of trusting to the evidence of those of other folk. Undoubtedly it is very convenient to rely on hearsay, but there can be no question that it fosters dilatoriness and a neglect of individual duty, and should therefore be discouraged as far as possible. People believe only half what they hear, and, though it may concern never so grave a grievance, are content to do no more than join in the general lukewarm cry of condemnation, leaving the vigorous application of a remedy to those who have inquired into what is amiss, and who are therefore in a position to know all about it. It is so with this iniquitous boy literature and the sudden outcry against it. Everybody believes it to be odious and abominable because everybody says so: and so the dog, and most deservedly, gets a bad name—but he is *not* hanged; he is simply avoided. Because he is such a mangy, ill-looking cur, offensive alike to the nose and to the touch, all decent people shrink away from him. But he would much rather have their room than their company, and grins to himself as they give him the path, and permit him to continue his career of ravening and rending. He must be discovered in the act of mauling one of our little ones before we are moved to take hold of the brute and strangle him.

Now, it may be fearlessly asserted that there never lived an animal of prey of uglier type than this two-legged creature, who poisons the minds of little children to make his bread. Never a more dangerous one, for his manginess is hidden under a sleek and glossy coat, and lips of seeming innocence conceal his cruel teeth. His subtlety, too, is more than canine. He is gifted with a devilish power of beguiling boys and girls to take to him and nourish him in secret. Beware of him, O careful parents of little lads! He is as cunning as the fabled vampire. Already he may have bitten your little rosy-cheeked son Jack. He may be lurking at this very moment in that young gentleman's private chamber, little as you suspect it, polluting his mind and smoothing the way that leads to swift destruction. You may scout the idea with indignation, knowing your Jack to be a boy of honest mind, and one least of all likely to conceal matters of this kind from you; but, my dear sir, pray bear it in mind that nine-tenths of the parents of England are as ready as yourself to stand forward and vouch for the purity of *their* Jacks and Jills: but for all that, it is estimated that *upwards of a million* of these weekly pen'orths of abomination find customers.

I find, on looking through my "weekly numbers", that one "plot serves for the construction of the whole. It is a simple and at the same time comprehensive plot, and may be briefly summarized as a mocking and laughing to scorn of the full number of the Ten Commandments. The main arguments are, that there is no creature so noble as the thief, and that the noblest fellow's primest reward consists in boundless debauchery, in which intoxicating liquors and the loveliest of her sex, of course, figure most conspicuously. Here is a little ditty that may more clearly express my meaning. It is extracted from No. 5 of a stirring romance entitled "Tyburn Tree":

"Let the asses who choose drive the plough or the spade,
Let the noodles of commerce get guineas by trade,
Let the sailor for wealth skim the wild raging sea,
I envy not either—the high road for me!

"Brave fellows who, scorning to flinch or to falter,
Defy full-wigged beaks, and don't care for the halter;
Who taxes alike spendthrift, miser, and churl,
Then is off with light heart to his crib and his girl.

"And if, boys, at Tyburn, our exit we make,
A curse on the sneak who shall peach, or shall shake;
Let's swear to be faithful, if such our end be,
And manfully drop, like ripe fruit, from the tree."

The talented author, however, does not seem to regard this wind-up of the convicted ruffian's existence as a *sine qua non*, for at page 40 of his story he feelingly remarks: "Thank God! the torture of the Inquisition is now abolished, as we trust that the gallows will be before long. *But we must not moralize.*" Well, to be sure it does seem a little out of place, considering that a little further on our author puts into the mouth of one of his most famous characters such a sentence as the following:

"Who the devil would be chained to a dull shop, to plod

APPENDIX I

for paltry shillings, when he could jump on the back of his good steed, cry 'Stand and deliver' to the first he meets, and return to his girl and his glass with golden-lined pockets?"

There is always a banding together by means of some terrible oath amongst the ruffians and murderers of penny romance. Wretched little London errand boys, following to the best of their ability in the footsteps of their heroes, not uncommonly imitate them in this respect. To be sure they cannot hope just at present to get up so imposing a ceremony as the "Tyburn Tree" band engaged in, but no doubt it has furnished them many valuable hints.

"A large goblet nearly filled with red wine was brought and placed on a low stool; on either side of this were laid a dagger, a phial of deadly poison, a halter, a loaded pistol, and a hideous-looking human skull from which the hair had not yet all fallen away, and which had an earthy and charnel-like odour.

"All the lights in the hall excepting the one which hung immediately over the low stool, and the fearful things placed thereupon, were then extinguished, and the red light now glaring on the instruments of death and on the grinning skull produced a fearful effect!

"One of the gang, who had a rude lancet in his hand, then commanded Hawkins to bare his left arm. This having been done, he was made to kneel down, and the lancet having made an incision into one of the small veins at the bend of the elbow, the blood which streamed from the orifice was suffered to fall into the wine goblet, and when about the sixth part of a pint had issued, the flow was stopped and the slight wound bandaged up.

" 'Lieutenant, administer the oath!' commanded Captain Fury.

"Fresnean now requested Hawkins to repeat after him:

" 'I hereby, in the presence of God, man, and devil, bind myself to serve as a freetrader in this gang; to obey my captain in all his commands, whether at the peril of my life or otherwise; to keep faithfully all his secrets, and never to betray those with whom I am associated. Also to guard against all treachery; in the performance of my duties to spare neither friend nor foe—young or old—man, woman, or child; and if guilty of traitorhood, to agree to take my choice of halter, poison, or dagger, and never until death to quit the Black Gang.'

"As soon as Hawkins repeated the words of this oath, the goblet of mixed wine and blood was handed to him, and he was ordered to drink to the dregs the fearful mixture. The cord, the poison, and the dagger were then handed to him, the halter being dropped over his neck, the poison phial placed to his lips, and the dagger's point placed to his breast. His hands also, during the speaking of these words, were placed on the hideous relic of mortality.

"It was the head of a former member of the gang. Pointing to it, Captain Fury informed Hawkins that the crime of which the man to whom it once belonged had been guilty, had been a violation of his oath, and that his skull would be so used should he be guilty of a similar offence."

And so, having bound himself in the eyes of "God, man, and devil", the new member of the villainous brotherhood was entitled to participate in the manifold advantages the high distinction confers. Chief among these is the companionship of "female beauty". It is in this branch of his profession that the cankerer of young minds shines brightest. His tactics are invariable. Awaiting the return of every "highwayman", or "burglar", or "burker" of his collection is a "lovely young female", who as soon as he takes his seat perches herself on his knee, and enfolds his neck with her "soft, plump arms, white as alabaster".

But further to select from the ugly batch of seventeen would be to suggest the possibility that in only a few instances were they so very bad. This would be conveying a false impression. Undoubtedly, some of the weekly numbers contain more of obscenity and flagrant indecency than others; but of the ingredients indicated they are one and all composed, and differ only in proportion and mixing. In every one of the "romances" in question there is a highwayman, or a burglar, or a footpad, who is wonderfully successful in all he undertakes, and with whom guineas are as common as nuts in a squirrel's nest. In every instance there exists the fiercest hatred between the "hero" and the law, and it is the author's aim to show constantly what a purblind, weak-minded affair the law is; and considering how very little a "daring spirit" has to encounter in defying it, and how that same defying it means every luxury that can be desired without the mean, degrading drudgery of working for it, what a wonder it is that there are so many "asses who drive the plough or the spade", and so few valiant ones "who defy full-wigged beaks, and don't care for the halter". This is the theme never-ending—this and the other deadly pernicious ingredient, the "lovely wanton", in a description of whose "charms", from her eyes to her heels, the author wallows with evident great personal gratification.

What more remains to be said, except once again to apologize to my readers for so boldly uncovering the unsavoury stew and clapping it so immediately under their nostrils? It is a most unthankful task to do so; but the effect will be salutary, I hope and believe. It is hard to credit that fathers of families would so long have endured the existence of the "Boy Highwayman", or the "Boy Burglar", or "Tyburn Dick", if they really knew the monsters each and every one of these worthies were.

APPENDIX 2

"Horrible Murder And Human Pie-Makers"
Anonymous

THIS REPORT, WHICH may well have been one of the major sources for the story of Sweeney Todd, was published in 1825 in the penny magazine, *The Tell Tale*. It is the only known written English account of the dreadful crime.

*   *   *

In the Rue-de-la-Harpe, which is a long dismal ancient street in the faubourg of St Marcell, is a space or gap in the line of building upon which formerly stood two dwelling-houses, instead of which stands now a melancholy memorial, signifying, that upon this spot no human habitation shall ever be erected, no human being ever must reside!

Curiosity will, of course, be greatly excited to ascertain what it was that rendered this devoted spot so obnoxious to humanity, and yet so interesting to history.

Two attached and opulent neighbours, residing in some province, not very remote from the French capital, having occasion to go to town on certain money transactions, agreed to travel thence and to return together, which was to be done with as much expedition as possible. They were on foot, a very common way even at present, for persons of much respectability to travel in France, and were attended, as most pedestrians are, by a faithful dog.

APPENDIX 2   373

Upon their arrival at the Rue-de-la-Harpe, they stepped into the shop of a peruquier to be shaved, before they would proceed to business, or enter into the more fashionable streets. So limited was their time, and peremptory was their return, that the first man who was shaved, proposed to his companion, that while he was undergoing the operation of the razor, he who was already shaven would run and execute a small commission in the neighbourhood, promising that he would be back before the other was ready to move. For this purpose he left the shop of the barber.

On returning, to his great surprise and vexation, he was informed that his friend was gone; but as the dog, which was the dog of the absentee, was sitting outside of the door, the other presumed he was only gone out for the moment, perhaps in pursuit of him; so expecting him back every moment, he chatted to the barber whilst he waited his return.

Such a considerable time elapsed that the stranger now became quite impatient, he went in and out, up and down the street, still the dog remained stationed at the door. "Did he leave no message?" "No"; all the barber knew was, that when he was shaved he went away. "It was certainly very odd."

The dog remaining stationed at the door was to the traveller conclusive evidence that his master was not far off; he went in and out, up and down the street again. Still no signs of him whatever.

Impatience now became alarm; alarm became sympathetic. The poor animal exhibited marks of restlessness in yelps and in howlings, which so affected the sensibility of the stranger, that he threw out some insinuations not much to the credit of the barber, who indignantly ordered him to quit his boutique.

Upon quitting the shop he found it impossible to remove the dog from the door. No whistling, no calling, no patting would do, stir he would not.

In his agony, the afflicted man raised a crowd about the door, to whom he told his lamentable story. The dog became an object of universal interest, and of close attention. He shivered and he howled, but no seduction, no caressing, no experiment, could make him desert his post.

By some of the populace it was proposed to send for the police, by others it was proposed a remedy more summary, namely to force in and search the house, which was immediately done. The crowd burst in, every apartment was searched, but in vain. There was no trace whatever of the countryman.

During this investigation, the dog still remained sentinel at the shop-door, which was bolted within to keep out the crowd, which was immense outside.

After a fruitless search and much altercation, the barber, who had prevailed upon those who had forced in to quit his house, came to the door, and was haranguing the populace, declaring most solemnly his innocence, when the dog suddenly sprang upon him, flew at his throat in such a state of terrific exasperation, that his victim fainted, and was with the utmost difficulty rescued from being torn to pieces. The dog seemed to be in a state of intellectual agony and fury.

It was now proposed to give the animal his way, to see what course he would pursue. The moment he was let loose, he flew through the shop, darted down-stairs into a dark cellar, where he set up the most dismal howlings and lamentations.

Lights being procured, an aperture was discovered in the wall communicating to the next house, which was immediately surrounded, in the cellar whereof was found the body of the unfortunate man who had been missing. The person who kept this shop was a patissier.

It is unnecessary to say that those miscreants were brought to trial and executed. The facts that appeared upon their trial, and afterwards upon confession, were these:

Those incautious travellers, whilst in the shop of this fiend, unhappily talked of the money they had about them, and the wretch, who was a robber and murderer by profession, as soon as the one turned his back, drew his razor across the throat of the other and plundered him.

The remainder of the story is almost too horrible for human ears, but is not upon that account the less credible.

The pastry-cook, whose shop was so remarkable for savoury patties that they were sent for to the Rue-de-la Harpe, from the most distant parts of Paris, was the partner of this peruquier, and to those who were murdered by the razor of the one were concealed by the knife of the other in those very identical patties, by which, independently of his partnership in those frequent robberies, he had made a fortune.

This case was of so terrific a nature, it was made part of the sentence of the law, that besides the execution of the monsters upon the rack, the houses in which they perpetrated those infernal deeds, should be pulled down, and that the spot on which they stood should be marked out to posterity with horror and execration.

APPENDIX 3

"To My Readers"
by George Reynolds

THIS ATTACK ON one of his plagiarists was published by Reynolds in his *Miscellany* in November 1848. The tone of the article is typical of several that the author wrote; but is particularly interesting in that the Mr Stiff referred to was one of Reynolds' first employers.

* * *

I should not again have intruded my private affairs upon the public, had not the conduct of Mr Stiff placed me in the position of a man that must either endure a systematic and cold-blooded persecution with the grovelling submission of a spaniel, or at once speak out boldly in his own defence. Not contented with having started that miserable thing entitled *Reynolds's Magazine*, with the avowed object to crush and ruin me altogether, this man pursues me with the most rancorous hatred and the most unparalleled malevolence. Thank God, I can afford to put up with all these despicable outpourings of a little mind's vulgar spite; and having killed *Reynolds's Magazine*, notwithstanding all the magnificent blusterings and vapourings of its proprietor, I might even be satisfied by treating him and his proceedings with silent contempt: but I deem it to be a duty alike to myself and to the patrons of my writings to give the ensuing explanations.

APPENDIX 3   377

Several weeks ago an article upon "The Mysteries of London" appeared in the columns of the *Weekly Times*, of which Mr Stiff is the proprietor. This pseudo-review, which was written to the express order of Mr Stiff, bestowed all kinds of Billingsgate abuse upon the work which it pretended to criticize. How any respectable Editor could have lent himself to such a disgraceful proceeding—or how any literary man could consent to do Mr Stiff's dirty work rather than assert his independence and say boldly, "*I will not be made a tool to commit a cowardly and assassin-like assault upon an individual who never injured me*"—I must leave the public to judge. The article concluded by intimating that Mr Stiff intended to issue a *new* work entitled "The Mysteries of London", and that he was looking out for "a competent person to carry out the original design". Mr Thomas Miller was the gentleman thus selected; and he accordingly entered into arrangements with Mr Stiff for the projected publication.

The agreements between Mr Miller and Mr Stiff were signed, sealed, and delivered—the placards and bills announcing the work were printed and ready for issue—the manuscript of the first Number was in Mr Stiff's hands—and an advertisement was already in print, to appear on the last page of *my* concluding Number of the Second Series—when, lo and behold! Mr Stiff sent a lawyer named Moss to my solicitor to propose arrangements for *me* to write a Third Series of "The Mysteries of London" for *him!!!*

Mr Davis communicated this circumstance to me; and I agreed to meet Mr Stiff to talk over the matter. Without revealing to Mr Davis my real sentiments, I wished to see how far human impudence could really go. Accordingly Mr Davis and myself had an interview with Mr Stiff and Mr Moss, on Wednesday afternoon, September 13th; and on that occasion Mr Stiff proposed to me the ensuing terms: "That I should write the Third Series of 'The Mysteries of London' for him at the rate of £5 per Number; and that I should become the Editor of the *London Journal* (his property) at a similar salary; he thus offering to engage my services at £10 per week for two years certain." He added that he should unhesitatingly "throw Miller overboard" for me, and turn away the gentleman already managing the *London Journal*. He likewise observed that having just purchased a work called "Godfrey Malvern" of Mr Miller, he had him completely in his power and could do with him just as he chose. The propositions were *reduced to writing* by Mr Moss, *and the document was forwarded to Mr Davis in whose possession it now remains.*

Thus was it, then, that after all the abuse which Mr Stiff had heaped upon me through the medium of his various publications—after all the unfavourable opinions his dirty scribes, acting in obedience to his orders, had passed upon "The Mysteries of London", and after all his boasting about getting "a competent person to carry out the original design" —and after all his despicable but not the less malevolent attempts to run me down as an author—he comes to me at the last moment, begging and praying that I will write him a Third Series of the much-reviled book, and proposing to break off all his solemnly contracted agreements with Mr Miller! And mark—the interview thus alluded to, took place *the day before* the *last* Number of my Second Series was to appear, and consequently only seven days before he proposed to issue the *first* Number of the Third Series. Thus, even at the very last moment, did he apply to me and express his anxiety that I—and I alone—should continue to write "The Mysteries of London".

I will candidly confess that I did not give him a decisive answer on the occasion. I wished to get the proposal in black and white in order that I might acquire positive proof that the attacks which had appeared in his publications upon my writings were dictated solely by a spirit of malevolence, and were not the opinions of an honest criticism. For it stands to reason that if Mr Stiff really entertained the sentiments expressed in those diabolical attacks, he would not have come begging and praying that I would continue to write for him. Indeed, it must have been sadly galling to his feelings to make such proposals to me at all, after everything that had taken place.

The above statement I should not have thought it worth while to make public, had not the *Weekly Times* renewed its spiteful onslaughts upon me in its Number of the 8th of October: but I can no longer refrain from convincing the public that a paper, professing liberalism, is made the vehicle of a private vindictiveness which would be detestable even on the part of a barbarian, but which is doubly reprehensible on that of an Englishman.

BIBLIOGRAPHY

Algar, Frank. "T. P. Prest", *Reckless Ralph's Dime Novel Roundup*, January 1950.

Altick, Richard. *Victorian Studies in Scarlet*. Dent, 1973.

Atkinson, N. *Eugène Sue et le Roman-Feuilleton*. Nemours, 1929.

Block, A. *The English Novel, 1740–1850*. London, 1939.

Catling, T. "The Founder of Lloyd's". *Lloyd's News*, November 1902.

Coke, Desmond. "Penny Dreadfuls". *The Connoisseur*, November 1930.

Collins, Wilkie. *My Miscellanies*. Murray, 1863.

Dalziel, Margaret. *Popular Fiction 100 Years Ago*. Cohen & West, 1957.

Disher, R. W. "Penny Dreadfuls". *Pilot Papers*, March 1847.

Dixon, J. Hepworth. "Literature of the Lower Orders". *Daily News*, 1847.

Dugdale, W. "Mischievous Literature". *The Bookseller*, 1868.

Fiedler, Leslie A. *Love and Death in the American Novel*. Cape, 1967.

Frost, Thomas. *Forty Years' Recollections*. London, 1880.

Greenwood, James. *The Wilds of London*. Chatto and Windus, 1874.

Haining, Peter. *Great British Tales of Terror*. Gollancz, 1972. *Great Tales of Terror from Europe and America*. Gollancz, 1972.

Harrison, C. P. "Cheap Literature Past and Present". *Companion to The British Almanack*, 1873.

(Hingston) "The Late Mr E. P. Hingston". *Era*, June 1876.

Hoare, Archdeacon C. J. "The Penny Press". *The Englishwoman's Magazine*, 1850.

Hunter, J. V. B. Stewart. "George Reynolds". *Book Handbook*, 1947.

James, Louis. *Fiction For The Working Man*. Oxford University Press, 1963.

Knight, Charles. *Old Printer and Modern Press*. London, 1854. *Passages of a Working Life*. London, 1864.

Lanarch, S. "Edward Lloyd". *The Story Paper Collector*. January 1957.

Medcraft, John. *Bibliography of the Penny Bloods of Edward Lloyd*. Privately printed, Dundee, 1945. "Crimes that inspired Penny Bloods". *Collector's Miscellany*, May 1949. "The Gothic Novel in Penny Number Fiction". *Collector's Miscellany*, June 1947. "The Lure of the Fearsome Title". *Collector's Miscellany*, September 1949.

Miller, W. "G. W. M. Reynolds and Pickwick". *Dickensian*, January 1917.

Nicholson, Renton. *Cockney Adventures*. London, 1838.

Reynolds, G. W. M. *Modern Literature of France*. George Peirce, 1841.

Roberts, W. "Lloyd's Penny Bloods". *Book Collector's Quarterly*, 1935.

Rollington, Ralph. "A History of Boys' Periodicals". Leicester, 1913.

Sadleir, Michael. *Collecting Yellowbacks*. London, 1938. *Nineteenth Century Fiction*. Constable, 1951. *Things Past*. Constable, 1951.

Sala, G. A. *Charles Dickens*. London, 1870. *London up to Date*. London, 1894.

Stonehill, C. A. *Catalogue of 19th Century Books*. Stonehill, 1935.

Summers, Montague. *A Gothic Bibliography*. Fortune Press, 1940. *The Gothic Quest*. Fortune Press, 1942.

Thackeray, W. M. "Half-a-crown's worth of Cheap Knowledge". *Fraser's Magazine*, 1838.

Turner, E. S. *Boys Will Be Boys*. Michael Joseph, 1948.

Watts, W. W. *Shilling Shockers of the Gothic School*. Cambridge, Mass., 1932.

Wilson, John James. "Penny Dreadfuls and Penny Bloods." *The Connoisseur*, April 1932.

Worsley, T. C. *Juvenile Depravity*. London, 1850.